The True Chronicle

The Children of Valdelaine

Sean Dillon

For Mary,

Acknowledgements

Special thanks to my wife,
Mary,
and to my brother,
Paul.

with best wishes

Sean Dillon

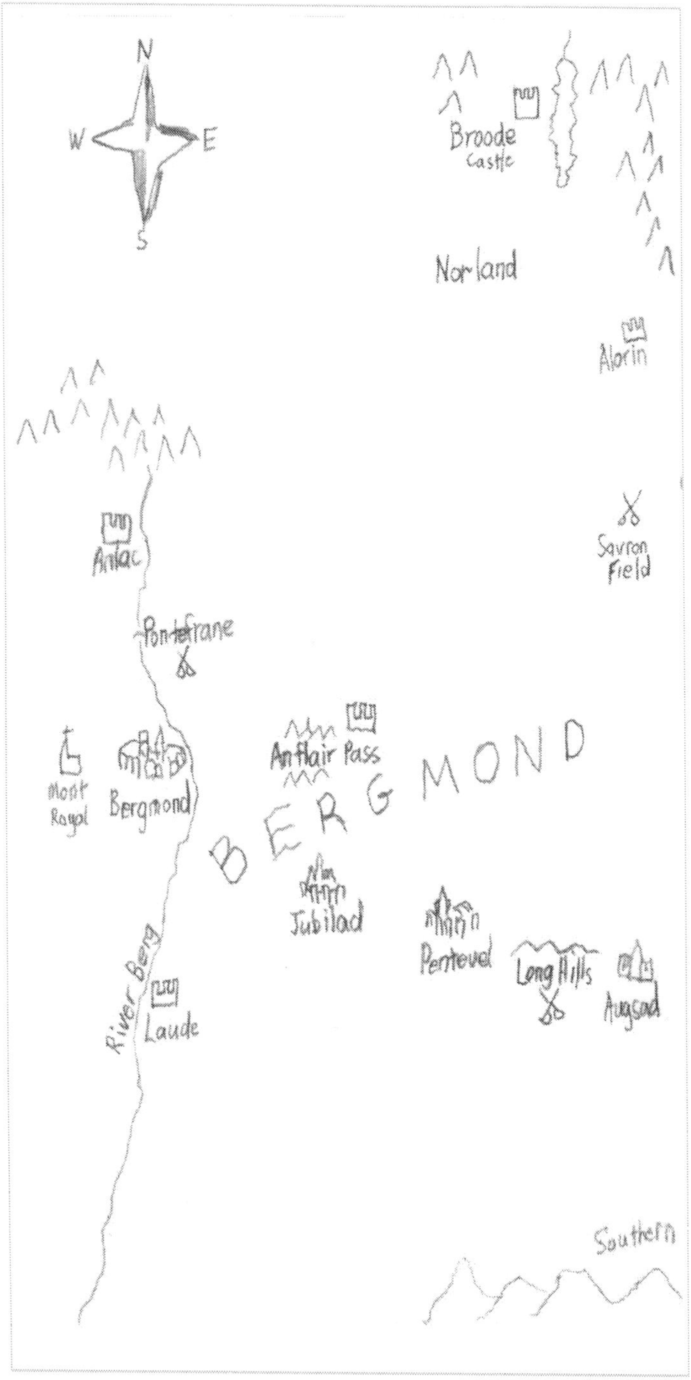
N
W
E
S
Broode Castle
Norland
Alorin
Antac
Savron Field
Pontefrane
Anflair Pass
Mont Royal
Bergmond
BERGMOND
Jubilad
Penteuel
Long Hills
Augcad
River Berg
Laude
Southern

Northern Marshes

Borderland
Countries

Borderland
Fort

Fortrue

Elvendene

Ronclara

Valdelaine

Convent
of
St. Catherine

River Gavenne

Ostmontane

E S M O R

The
Lakes

Holgen

The Golden
Plain

Belmont

River Gavette

Campialdo

Gavenne
Bridge

Pelaine

St. Michel

Deer Park

Esmor

Frontier
Line

Rocharden

Mountains

Table of Illustrations

Front Cover: Mary Dillon

Book Design: Paul Dillon

Illustrations: Sean Dillon

Also available as a Kindle e-book on Amazon.

Table of Contents

Prologue

*L*ong, long ages ago, when the great king of the Britons gave up his life in defence of his country, of justice and of freedom, the great golden light that shone upon his noble reign was dimmed and finally darkened by a succession of invaders, his noble sword was thrown upon the lake, there to remain in its depths for all time. In the aftermath of this wonder age, his knights dispersed to many lands. Some went to Lyonesse, some to Cymru. Others crossed the sea to Ireland finding refuge with Irish kings, others still crossed the other sea to Brittany, from there taking service with the Frankish kings. These latter prospered and their descendants grew in strength and numbers. Finally after the battle of Tours, King Charles gave them a land of their own on either side of the river Gavenne. This principality was land previously occupied by the Moors, and the wandering Britons, as the they were called, set up a vassal kingdom with the Frankish king as their overlord. Over time however the eastern part of the kingdom broke away from the west, so called after the city of Bergmond. Thus there were two kingdoms – the Esmorins were always aggrieved at the splendid mercantile cities of Bergmond. In their turn the Bergmondese envied Esmor, its beautiful rich land, called the Golden Plain. A particular bone of contention was the fertile land which lay west of the Gavenne and east of the mountains of the Ostmontane. Bergmond wanted it, took it many times, but Esmor always won it back again.

Some are blessed to be born in an age of peace but, like all my generation, I was destined to sweat out my young years in a hectic and tumultuous conflict that nearly destroyed both our kingdoms. All of this took place in my youthful years – some fifty years ago now. In the midst of that far off conflagration a famous legend was born concerning two young people – each one from opposite sides of the conflict. It was, of course, the legend of Germaine and Ioni. The legend was to grow and grow over time, thanks to the poetic exaggerations of rhymesters, storytellers and troubadours. With the onset of old age new awarenesses creeps into the soul; there is the sense of mortality of course, but in my case there was this need to check the excesses of the legend as best I could. Far and wide, there are stories of Germaine and Ioni which I know never took place at all; unbelievably, even to this day new stories continue to be created. That, it seems, is the way of things. So far did the legend grow from the truth that, as the years passed I gradually felt it had fallen to my lot to set forth without embellishment the true chronicle of them, of Germaine and Ioni, as best I could.

This narrative, then, is the true story of them, and I might add that my sources for it are of the highest order. For, in truth, the Lady Ioni de Valdelaine was my own sister. Germaine, as everyone knows, was the son of the Duke of Anlac and was undoubtedly, even in his early youth the greatest soldier of his age. As I left my home when Ioni was but a baby, I knew little of her until by a happy chance we were to meet when she was in her teenage years. A happy and loving bond was to grow between us. As for Germaine I came to know him in the months after the battle of Elvendene when I was stationed at the fortress of Fontrue. I am much in debt to my cousin, the Lady Eleanor de Ronclava for her many letters which shed so much light on life in Valdelaine when I was away in the wars. Equally, Count Michael, cousin to the king of Esmor, in whose service I learned my trade of knighthood, has been of great help, often regaling me with details of battles fought and with accounts of his thoughts before and after each military encounter. Many others have contributed to my story, too numerous to mention here. Nevertheless I must make mention of my younger brother Eris who generously supplied details of his capture by the Countess of Norland, famously known at the time as the 'Witch of Norland', and his subsequent imprisonment there. It is not often in history that three young members of the same family are privileged with an extraordinary influence on the great events of the age in which they lived, but so it was with us. For myself, I now retain few memories of that time. What comes to my old mind are dreams of early childhood – endless days of happiness and adventures in summer meadows.

Chapter I: Valdelaine

*O*n a summer day when she was just eleven, Ioni stood, tied hand and foot to an oak tree which faced onto one of the great fields by the castle of Valdelaine. It had been nine year old Eris who had tied her to the tree. He was now at the far side of the great field, mounted on Talon, his father's great war horse, which he had somehow stolen from the stables. Eris sat there, quite tiny, on the huge horse, covered in armour made of pewter pots and pans, also stolen, as it so happened, from the kitchens. At a given moment, Ioni then proceeded to scream for help. Across the field, Eris dug in imaginary spurs and Talon began to lumber forward gathering speed as Eris urged him on.

The great hooves were thundering now as Eris cheered and charged at the great tree where Ioni was bound. At the last minute, Eris pulled the reins to halt Talon and dismount gallantly to rescue the fair maiden. But Talon had other thoughts, halted abruptly of his own accord, and Eris shot out over the horse's neck and head, somersaulted through the air, and ended on the ground in a seated position. Ioni screamed at first but then burst into laughter at the sight of Eris on the ground and Talon walking nonchalantly away. Eris was now laughing too, and his pewter pot helmet fell from his head.

"Stop laughing Ioni," shouted Eris, chuckling himself, and raising himself from the ground. He solemnly drew his sword, a fire poker, from his rope belt, laughed again and shouted.

"Stop laughing Ioni! I haven't slain the dragon yet!" He was panting from the effort of getting up.

But the tears of fun were streaming down Ioni's face as Eris attacked a bunch of nettles and brambles with his sword poker. The dragon despatched, Eris approached Ioni and shouted.

"Fear not, my Lady. For I have slain... I have slain... the..." But more laughter permitted no more noble words, and he fell over again, the poker falling on top of him.

The fair lady, once set free, Eris retrieved his sword, and then his helmet. Taking Ioni by the hand, he then set off across the field calling out to Talon who was contentedly munching grass quite a distance away.

"See, my Lady, I am calling my great war horse," Eris shouted but then let go of Ioni's hand to reach behind himself and clasp his buttocks. "Oh," Eris cried and laughed, "My behind is sore!"

A great booming voice came from the other corner of the field.

"Not nearly as sore as it will be when the master hears of this".

The two children looked round suddenly, and saw the huge form of Ander, the chief stable man, storming across the field. The two children were rooted to the ground as Ander passed them with an angry glare, and called Talon who came to him without delay. They were still rooted to the ground when the tall man and the huge horse stood before them.

"I am taking Talon back to the stable," boomed Ander, "and the two of you can walk in front of me. I don't know what will happen to you, young lady," he said looking at Ioni, then he glared down at Eris. "I think you know the whipping you'll get from the master before this day is over! Now march on, the two of you, where I can keep an eye on you!"

So the little procession moved off across the field toward the castle grounds, Ioni at the head, holding Eris' hand in hers, Anders following with the war horse plodding steadily behind.

Both children were still in a kind of shock at being caught, but Ioni's mind was whirling in an effort to think of some solution to their plight. They walked on in silence, however Ioni stole a glance at her brother's face. Her eyes widened with surprise. Eris was still laughing silently, his face beaming with the fun of the day. Ioni pulled at his sleeve.

"What are we going to tell Papa!"

"Don't know," said Eris gulping on his laughter again. Ioni pulled his arm again.

"Be serious!" she breathed, "and think of something to tell Papa!"

"I'll think of something," Eris said pursing his lips, and trying to keep a straight face.

Ioni was miserable. How could Eris be merry? She knew if Papa became angry at Eris for stealing Talon from the stables just to play games, then he was in trouble. To teach him a lesson, if nothing else, he would be fairly thrashed. It didn't seem to bother Eris, who had extracted a little apple from one of his pockets, and was munching on it, matter of fact. To be fair to herself, Ioni had gasped with horror when she saw Eris emerge from the grounds with the war horse; she had remonstrated with him to take Talon back to the stables and bring out one of the ponies. But Eris had raised himself to his full height, looked at her comically and said, "What's to fear, Ioni? Very soon I will be a knight of the realm myself."

"Stop worrying Ioni. Talon will not be missed. No one saw me!" and he had climbed, with some difficulty, it must be said, onto the great horse.

On entering the courtyard the two culprits were fast placed in custody, one at each end of the wooden kitchen table where Margreth kept an eye on them. Ioni pleaded with Margreth to be allowed up to the embroidery chamber to see her mother. She could tell mother it was her fault, that she had put Eris up to taking Talon. Margreth was not impressed, she knew Ioni would never do such a thing; her mother would never believe such a story either. Eris, though, was impressed that Ioni should make such a bold bid to save him. He also began thinking of escape. He could make a dash for it, hide in the barn or stable until the storm had blown over. However, when Leifing, the steward, appeared at the kitchen door, Eris knew his options were narrowing. Liefing called him, and he disappeared with the steward but not before he glanced back at Ioni, a comical grimace on his face.

Ioni was no longer amused, she placed her hands and head on the table, and began to cry quietly at the sudden turn in the events of the day, at the loss of happiness, at the pain and guilt she now felt in her own heart.

When Eris finally faced his father, the realisation came that he was not going to escape from the consequences of this day's adventure. A little nervousness came over him and, as he answered his father's questions, his eyes blinked a little. Finally his heart almost lifted again as he was offered a choice of penalty – he could escape the strap on the table before him for a week's imprisonment in a room in the castle. To a child a week can seem like an eternity, so much sunshine and adventure to be missed out on, so much companionship denied.

An hour and more later Eris, hot with pain, panting and sobbing, fell mercifully into a childish sleep in the arms of Margreth. By the fire in the embroidery chamber, Ioni sat silently with mother, her heart wondering how she could have saved the shattered patches of the day. And wonder though she might, no answer came upon her heart.

The following day Eris was very much on the mend. His aches and pains were laughed and pranked away; he spent the morning in boisterous play with his comrades, the boys of the stable hands. He spent the afternoon upstream near the rapids fishing with the others, all the tragedy of the previous day forgotten in the thrills of new adventures. At the evening meal he did as he always did, regaled the family with tales of the happenings of the day. His parents, Lord Henry and Lady Marie de Valdelaine indulged him as he spoke, for in truth, Eris was as entertaining and comical as any court jester.

"Did you catch any fish," Lord Henry asked smiling at the boy.

"Uhm, yes two!" chirped Eris. "But Joseph, Ander's boy, he caught more. Methinks he has some secret, like as if he can talk the fish out of the water. Papa! Can a person talk a fish out of the water – if he learned the right words, I mean?"

His father chuckled.

"I don't know, Eris!" Lord Henry said. "But I'm sure you could talk to fish too – but I've never heard of fishing done in that way!"

"But suppose I had secret powers, Papa," Eris was enjoying the idea as he looked around the table. "I could lure – lure them to me, could I not?"

"I suppose so," the father indulged him again. "But then fishing would be too easy and not much fun."

His mother spoke.

"As long as the fish do not have magical powers too," she said, "and begin to lure you into the water."

There was laughter as Eris' face changed from comical grin to repugnant grimace.

"Now be a good boy," Marie said to him, "and use your magical powers to finish your food!"

At that Eris and his father caught knowing glances – on mother's orders it was time to finish supper, and they did so.

*   *   *

"He must leave us. You know that, Marie," Lord Henry addressed these words to his wife when they were alone together. Marie put down her embroidery, gazed at the fire and sighed.

"I will miss him," she murmured quietly. "I will miss him terribly!"

Henry looked away into the distance.

"Already we have kept him too long," he said quietly. "He should have been away to the Belmonts two years ago, but our hearts got the better of us. For his own sake, he must go."

Marie continued her stitching. She knew in her heart that Henry was right. Eris would have to make his own way in the world. As the eldest son, Jean would inherit Valdelaine; Ioni would marry well, hopefully. But Eris would have to leave and learn the trade of knighthood. To survive at all, he would have to sell his skills as a hearth knight to some powerful lord, near or far. If he was lucky, he might be called into the service of the king or spend his days travelling from joust to joust, until he made himself some fortune, and could settle down in life. Two years past, the time had come for him to leave Valdelaine, go to Lord Belmont, and begin his training, but at that time no one wanted him to go. And so, Eris had stayed on. But the day was surely coming when his future life would be nothing if he did not depart and take up the call of knighthood, as his ancestors had done for centuries.

"Will you send a messenger to the Belmonts?" Marie asked finally.

"I have been thinking about this," Henry answered. "Jean is already in the service of Count Michael. Why not ask the count to take Eris also? God knows the count owes me the favour. And then, well, Jean could keep an eye out for young Eris."

Marie thought about what Henry had just said and was pleased at the idea. Jean and Eris, the two brothers, together in the service of the count; now, that was a good idea.

"Will you write to the count?" Marie asked.

"I'll do even better than that," Henry cleared his throat. "I will ask the count to release Jean to come and fetch the boy. In that way we will have a chance to have Jean here for a while."

Marie smiled and brightened up.

"My God!" she beamed. "It has been so long since we've seen our eldest son! He must have grown so much by now. Henry, I would dearly love to see him. Will you write to Count Michael?"

"Tomorrow!" Henry said emphatically.

"It is a splendid idea! I must go tell Ioni!"

Weeks passed and finally, news arrived to say that Jean was on his way back to Valdelaine. The message had come to Valdelaine carried by a young squire of Jean's company who had ridden ahead to bear the good news. Every one there thrilled with excitement at the prospect of Jean's homecoming, the family had not seen him for eight years. Ioni had no memory of her older brother as she had been only three when he had departed for the count's service. With the rest of the family, Ioni was possessed with an intense sense of anticipation and curiosity.

The family had assembled to welcome Jean in the comfort of the upper hall. Everyone was there, Lord Henry and Lady Marie, Ioni, Eris, even Uncle Robert with his two girls Fleur and little Anna. When the steward Liefing pushed open the doors and announced him, Jean had come striding across the threshold. There were gasps of amazement, murmurs of approval; even Lord Henry murmured "My God! Look at him now!" The tall dark haired youth of fifteen who now swaggered down the hall to greet them, sword at hip and helmet held close, was indeed, a far, far cry from the chubby little seven year old boy who had departed all those years ago. Jet black hair fell to his shoulders in curls; dark piercing eyes smiled as he moved forward, and at length halted before the family group, and bowed. For a tiny second the family stood there entranced, as though they were seeing an apparition. Jean simply looked at each one in turn, reached out his arms and said, "It is I, Jean? Aren't you going to greet me?"

With that the family moved upon him, his mother could contain her joy no more and embraced him fondly. One by one they all held him as though he were a precious treasure which had been just found.

As with all the others in the days that followed, Ioni continued to be entranced at the presence of Jean; for her, he was the older brother she had never known. She loved every moment spent in his company, and found herself observing him and his traits with fascination. Polite and attentive he was at all times; he was quite reserved in all his words and actions. He seemed quite unaware of those extraordinary good looks of his, especially when he smiled, and his eyes brightened. When he laughed he did so heartily but this was not very often, and he eagerly sought solitude whenever it could be afforded him. Ioni did not understand this at first, and said as much to her mother. Marie explained to her that one day Jean would be the future Lord of Valdelaine, and as such he was in some way already carrying the burden of this within himself. However, Ioni continued to seek his companionship as much as possible and was largely pleased though she felt sure that Jean thought of her as merely a little child. No matter how much she tried with him, there seemed to be that invisible, impenetrable wall surrounding him, which he was not prepared to unravel for her, nor for anyone else. How could anyone be so wonderful, and yet be so remote in himself, she wondered, and would she ever really know him?

Ioni's face glowed as she expressed her joy and wonder to her younger brother Eris.

"Is it not wonderful to see our brother Jean, and have him here among us in Valdelaine?" she gushed. Eris, accustomed to agreeing with his sister's outbursts of emotion, was compelled to consent though he could not see what all the fuss was about.

"Ahem? Yes, it is, Ioni!" he responded. "It is, indeed, very wonderful. You know his sword and his helmet are the best part, I really like them! But they are only on loan to him from Count Michael, they are not his to keep, mind you!"

"It is not the sword and helmet I'm talking about, Eris!" Ioni flashed a look of indignation at her brother. "I'm talking about Jean himself – bother his sword and helmet! It is so precious to have him among us!"

Eris picked up a piece of stick and threw it for one of the dogs.

"Well, yes, I suppose so!" he said. "But one day, Ioni, I will carry a sword like that too!"

Ioni could only shake her head a little, and smile as Eris turned and looked earnestly at her.

"Yes, Eris! I'm sure you will!" she said, and walked on. Then looking back at Eris she said, "Someday, Eris, you will have to carry your own sword. Though I hope there will be no wars in our time. I should hate to think that Jean, yes, and even you, may have to fight in horrible battles and suffer or be killed. I could not bear it."

"Oh!" replied Eris. "I hope there will be plenty of battles and that I'll be a great warrior!"

"Eris!" Ioni scowled at him. "Wars are terrible. And what do you know of them anyway! Here at home you have had a wonderful life – you've had nothing to do but play all day! You are going to grow up fast when you go to Count Michael. You'll have work to do; you'll have to learn the skills of war! But up to now you have been spoilt, utterly spoilt!"

Eris looked at Ioni, and was mystified. He looked away from her to the distant skies. Either way, he could not understand her words anymore than he could understand the shafts of light that fell between the clouds downwards to the fields below. Words like that were beyond him. This was his sister speaking and what could she know? Like all boys between the ages of seven and fourteen or so, he was in a kind of golden age where he was the lord of the universe, and nothing could assail him. And talk of being spoilt or talk of difficult times ahead had no meaning for him. No, the sun shone from the heavens, the earth was green and he was part of it – no more to be said. There simply wasn't anything in the world that could ever bring him down, and this was as sure as the blood in his veins.

"You have never had to take responsibility for anything," Ioni said.

"You talk just like our mother," Eris remarked as he patted the dog's head, and searched for another stick to throw. Just then their attention was taken by the sound of hooves on the wooden bridge which spanned the river. Their father and Jean and the other knights were returning from a hunt; they looked magnificent as they trooped up the causeway towards the main gates. "Papa! Jean!" they both shouted but their voices were carried elsewhere in the breeze.

"I wish Jean could spend more time with us!" sighed Ioni.

"We'll have good supper tonight!" mused Eris who then ran on across the grass, and up onto the causeway disappearing into the courtyards. But as she watched Eris chase after the homecoming hunters she could not resist a pang of regret within her heart that, somehow the childhood spent with Eris was now to pass away.

Some hours later Ioni had successfully contrived a means to be alone with Jean, and as always, she loved every moment spent with him. The way he spoke, the very look of him, his every gesture she was etching on her memory, to be held in her heart until she might see him again. With her mind she poked at his mind to get him to speak, and to keep him talking. For her, Jean was the wonder of the age, as it were, and his coming into her life at this stage was the most important event ever to happen at Valdelaine.

"It must have been difficult to leave home at such an early age," Ioni prompted, and Jean smiled, folded his arms and gave her all his attention as he spoke.

"Not really, Ioni," Jean's eyes twinkled. "You see, for a boy, it was like the beginning of a great adventure. Oh there were difficulties, I grant you. They don't make a knight of someone of seven years, as you know. We start out at the bottom of the pile, as it were, as mere pageboys. We served the master, Count Michael, and waited on him; of course everyone looked down on us as if we were nothing. But it had its rewards too; I saw some of the world beyond Valdelaine. I saw the great men and women of our country. I saw the king and queen many times.

"Ah!" gasped Ioni. "You have seen the queen and her ladies! Tell me are they beautiful?"

"I suppose so," said Jean with a little chuckle. "But you should know Ioni, that nobility and beauty don't always come together. Some of the ladies are quite plain of face, and they cover their faces and lips with coloured powder to make themselves look better than they are! But of course their clothes and gowns are magnificent. By the same token, Ioni, I hope that you, my dear sister, will not take to using coloured powders on your face."

"Why do you say that, Jean?" Ioni asked. "I mean, a little colour here and there is no harm, is it? I want to look beautiful too!"

Jean put his hand to his mouth to stifle a little laugh and then smiled, gazing intently at his sister, who was still staring at him questioningly.

"I see, Ioni," Jean said. "Maybe you do not know or maybe nobody has told you?"

"Has told me what, Jean?" Ioni exclaimed. After a silence, Jean spoke.

"Please listen to me, my new found sister. You were a baby when last I saw you. But you are not a baby now. You are a young woman, and you are beautiful as you are – you do not need colours on your face."

Her heart melted as she heard these words, but of course they were the words of a kind older brother. What else would he say? She told him as much but thanked him for the kind compliment.

"Nay! I jest not, my sister!" he said. "You have a face and an expression so beautiful – why it could start a war, or better still, it could end a war!"

She looked at him lovingly.

"Which brings me to my next question, Ioni. How goes it with you and our friend Leon Belmont?"

Ioni gasped and went quiet for a moment.

"Are things not well between you both?" Jean probed. Ioni bowed her head into her hands, and finally she shook her head and looked at him, troubled and pleading.

"I will speak plainly, my Lord!" she said.

"Please do, Ioni," he replied.

"I no longer wish to marry him!" she said miserably.

"Oh!" said Jean. "I understood you were both very fond of each other. An alliance with the Belmonts would be very good for us Valdelaines. What was wrong with him?"

"Nothing! Simply nothing!" Ioni moaned. "But I was only a child when he was page here. It was wonderful to have his attention when I was girl, trotting after him everywhere. But it was only a childish thing on my part. And then towards the end of his time here when he was squire to father, well, he constantly put it out that we Valdelaines were – well, shall we say, inferior nobility. But at that time, I had felt my adoration of him had passed. Now I know I don't love him. Forgive me, my Lord!"

"I see," he said kindly. "Call me Jean, Ioni, please and not 'My Lord.' Have you spoken of this to mother and father?"

"No!" said Ioni. "God knows I've hinted at it often enough to Mama, but I can't bring myself to tell Papa. Not yet!" Then she looked at Jean and added "Forgive me, Jean, I had not meant to disappoint you!"

"And you're sure you would not be happy with Leon?"

"I'm sure of it, Jean," she moaned.

"I see!" he said promptly. "I know it was just an understanding, and that no betrothal promises were made. Maybe I can help you in all of this."

"That would be wonderful!" Ioni's face lit up.

"Perhaps you should give it another year or so," he said, "and then break it all gently to Mama and Papa. They will, of course, immediately write to me with your story. I will then write to both of them defending your choice. I will protest strongly on your behalf that I wish to see you happy in life, even if it means losing Belmont. I promise you that I will do that – whatever their own thoughts. Mama and Papa are bound to be swayed by my opinions!"

"Oh God, Jean," Ioni said almost in tears as she came to him, knelt before him, and kissed his hands. He then held her hands warmly and said, "All through our history we have been called many names, as you know – the Merry Valdelaines, the Mad Valdelaines, but I assure you, we were never called 'The Sad Valdelaines'!" Ioni laughed heartily and looked lovingly up at her brother. She kissed his hands again.

"On your feet, Ioni!" he ordered. "And let us seal our arrangement with an embrace!" She lifted her gowns to allow her to rise, and he held her in an embrace.

"It should be the motto of our family crest I suppose," he said. "Mad But Not Sad!"

And they both laughed, and he added, "Though our motto is not a bad one. Courage And Truth. A good motto."

"Yes!" chirped Ioni, still in the comfort of his arms. Then he took her arms and held her away from him and looked at her with much sternness.

"But wait, Sister!" he raised his voice. "Am I to understand that you have found another lover besides Belmont! Confess, Sister, confess!"

Her upper arms were still held in his firm grip and her face was looking up at his, smiling.

"No, my Lord and brother. I have found no other lover, nor do I wish to find one," and she added, "for now, at any rate!"

He embraced her again, and said quietly, "Trouble yourself no more with this matter, Ioni. I will see that everything goes as you wish! It has been a joy to find you and to know you after all these years!"

Ioni curtseyed low before leaving Jean, who in turn, smiled and shook his head.

It was late afternoon when Ioni sauntered towards the kitchen to find Margreth. Her mind and heart were still mesmerised by her conversation with her brother Jean. Her cousins Fleur and Anna were up in the old tower visiting their father, Uncle Robert. Eris was away with the servant boys up the river somewhere. It was a quiet time of day and she found Margreth seated at the kitchen table in deep conversation with Mère Clothilde, the lady from the village, who was Margreth's closest friend and confidante. The two women looked up as Ioni entered, and they could see from her face that she was flushed with joy and contentment.

"Ah! Greetings, my child!" Margreth called out. "Come and sit with us and have some milk to drink!"

"Greetings, my Lady!" said Mère Clothilde as Ioni took a chair and sat down. "You look so well, and, indeed, you look well contented!"

Margreth took Ioni's hand while Clothilde poured some cool milk into a pewter mug.

"Tell me, my child, what has you thus content this day?"

Ioni beamed at the two women and sighed.

"Oh! Margreth," she said, "I have had such a wonderful conversation with my brother Jean. Margreth! He is so good to talk to! I could talk with him forever! But I get so little time with him alone, you know! It is lovely to talk to him – he talks to me as if I were, you know, all grown up. He makes me feel so grown up too! What a shame he cannot be here with us all the time!"

"Aye! What a shame indeed, child!" rejoined Margreth. "But you know very well that young Lord Jean must go far away – to learn all he must know in order to be lord and master here in Valdelaine, one day!"

"I know, Margreth, I know," said Ioni, a little sadly as she began to sip her mug of milk. "But it has been wonderful to meet him!"

"Of course, of course, child," Margreth said. "Let me tell you that it has been so good for me to see him so well, so strong, so sure – not to mention, so good looking. But he was always such a dear and lovable boy!"

"A noble young lad, if ever there was one," said Mère Clothide, nodding her head.

"For a long time after he left us," said Margreth, "I fretted for him and worried so much. Indeed I prayed for him day and night – oh! For many years after. And now to see him so well – indeed, his time at Count Michael's has done him nothing but good! And my prayers for him too!"

"Thank the Lord!" Mère Clothilde exclaimed. "Thank the Lord again, I say, that he suffered no ill to his mind!"

Ioni's face had grown serious, and her wide eyes looked questioningly at Margreth and then at Mère Clothilde and then back to Margreth again.

"Instead," Mère Clothilde was still speaking, "the young lord went from strength to strength, and he never looked back from that day forward –"

The two women went suddenly silent as observing Ioni they both realised that she had known nothing of which they had been speaking. Margreth's face flushed red.

"Did," Ioni said hesitating. "Did something happen – did something happen to my brother – when he was young? Was he ill? Tell me, tell me!" Ioni looked at both women for an answer. After a long pause, Margreth took a deep breath and said quietly to Ioni.

"Ioni, your brother Jean – well, it seems something strange happened to the poor boy. Why yes! He was ill for a while."

"Oh!" said Ioni. "He must have been very ill. Imagine! And now he is so well!"

Ioni pretended to forget her surprise that Jean had been ill in his childhood. But the following day, finding Margreth again, alone this time; Ioni pressed her to tell the details of Jean's illness. Margreth placed her arms around Ioni and held her close.

"My child, we thought you knew, that someone might have told you," Margreth said reverently. "In fact, there is nothing to tell but this. Jean was never ill in his young life. But, deep upon a winter's night, the poor boy was found alone on the stairs of the new tower. He was wearing nothing but his little nightshirt, and in his hand he was holding the wooden dagger that his father had made for him. His face was deathly pale and perspiration had broken through his little body. My Lord and Lady had been woken by his scream, and when they found him there, all he could say was that he had heard something strange in the night. When no one else had heard anything, and all were fast asleep all about, it seemed he took the dagger with him to drive it away, whatever he thought it was. Your father had the house searched, found that the house dogs were all asleep by the fire in the upper hall. Nothing was found, but something had frightened the child. Poor little thing! He became quiet in himself after that, and some months later he left us for service to the count. Everyone said he must have had a troubled dream, but I was never sure of that. Knowing the child as I did, I always felt something strange had happened, though I said nothing at the time I was compelled to pray for him as much as I could, and leave the boy to the love and mercy of God."

"Has he ever spoken of this, to anyone," Ioni said appalled.

"Never, Ioni, and I doubt if he will," Margreth answered, hugging Ioni. "Perhaps it is best to let him live as best he knows how. But look! What a splendid young man he has become!"

*   *   *

Even within the short span of one lifetime so many changes take place in the life of the human being. From far off lands new learning along with new books and treatises come our way, bringing new thoughts and ideas. New instruments of measurement like the astrolabe and quadrant transform our methods. Apothecaries and alchemists insist on new remedies for age old infirmities. All of which did not even exist in the years of our youth. People put such faith in the new ideas: in the future they will mend the way we live on this earth, we are told. One wonders what will happen to people's faith in God – what with so many new philosophies and new mechanisms in life? However, nothing new seems to explain the truly extraordinary things that may occur even in a very ordinary life. Yes, we have had witchcraft and future-seeing in plenty, but in the life of the human being are there not extraordinary phenomena which seem to elude explanation by our most learned teachers?

Who can speak of such things when the very skin of reality is perforated, and the powers from a world beyond ours occasionally penetrate our given world?

Though a few of the anecdotes are stories of comfort, by far the most are tales of events which terrify the person involved. And so the question which arises from the soul is: to what purpose is it that such random and unheralded events take place at all, given that the wise people insist that our world along with the celestial bodies all move upon a pre-ordained plan? If indeed there is a Dragonwelt existing side by side with our natural world, we may reasonably ask why it is allowed occasionally to impinge itself on our existence, why would we need to be terrified by it, as if we had not enough terrors in our normal life? Any possible explanation seems to be beyond the ken of our philosophers and to be equally beyond the scope of our mechanical devices. The anecdotes referred to here are not those of highly inventive and imaginative people – they are, rather, the stories of people of sound mind. Whatever is in the scheme of things, there always seems to be more there than we can account for.

*   *   *

In the middle of the night, Jean was awakened by a noise that sounded like something scratching at the timbers of the chamber door. As the sound continued and as no one else seemed to hear it Jean stirred himself, got up, and moved towards the door. He opened the door and could see nothing in the darkness, though he could hear the snoring of the houseboys who slept on pallets of straw by the doorway. Thinking the sound might have been caused by one of the housedogs, he moved to close the door when his attention was arrested by a swirling sound that seemed to come from the exit to the staircase. He jumped with fright, slammed the door and ran to his bedside where he found his little wooden dagger. Clutching the dagger tightly he slipped into his bed and pulled the coverings about him. Mercifully, there was only silence, and he began to relax. What followed sounded like a great claw scraping a long downward stroke on the door. Jean froze in terror and sat up, his grip tight on the little dagger. Another long scrape followed this time accompanied by a long deep growl that seemed to drain the life from Jean's little body. His heart too was drained by terror as he once more left the safety of the bed and moved towards the door. He would always remember in after years, how, as he pulled open the door, it seemed as if, there in the darkness, the blood seeped from his veins and he felt his heart go white with terror. Once more, there was nothing there, nothing to be seen or heard. Then suddenly, came the weird, unearthly growl from the pit of the stairs. Jean screamed with fright, but strangely, with nothing but the dagger for protection, he found himself moving towards the ominous stairs. Again, in after years, he would remember it like a kind of death, as he moved toward the snarls and growls, with nothing of life left inside him, only a white light in his heart, yes, a white light, compelling him to place himself between those he loved and the horror which was now retreating down into the darkness. Lights came on, people came out alarmed by his scream, gathered round him asking questions, but Jean was dumb with fright and with the return of normality. He opened his mouth to speak but no words came to him. His father lifted him up, ordered a search of the house, and put Jean to bed.

Like all little boys, Jean put the horrible experience into a box and left it deep in some cellar of his mind. Whether or not he would revisit that cellar ever again he did not know. A warm gentle boy became only more gentle, and indeed, he became compassionate towards people, animals and towards everything that is contained in the world which we normally inhabit, cherishing everything, as though he knew that everything was equally vulnerable, and could be threatened at any time.

*　　*　　*

Thus it came about that Ioni had the opportunity to meet her elder brother Jean. For a brief period of three weeks and for the first time in her life she was able to enjoy the companionship of both her brothers. At times she wondered how soon or, if ever, the three of them would meet in one place again. The times she spent with Jean were relished beyond measure, and the evening meals were special treats, all of the Valdelaine family being together around the table. These family gatherings were the merriest of times, the parents were eager to hear as much as possible about Jean's life at the count's castle near Esmor. Jean had some fascinating stories to tell of the great and mighty nobility, men and women, whose world he now shared, but most of his tales concerned the great Count Michael himself. Ioni was to learn from Jean's stories that even though the count was a great statesman and commander, he was also a warm hearted man, possessed of a great sense of humour. Eris too was most interested in stories of the count, as soon he would be in the service of the great man, first as pageboy, then as squire.

The day before he was due to leave Eris played his last batch of games with the servant boys and stable boys. Then he took his own horse, the year old Strang, downriver, where he bathed in the cool waters of the Gavenne. Upon arrival back at the castle, he amused the kitchen girls with some stories, stole a batch of pancakes, and later ate a hearty supper. After this, his mother and sister presented him with two newly sewn tunics with the Valdelaine colours deftly sewn into the front. When mother departed he had a little chat by the fire with Ioni.

"You know, Ioni. I will be learning to play the lute at Esmor," he said with enthusiasm. "Then we can both play together!"

"Only when you come back to us, silly," Ioni smiled at him. "That may take a long time – Oh God! Eris, I am going to miss you so much! I'm going to miss the times we had together! Still I'm so proud of you going away to be a knight – you must be so brave!"

"Of course, Ioni," Eris smiled, "I am very brave, as you know!"

There was a little silence between them and then Ioni spoke.

"Will you miss me?"

Eris had not thought about missing Ioni – girls' questions were so difficult to answer – but if he even gave in to the thought of missing her, who knows what floods of grief might rush over him and sweep his heart away. He tried to speak but, for once, he was not able. Even the sight of Ioni, so lovely in the firelight, wrapped in her blue mantle and smiling at him, her piercing eyes seeming to search him blood and bone; this sight was proving too much for him.

"I think…" he blurted, but could speak no more.

Ioni was moving towards him and, placing a kiss on his cheek, whispered in his ear.

"I know you will miss me! Now good night and sleep well!"

He watched her walk away down the passageway, this sister who had been the wondrous audience of his life. He longed to race after her and say thanks and tell her that he loved her. But such expressions would open such floodgates of feeling and of tears that he could not bear, as they would surely sweep him from the face of the earth. He watched her stop at the end of the corridor, turn around and raise her hand in farewell. Eris gulped and kept the floodgates shut.

The following morning, Eris, looking quite dapper in his new tunic, mounted his yearling, Strang, smiled and waved goodbye to all. Hooves clattered on stone as the little cavalcade left the courtyard and moved down the causeway to the bridge. Ioni ran to the main gate to see them cross the bridge and take the road, the long road to Esmor. A little pang arose in her heart as she wondered when she would see her two brothers again.

*   *   *

When she reflected upon her life of fourteen years, Ioni could only see a life of simplicity and obedience to her parent's wishes. Always, from a comfortable distance, she had watched the antics of Eris, who was so wild and lovable, in his many acts of boyish disobedience, and the drama that went with such occasions. How many times he had done something truly awful, only to be punished and then totally forgiven and loved at the end. She had wondered what it would be like to do something really bold, as Eris would do, to be caught in the act, to be taken a kind of prisoner, punished and pardoned, only to live on again for the next adventure. But she could never think of anything. It was not in her nature, she would prefer the part of young lady to the part of young lord, in spite of all its reckless adventure. Her elders, especially her parents, had their respected place in the scheme of things and she could never figure out how to challenge that. Until one summer afternoon when she was twelve.

The rapids up the river had always enchanted her with their rushing waters and cascading sounds. Often, on the summer days she had strolled with the other girls and watched in wonder as the two great parts of the river emerged from the woods, rejoined, and then gushed over the rocks, roving downstream together past the fortress and the village. Of course, in summer the river was low and the great stones stood high out of the water; in places, one could move safely from one stone to another, but not too far; only the boys ever crossed the entire river, stone to stone, side to side. Ioni seated herself upon one of the stones leaving the other girls to chatter among themselves on the riverbank.

The sense of the breeze on her face, in her ears the unending sound of the cascade, the reflected light off the waters, all these held her there, soothed and relaxed. Time went by gently and being in this place was truly peaceful. As she sat there, with her arms wrapped about her knees, she felt her body relaxing and she thought to herself how lucky she was just to be there in the midst of the summer day. And time went by again. At length, whatever change came in the light, whatever little cloud crossed the face of the sun, she sat upright, shivered a little, and was taken from her daydreams. She looked about and saw the others a little distance away down the bank. She shook herself, sighed and raised her body until she stood on the stone. On an impulse she stepped back to where the rock jutted out from under the grassy bank, then she walked again across the first rock and hopped easily from one great stone to the next, with her eye, measuring each width of water below. She stopped and looked about her and was thrilled to have gotten so far, how differently everything looked from out here. If anyone was there to see, they would have observed a girl in a red dress standing on a large rock about one third of the way across the rapids. She wondered how she had never done this before especially when she had seen Eris and the other boys do so. Maybe she had been afraid then, but now she suppressed all fear, as she was gaining the middle of the stream where she met wider gaps with greater torrents rushing between. These, of course gave her pause for thought, but exhilarated by each new challenge, she would retrace her steps upon some stone, gather the skirts of her new dress, taking up her courage she would leap great strides to bring her to safe foothold on each new destined stone. At last she won the little game she had set herself and stepped to the far shore of the river. There she gasped for breath and laughed heartily and then turned to survey the mighty journey she had come, above the torrent. She smiled, down river she could see the castle, the bridge and the village. Across the divide, she could see the others as they gradually became aware of her absence and then as their searching eyes found her far away across the river. "Ioni!" they screamed but their voices were eerily faint against the noise of the waters.

Ander, the chief stableman had heard the screaming down by the river, had run to the rapids and was now stepping from stone to stone out into the river. He called to Ioni to stay where she was, not to re-cross except by going downstream to the wooden bridge. Ioni refused, and gathering the skirts of her red dress began to jump the stones again. Ander was coming closer to her now but she refused to stop and continued leaping from stone to stone. As she leapt one of the wider gaps, she missed her footing and went down. There was hardness of stone and cold of water as she slid helplessly down, plunging into the swirling waters of the tail-race. For an instant, she was buoyant but sank below the surface down into the eerie silence under the water. There a world of green and brown with the blue surface away above her. The red dress she thought, how she had looked forward to wearing it for the first time, and now... For an instant she broke surface, saw the sky and gulped in the air. Then it was down with her again, into that dreamlike world below. Then came the strange sense that this is what her life had been and in a few seconds she would be no more; an almost hopeless acceptance of her fate. Only for an instant though; as her feet touched ground down there, it was as if a new person had taken over her and she was struggling now, fighting with every limb to climb in the water to the surface. This time the force of her struggling caused her to shoot up out of the water. This time too, something inside her did not wish to revisit the world beneath the waves and she thrashed about determined to stay on top of the water, even if the red dress was dragging her down. She began to sink again, when she was grabbed by the hair of her head and pulled above water by the strong arms of Ander.

When the excitement over Ioni's near drowning incident had died down and people no longer spoke of it, Ioni was quite happy. Obviously, she never discussed the matter beyond the outpouring of her emotions to her mother the evening it had occurred. Marie had been patient and gentle with her daughter, chiding her gently not to dwell on it, and urging her not to preoccupy herself with feelings of guilt about it. Slowly her mother's comforting had soothed Ioni's heart. After that Ioni did not refer to it nor did she need to. When she did think about it she felt grateful to be alive and she felt thankful to have been so lucky. For those terrifying moments under the waters of the river, she had momentarily accepted her short life was ending, and though her own struggles and Ander's rescue had brought her to safety, the memory of her own possible death down there was as close to death as she ever wanted to be. Having almost lost life, she was now most earnest about preserving life. It seemed now, that the boundary between life and death was so fragile, that she never wished to tempt fate again, to visit that frontier again. In fact, during the years that followed, Ioni's life was marked by an obedience to her parents, by a respect for the forces of nature, and by a caution in her dealings with all aspects of her life.

There was a deeper element within Ioni, not born of thought nor reflection, but like a light of intuition and perspective, that grew within her and was changing her spirit from day to day. Certainly she saw things and people differently, patience and tolerance had grown within her, and insignificant things were no longer important. Having been snatched from the grasp of death itself, she had been given another chance at life, and she felt so grateful for this; she sensed within, the responsibility to cherish the life she now had, and to live it with love and gratitude. Added to this, she also felt an insight from time to time that her life was so special, that she perhaps had some special destiny to fulfil, a condition perhaps, of being allowed to be alive. What her special destiny might be, she had no idea, of course, but that feeling grew within her, that her place in this life would be such that she had never dreamed of. God, or the universe, had allowed her existence to continue beyond the awful moment; might it not be reasonable to believe, that maybe she was allowed to live for some special reason? However, more often than not, Ioni dismissed these feelings as just possibly tricks of fantasy, but unknown almost to herself, she was changing within herself, changing forever.

*   *   *

Apart from her parents, there was Uncle Robert. He lived in the topmost chambers of the old tower with his wolfhound and his raven. He did not play any obviously active part in the life of Valdelaine, though there was always a keen sense of his presence about, especially for Ioni. After the death of his wife, the Lady Fleur, Robert had returned to Valdelaine from his own estates, bringing his two daughters Fleur and Anna with him. He had promptly occupied the top of the tower leaving the two girls in the care and company of Ioni, who was very glad to have them in her daily life. But Robert did not abandon the girls, in fact quite the opposite. It became an unfailing part of daily life, for the girls to abandon what they were doing, climb the steps of the old tower and be greeted by the barking of the wolfhound and the squawking cough of the raven, and finally by the smiling, bright eyed face of their father. On their arrival on the landing he would enfold them together, and in turns in long embraces, as if he had not seen them for years.

"Ah! There it is! My children, my beloved children," he would say. "How wonderful to see you again. Ah! My children, my children!" And he would bundle them into his chamber with much noise from dog and raven. The scene was not without a sense of tragedy at times, and these moments were too much for poor Fleur who would be tearful for a while. However, for Anna, these visits to father were as natural as any part of life; frequently she would stand in front of the wolfhound, scolding him until he would finally stop barking and stretch himself before the fire. Anna was also perfectly at ease with the raven and would greet him and converse with him, the great bird's eyes looking down at her from its high perch in the corner. Strange as it seems, a child of four years can converse with a bird, for instance, because somewhere inside the magic of a child's mind there is a room for the possibility that communication is taking place and is not a waste of time. So with Anna, as she frequently held long conversations with both of Uncle Robert's companions, sometimes even falling asleep on the great chest of the wolfhound, who dared not move until the child awoke. Frequently Ioni came along on these visitations, which usually proved fascinating and entertaining for everybody. In spite of the tragedy of Aunt Fleur's loss, and in spite of the state of Robert's mind,

Ioni had always had a curious sense of ease and happiness in her uncle's presence. Whatever had been damaged in him did not seem to matter. What was left was this quaint man in long robes, grey hair and wispy beard, luminous through his entire being, shone a benign and wonderful energy. Being in Robert's presence seemed like being in the happy presence of God himself, though Robert professed to being a heretic. There were other reasons for feeling grateful to Robert: he was the one who, from the beginning had urged Ioni to learn to read and write. When others had thought this a waste of time, Robert had begged Ioni to study, had supplied her with plenty to read until she had become a reader in her own right. From romantic tales to tracts on religion or philosophy, books had never failed to enchant her young mind, and eventually she was never without a book of some kind.

*   *   *

By any standards the castle at Valdelaine was a well protected and strong fortress, almost as large as any in the land of Esmor. Only Holgen Fort, between the Gavenne lakes to the south, and Borderlands and Fontrue in the high border country far away to the west, were larger. Valdelaine was set on a high bluff of rock which ran at an angle to the Gavenne. The eastern end was closest to the river and a great arched causeway led downward from the main gate connecting with the wooden bridge which spanned the river. The village began some distance beyond the bridge. Because of the angle of the rock, the western end of the castle was separated by fifty yards of green lawn from the river bank. At the foot of the sheer rock there was a moat, which was kept dry, save in times of attack when sluice gates at the riverbank could be opened, flooding the moat in a short time. A would-be assailant, having crossed the river, the lawn, and the moat, would then be faced with a climb of the fifty foot sheer rock face before reaching the castle walls, which rose yet again to a height of another sixty feet. The entire outer walls enclosed a rectangular area eighty yards by fifty. Each corner of this rectangle was protected by strong round turrets. Two smaller turrets at the eastern end protected the main gate. Inside the gate the ground continued to rise until it levelled out forming a courtyard about the colossal keep, which was called the old tower. From here a two story building stretched across the bawn where it joined the second keep which was called the new tower. Thus it was possible to access both towers from both floors of the castle house. This two storey ran close enough to the southern wall which overlooked the river.

It ran close to the southern rampart and the two were linked at the upper height by a great arch. This supported an enclosed passageway complete with roof, windows and doorway opening onto the south rampart and giving a magnificent view of the river below, the village, the open land and the forest beyond.

On the north side of the castle the bailey was wide, and outhouses and stables were set against the west, north and east walls. As well as this, into the north rampart an extra turret had been set, midway down its course.

In its long history, as any Valdelaine could tell you, the castle had never been taken – its inhabitants and garrison may have surrendered – but never had Valdelaine been taken by force of arms. What had started out its life a thousand years before as a Roman fort on a high rock, had gradually extended over the centuries to the towering edifice it is today. Legend has it that the Roman general who constructed the fort named the place for his wife;

Vall de Helena, thus the name Valdelaine, the Valley of Helen.

"*Ye Valdelaines of ancient glory*
The Golden Plains most precious gem
The lofty halls of many a story
Still generations follow them."

Chapter II: The Beckoning

*I*oni was now fourteen and was beginning to grow tall; the first intimations of her eventual beauty were becoming apparent in her manner, in her bearing and in her bodily form. She was a young woman now with dreams and hopes like any other of her age. Though she was not to know it at the time, the very seeds of her eventual destiny were about to come to her, gather round her and fill her awareness to overflowing. Unforeseen, and with a touch of good fortune, events would now overtake her which would bring the great wide world beyond Valdelaine into her own home, into her mind and understanding. Like the pebbles that might turn a little stream at its earliest flow, events would take place under her very roof which would thrust upon her the path in life she would eventually take.

"Make haste, Ioni!" her mother called to her one summer morning, "for I have wonderful news for you, my love. Take a deep breath my love!"

Ioni obeyed, took a deep breath, but then burst out laughing, "Mother, what is it? Tell me, tell me!"

"Well, my child, it is this. The king and queen – you have heard of them surely?"

"Of course, mother. Tell me or I'll burst! What news of the king and queen?"

"Ioni, the king and queen of Esmor are to visit us in two months or so!"

Ioni gasped, unable to contain her joy.

"Our king and queen are to visit us, mother! I've never heard anything so... well shall we say, wonderful!" Ioni swirled about in a little pirouette of joy and wonder, her head sideways and her arms outstretched. When she stood still again Marie said:

"And there is more good news, Ioni – their majesties are to be in residence here for the best part of the coming year. The entire court of Esmor is coming too. My child, for the coming year, our beloved Esmor will be ruled from Valdelaine!"

Ioni stood open mouthed before the smiling Marie. "Is it really true?" she gasped.

"Yes, quite true!"

Ioni let her excitement go with loud whoops as she took her mother and danced about the floor with her. More whoops, happy shrieks and finally they both stopped, out of breath but bending over with laughter. It was then Marie's turn to take hold of her daughter and say,

"We have much to do, Ioni!" and they laughed again.

The first preparation for the royal visit was to send for the 'Ronclavas' to come with all possible haste. The 'Ronclavas' as the Valdelaines called them, were Ioni's uncle Raymond, her father's brother. He would be accompanied by his wife the Lady Blanche de Ronclava, and their two daughters young Lady Eleanor aged fourteen and young Lady Clara, aged ten. Ronclava was the name of the region, forty miles upriver where they kept a castle and an estate almost equal in size to that of Valdelaine.

Within a week Raymond and his family and servants arrived. Unlike his two brothers Lord Henry and Uncle Robert, Raymond was a tough, plain, wedge of a man. Though he had little to say beyond 'yes' and 'no' Raymond had the gift of being a shrewd manager when it came to keeping vast estates functioning to their best.

This latter gift of Raymond's would be put to good use, thus leaving the Valdelaines free to bestow all their attention on the illustrious guests they were about to receive. By contrast, Raymond's wife, Blanche, was still beautiful in middle age, her elegance and her height, her imperious manner gave her a sense of presence, which in Ioni's opinion made her a formidable matriarch. Her sterling qualities would be a support to Marie when the royal visitors were installed. Whatever Raymond and Blanche might have in common was a mystery to everyone else, for to outward appearances they seemed complete opposites. Their eldest daughter, Eleanor, the same age as Ioni, took after her mother in many ways. She, too, was tall and elegant, her bright blonde tresses cascading to her shoulders and halfway down her back. To Ioni's mind however Cousin Eleanor was rather too elegant, too fond of bright dresses and fashionable jewellery, too much of a chatterbox and altogether too taken with being the centre of attention. No, Eleanor was absolutely not to Ioni's taste and she doubted she would ever find anything in her cousin which might yield to mutual affection. Au contraire! Ioni was determined to avoid the loud and elegant Eleanor and leave her to those who might appreciate her. By contrast with Eleanor, the ten year old Clara was dark haired, calm and gentle in herself, soft hearted and quietly humorous and was the perfect object of Ioni's affections.

Thus it was that, thanks to the royal visit, Ioni had the joy of having all her wider family, uncle, aunt, cousins under one roof. Inwardly, during her prayers she thanked God for such varied companionship and the joys that went with it. Ioni reflected too on the other cousins she had never met, those on her mother's side. But Rocharden, her mother's birthplace was far far to the south – too far away. But might it not be possible during the royal stay

that even the Rochardens, or some of them, would come
to attend the royal couple. Other knights from the south
would come so why not the Rochardens? Ioni mentioned
all of this to her mother who smiled gently and said
"When their majesties of Esmor arrive, Ioni, there will be
Rochardens in their escort! Believe me you will meet
some of my nephews and some of my nieces – all your
cousins!"

"Mama!" was all Ioni could say.

When she was alone again Ioni's imagination
stretched out to the dizzying galaxy of people who would
come to Valdelaine. Great names that she had only heard
of but never met, first cousins she had only known in
Marie's stories of Rocharden. But deepest down in her
heart, her affections held her most secret longing. After
all, if Count Michael was to be in Valdelaine, so too
would be his squire and page, Jean and Eris, her very own
brothers. And Ioni's heart was set on coming to know her
older brother Jean even better. She had only once met
him before and loved his company, back when she was
just eleven. Now she would make up for all the lost time
of both their lives.

And so the weeks rolled on, and as they did so, all
of Esmor seemed to converge on Valdelaine, as so many
knights, courtiers and people of any importance arrived to
prepare the way for the royal couple. Armies of servants
and handmaids arrived also. These days whenever she
looked down from the south rampart upon the fields about
the castle or those that stretched away beyond the river
Ioni could scarcely believe her eyes. Brightly coloured
pavilions and tents filled every space, and hundreds of
banners of every colour fluttered on the breeze. Valdelaine had become a city of canvas which seemed to stretch
further and further with each passing day. And all the

people! Ioni had never seen so many in one place, all going about their duties in such organised determination. These days, every day she would climb the steps and over the covered passageway that led from the upper story hall and out on to the rampart to look down upon the scene which never failed to take her breath away. Another week Ioni would have to wait before the arrival of Esmor's king and queen. In the meantime the Valdelaine family would move to the old tower, leaving their quarters in the new tower at the disposal of the royal family, their menservants and ladies in waiting. Ioni and her cousins enjoyed the move as it became like a game to them, setting up the rooms of the old tower. The servants moved chests of clothes, washing ewers, chairs and tables and wall hanging tapestries. Ioni and her cousins now lived on the topmost but one of the floors of the old tower. Uncle Robert, at the topmost floor would be left undisturbed, happy as he was with his wines, his raven and his wolfhound. They would share chambers as well; Ioni with Fleur and Anna, Eleanor with Clara. On the floor beneath them, Lord Henry and Lady Marie, with Lord Raymond and Lady Blanche took up their residence. The remaining two lower floors of the tower were left free, but furnished, in the event of an emergency or overflow!

On it came, then, the golden day. At noon, from the south beyond the village and the fields came the first distant sounds of trumpets heralding the approach of the royal family. Thereafter, the trumpets sounded at intervals, each blast louder than the last. Ioni could hardly contain her excitement as she stood with her cousins on the little balcony which overhung the great main door. Below, in the courtyard, stood her parents patiently waiting with Uncle Raymond and Aunt Blanche. From the courtyard to the bridge two rows of knights stood facing each other in silence, forming the guard of honour. The next blast of trumpets was so loud that Ioni knew the royal cavalcade was at the village; and suddenly, in answer from the top of the south ramparts the trumpeters of Valdelaine sounded off their blaring tones of welcome. The outriding knights reached the courtyard and dismounted, they were followed by various court dignitaries. Behind them came a lone rider bearing the royal banner – Ioni knew that from his height and bearing this must be Count Michael, cousin to the king and commander of all the forces of Esmor. Finally, escorted by a large troop of knights, the king and queen came under the archway of the main gate, up the rise and wheeled into the courtyard. Ioni stood entranced by the sight below. The royal couple came to a halt but did not dismount, a couple of pageboys in royal livery came forward to hold the royal horses. The lords and knights of Valdelaine, the ladies also, knelt before their majesties. They were resplendent in their attire, King John and Queen Isabel, likewise the prince and princesses. The king was in full armour, the rim of his helmet decorated by a gold crown, his surcoat was saffron edged with purple. The queen wore a silk gown, a pale shade of saffron, neck, sleeves and hems edged in gold. Above her purple cloak her scarf and veil were white, she too wore a golden coronet. Their white horses were richly decorated with long pale saffron cloth, rich with embroidered emblems, edged in braid, with golden tassels which swung to and fro. The horses wore head and chest armour embellished with gold and diamonds, an ancient gift from one of the kings of Bergmond. The prince and princesses were similarly arrayed. The king, Ioni noted, was fresh of face though his beard was grey white. The queen had a soft rounded face, high cheekbones and eyes and lips that were so harmonious they gave her a look of gentle beauty.

At a signal, Ioni's father rose from his knees and made a speech of welcome to the monarchs. In turn the king and then the queen made speeches of gratitude for their welcome. Then the king dismounted and the tall Count Michael moved forward to assist the queen to the ground. The formalities over, it was smiles and greetings all around. Ioni's mother curtseyed to the queen who held out her hands to her and embraced her. At this moment Ioni and her cousins were ushered away from the balcony and down to the great hall, where in a few moments they would be presented to the royal couple.

Rushing headlong into the great hall the girls, especially Ioni, could scarce believe their eyes. Those standing with Uncle Robert were Ioni's brothers, Jean and Eris. Breathless Ioni raced arms outstretched into the arms of Jean. Ioni held him fondly and tight. He smiled indulgently down at her, caressing the dark auburn hair pressed to his chest. Tears of sheer joy had welled up in her eyes and then she turned to embrace Eris who was now, almost as tall as she. Eris shrank a little at Ioni's wild embrace until he was almost out of breath. "Oh Eris, it is good to see you!" Clearing his throat and regaining his breath Eris gasped, "It is wonderful to see you too, Ioni." Flushed with boyish embarrassment he quickly wiped away Ioni's kisses when she was not looking!

And then the king and queen entered the hall, surrounded by courtiers. Ioni's parents presented each one to their majesties. When her turn came Ioni curtseyed low – but still could not resist a little peep at the queen's kindly countenance. The last to be presented was Robert's daughter Fleur who held her four year old sister Anna in her arms. "And who is this young girl, Lady Fleur?" "This is my sister, Lady Anna!" The queen drew close to Anna and smiled, something in the queen's countenance triggered a response in the child such that she reached out both her little arms to the great lady. The queen took Anna in her arms and hugged her. "Well, Lady Anna, tell me," the queen's eyes alive with merriment, "will you become a great lady one day?" Without hesitation Anna looked into the queen's gentle eyes and said, "Yes your – majesty." Anna said when she could say the word, "And I will most certainly marry a handsome prince!" "Oh?" the queen exclaimed merrily and answered, "Perhaps you will, Lady Anna, perhaps you will." "Charming!" the queen said as she handed the little girl back to Fleur.

With that, the stewards ushered the royal entourage down the hall to the new tower. There they would rest after their journey, take some light refreshments, wash, change and rest. They would not be seen for the rest of the day, appearing only for the great banquet of welcome in their honour. There would be dancing and music. The royal family would dine on the high dais at the end of the hall and rows of tables and trestles would fill the long hall, to be occupied by all the guests of honour. The Valdelaines and Ronclavas, as hosts would dine at the first table to the right below the dais. That night their majesties departed early, leaving the festivities which went on for some hours. The Valdelaines retired soon after. On the way up the stairs Ioni and her cousins were full of chatter and giggles and had intended spending an hour chattering about the day, but when their maids had helped them to bed, they slept quickly and soundly. It had been a long, long day.

Within two months or so, life had settled into its new routine and already Ioni was beginning to wonder at how she had lived her former life at Valdelaine. It was a whirlwind time for her as she had been first introduced to the king and queen, and thereafter to so many of the great

and famous of the land. So many young men had presented themselves to her as possible suitors, and would
continue to do so. While she was charmed and excited by
the attentions of so many handsome young knights and
squires, she struck a happy balance between being courteous and kindly with everyone, while involving herself
with none. There was hardly a day without celebration of
some kind – jousting tournaments and hunting by day,
music and dancing by night. Ioni was never without
dancing partners at the evening revels, and she enjoyed
the the fun, the gallantry of the young men and their enthusiasm for her. Her cousin Eleanor was a good deal
more content in her emotional encounters, and was a
wonderful flirt – enchanting the young men with her wit,
her interesting conversation, testing out her womanly
wiles to the limits allowed. But Ioni had other concerns,
she watched amazed as her parents managed the entire
pageant with warm and unerring ease; it was every bit as
much a happy time for them, a time of happy reunion with
so many friends of earlier years. Her mother's relatives
had come in the royal escort – the Rochardens, her
mother's brother and two nephews, whom Ioni had not
previously met. She was struck by the close family resemblance between her mother and her brother Louis –
and the two cousins were all but copies of her brother
Jean. She was struck too, and slightly mystified at the
easy going attitude of her Uncle Louis towards her mother
– there was something there she could not define. Uncle
Louis constantly treated mother as if she had been some
winsome wild child, whereas Ioni knew for certain that
mother was nothing less than a living saint. Ioni made no
comment about it, they were after all, brother and sister –
but it was interesting none the less. And so Ioni watched

in delight as, over time, it seemed that the entire kingdom of Esmor came to Valdelaine.

And so it did, for the great hall and lower chambers of the new tower were now the seat of government of Esmor. From here, the king ruled his kingdom. Morning and sometimes afternoons, the king held his court and council meetings, settled disputes and passed new laws, ordered imprisonments and even executions. In the great hall the king received embassies, archbishops, delegations and deputations. Dignitaries from other lands came to pay their respect, from northern Spain they came, from Savoy and Italy, from the Rhineland, and of course, from the kingdom of the Franks. The king knew well that Esmor needed all the allies it could muster – Esmor was a small David compared to its Goliath neighbour Bergmond. The latter was often a friend but equally as often an enemy – the great burden of every Esmorin king was the constant vigil of keeping a close eye on Bergmond and all its doings. Relations with the latter had been reasonably good these past fifteen years – but as everyone knew, at least once in every generation the lion of Bergmond roared and when it did the consequences were usually serious. Of particular concern to the king was this Heiligebund or Holy League of knights formed over twenty years before in Bergmond. The original aims of this bund had been the protection of the Bergmond monarchy and its succession. Leopold King of Bergmond was now old and feeble and he had not produced an heir to the throne. The league's aim was to foster unity among the Bergmondese in the event of an empty throne and facilitate the choosing of a new king peacefully, without the awful prospect of a civil war of succession. Worthy aims indeed, but his majesty of Esmor through his spies had learned that the leadership of this league had been infiltrated by a clique of warmongering barons who were intent on bending the league to suit their own ambitions. Therein lay the cause of King John's concern. If the lion of Bergmond roared again – the league had now given it sharp and warlike teeth!

Blissfully unaware of the king's troubles Ioni continued to revel in her new life. She was glad that Eris had retained so many of his comical childhood traits. While serving food at each banquet to his master, Count Michael, he would invariably catch her eye as he passed, and wink, grimace or pull a funny face as he passed. She had little time for such fripperies now, but occasionally he could still make her smile and giggle. He was quite adept at dodging his post for a few moments to convey some item of food or drink to his parents, who would regard him with scolding eyes, at which he would bow deeply with a flourish, and turn away on his heel with a mischievous grin on his face. Frequently, amid the bustle of court life, Eris found opportunities to visit Ioni, who had grown tall and stood some inches over him. Both of them had changed much in the years since childhood. She was now a young woman and he was on the threshold of manhood. Somewhere, sometime, the old bond between them would reassert itself again, she assured herself. For now however, amid the hosts of charming young men who thronged the halls of Valdelaine, Ioni felt she had quite outgrown the company of her baby brother, and, on meeting Eris would look down on him in mock distain, and enquire of him:

"What is it you require of me, little pageboy?"

At which he would chirp something like "My compliments to your Ladyship. Why I require nothing but to visit my favourite sister!"

"You have only one sister, Eris," she would retort. "And that sister is me! What do you require of me?"

And then the years would fall away as Eris would regale her with stories of his latest adventures in the count's service, never failing to charm her as he had done so often in earlier times.

"The count has permitted me to train with weapons," he told her one day. "At last, weapons!"

"Oh dear," she said. "I fear you will do yourself an injury!"

"I already did, or nearly did. The other day I was permitted to mount horse and charge at the quintain with a lance. It caught me, though, and I was thrown off the horse! I had to get up quickly, as Count Michael took a swipe at me, intending to kick my arse! But I dodged him, which was just as well for my rear end, as his leg is very long and his foot is very big! Anyway, Ioni, tell me what news is there of Himself and Her Majesty? I hardly ever see them!"

'Himself' and 'Her Majesty' were Eris' words for their father and mother, Lord and Lady Valdelaine. Though he loved them dearly, Eris could poke fun at them too.

"They are very well, Eris. Especially now, with so much going on about them. They are quite enjoying it all!"

After a long pause, Eris asked:

"And what do you think of Count Michael?"

Now there was a question for Ioni as, since his arrival in Valdelaine she had held him in the highest esteem. Count Michael stood high at seven feet tall, his face was strong and ruddy and his thick dark hair was streaked with white. The man towered above everyone, though he smiled a lot and there was always laughter where he kept company. Garrulous and chatty, he seemed to have time for everyone; warm and generous, he loved a jolly feast, a good joust or a daring hunt. Count John Vaune de St. Michel, or Count Michael, as everyone called him was the king's cousin and the king's strong right hand. Known among his troops as the Archangel, he had lived up to the title all his life, protecting the monarch, protecting the realm. He had put to flight all enemies who dared cross Esmor's frontiers; time and again he had been called on to rid his country of marauding invaders and time and again he had risen to every occasion, such that the title the Archangel had carried more than a grain of truth. He had revelled in every challenge and despite his humour and bluffness was a most shrewd tactician in war, with an uncanny flair for turning seeming defeat into victory.

In answer to the question put to her by Eris, Ioni's reply was,

"He is in every way a towering hero, a man who, in this age, stands above all others! And now, little page, pray be gone. My duties call, as I'm seeing our brother Jean quite soon!"

"My word, Ioni, but you're becoming quite a lady!" said Eris with a smile.

This time round, Jean had been good to Ioni, whenever she had sought his company. In turn, he felt a kind of responsibility towards her; but there was more to it than just that – he, likewise enjoyed her company. A sense had grown within him about her, a strange joyful sense that he was in the presence of someone quite out of the ordinary. He could not quite express it for himself but he felt a great and benign energy that seemed to emanate from her – warm, strong and wise. And this sense was not merely for one or two days only – it was there every day. He had been as good as his word to her on his promise of three years before, to smooth out for her the issue of her change of heart with regard to her previously mooted betrothal to Leon Belmont. Along with so many others Leon was now at Valdelaine again, but his presence did not bother her. In the way of things she could not avoid meeting Leon from time to time, and though she had entered a phase of dislike towards him, she was always courteous, always her self-contained self with him. As for Jean, she continued to grow in wonder at him, he was now so much taller than before and still so interesting she was sure they would now be friends for life. She was learning more and more about him. He was solicitous for her welfare, for that of his parents and brother Eris, he seemed to carry all of his loved ones as a kind of burden within himself. Her intuition told her that he did not lack physical courage but with other people he was tactful and polite but never expansive. She did not love him less for this, she found his gentleness, his love of solitude all the more intriguing.

Jean did not lack physical courage, this she had seen many times already for he was in his last year of knightly training, and so he engaged heartily in every competition, every challenge, every feat of arms. Only the other day in the company of her father and Count Michael she had watched him take up a challenge to combat with sword and shield. His opponent seemed the stronger, and Jean was forced back a number of times. The knight now launched a fearsome attack upon Jean, hammering repeatedly upon his shield and driving Jean back step for step until, with a mighty stroke he knocked Jean's shield right out of his grip sending it spinning across the bawn and wounding Jean's left hand. But Jean wasn't in the least dismayed. Without his shield and with his opponent bearing down on him for the 'kill', Jean stood sideways on to present a slim target to his attacker, pointed and parried with his sword and then catching his opponent on the wrong foot he launched his own fierce attack at the other man's shield, hacking and hacking again, giving him no time to resume his stance, then with one sideways blow to the shield, coming on the rebound Jean brought his sword full force across to his opponent's sword, such force indeed that swept the man's sword out of his grasp, sending it spinning head over point until it found rest in the bawn some yards away. Their breath regained the two men embraced, complimenting each other on their skill. Then Jean retrieved his shield and smiled a happy smile. Within a moment however the smile was gone from his face as though he had other things to do or think about.

When he approached his father, Ioni and Count Michael they were full of praise for the manner in which, without a shield he had gone into attack with sword only and deftly won the contest.

"That was well done, Jean," his father said.

"You were wonderful," said Ioni.

"I think I trained you well!" laughed Count Michael.

Jean thanked them politely and smiled, divesting himself of arms and armour and giving them to a page. And by then, the other far off look had returned to his eye, the other Jean had reappeared. He who had enjoyed the combat, but once over, Jean's eyes seemed to say "There are other wondrous things to do – there's more to life than knightly combat. And now to other things!"

And Ioni had taken all this in and found it all the more endearing in a man like her brother.

"Shall we walk a little," he said to Ioni, smiling, "and talk a little, too, for I have need to hear what you might have to say!"

As they walked across the bridge and out among the pavilions in the fields, Ioni said:

"You know, Jean, I never knew I had a brother quite like you. So brave in combat and yet so free of combat when it is all over. Free for other things and people. Free to be at peace in your own company!"

Apart altogether from her natural reasons for seeking out her older brother's company so much, Ioni had another reason too – the fact was she had very little time in which to do so. The girls of the Valdelaine household were obliged to wait on the queen in her chambers for a number of hours each day, sometimes in the mornings, sometimes in the afternoons, especially if her majesty had no important visitors at those times. The girls would enter the chamber, curtsey to the queen and then join her, seated about her on chairs or cushions. They would chat with the queen while doing their embroidery; they would entertain her with stories and sing songs to her, accompanied on lutes and other instruments. They would observe and learn the niceties of court etiquette, and quite often the queen would read aloud romantic stories and poems. These last the girls loved most for invariably they were romantic stories of gallant knights and noble ladies. Thus the time spent with the queen was both an education and an entertainment.

On their first visit to the queen, however, the girls were not calm at all, but were all in a tizzy with excitement. Even the night before, they spent some hours chattering together about what they might say to her majesty, while at the same time running to every room available, pulling and dragging at every clothes chest for clothes, and pestering every female family adult, requesting to borrow jewellery, brooches, earrings and all kinds of trinkets.

"Now, Anna," Fleur was breathless as she instructed her little sister. "Tomorrow you must be on your best behaviour, all the time mind, all the time we are with the queen. We don't want her majesty thinking you are a silly little girl, no, you must behave like a perfect young lady, you understand?"

"Yes Fleur. Yes Fleur," Anna was saying, her eyes rolling to heaven and giggling with amusement to see her sister so excited. She had never seen Fleur and the other girls in such a frenzy of dressing up and rehearsing their bows and curtseys, not to mention their words of address to the queen.

"You'll be dressed in a new dress specially made for you," panted Fleur. "You are to walk straight, sit up straight, don't dribble and spoil your dress. And for heaven's sake, Anna, make sure you go to the privy and make a good pee before we visit her majesty. When you're offered something to eat – eat slowly mind, don't gobble your food – and burp quietly. Oh God!" She turned to her cousin Clara, who had been amusedly watching her efforts at preparing Anna for the ordeal. "Clara, could you find me some veils, I want to try them all."

As it happened, all the veils were now with Eleanor next door and, being Eleanor, she called everyone in to view her efforts at dressing up and comment on them. In a moment everyone abandoned their own concerns to see how Eleanor was doing, and gathered round her not in admiration but with hilarious laughter. Eleanor had put on a dress twice too big for her, on her head she wore a painted wooden crown, a toy, over a veil that stretched to the ground. She had poked some cloths into her slippers to make her look taller, but they made her wobble quite a bit when she tried to display her walk to the others.

"You may all laugh and giggle!" she sniffed, "But when the queen meets me tomorrow –" she didn't finish the sentence for she lost her balance and fell over into the arms of Fleur and Clara! Then Eleanor proceeded to get everyone to play the parts, Fleur she put seated on a chair which was elevated because she had placed it on a clothes chest. Ioni and Clara she placed on either side of 'Queen Fleur'. Anna she took by the hand as lady in waiting. Then, from the door, Eleanor and Anna walked solemnly, heads erect, eyes down, step for step towards the royal trio at the far end of the room. Eleanor barely managed the huge green dress, and wobbled a little in her high slippers. On approaching the 'queen' Eleanor and Anna curtseyed beautifully.

"You may rise, young lady," Queen Fleur said, "and pray tell me what is your name, child?"

Eleanor stood to her full height and, with a twinkle in her eye, said:

"Majesty, I am the Lady Eleanor de Ronclava. You may have my permission to call me Eleanor, and my I say, your Majesty, how well you look this morning. Furthermore I might add – how exquisitely fortunate you are to make my acquaintance!"

At this, the little charade ended as the girls could not contain their peals of laughter. Later Ioni would remember all of this, how Eleanor had taken it on herself to amuse everyone and take the tension from the frenzied hour. Later Ioni would remember Eleanor.

On the morrow the girls approached the queen's chambers with some trepidation, but they need not have worried, as the queen made them welcome and quickly put them all at their ease. Her majesty Queen Isobel sat on a beautiful chair in the centre of the room, and all her ladies in waiting stood in groups around her. Ioni gasped when she saw how the chamber had been changed. Instead of the few old wall hangings, the walls were now covered with multicoloured tapestries, the furnishings in the room were exquisite, their gold edgings glimmering in the light of the warm fire. The girls were seated nearest the queen on chairs or large cushions.

Isobel, Queen of Esmor was in late middle age, yet her round kindly face had lost none of its handsomeness. Her blue eyes seemed to smile, at all times, and she delighted in the company of the young girls. Altogether, by the time they departed from her majesty's presence, they were already looking forward to their next encounter with their monarch.

As time passed, the queen had taken an interest in Ioni's singing voice; it was a voice that was strong, round and true. Privately she put it to Ioni that her voice was of exceptional quality but that it could do with some formal training. One of the queen's ladies, Marie de Claire was an excellent singer and a very good singing teacher. Ioni agreed to take lessons from the Lady Marie and within eight weeks of daily practice Ioni's voice was controlled and enlarged so much that, at banquets and soirees her voice filled the great hall from end to end and echoed high among the rafters. Ioni was to sing many times, not alone for the king and queen, but for the many visitors who continued to throng to Valdelaine.

*   *   *

"Who are they?" Ioni exclaimed as she and Jean watched yet another cavalcade draw close to Valdelaine.

"If I am not mistaken that may be Raxtene!"

Erak Osthene, self styled king of the people of the mountains in the far south, rode at the head of a retinue of nigh a hundred men. Ioni was struck by their outlandish appearance and dress for they wore little armour, only woollens and leather; they kept their hair long and carried beards and fearsome moustaches. They each carried weapons in plenty, especially battle axes, broadswords and maces, and strapped to the back of each trooper was a long and ugly halberd. The people of the southern mountains had always maintained their independence, for who in his right mind would try to conquer a people who lived in a land of high plateaus and delving ravines, a land of high rock and plunging cataracts, a land famous for its wolves, its bears and its fabled monsters? The king of Bergmond claimed sovereignty over the mountain people, but they, in turn swore fealty to no one and were experts at playing off Esmor against Bergmond and vice versa.

"Things must be serious when Raxtene comes to us, or if we have invited him," Jean mused.

"What do you mean?" Ioni queried.

"Well, one wonders why he would come to us, unless our king saw signs of trouble to come. Trouble for us, I mean, trouble from the direction of Bergmond. Perhaps the king seeks some kind of alliance with Raxtene!"

"What kind of trouble, Jean, do you mean war? Have we not been at peace with Bergmond now for many years?"

"I'm sure I have no idea, Ioni," Jean said as the cavalcade passed them. "But it is very interesting – curious, that this should happen. Those people have made war on the southern reaches of Esmor – almost at will, whenever they fancied, as it were. And now they are to be allies, or so it seems. You should ask mother about Raxtene's people – I'm sure they raided Rocharden many times when she was growing up!"

"I see!" said Ioni. "Mama doesn't speak of her childhood much, nor of Rocharden neither. She never mentioned... these."

They watched as the cavalcade stopped, dismounted and began making fires and tents. They were quite outlandish, she thought.

Before the day was out Ioni was to meet Raxtene in person, for Count Michael presented him to the family. The giant man greeted Lord Henry courteously; then as his eyes moved to look at Lady Marie his face broadened into a genial smile. He took both her hands into his, bowed and kissed them.

"It is good to see you again, my Lady," he said, still holding her little hands in his. "It has been a long, long time since last we met!"

Marie took a deep breath, returning his smile.

"It has indeed, my Lord; I am grateful that you are strong and well."

He then gave Ioni a little bow and passed on to greet Jean and Eris.

Ioni gave her mother a little nudge and whispered:

"Mother! I am amazed! How could you ever have known a man such as this?"

Marie looked straight ahead, but on her face there was her eye-fluttering smile!

"You forget, my child," she said, "that I am a Rocharden, we met the mountain people all the time. I was barely a child at the time."

And that was one of Marie's occasional golden fibs she kept solely for her children. She did not say which end of her childhood she was barely at – at the time. In fact she was a hale and feisty fifteen years at the time she had last seen Raxtene. The second golden fib was that Raxtene and his mountain moss troopers were not paying social calls to Rocharden, not at all! In fact they were frequently besieging Rocharden and plundering the southern lands of both Esmor and Bergmond at the time. It was only in after years that Count Michael had gradually come to an understanding with Raxtene – for he had crossed the wild man's palms with sliver to keep him sweet and mostly on the Esmor side. The two had become friends over the years. At any rate, Marie was no longer the wild child she had been at the time – crossing the threshold of Valdelaine as Lord Henry's wife had change her into the most lady-like of beings. Lord! But it was hard enough to rear her children to the paths of righteousness and she saw no reason to enlighten them as to her wild and wild-tempered childhood.

Raxtene and his entourage, to all outward appearances, enjoyed their time in Valdelaine. They stayed until after yuletide. When they began their long return journey to the south, the general feeling was that the embassy had been a success, although Count Michael did confide to Lord Henry that the king could never be absolutely sure of Raxtene – until he lined up his forces with those of Esmor, nobody could be sure of what he might do. If the affairs of state between the kingdoms of Esmor and Bergmond took a turn for the worse, Count Michael knew for certain that he would need Raxtene on his side. Esmor was small by comparison with Bergmond and the old saying held true, "Esmor has an army, but Bergmond has armies!"

In the early spring of the new year Valdelaine was the venue for a meeting with the representatives of Bergmond. It was a large embassy comprising diplomats, courtiers and military representatives. This embassy was led by the Duke of Anflair, cousin to King Leopold of Bergmond. He cut a dashing figure, with good looks and

reddish-blond hair – he was quite popular with the Esmorin court; friendly and charming, a soldier, a diplomat
and a courtier all rolled into one. Bergmond had sent
their most popular man. Ioni could not help but be
charmed by the duke and his immediate entourage. But
after these had come quite a vastly different bunch of rug-
ged-looking knights and barons. As they entered the great
hall, they looked out of place, with strange and grim
faces. Especially their leader, a huge giant of a man with
bulbous eyes and swelled red cheeks, thick lips that never
smiled; altogether it was a countenance in a perpetual
state of scowl. The men who followed him were much
the same, and all of them wore a black cloak with an embroidered silver dagger as though they belonged to a
unique group.

"Who is that man?" Ioni queried her mother as the
giant passed.

"That is Baron Gavron de Laude," Marie answered. "Seemingly he is one of the most powerful men
in Bergmond!"

"He makes me shudder!" whispered Ioni, as Gavron passed close to her, his towering figure encased in
armour and chainmail, surmounted by the great high conical helmet, made him look formidable and frightening.

In the following days, Ioni noted that Baron Gavron kept a bodyguard of twenty or so young men, very
young men, all dressed in the black and purple livery that
she had seen worn by the baron and his lieutenants, Baron
Agron and Baron Conrad. These young men proved
themselves admirable fighters, in tourneys and in feats of
arms. One of them in particular had caught Ioni's eye, a
dark haired smiling gallant called Philip, with whom she
willingly danced and chatted at the evening banquets.
From him she learned that they were handpicked at child-

hood and reared by Gavron to become eventually, it was hoped, an elite troop of knights dedicated to protecting King Leopold of Bergmond. She liked Philip, he was so cheerful and so gracious; she found also that he had a deeply reflective side to his nature and that endeared him even more to her.

Meanwhile, each day, the Duke of Anflair and the barons were in the great hall in deep conference with Count Michael and the king's courtiers. No one knew how well the embassy was going and Count Michael certainly made no one the wiser. For two long weeks the two sides argued and debated. The Bergmondese were adamant in their demands – that the rich country west of the Gavenne should be added to Bergmond. This was nothing new, that countryside had been long disputed. But the king was equally adamant that no territory should be ceded to Bergmond, even in return for a twenty year peace treaty, which the Bergmondese dangled before the Esmorins, like a carrot. Eventually the negotiations broke down and the Duke of Anflair took it on himself to broach Count Michael with the dark news, that sooner or later Bergmond would declare war. The duke was saddened but assured Count Michael that he would do everything he could to continue to find a path to peace. It would be difficult of course, with the warmongering Gavron and his allies, who would constantly do all in their power to persuade Bergmond to the brink of war and beyond. The two noblemen embraced and wished each other God's blessings. On the morrow the Bergmondese departed.

And so, spring came and with it the Eastertide. It had been the most wonderful time in her life for Ioni; she had seen and learned so much, she had made a myriad of friends, and she knew she would have so much to ponder on. Some weeks after Easter the king and queen were ready to depart for the city of Esmor. The royal couple were so grateful to Henry and Marie de Valdelaine and in reward for their munificent hospitality they gave a most surprising gift – Jean was knighted. As was normal, he spent the night in vigil of prayer – in the ground chamber of the old tower, which was used as a family chapel. The following morning, in the presence of his family and a throng of knights and courtiers, the king placed his sword upon Jean's shoulders and dubbed him knight.

Within a week Valdelaine was returned to its old self and the little city of pavilions and tents was gone. Jean and Eris, too, were gone, but Ioni was not troubled by their departure. Both she and her cousins would have so much to talk about in the months to follow. The Ronclavas stayed on for the summer and did not depart until autumn.

Ioni was happy, though unaware of the darker things that had taken place under the roof of her home, darkest of all were the seeds of war sown between the two kingdoms. The years would pass before the people she met in that time would again tread upon her consciousness, not in peaceful festival, however, but amid the harshness and horror of the oncoming conflict. The seeds of her destiny were taking root.

Chapter III: A Bitter Rainfall

*U*pon an evening, when the howling winds of March whipped the cold turrets of Valdelaine, Ioni sat with her mother by the warm fire that had been set for them in the solar room. Fleur and Anna had gone round to the upper reaches of the old tower to visit their father, Uncle Robert. Ioni's father, Lord Henry, was out and about on his estates, seeing tenants, visiting outlying villages, and generally surveying the progress of the spring ploughing. Given the inclemency of the weather, Ioni was disposed to enjoy this quiet time in her mother's company, all in the radiant warmth of the huge fire. She paused, heaved a sigh of contentment, putting down her embroidery, she looked at her mother.

"What are you thinking about, Mama?" Ioni said quietly. Marie smiled, and she too, placed her needlework on her lap.

"I am always thinking of so many things," Marie said, in a non committal way. Then, she added, "I was thinking of the boys, Jean and Eris. Wondering where they are, and what they are doing. They are so far away, and we get such little news of them."

Ioni smiled again at her mother.

"I am sure they are both well," she said, with a sigh. "Eris is fourteen now, and I'm sure he is growing up to be a fine young gentleman!"

They both smiled at this; their faces glowing in the firelight.

"I was also thinking of something else," Marie said. "I was thinking about you, Ioni!"

"About me, Mama!" Ioni chuckled. "What about me?"

Marie turned her head sideways, thoughtfully, the top of the long needle held against her cheek; then her head bent over her needlework again.

"The two boys are now seeing something of the world," she said. "Something of the world beyond Valdelaine. They are preparing themselves for life."

Oh Dear, Ioni mused silently, I wonder what this all means for me!

"I was thinking," said Marie. "Maybe, you should leave Valdelaine, even for a little while."

Ioni could not control her surprise, for now her dark eyes were large with amazement.

"Mama! I have no wish to leave you, nor Valdelaine!" Ioni said calmly. "Anyway where would I go – even for a little while!"

Marie gazed at her daughter.

"I think maybe you need to get away from Valdelaine and from all of us here – for a little while only!"

"Mama! I love all of us here! You know that!" Ioni said. "Why would I wish to leave, and where would I go?"

"You could go, and visit your cousins at Ronclava!" Marie said. Ronclava was where her uncle Raymond lived, a fine estate upriver and a fine castle on it.

"Mama! My relatives, at Ronclava, are very dear to me!" Ioni said, indignantly. "But I would not wish to spend a moment more than I had to, under the watchful eye of the Lady Blanche!"

Marie smiled, and even laughed silently.

"Blanche is not as bad as she is made out to be, you know!" she said. Ioni again looked at her mother.

"Mama, please don't send me to Ronclava," she said. "It would be constant warfare between Blanche and me – she's too fussy, too opinionated, I could not enjoy one moment of peace with her!"

"Of course I won't send you there, my love!" Marie said reassuringly. "It was only a thought! But you are becoming a young woman –"

"I am a young woman, Mama!" Ioni interjected. "And I don't wish to leave you!"

"I know, my child," Marie said soothingly. "But a few weeks away from me will not do you any harm. In fact, I feel sure it would do you good. Just for a little while."

Ioni paused in her pout, and bit her lip.

"But not to Ronclava!"

"No! Not to Ronclava," Marie said. "Not if you don't wish it, my love!"

Ioni breathed a sigh of relief and contentment, and was about to take up the embroidery again, when Marie said:

"You know, Ioni. It is only a thought; but you could spend some time at the abbey!"

Ioni's embroidery fell to the floor, and as she bent forward to pick it up, she looked up at Marie, and said:

"I have no wish to go to the abbey, Mother! Neither Ronclava nor the abbey attract me!

Marie returned eagerly to her work. It was getting dark outside so she took a taper and held it to the fire and then lit a candle on the mantel.

"Remember, my child, we are patrons of the abbey," Marie said. "I myself spent time there before I was married; and I found it beautiful, peaceful... The abbess and the nuns would greatly appreciate a visit from the daughter of the house of Valdelaine! It would do them good; they would feel, well, appreciated by such an honour!"

Ioni calmed herself down, and breathed gently once more. She had been quite ambushed by her mother's conversation; and, quite frankly, she was now quite out-manoeuvred by her mother's thoughts.

"So, you wish me to go and spend some time with the nuns at the abbey?" she said with a sigh.

"Yes, Ioni, my love, I do wish you to go there, for a while," Marie answered.

Ioni paused and thought for a moment.

"If it is your wish, Mama," she said, "then I will go. I will go."

"Thank you, my child," Marie said. "I would dearly love you to go, and... believe me, it will do you good!"

Ioni smiled, as her mother rose from her chair to embrace her. Mothers always have the knack of knowing what is good, she thought, as she embraced Marie.

Ioni turned to sit again, but whirled round to face Marie.

"But beware, Mother," she said in mock warning. "You shall be so lonely without me!"

With that both women embraced again, and laughed. Ioni begged to be excused; and made her way to the door. But, then, she paused, turned to Marie and said teasingly:

"You may live to regret this, you know! What if I decide to stay at the abbey and spend my life as a nun!"

Her mother turned towards her, chuckling,

"The ways of God are strange, my love," Marie said, coming towards Ioni. "What more could a mother desire on this earth than to give her daughter to the good Lord. But I doubt it will ever happen in your case, Ioni."

"Why, Mama!" cried Ioni. "How can you say that?"

Marie reached out, and lovingly cradled her daughter's face in the palms of her hands.

"The nuns spend long, long hours in prayer, my love," Marie said, smiling affectionately into Ioni's eyes. "Always, and ever, your prayers were so sweet. But, dear me, they were ever so short!"

"Mama!" Ioni said, smiling, and left the room.

The notion had occurred to her to invite Fleur along with her for company but her mother had turned down the idea. Marie had been quick to spot that with Fleur for company at the abbey, precious time would be lost in idle chat and banter and thus Ioni would hardly benefit in a spiritual manner from her time spent there. If Ioni wished for such companionship then she had better stay at home in Valdelaine. No, Marie had said, better you go alone, Ioni. And that had been that.

Two days later, Ioni departed, having said fond goodbyes to everyone.

"Keep you well, my child," Marie had said as she kissed Ioni goodbye. "Keep always well."

Ioni waved as the two wagons set off for St. Catherine's some fifteen miles away. The wagon in front, carried the young Lady Ioni, the other carried gifts for the abbey. Among these were some items of furniture, a batch of hens, some fresh meat and fish, and a roll of parchment for the abbey scriptorium.

Upon arrival at the abbey of St. Catherine, Ioni was greeted warmly by the Abbess Mère Brice, a tall, strong, and kindly woman. As is always the case, Ioni was fussed over, with great affection, by the sisters. How tall she had grown, how beautiful, and how delighted they all were to have her there, as such a special guest. But Ioni knew she was being spoiled by the sisters, and in her heart, she felt no real need for spoiling. Before falling asleep the previous night, Ioni had made a mental note on one thing: for this visit to the abbey, she would be the very soul of silence, humility and patience. This was not a time for frivolous idleness; it was, rather, a time to make ready her soul, in advance of whatever life might offer – good, bad or in between. As Jean and Eris had gone to Count Michael, to train for knighthood, so too, she was going to St. Catherine's to prepare for whatever might be in store for her. She smiled at the comparison. The sisters continued to spoil her. However, Ioni would have none of it. Heartily, she threw herself into the life of the abbey; she worked in the laundry, in the garden and in the fields. She attended all the daily hours of prayer and chant. For the first few nights, she had even risen for the hour of nocturnal prayer. When her head nodded, and her prayer book fell to the floor, Mère Brice had advised her only to attend the daytime hours and thus be refreshed by a full night's sleep. As Ioni was able to read and write she was allowed to spend much time in the scriptorium; this pleased her greatly, for she loved to read, and so spent happy hours working her way through the many manuscripts there.

When one week at the Abbey was done, Ioni was feeling more at home there, though at times she felt a little overpowered and perplexed by her new life. So many religious ideas, and so many ideas about God had assailed her mind and, far from reassuring her, had quite confused her. How to take it all in, she thought, I would need a life time to master it all. She was beginning to feel a little sorry for herself; lost as she was in this whirling milieu of godliness – that was St. Catherine's. How do the sisters manage to live this life? She wondered. A week here and I am no better than I was before, and indeed, no wiser in myself as to the things of God. Granted, the abbey was beautiful, and so atmospheric; it was easy to imagine that God or his angels and saints were close at hand, behind the stone of some Gothic column, or beyond the light of some holy lamp. She sighed deeply and wondered if she would ever make even a tiny beginning to it all. I am happy, but... a little lost, she thought.

In conference with Mère Brice, the abbess, Ioni spoke freely of the many thoughts and feelings that had flowed through her mind and heart, during the brief time she had spent, so far, at the abbey.

"In the evenings, when I glimpse the stars, from under the arches of the cloister, I have the feeling that God is so large. Then too, I realise my understanding is so small. In between, the gulf seems so large that I wonder if I can ever come nearer to God at all," Ioni told the abbess. A gentle smile came across Mère Brice's lips, and her eyes looked at Ioni with such compassion.

"But remember, Ioni," the abbess said. "God is always close to us – yes, even when we have no sensation, nor feeling, of His presence. Maybe you should keep in mind the wonderful words of St. Paul, as he spoke to the Athenians: he said of God: "In Him we live, we move, and we have our being!"

"We live, we move, and we have our being," Ioni slowly repeated the words.

"This teaches us," the abbess continued, "that God is all about us!"

"Like the air we breathe, Mother," Ioni said smiling at the comparison.

"Exactly!" exclaimed the abbess, smiling, also.

"But, Mother, there is something else," said Ioni. "When I see the faces of the sisters, as they go about their work and prayer, I am struck with wonder at... at..." Ioni struggled for words. "...at their faith, Mother. And then I think my own faith is so small, in comparison. I just wonder what it is they have, that, well, I do not have. My faith is small, my doubt seems large."

Mère Abbess paused a while, as she let Ioni's words sink in.

"Maybe what you do not realise, my child," she said patiently, "Is that, for each sister, her faith is like a candle that shines within a vast sea of doubt, just like your own! The difference is that each one of them takes that candle of faith, and brings it with her into her everyday living. There is no reason why you cannot do this in your own way! Every day, every one of them, takes up that little flame of faith, and then takes a chance on it, that... well, that God is with them."

"Takes a chance on it!" Ioni repeated slowly.

"Yes, my child," Mère Abbess said gently. "We cannot hope to have the simple feeling that God is close to us, at all times. Such feelings are transitory. On the other hand, faith is lived out in our lives, by taking a chance on God, day by day."

"Taking a chance on it!" Ioni again repeated the words of the abbess.

"Yes. But the chance you are taking in faith is not based on any old whim, my child," Mère Abbess continued. "You are taking a chance on God, and on His power, and on his promises!"

Ioni paused for a long time and then said, "You have given me much to reflect on, Mother. I shall think about these things."

"Then God be with you, my child," Mère Abbess said cheerily.

And so, Ioni continued her life at the abbey. She loved the hours spent in the scriptorium, watching the sisters write and illuminate the manuscripts. Sometimes she would take down other works to read, like annals and chronicles; of course, she was fascinated to have the opportunity to read the book entitled 'The Annals of Valdelaine.' This particular work contained so many stories about her ancestors and the last pages contained details of her very own parents' lives. The annals gave her a thrilling sense of continuity with Valdelaine and its past. Someday, in the future, the annals would mention Jean and Eris and – of course, herself. She wondered what it might have to say. Beyond all of this, she reminded herself that she had not come to St. Catherine's to read stories; so she dutifully took it upon herself to spend more time reading the religious works, the Holy Gospels and the Psalms.

For a long time, she had little enough success with the holy writings; she could read an entire page from end to end, but not be truly moved by it. There was so much to read. There was one evening, when one of the sisters was called away from her scribely duties, and Ioni sauntered over to the wooden desk, and hovered over the last unfinished page. As ever, her reading and translating brought her no comprehension at all. It was indeed a page from the bible that she knew, but the substance of the work meant quite little to her. But her heart lifted when she read the last sentence the sister had written. It read:

"Fear not; for I have redeemed thee, I have called thee by thy name; thou art mine. When thou passest through the waters, I will be with thee; and through the rivers, they shall not overflow thee."

Now there is something with meaning, Ioni thought happily, and she sat down to read it over, and over, again, until she could remember it all.

Later that night, as she lay on the hard bed of her cell she recalled the words 'Do not be afraid, *Ioni*, for I have redeemed you. I have called you by your name, *Ioni*, you are mine! The waters shall not overflow thee.'

She smiled with the sheer fascination of it all. All those hundreds of years ago, God had spoken those words to His holy, chosen, Hebrew people. And now, it was as if God was there with her, speaking the ancient words into her very soul.

Repeating the precious words over and over again, she gradually fell into a peaceful sleep.

By the third week she had spent at the abbey, Ioni had settled into the life there, and was content. This was due, in no small measure, to the peacefulness of the place. Ioni was the beneficiary of a sense of quiet orderliness, combined with a corresponding sense of being so free of care; free in her mind of burdens of ordinary life. For her, this was a treat and a tonic to the spirit, a kind of holiday from everyday care. The feeling had come to her gradually: one evening after she had worked in the fields she sat on the bed in her cell, and heaved a sigh of sheer joy, and wondered why she was so happy. It came to her that it was perhaps the combination of everything, the work, the prayer and the companionship of the sisters that gave her such peace of soul. She had come to know all of the sisters, the younger ones and the older ones. There were some titled ladies, like herself, in the community; there were merchants' daughters from the cities; there were strong country women too, rosy cheeked and matter of fact. She found she could talk with them all and was charmed to listen to stories of their varied experiences of life before entry to St. Catherine's. Accustomed as she was to being spoiled as the only daughter of a loving family, Ioni revelled in the company of the womenfolk of St.

Catherine's; she loved their insights, their cheerfulness, and above all, their common femininity. However, now that she was growing more and more content, Ioni continued her private exploration to find every grain of truth and wisdom as was possible in the time she was to spend there.

An afternoon of sunlight and cloud found Ioni working in the abbey garden with Sister Ethel, the gardener, who was quietly directing the labour of the day. In spite of the cool winds that invaded even the garden enclosure, Ioni found her body grow warm with the activity. When an hour had gone by in silence, Sister Ethel called Ioni and said to her,

"You have worked enough for today, my dear. Everything is done. You are free now, child. Go and take some time for yourself!"

Ioni was surprised that the day's work was over so soon, but she obediently left the wild fresh air, went to her cell and washed. She sat on the bed for a while wondering what she would do next and, thinking of nothing in particular, decided to venture to her favourite sanctuary, the scriptorium. When she got there, Ioni found the place empty; at this hour all the sisters were elsewhere, working in the fields beyond the abbey walls. Outside, the winds continued to rise and fall, and there, with nothing for company within, save the scripts and scrolls and the wooden desks and seats and shelves, Ioni was happy in the feeling of solitude. For a long time, she simply sat there, just listening to the sounds coming from beyond. Strange, she thought, how sweet solitude could be, and then her eye fell upon a copy of the Psalter, which she opened and began to read. The psalm in question was one of great comfort, about the mercy and compassion of God, and Ioni was savouring every word. She had passed the verse without heed but suddenly took a sharp intake of breath as she re-read it:

'Who redeemeth thy life from destruction; who crowneth thee with loving kindness and tender mercies.'

Again, she took a deep breath, and again she read the verse to make sure it was really there. And the verse was true and it was true of her, Ioni.

God redeemeth thy life from destruction!

Her mind flooded with the memory of that day, years before, as she had struggled amid the swirling waters of the Gavenne.

Had she herself not been lifted from the waters of death, to live again, to live again, when one moment more, and she was lost in the torrent forever?

"He hath redeemed your life from – destruction," she whispered.

And so God had done – had done for her, that she might live on. Live, thought Ioni, live on, to what end, who knows? But live!

"He hath crowned you with loving kindness and compassion," she said aloud.

And so He had. She had been the child of good fortune and blessings from the moment of her birth; adored by her family, and loved by all who met her. She was the daughter of the woman she admired and loved most in all the world; she was crowned with the loving kindness of the great Marie de Valdelaine. This was a love she must now treasure, as never before. This was a love she must return, and return a million times over, with all her heart and soul. It was Marie who had asked her to come to this place, it was Marie who had been her treasure and who had continued to bless her, time and again, through all her life.

*   *   *

So far the day had been uneventful, Ioni was with a group of the sisters, working in the abbey fields; the spring afternoon was cool and a blustery wind set the sisters veils fluttering but there was no way out of such work as the cold earth had to be turned for the planting of vegetables. They were all out of breath at times as the work was strenuous; Ioni was enjoying the silent companionship of the nuns and also the work in hand. She could feel her body and her cheeks grow warm in the cold air as she dug into the soil, lifted it and broke it. She stood for breath at one moment and caught the eye of the sister next to her who gave her a knowing smile and a nod of the head. Tonight there would be aching muscles and sore hands, especially for Ioni who was unaccustomed to manual work. Ioni smiled briefly, cast her eyes downward and continued with her task. After an hour or so they paused and Ioni watched with pleasure the amount of the work done and the area of ground turned. There was rain falling now, and Sister Ethel, the gardener, bade them all leave to go, and indeed to run as fast as possible as the rain was beginning to spill a downpour. And run they did, with shrieks and laughter and billowing veils along the path from the fields to the shelter of the abbey walls. In her cell, Ioni quickly changed her dress and dried her long hair as best she could, exhilarated by the sense of being so warm in the cool air. In the refectory, she sat with the others, silently welcoming the warm soup and the dry bread. Although she did notice that Mère Abbess was missing from her usual place at the upper table, Ioni relished the simple meal as though it were a sumptuous banquet.

Later, after prayers, Ioni had just seated herself in her place on a bench in the little scriptorium, had opened a page of the book which was her study for the evening when she was lightly tapped on the shoulder by Sister Anne who murmured gently into her ear, "Ioni, dearest young lady, Mère Abbess wishes to see you in her study chamber." It was a moment before these words and the summons they contained sank in. Ioni whispered "Yes, Sister!" and rose from the bench, walked down between the rows of tables to the door which she closed behind her as silently as possible. At the end of the stone passage-way she was surprised to find Mère Abbess there, smiling at her almost compassionately, with eyes that seemed to be searching her face intently.

"Ah! There you are, Ioni," Mother said tenderly and took Ioni's hand gently. "Please come with me now, my child, for I have something to tell you." Puzzled, Ioni said, "Yes, Mother," and allowed herself to be conveyed by Mother's hand in the failing light of the evening. Ioni glanced sideways at Mother, more curious than ever now at being summoned at such an hour by the abbess. They stopped in the passage a few paces from the door of Mother's study. Mother pressed Ioni's hand in hers and said,

"Ioni, my child. Are you – are you a brave girl?"

What a question, Ioni thought, mystified, am I a brave girl? God, what a question! And how should I know, anyway, whether I'm brave or not?

"I don't know, Mother," she said.

Mother was now trembling a little and, looking away, spoke again,

"Ioni, child, you were here with us when Frère Benedict spoke to us about the Cross. About the Cross of Our Lord, you remember, and how we, all of us, must bear our own cross in this life."

What was this good woman talking about, Ioni thought to herself but answered "Yes, Mother!"

In fact she remembered the sermon clearly and had been quite impressed with it, such as it was. They were now at the study door which the abbess was opening.

"My child," said Mother looking intently up at Jesus' face, "I must ask you now to be brave and to bear a heavy cross."

They were now in the chamber standing near the writing table where Mother was lighting candles. Outside the window, in the last of the spring daylight the rain continued to pour. Ioni, still completely mystified, guessing that perhaps Mother Abbess was about to bid her to some extraordinary act of penitence, prepared herself for whatever must be. Mother reached out and held both Ioni's arms.

"My child, there has been – bad news. Very bad news."

Oh God! Ioni thought. This was what all this ceremonial had been about. Bad news! But who? Oh God, it is Eris. No, Father has been injured. No Jean.

"Your mother," said the Abbess, solemnly. "Your mother, Ioni. Your mother is dying, my child."

There was a moment of helpless searching within her, and then Ioni feeling weak, fell into a chair. She shook and shivered and the tears ran down her cheeks. How could it be mother, she thought, all the others… and she could think no more. She was in the arms of Mère Abbess, that she was sure of. And the rain, the rain outside the window, that too she was sure of. For moments she was numb and then the panic, of realising the words "Your mother is dying."

I must go to her. What has happened to her! Quickly, I must go to her. There is no time to be lost!

No! Her heart screamed as she wept... not mother, not Mother!

And her strength failed. She wept in the arms that were holding her.

Somewhere behind her there was a knock on the door and Mother called "Enter!" There were other nuns about her now, embracing, weeping.

"Take her to her cell," Mother said. "I will meet you there, my child, in a few moments."

Down the passageway the little cortege of nuns passed, supporting her, weeping and murmuring. Ioni recognised the chapel door.

"No!" Ioni gasped. "Let me enter there, a moment. A moment with God, I beg you!"

She was unclasped, and the door was opened for her.

"Alone, I beg you!"

She walked, pace for pace now until she was standing before the little silent altar. She breathed and just looked at the altar and the cross. She shook a little but her tears were gone. She whispered in the silent air to a God she could neither see, nor hear.

"If you are there," she heard herself whisper, "I need you now. Whatever my lack of goodness, whatever my faults and sins, my lack of prayer and devotion – I need you now, whoever, whatever you may be!"

And she knelt before the altar, all her thoughts were gone, only the sense of being there, alone, came to her. Moments later she emerged from the chapel. There were other nuns reaching to her in sorrow. Finally she reached the inside of her cell. The sisters embraced her each in turn and departed. Only Mother Abbess was left with her now.

"I have not told you the full truth," the abbess spoke, Ioni stood breathless with her back to the cell wall. "I told you, your mother was dying. Sadly there is no need for haste, my child, and there is not a thing you can do now. My child – your mother is dead!"

Ioni simply allowed her body to lean backward for support against the wall which she found. She gazed about her. So that is it, she thought. All the haste, all the hurry in the world is of no use. Try as I might to reach her, she has gone from me. Already. In my young, little life. She, of all people. She has gone!

"Alas!" Ioni cleared her throat. "As you say, there's nothing I can do now!"

Late that night, Ioni finally gained the comfort and familiarity of her own bedroom chamber at Valdelaine. Jean had ridden out to collect her from the abbey; she had been conveyed homeward in a little carriage, escorted by Jean and a group of torch bearing outriders. She had seen her mother's face, beautiful and serene in death. Indeed she had gazed at that face for a long time, surrounded as she was by family and friends, in the candlelight of the great bedchamber. The day's events had played strange tricks on her, standing there with her father and Jean she had been greeted by people she failed to recognise in her grief, only to recognise them some time later. Her uncle Raymond had spoken words of comfort to her, but she had not known who he was.

Now she stood by the window of her chamber. How the world, nay, the universe itself, had changed in so short a time. The rain that had poured all day began to ease and fade away. What a bitter rain, she thought, as she remembered its first drops falling upon her that afternoon, then all the interim of shock and pain, a few hours that had its terrible sway upon her world, and, like a thief, was now waning away far into the night.

The journey to the abbey was retraced two days later as the remains of Marie de Valdelaine were brought there for burial in the family crypt. Standing there in the little chapel, Ioni felt weary and thought how much had changed for Valdelaine in a few short days. Her father, Lord Henry, and her uncles, Lord Raymond and Lord Robert, and her brother Jean surrounded her as the coffin was placed in its resting place to the sound of the abbey choir singing the plaintive notes of the Miserere. The last sight of the coffin brought a powerful twinge-like sensation in Ioni's breast, and tears flowed unbidden down her cheeks. Something so precious as a mother and her love – these are now lost to me for all of my life.

Later, the Valdelaine mourners made their way back to the castle and Ioni recalled the lines of villagers and peasants who had paid their respects to the dead with bouquets of spring flowers.

Chapter IV: Mistress of Valdelaine

*T*he first effects of the war were felt in Valdelaine long before any kind of fighting took
place. For one thing, Ioni's father, despite all his protests,
would be obliged to depart his castle and lands and join
the king in Esmor to serve on the royal council. It was
Count Michael who had insisted that Henry leave Valdelaine and take his place on the council. The count knew
Henry too well from their youth, valued his opinion and
experience greatly, and refused even to consider a wartime council without the presence of the Lord of Valdelaine. In vain were Henry's pleas that both his sons, Jean
and Eris, were already in the service of the count and that
Valdelaine needed his presence to manage its estates and
look after its affairs in general.   In yet another letter, the
count insisted that Henry join the king "for the sake of the
bonds of loyalty and friendship forged in our youth in the
defence of our country and our noble king." Henry could
not refuse this, the count was no fool, and if he insisted on
something then there had to be good reason for it.

"So there you have it," Henry said to Ioni as he
finished reading aloud from Count Michael's letter.

"I don't seem to have a way out of this, Ioni. It
seems that Valdelaine is to be emptied of all its men folk.
I'm afraid I will have to leave and join the king. As you
have just heard, Count Michael is quite insistent that I
go."

Ioni was standing before the table in the great hall
where her father was seated. She placed her hands on the
table and looked at Henry and said,

"I had hoped, Father, that you would be left here
with us, in the event of a war."

"I had hoped so too, my child," said Henry looking fixedly at her. "But it seems our country is in a grave situation and the king is pulling older men than me out of their estates and pressing everyone into service of some kind. I am sorry, Ioni, but I will be leaving, and soon, too, the count's messenger awaits to carry my reply to court within the hour."

Ioni drew in a deep breath, inside herself she felt deeply disappointed and not a little angry at her father's news. Henry pushed back his chair and arose, the letter still in his hand; he walked around the table to where Ioni stood and placed his hand on her shoulder. He stood for a moment gazing into some distance.

"Do you remember, once," he began solemnly, "that I told you that I longed for another boy when you were born."

"Yes I do, Father," Ioni said, casting her eyes downward.

"But I also told you," Henry went on, pressing his hand gently on her shoulder, "that, as the years went by I came to love you as my daughter. I loved everything about you, Ioni, but to me you became both a son and a daughter. I love your wisdom and your courage."

Ioni lifted her head to look at him and lifted her hand upwards to let it rest on his hand on her shoulder.

"Thank you, Father," she smiled, lovingly at him, a little tear welled in her eye and she blinked it away. Henry turned to face her and placed both his hands on her upper arms.

"Oh child," he sighed, "I fear that I must now call on that wisdom and courage, and ask you to carry a burden for all of us."

Ioni looked at him, eyes now wide with puzzlement.

"I must ask you," he said, "to take charge here in Valdelaine. You are the Lady of the house, but I must ask you to manage the entire estate while this war lasts."

Ioni was about to speak, but no words came, the task before her seemed immense.

"You will manage very well," Father said encouragingly. "Everything will go on, more or less as it always has done."

Ioni stared at him now, her mouth wide open.

"But Papa, I'm only eighteen, how will I –"

"You will manage," Father smiled into her eyes. "Uncle Raymond, Aunt Blanche and all their family are to arrive here, ostensibly, to look after you and all of Valdelaine. So do not worry, you will have plenty of help and counsel. The stewards, Frère Benedict, even Robert, the old goat – they will all be here to help you!"

Ioni almost laughed. "But how am I to manage all of them, Papa? I'm a child to all of them! I daren't stand up to Uncle Raymond, let alone Aunt Blanche!"

"You are a Valdelaine as much as any of them," father smiled. "You'll be able for any of them. And besides, if you take my advice, don't take them on, rather be present to them all, be at the heart of everything – let them think they are in charge, but, as I said, I need you to be at the heart of everything here, while I am gone. I trust your wisdom, Ioni. I trust you completely."

"Oh Papa!" Ioni sighed and embraced her father.

"Furthermore," said Henry gently enfolding her in his arms, "Remember your two brothers Jean and Eris as they enter the field for the first time – you will not go far wrong, my child!"

"Yes Papa," Ioni murmured.

Ioni departed from her father's presence with feelings that both daunted and exhilarated her at the same time.

Knowing that his absence could be for quite a long time, Henry had asked his brother Lord Raymond and his family to leave their estates in the hands of their stewards and to come to live in Valdelaine for the duration of his absence. They would provide help and company for Ioni, as she would now be running the large Valdelaine estate virtually alone. Uncle Robert, of course was already living in Valdelaine and had been doing so for some years since his wife, the Lady Fleur had died, his daughters Fleur and Anna had come to Valdelaine with him. It was of course, doubtful whether Uncle Robert could be much help to anyone. After Fleur had died, some of his mind had been lost, and he spent his life a recluse in the upper chambers of the old tower, studying his books and writing, with nothing save his great wolfhound and his pet raven for company. Though his daughters and Ioni visited him every day, he seemed to enjoy their visits, but he took no other interest in their welfare. It would be left to Uncle Raymond and his wife, Lady Blanche to assist Ioni with the vast task of managing a large castle like Valdelaine and its attendant estates and manors. Frère Benedict, who was the priest in the village, would be on hand as always to assist the family, particularly with financial and legal matters. The Frère could read and write in many languages including Latin and was quite a wizard when it came to all kinds of documentation.

I must learn and learn quickly, Ioni reflected, I am now responsible for Valdelaine, with father gone to the royal court, Eris in service to Count Michael, and Jean already knighted and in command of some troops in the Borderlands. Ioni felt just a little daunted by the size of the task ahead, but she was quite excited too. She was looking forward to having so much responsibility and power. Being determined that it would be she, Ioni, who would wield power in Valdelaine and, though she loved her uncles, aunts and cousins, she would not be a mere puppet in their hands. Authority was hers, and she would assert it, always making it known, gently and firmly, that she was in charge. She owed it to her dead mother; she owed it to her father and brothers that, no matter what befell, Valdelaine would not suffer in any way as a result of her stewardship. Gracefully she would accept the counsel of other people, but she would make decisions herself. After all, she had only to think, what would father have done, what would mother have done? As she thought about it, Ioni knew she would throw her heart into her new life, and she smiled.

Some weeks before he had departed, Henry had broached the subject of marriage with her.

"You are now almost of marriageable age," he had said. "Should you wish to do so soon, then it might be a good thing to be betrothed to Leon before the war takes him far afield."

"Father, I have no wish to marry Leon," she had said quietly, firmly. Father had looked up somewhat puzzled and a deep frown furrowed his brow. Leon had spent his early fostering years at Valdelaine, and in the minds of many people, Ioni and he would make a perfect match.

"But you were promised to him as a child!" he said.

"In all that time," Ioni said, "He never wrote to me. He never sent any gifts or tokens of love to me. When he did finally visit when I was fourteen, I did not find him pleasing to me in spite of his wealth and goodly inheritance!"

"No?" said father quizzically, the frown gone.

"No Father," Ioni continued. "After that time I was nearly drowned in the river, and Ander saved me, I realised, then, that I had only one precious life to live and that I would prefer to give myself to someone who loved me, who really loved me!"

"And what about Leon?" quizzed Father. "He seems a fine fellow. He's a distant relative and will inherit vast estates. He would be a very good match for you. And you'll find he will get to love you once you're married."

"I doubt it," Ioni said gently. "When he was here I found Leon to be vain, self centred and rather pompous. I felt nothing for him, and, in his time here he impressed on me the great favour that he was doing for me by proposing to marry me and the great favour he was doing you and all our family by taking me off your hands!"

"So you have no desire to marry him?" Father asked.

"Father, I have no desire to marry a man who thinks so little of me and of all of us Valdelaines," Ioni said gently and quietly. "However, Father, if you were to insist on my marrying him..."

"Insist?" spoke Father loudly. "Never! I have only one daughter, and she is dear to my heart, so dear that I would not force this issue."

Ioni smiled for the first time.

"Oh Father," she cried. "Will you allow me to revoke the promise?"

"Of course!" Father said. "I will do more, I will write to Leon's family on the matter and that will be the end of that!" He was laughing and father and daughter arose and embraced.

"Thank you, Father," Ioni said, hugging him. "You will not regret it, I promise you!"

As she stood there in his arms, Ioni was happy for yet another reason. Especially with the war looming, there would be many young knights calling at Valdelaine. They would attempt to woo her, charm her, and maybe offer their hand. There would be so many to choose from. Ioni's heart was happy at such a thought. But father had been reading her thoughts and released his embrace of her and looked into her eyes.

"Of course, when you think about it," he said with a merry twinkle in his eye, "there will be lots of fiery young knights calling this way! And calling to see you!"

"Oh Father," Ioni blushed and looked away.

"Oh yes, Ioni," Father boomed, "lots of gallant young men. In fact you will have your hands full just keeping them all at bay!" His booming laughter echoed around the hall.

"Oh Father," Ioni more abashed than ever, said "I'm sure I shall keep my distance…"

"Keep your distance, oh dear!" laughed father. Ioni drew herself to full height, tossed back the hair from her face, in full control of herself again, placed one hand on her hip and raised up the finger of the other hand as she said in mock seriousness,

"What kind of lady do you think I am, Father? You forget I shall now be Lady of Valdelaine. And with these fiery young knights, as you call them, I shall be haughty, distant and disdainful, such that I will frighten them all away again!"

Father laughed again, and again took her in his arms.

"Heaven help them, then!" he chuckled. "If you are going to be disdainful as you say! But, be serious for a minute, Ioni." He paused a moment, looking at her. "I pray that you will be able to manage Valdelaine while we are all away. Do you feel up to the task before you? Because if not I can send you help."

Ioni looked at him and smiled at him sweetly.

"I think you will find, Father," she said, "that even though I am a girl, I will be as good a soldier as either Jean or Eris. After all I am a Valdelaine and that alone should count for something."

They were both looking at each other intently and smiling.

"You are a good daughter," he said, "and as I told you before – in you, I feel I have both a son and daughter."

"Thank you, Father," she smiled with a tear in the eye. "I will not fail you!"

As the days passed before Henry's departure, she came to view Valdelaine in a very new light; the place was no longer just her home, it was now her responsibility as well. She made mental notes of every nook and cranny; she took time to speak with Liefing the steward, quizzing him as to all of his responsibilities; she spent time also with Frère Benedict acquainting herself as much as possible with the legal, clerical and financial state of the estate. In the evenings, she took walks outside the walls, standing frequently to gaze back at the great pile of Castle Valdelaine. It was now all in her hands, and this thought sent a thrill of excitement through her, she would manage it all so well, she mused to herself. She felt a thrill of pride that all of this was now entrusted to her. But she did want, more than anything else, to converse with her father at length for one last time before his departure; there was so much she wanted to ask him, she wanted the benefits of his insights before she embarked on her new role as Lady of the Castle.

"Try to see everything, Ioni, hear everything, know everything," her father said to her when they were alone together in his study chamber the evening before his departure. "But don't feel you need to act on everything, you know. Most situations will resolve themselves – without your intervention. It is as if you are standing on top of a great tower full of people – all of them will be getting on with their particular tasks and bear in mind that they know their responsibilities and are capable in their own particular work. Yes of course, you will see something wrong here, something amiss there, but you can learn to tolerate moderate failure here and there. As long as the whole thing works, as long as Valdelaine is surviving you can afford to overlook small problems and failures in those around you."

Ioni smiled and took her father's hand.

"Much like Mama did!" Ioni said.

"Yes indeed," said Henry smiling too. "Your mother and your Aunt Fleur, having married into the Valdelaines, achieved more by their humility, sweetness and reasonableness than could have been achieved by all the harshness in the world. They had the gift of turning a blind eye to trivial faults in others. They met everyone, the great and the small, with so much charm and, indeed, courtesy, that the house of Valdelaine became loved and respected, rather than feared. We are privileged in our life as nobility, Ioni. We rule over the people, but with that privilege goes the responsibility for the safety and well being of our people. You cannot get away from the fact – privilege and responsibility are two sides of the same coin. Both your mother and Aunt Fleur taught us Valde-laines that precious lesson, Heaven bless them both."

Ioni was silent for a while, she loved her father's wisdom and was now savouring every word he said. Then she looked at him again and grasped his hand, and said,

"But Papa, what of unforeseen events and, say, sudden emergencies, how shall I cope with them?"

Henry smiled at her and said,

"Again, back to your mother. She always said that the sudden crisis was, in fact, the easiest to manage!"

"The easiest Papa," exclaimed Ioni, "I don't understand!"

"Well," said Henry, "Mother used to say that, in the case of the sudden crisis, we get the grace to see, and do, what is for the best at the time. There isn't time to think, you see, and so, without realising it we take hold of the crisis, and by doing so, we settle it. So, remember Mother, and don't worry about sudden disasters! They are the easiest to manage!"

Ioni was enthralled by her father's words, in so short a time he was teaching her so much.

"Oh Papa!" she gasped and kissed his hand. "I have so much to learn. I wish you were here for a longer time, I would know so much!"

"When I was young and away on knight service," Father said, "I was often unsure of the correct course of action to take. I began to recall my own father and I would ask myself 'What would he have done?' And, mostly, the answer came to me right and true."

Ioni smiled again. "So you think that if I am in doubt, I have only to remember you and Mama, and then I'll know what I have to do. I wonder, will it be that simple, Papa?"

"You will see for yourself," said Henry, "when the time comes."

There was a time of silence between them as Ioni pondered all that her father was saying, she wanted to remember every word he said, and more than that, she wanted every precious word to sink in deeply into her soul. As she gazed at him, she felt her heart glow with love and admiration for him.

"I know that you are young," he said eventually. "When I was young I was often placed in command of companies of men. At first, I was too harsh on people, fearing the loss of authority, fearing to lose face before others if things went wrong. But soon I realised that, in fact, the men I commanded were older than I was, with more experience of life and war than I had. I suppose I felt quite alone at the time, but gradually I came to appreciate them. I came to know their concerns, their stories of home, of wives and loved ones and children. Somewhere inside of me, I began to store up so much regard and respect for these men and it changed the way I dealt with them. Somehow I must have made it clear to them that I loved and respected them. It was very gratifying and, indeed humbling, that these good men entrusted their lives to me and I resolved that I would not fail them, if I could help it. You know, years afterwards, in my early thirties, I met these men – again in war. I could tell clearly that they were so happy to serve with me, they knew I would do my best for them. There were times when I lost opportunities of advancement in the service of the king because of my attitudes – but, that was as nothing compared to the confidence and joy that shone in their eyes, each time I took command. They felt that, how shall I put it, they felt that I cared about them and, to be truthful, I really did care for them."

"So, the secret is to care about the people here," Ioni murmured, tossing back her hair again. "But I do care about them all!"

"Then let that care guide you!" Father said placing his hand on her shoulder. "And, by the way! Always remember, not to make a hasty decision about anything if you have time to dwell on it and think it over. In twenty four hours and after a good night's sleep problems always look so much different. In fact, given that kind of time lapse, most things solve themselves. Now, believe me, I must go and prepare for my departure."

As she embraced him she said, "I have much to remember, Papa!"

The following dawn, Lord Henry said his good-byes and left Valdelaine to join the king and his council at Esmor. With all her heart, Ioni threw herself into the work of governing Valdelaine and its estates. In the early morning she met the maids and servants to discuss their work and deal with any problems. After breakfast she met with Ander, the chief stableman. In the late morning she would meet stewards and the manor lords of outlying areas. At times she would send to the village for Frère Benedict to help her. Frère Benedict was given a house in the village, he ministered to the spiritual needs of the local people and conducted religious services in that house, as yet Valdelaine had no proper church. Over time, Frère Benedict earned the affection and respect of the Valdelaine folk, and was invariably treated as a member of the family. Now Ioni would find in him a trusted advisor and indeed, something of a personal mentor too.

Some weeks passed before the Valdelaines of Ronclava arrived, and in this time, Ioni was able to establish herself, with everyone, as the lady of the house. Then

Raymond and Blanche arrived with their daughters, Eleanor and Clara. Raymond was red faced and round, a man of few words, down to earth and full of common sense. By contrast, Aunt Blanche was tall and elegant, held very strong opinions on everything and was quite a difficult woman to oppose. Ioni would have to find her way with Blanche, to try and strike a balance between conceding to the woman in trivial things, while holding firm on essentials. As Lady of Ronclava, Blanche was used to authority and to having her own way, and would naturally expect a say in the running of Valdelaine. Ioni knew that Blanche would need diplomatic handling if she was to preserve family peace. It would be no easy task.

For company, Ioni would now have not only Fleur and five year old Anna, Robert's daughters; she would also have the companionship of Eleanor and Clara, Raymond's children. The tall, fair haired Eleanor was Ioni's own age and as chatty and opinionated as her mother, but good company, nonetheless. Clara, three years younger than Ioni, was dark in looks and very calm in character, and this made her good company too. Clara's quietness of spirit and gentle penetrating humour made her a complete contrast to the more flamboyant, garrulous Eleanor. Thus, Ioni had now four very different female cousins to amuse herself with, Eleanor, Clara, Fleur and little Anna. Ioni would spend time with all of them in the late afternoons and evenings. When the weather was mild, Ioni loved to ride out accompanied by Clara and Fleur; Eleanor was not fond of riding. In harsher weather, all the girls met in the solar room for embroidery and convivial company. Not having had sisters of her own, Ioni thoroughly enjoyed these evening sessions with her cousins. Each of them contributed in their own way to Ioni's happiness at this time. Ioni observed how Eleanor, above all could deal with her mother, Aunt Blanche; Eleanor had a combination of defiance and cajoling, sufficient to deflect the sharper elements in her mother's character. And Ioni was learning from this, quietly but surely.

In the time that followed, Ioni had to reassess her previous opinion of her fair Cousin Eleanor. Previously, Ioni had thought her to be little more than a grown up ninny, with her flowing golden hair, her penchant for the most fashionable clothing and her unwavering flirtatious manner with every man she met. Quick witted, Eleanor possessed a powerful command of language, which seemed to flow from her wherever she went. All of this made her a constant centre of attention and frequently Ioni found herself having to repress some odd pangs of jealousy towards her. But these were not serious, after all, she reflected, I am the lady of the house, I have my responsibilities to everyone here. So Ioni decided it was best to let Eleanor be Eleanor. Gradually, Ioni became aware of a deeper side to her cousin and she was happy that she had found it; they would not become rivals after all. Strange though it seemed at first, Eleanor proved herself to be most generous with everything she had, her most treasured possessions actually meant nothing to her and were given away at a whim.

Neither did time seem to matter to Eleanor and those who needed to chatter the night away found in her a witty companion, while those who needed to confide their troubles to a trusted heart found in her a sure and reflective confidante. It was not that Ioni herself would ever confide in her but it was comforting to find that there was more to her cousin than the good looks, the fashionable gowns and the stories that never lost with Eleanor's telling of them.

Upon a weary evening, Ioni stood for a moment within her father's study and sighed; even though she had enjoyed her day, inexplicably she was feeling quite out of sorts, cranky and tearful, and longing to be alone. She heard footsteps on the passageway outside and then Eleanor breezed into the study, all flowing hair and swishing white gown and an angry look upon her face. Standing before Ioni, Eleanor, almost out of breath, blurted out at her,

"I thought you promised Fleur some new coloured threads for her embroidery piece. Ioni, she still doesn't have them and she cannot finish her masterpiece."

"Oh!" Ioni said, taken aback. Yes, she had fervently promised Fleur her threads quite some days ago. "Oh! Dear! It must have slipped my mind – I forgot."

Ioni felt even more weary and was lost for words. Her old problem, how to keep everyone happy and then find the right words when she failed to do so.

"I must have forgotten!" was all she could say.

"You must have forgotten, Cousin," Eleanor retorted. "Ioni, dear, you know you cannot forget a promise – especially to Cousin Fleur!"

Ioni was stung with these words of reproach. After all she had been Fleur's companion for years, and now, here was Eleanor, all hot and bothered, with new found concern for their mutual cousin. She tried to speak but could think of nothing – the old feeling of not knowing what to do or say in the heat of the moment.

"What's the matter, Ioni?" Eleanor demanded. "Are you fallen dumb or something?"

But Ioni's mouth just opened a little in a grimace and her eyes crinkled almost half closed and welled up with tears. On seeing this Eleanor, in a storm a moment before, simply reached out her arms and took Ioni in a close embrace.

"Dear God!" breathed Eleanor into Ioni's ear. "I'm so sorry, Ioni. I should never have flown at you like that! I'm stupid and I forget sometimes. You have so much responsibility to bear. Please forgive me!" Eleanor was holding her cousin even closer and for an instant her cheek brushed against Ioni's forehead.

"My God, Ioni!" she exclaimed. "You're burning! What's the matter!" and she placed her cool hands to Ioni's cheeks while Ioni sniffed her sobs to a halt.

"I think I'm tired, Eleanor," she said weakly. "I may have a little fever!"

"A little fever; your burning alive!" Placing her arms around Ioni, Eleanor took her cousin to her again.

"I'm so ashamed, Ioni," she said. "We are all so fond of you, you know. I know, I know I did the wrong thing just now, and I know I may not be your closest friend, Ioni. But, I would do anything you would ever ask of me – and I'll be careful never to hurt you again! This much I can promise you!"

Ioni could only look downward through her blurred eyes.

"Now!" Eleanor said. "I'm taking you to your room and putting you to bed. I'll fetch drinks and potions

for you. Mother has all kinds of potions! For just everything!"

Hours later Ioni awoke from her sleep to find candles still lighting in her room. And there was more than
that: sprawled into a chair was Eleanor, fast asleep, with
her legs stretched out in front of her and her slippered feet
resting at the foot of the bed. Ioni smiled and returned to
her dreams.

Life went on its normal fashion at Valdelaine, Ioni
smiled to herself and was well pleased. From her vantage
point of authority, she could see that each part of the very
large life of her castle and her estate was proceeding well;
the kitchens and dairy functioned as they should; the stables were well managed; in the home, farm and village the
work went on as usual. Ioni left it to Uncle Raymond to
deal with outlying manors, both manor lords and local
people. The new regime at Valdelaine had its sense of
novelty for everyone concerned; with Ioni in charge, just
about everyone gave her all the approval and leeway she
needed to fulfil her task. She was pleased and immensely
happy at this time, and though weary at the end of each
day, she felt a thrill of sheer excitement in being involved
with so much, and with the novelty of every task. As was
expected, it was not in her nature to be bossy, nor offi-
cious, nor did she lord it over anyone. In manner, she remained the same Ioni that she had always been, this
brought great pleasure to people of every degree, and the
universal response to her was one of affection and overflowing goodwill. No one had ever had the experience of
having the young daughter of the house in sole charge and
in supreme command; they found it all a refreshing novelty to be called to task and praised for work by the
"young mistress" as she was invariably called. The older

people smiled at the sight of her, tiny among huge hearth knights or stable hands, calling for what she wanted done. Explaining, pleading and expounding, her girlish voice and ready smile were enough to charm the toughest hearts. The way that Ioni put things to people, it felt as if she were asking for their help and expertise, such that it was impossible to refuse her. If there was a problem with a task, people felt at ease in explaining any difficulty to her, smiling indulgently at the youth and charm of the girl who was now mistress.

Delighted as she was with the manner in which life was proceeding at Valdelaine, Ioni was not unaware of the fact that there would inevitably be occasional difficulties and problems which would try her patience as much as they challenged her judgement. She knew that she was still learning her role as mistress, and that she would be learning for some time yet. She comforted herself with the thought that, if she saw through the first year of her tenure capably, with its normal events and issues, then she would have gained a great deal of knowledge and experience; and this would form a foundation of wisdom with which to govern the ensuing years.

Her first surprise came one morning when, in the courtyard one day she encountered the two youngest hearth knights Gilbert de Blaine and Simon de Valent. They had just ridden in and dismounted having returned from some errand in the outlying districts. As they chatted affably with the young mistress they acquainted her with the fact that they were finding the routine of life at Valdelaine too quiet and irksome for their young spirits and longed to be away to Count Michael and the war. Ioni recalled that her father Lord Henry had sent a troop of some forty knights and manor lords to the service of the count who was campaigning in the southern regions of

Esmor. To defend Valdelaine and its surrounding region Ioni was left with a mere twelve knights, most of whom were older or married or incapacitated. She gently explained to the two young bloods now pacing the courtyard with her that she was fearful of losing even one of her knights to the war. She added that bandits from the Fens of Aren had been seen on the roads not far off from Valdelaine.

"But I will consider something," she told the two young men. "If it is truly your wish to depart for the south then you will have to wait some time. As you know, every week that passes, there are knights and soldiers from the northern parts of Esmor calling here for shelter as they make their way to Count Michael. If it should happen, that, at my request, any of them cared to take service here rather than proceed to the war, then of course you will have my permission to go. Though I shall miss both or you, and though I would prefer you both here, I shall not stand in your way!"

Both the young men smiled down at her and thanked her.

"Pray Gilbert, and you Simon, do not let me down, fight well and come home safely!" The two laughed and thanked her again. Later when Ioni remembered it, Gilbert and Simon's request had come as a complete surprise, but she was happy that she was able to come up with the solution there and then, on the spot. She knew that not all solutions would come to her so readily but she was pleased nonetheless.

Some days later Ioni was to deal with yet another unforeseen situation, but one quite different from that of the two young knights. In the mornings, at this time, she was busy in the great hall with small delegations of peasant folk from all parts of the estate, all come to pay their allotted taxes. Ioni sat at the high table flanked by Liefing standing at her right, while Uncle Raymond and Frère Benedict were seated at her left. Liefing would introduce each peasant by name indicating also from which part of the estate the man had come. It was an opportunity for Ioni, not alone to receive their hard earned tax money, but also to get to know each one by name and by place. The money was checked by Lord Raymond, while Frère Benedict would write in the amount and the man's name in the book of accounts. On a particular morning everything had proceeded much to Ioni's satisfaction, when the last peasant man, big, burly and bronze-faced, presented himself. The man had stepped forward and, on finding himself facing the young lady hastily removed the cowl that covered his head.

"Peter of Ravenswood," Liefing said.

"Greetings, Peter of Ravenswood," Ioni said. "Pray place your tax money on the table here, that we may account for it!"

The man paused for a moment, looked embarrassed as he scratched his head and shuffled from one foot to the other.

"I be Peter of Ravenswood, Ladyship, Lordships," he said in a hoarse voice. "I don't be here for paying of tax, Ladyship, I be here for whipping!"

"For whipping?" Ioni exclaimed uncomprehending. And it took another few seconds before she realised the man's meaning. Uncle Raymond leaned towards Ioni and murmured in her ear.

"This one has not paid his due taxes for two years!" he explained.

Taken aback, Ioni felt a little queasy for a second – she certainly had no heart for sending this man to the whipping post in the courtyard this morning. Was this part of her duty too, she wondered?

"It is the normal thing," Raymond was whispering in her ear again. "No payment of tax for two years, then the penalty is a good whipping. Don't worry, Ioni, I'll see to it, he has a strong back and the whipping will do him no harm!" Ioni huddled together with Raymond and the Frère and said,

"Uncle, I hate the idea! Can we not find another way of punishing him? What good will come of a whipping, it won't pay the tax!"

"No?" said Raymond. "It will make him work all the harder so that he pays next year!"

"I'm not in the mood for this," Ioni whispered intensely.

"If you don't," whispered Raymond, "then every damned serf in Ravenswood will be here – with plenty tall stories – and no tax!"

"Unless we can temper justice with a little mercy," said Benedict, ignoring Raymond and looking pleadingly at Ioni.

At which point, Ioni took a deep breath, placed her hands on the table, and looked up at the hapless serf.

"What am I to do with you, Peter of Ravenswood?"

"Like I said, Ladyship, Lordships, I be here for whipping. I have only made enough from crops to feed my family, and no more. And that's the truth, Ladyship!"

Ioni looked at him a moment and said,

"How many people in your family must you feed then?"

"Well, Ladyship, there be my father and mother, my wife and my six children."

"I see," said Ioni, tapping her fingers on the table. "Tell me, how old is your first son?"

"He be nigh on sixteen years, Ladyship!"

"I see," Ioni murmured and then looking up at Peter again she said, "Then this boy of yours is well able to work then, and help you with your work!"

"Oh right and true, Ladyship. The boy be a good worker, in truth!"

Ioni heaved a sigh and looked at Peter reproachfully.

"And still you pay no taxes," she called out, "even with the help of your eldest boy!"

The big peasant paused, looked glum and red faced and said,

"Please, Ladyship, things have been rare hard for us these times."

Ioni sat back and sighed again, tapping her hands on the table, pondering the situation.

"What age is your oldest daughter?" she asked.

"She be fifteen or near it, Ladyship."

"Very well then," Ioni said at length. "I shall have payment of some kind from you. But first you will return to Ravenswood and prepare this daughter of yours to come and work here for us in Castle Valdelaine. for, shall we say, six months. She will work here for her food and lodging, and that only. At the end of six months you are to return here and fetch her home!"

"Yes, Ladyship," croaked Peter, astonished and relieved. "I thank your Ladyship!"

"Very well," said Ioni. "Report here again to me in six months. I wish to hear of good progress from you then, in the matter of your holding and in the matter of tax. Now, tell me, how did you travel from Ravenswood this morning?"

"Why, I walked, Ladyship, as always I do."

"And how do you intend to return to Ravenswood today!"

"Why, like I came, Ladyship, by walking!"

"Hmm," Ioni was murmuring. "That is a journey of nearly thirty miles in all."

"I believe so, Ladyship."

Ioni nodded and turned to Liefing and said,

"Pray see to it that this man has food and drink before he sets out homeward. And provide him with enough for his family's supper." And then once more, lifting her head to Peter she said,

"Now, go! Peter of Ravenswood!"

Uncle Raymond sat back in his chair, folded his arms, cleared his throat and shook his head from side to side as he watched the lucky peasant shuffle his way down the length of the great hall. For a brief moment Raymond exchanged knowing glances with the grinning Frère Benedict. Those knowing glances said 'this young Ioni takes after her mother, more and more, every day!'

A little unnerved, Ioni remained in the great hall after the others had departed. It was quiet here for the moment, and she could relax and reflect awhile before dinner was announced. Did I do the right thing? She wondered. Even if I did, how do I know which is the right course of action at any time? That is the trouble, when you are young and know nothing – when am I ever going to know everything, she mused. For the moment it will have to do, she thought, at the time, I felt it was for the best. Beneath the turmoil of one's surface feelings, there is a sure sense in the heart, that yes, it was the best I could do.

The door at the end of the hall opened and Ioni was glad to see her cousin Fleur approach. When Fleur was seated Ioni was able to confide in her all the stories of the morning as, in these new times, her cousin was the best confidante Ioni had. There was a little silence when Ioni finished her tales and then Fleur said,

"How are you getting on with our cousin Eleanor?"

Ioni paused to think a moment and said,

"Hmm. I am getting on rather well with Eleanor, at least I think so. Why do you ask?"

Fleur looked away into the distance and then turned towards Ioni again and said,

"I just wondered. You see when the news first came that the Ronclavas would be staying here – well I became a bit afraid... you know... that you and Eleanor would become best friends and that I would be left out and would lose you!"

Ioni's eyes widened with surprise and she snapped,

"Don't be a goose, Fleur! How could you think such a thing!"

"I don't know, Ioni. I just got a strange feeling that you and Eleanor would get on so well that I would be left behind! It was just a feeling!"

"Well you can forget that particular feeling, Fleur. I mean, what would I do without you – you are my cousin, my best friend and – finish the phrase..."

"Your only sister," Fleur smiled.

"Always and forever," Ioni added. Fleur reached out her hand across the table and took Ioni's hand.

"Fleur, if you were not with me here, I don't know what I would do!"

And there was a moment of clasped hands and the eyes of the two girls embraced, with silent feeling. After a pause Ioni said,

"Fleur, as we both know, Eleanor is something of a whirlwind, she sweeps people off their feet. As well as this, have you noticed how she draws people to her – if there is a gathering of people, she is there holding them all together. But while we are getting on well, Eleanor and myself are not close, I enjoy her company, but we are not close to each other – as are you and I."

"I see," whispered Fleur.

"But bear in mind, Fleur, that beneath all that gaiety of Eleanor's, I think there is a strong decent streak – something worth bearing in mind, Fleur. She's not all flurry and no substance. Anyway! She and I are not close like us!"

And Fleur smiled. One of the maids called from the hall door to announce that dinner was being served so the girls arose and walked arm in arm upstairs to the family dining hall.

"I envy you, Ioni, that you are so strong. I still go into floods of tears when anything goes wrong!"

"But why is that so, Fleur?"

"When I get upset about things, it is still that my heart grieves for my mother – I can't seem to control this, not yet anyway. When am I going to grow up and not grieve so easily at everything? But you are strong, Ioni, it is only a year and a half since your beloved Mama died so suddenly, yet you cope with it and do not cry about it. How is this?"

"Well, as you know, Fleur, I cried a lot for the first six months, but gradually, I was thinking about her and about her life before she met Papa. It helped me greatly to know that, in her youth she lived a very full and adventurous youth. Oh yes, the Mama that we knew, Fleur, was so devout, so gentle and loving – but her young years were anything but gentle, as you may know. So it helped me to think that Mama would not want me to grieve, no. On the contrary, Mama would want me to live and love life as she had loved it and relish every moment as she did. These reflections helped me greatly and maybe you should think of your dear Mama, not in a grieving way – she would wish you to live life like a kind of adventure – and not waste your time in tears."

"I see," said Fleur quietly. "Maybe I will try and see it all that way, and the sooner the better or I shall grow up a weeping willow! But come, Ioni, tell me something of Lady Marie's early life."

"Well," said Ioni, "she grew up in Rocharden and was a wild child. Why, during a siege by the Bergmondese, she tired of nursing the wounded soldiers one day, when the fighting was thick on the ramparts. She turned about and took a lance from a dead soldier and donned his helmet as well. She lifted her skirts and ran up the steps and joined the men fighting there! Can you imagine! The girl we knew later as Lady Valdelaine in the thick of the fighting! She even threw spears, though I doubt her aim was very good! But once on the rampart as she was carrying water to the men, she heard a crunching sound as a scaling ladder was placed against the wall; when she looked down she saw an attacker come level with her. He was as much surprised to see a girl wearing a helmet, having no weapon herself, she threw bucket, water and all at him causing him to fall down to his death below. On seeing this, the Rocharden troops gave her a loud cheer, redoubled their efforts and held off the Bergmondese!"

Fleur's face was aglow with wonder.

"Soon after that my mother was travelling in a convoy to somewhere or other, and was ambushed by the mountain people. She was taken prisoner and lived among the mountain people. They hoped she would marry one of their own chiefs, but, with the help of a kindly mountain woman who took pity on her, she escaped to the lowlands!"

"What happened to her then?" asked Fleur excitedly.

"Believing she would be pursued she found refuge in a convent and remained there another half year, and lived as a nun!"

"My goodness!" chirped Fleur. "Did she tell you all this herself?"

"Oh no! Mother never talked of her early life – I heard all of these stories from various people only after she had died. This was how I came to know her life, well, before she ever came to Valdelaine."

"And how did she ever get home?"

"Well she left the convent which was in Bergmond territory, and took to the roads, pretending she was a beggar woman who had lost her husband! And after many adventures she finally reached the great Abbey of Campaldo where she made herself known to the abbot there. A young monk named Roland befriended her and wrote to Esmor to the king for someone to come and fetch her. Finally a knight from Esmor came to escort her home – and his name was Henry Valdelaine!"

"My God!" Fleur gasped. "Your father!"

"Yes. The very one. I don't know what they talked about on the way back, but instead of going south to her home in Rocharden, they went on eastward to Belmont, by which time they were in love. And when they reached Valdelaine they were married. And the rest you know!"

"My god! What a wonderful story, and what a different Marie to the one we knew!"

"Well my point is that your own mother, the lovely Fleur de Ronclava, must have had such an interesting life before Uncle Robert came along."

Fleur's eyes were filled with wonder.

"Yes, I must think about my mother, like you think of yours, and I suspect there's a lot of stories there, that I've never heard. I might ask Papa to tell me more about her – if he can talk about her."

"We could both go to him, pretend nothing, and gradually get him talking about her. I can certainly help you in this – because I know there are some wonderful stories about her, I can't remember them right now, but I will when I get time to think."

"We can try. I would love to see my Mama, in her young days, if only through the mind's eye of memory!"

"And then we need not grieve so much when we get to know her as she was then!"

Ioni had been careful not to tell Fleur that so much of the stories of Marie de Valdelaine had come to her via Uncle Robert, Fleur's own father. When she first confided her grief to him he had comforted her, not least with the tales of Marie's childhood and youth. These had been such comfort to her in that they gave her an image of a young woman she could never have imagined, bright, cheerful and at her best when she was most vulnerable. And thus the strength of the mother was now strengthening the daughter. Breaking their conversation one of the maids opened the door of the hall and announced that dinner was being served, so the two girls arose together and walked arm in arm upstairs to the family dining hall above. This was the hall which the family used for meals when there were few guests at Valdelaine or indeed, when the place was overcrowded. Smaller than the great hall, it had an atmosphere of warmth and intimacy.

Later that afternoon Ioni went riding accompanied by Fleur and the two young knights Gilbert and Simon. The road led through the thick forest south of the river. They paused at the Issel stream which gurgled its way across the road to join the great river Gavenne just a half mile northward. The two girls had dismounted and left the horses to the care of the two knights, while they took a little walk in the sun and shade of the forest road.

"What lies beyond these woods, Ioni?" Fleur asked.

"Well, the road leads to some open areas which have been cleared in the last hundred years. Some day they may be arable and contain manors and villages – some day, as the clearing of forest takes a long time. Further, there is more forest and then the great wide open spaces which are the Fens of Aren, full of streams and lakes. After that it is the long road to Fontrue to Borderlands and the Bergmond frontier."

"Do you think the boys, I mean Jean and Eris might be over that way with the army!"

"I think not," said Ioni, enjoying the woodland walk and the company of her cousin. "From what I hear most of the fighting is away to the south, beyond the lakes, places like Rocharden!"

"I'm glad it is not anywhere near us, it is good to think we are so far away and so safe!"

"Oh yes," said Ioni happily, glancing back to where they had left Gilbert and Simon at Issel ford. Then she stopped suddenly, and Fleur stopped too, and looked at her. "Though having said that, Fleur, the bandit people who inhabit the Fens have become more and more emboldened as the war goes on – they have come out of the Fens to raid and rob, and have been seen a number of times on this very road!"

"I see," said Fleur, wide eyed. "We'd best not stray too far from the men, then."

"Uncle Raymond will be patrolling that side of Valdelaine in the months to come."

"I see, but you look worried, Ioni. Surely Raymond and our knights will be more than enough for any bandits. We are safe, surely?"

"That is not what concerns me, Fleur. What concerns me is that Uncle Raymond either drives off the bandits, back to the Fens, or kills them on the spot!"

"Oh dear!"

"Fleur, the last thing I want now is prisoners being taken to the dungeon in Valdelaine. I hate even to think about it. First the dungeons and then the ghastly hangings. I hate the thought of it!"

As they gazed one last time at the road as it wound westward through the forest, Ioni felt a little shudder pass through her; she turned to Fleur and said,

"Anyway! Let us leave it for now, and get back to our escort!"

And so the girls turned about, rejoined the men, and had a good gallop home. From that day forward, any time that Ioni rode out alone, she was followed, at Fleur's insistence, by two of the knights keeping a discreet distance but keeping her in view all the time.

When they returned to Valdelaine, as they rode under the archway of the main gate, they were surprised and delighted at the sight which greeted them in the courtyard. A group of merchants from some far off city had arrived in a train of wagons and carriages. Everyone in Valdelaine had come out to the courtyard to see the merchants and to view the wagons laden with beautiful things of all kinds. There was furniture; there were great bolts of silk and wool cloth, boxes of ermine and caskets containing readymade dresses, cloaks and headwear. When Ioni had dismounted and greeted the merchants, she invited them to sup in the great hall. Much of the merchandise was then hauled into the hall for scrutiny by all. The girls held up the silk dresses, Ioni carefully fingered the wool and silk cloths, the men folk looked at the leatherwork, jerkins, belts, scabbards, dirk holders, boots and shoes. Amid the hubbub Eleanor's voice could be heard as she squeaked with delight at each new item, and of course the girls laughed. There was a whoop of delight from the females, as the first jewellery caskets were opened. Aunt Blanche was seated, still holding her staff to point at one item or other she wished to purchase. Ioni found silks that she would have loved, but decided that her purchases would be small. She bought some wool cloth of saffron and some of purple – these would make excellent fresh new tunics for Jean and Eris to replace the ones which must be wearing thin in their wartime travels. She also purchased cloths of blue and white – she would make a tunic for Leon Belmont, her friend of childhood times. She bought a piece of jewellery for Fleur – and she bought some books for Uncle Robert. And so the haggling and buying went on but Ioni retired to her chamber, tired but happy after yet another eventful day. Her last thought was of Jean and Eris; how dashing they would look in their new tunics of purple and saffron, the colours of Valdelaine.

The merchants stayed two days, were well housed and fed in that time and then departed. War time was good for merchants as much as anything, given the demand for so many commodities which would have been less in demand during peace time. Not that Valdelaine was completely dependent on outside manufacture, as Lord Raymond had commissioned the blacksmith to make three new swords, a number of pike heads and a number of shields. He had also sent to the expert smiths of Esmor for two new hauberks complete with chain mail. The castle armoury had been depleted somewhat after the Valdelaine men folk had departed for the war.

In the coming weeks Ioni was watchful for every troop of knights that visited Valdelaine on their journey southward, to where the war was raging. These knights were mostly young men eager to experience real combat for the first time and very anxious not to miss out on the opportunity to fight, for which they had been training since their childhood. Time after time, Ioni offered them service in Valdelaine, so that Gilbert and Simon could be released for campaigning. But it was to no avail. These men of Northern Esmor were keen for battle only, and gently and politely rejected any suggestions of remaining in Valdelaine while the war raged. Ioni was beginning to believe that she would never find replacements for her two young knights.

One day, however, a troop of some fifteen knights called to Valdelaine for shelter and respite. They had travelled a great distance, they said, all the way from the Kingdom of the Franks: they needed time to rest before proceeding onward. Ioni was quite happy to accommodate them – and the longer they stayed, the more time she would have to know them and possibly persuade some of them to stay. As they were Franks, then they were not committed to the war, mercenary adventurers they were – and some might be easy to persuade, she thought.

When they had rested some four days, the Frankishmen were eager and ready to take up their journey once more. From their arrival, Ioni had put it to their leaders that she wished some of them would stay on. The morning of their departure she was approached by two of the knights who announced they would be happy to take service in Valdelaine, for the time being at least. The two men in question were Claude de Chalons and Antoine de Cher; Claude was in his early thirties, handsome, fair-haired, with a friendly smile; Antoine was older, of huge girth and height, and gruff compared to his companion. As Ioni appraised them during their conversation, she became convinced they would make trusty replacements for Gilbert and Simon, but she did send for Lord Raymond, who came, and with his usual bland look, approved of them both.

Both Gilbert and Simon had already packed all their equipment, clothing and pavilions and were ready to go at any moment. Ioni found them in the courtyard and delivered the good news; when their initial joy subsided they thanked Ioni profusely. Within a short time they were ready and in the saddle themselves amid the hustle and bustle in the bailey, as the Frankishmen were preparing to leave. As the column formed up and began to pass under the archway, Ioni stood at the stone steps before the main door and waved goodbye. When their turn came to move out Gilbert and Simon raised their hands in farewell and then they were gone into the morning.

At the end of the upper hall there was a little archway in the wall and this led across a covered bridge which lined the keep to the south rampart via a little doorway and a short flight of stone steps. One of Ioni's pleasures was to make her way thus to the south rampart and stand there awhile, enjoying the summer air and the marvellous view out over the fields, the river, the village and the forest. The terrain to the south was flat and from there one could see all the way to the horizon. To her left as she gazed out the sturdy pile of the old tower still

loomed above her. To the right the rampart led along to
the corner turret and then veered back out of sight behind
the colossus that was the new tower. The stone all about
her took in the heat of the day which was swiftly cooled
by breezes from the river. It was one of her favourite
places, where she could smile and breathe with satisfaction as she surveyed the scene. This is my little kingdom
such as it is, and I am the queen of it all, she would say to
herself. Leaning against the battlement wall she would
place her arms on the crenellation and rest her head there.
Her mind idle, she would inevitably dream of the day
when all the Valdelaines would come home, riding from
the forest, coming via the curve in the road past the village, then across the bridge and up the causeway – back
into her life and heart. Sometimes she would daydream
about some great knight on horseback, all colours, armour
and banners, coming that very road, coming to pledge his
love to her forever. Daydreams, Ioni, daydreams she
would tell herself – but then, I must dream of something,
must I not? Long ago, her mother Marie had warned her
that daydreams were a waste of time; but she loved her
daydreams. Here upon the ramparts, after a full midday
meal and in the warmth of the lazy afternoon her dreams
transported her to another world for just a while and then
she woke from them, gladdened in heart and renewed in
spirit.

Upon entry once more to the upper hall, she found
it empty save for Lady Blanche who was sweeping down
the length of the hall like a galleon in full sail. Dressed in
a long wide white robe, her head surmounted by a high
steeple henin, she carried her staff, a polished wooden
pole with an ornate top of brass. When she saw Ioni she
approached, stood her full height and began to lecture Ioni
on the perils of slovenly and idle servants – the servants in

question being the Valdelaine girls and women with whom Aunt Blanche had launched a kind of war of attrition. Ioni just listened patiently, said little, agreeing with everything Blanche was saying, with the sweetest smile she could muster. Then she made her excuses to Blanche and departed. She went to fetch Fleur and Clara to join her in her usual afternoon ride.

The following day Ioni was just in time to witness the later stages of one of her Aunt's tirades against a group of the servant girls, who, on seeing Ioni approach, scurried away to their tasks as if they had been stung by bees. Blanche drew a deep breath, looked at Ioni and shook her head.

"You know, child," she said, "They are all too lackadaisical about everything they do! They need to liven up, or nothing will ever get done in this house!"

"I know, Aunt Blanche," Ioni said appeasingly. "But pray don't trouble yourself with them, you have more than enough to do yourself, and you are not here to be troubled by servants. I had hoped for you that this would be a time of rest. Pray do not trouble yourself with them! Leave them to me, Aunt Blanche, I will deal with them!"

Blanche seemed to fix Ioni with one eye, while the other followed the girls as they chased away to their duties. Blanche nodded, and fixed both eyes on Ioni.

"You need a firm hand with them, child. A firm hand!"

"I'll see to it, Aunt, I'll see to it," Ioni said sweetly.

Ioni had known it all along, of course, like a little glass splinter in her mind that sooner or later, somehow or other, Blanche would be a challenge. This great lady had been long accustomed to her authority in the management of her estate at Ronclava. She was long used to command and being obeyed without question, and the habits of a lifetime are not easily put aside; they weave into the very soul of the person, such that the person and the habits are indistinguishable. And the habit of authority was woven into Blanche and, in time must emerge again as she settled into life at Valdelaine. Ioni understood this; but the question for her was how to blend Blanche into life here, in a way that would keep life upon an even keel. She also understood that Blanche was not easily managed and that in the end, everything was Ioni's responsibility and hers only. How to keep Blanche sweet and everyone else content was not going to be easy. Maybe she would adapt easily to Valdelaine; on the other hand, she might not. Ioni was not completely at ease with the presence of Aunt Blanche. It wasn't any single issue in particular, just a growing vague sense Ioni had that Blanche would strive to become the authoritarian in Valdelaine that she had been in Ronclava. This was something Ioni did not want, Valdelaine was her domain, and hers only. Until ordered otherwise, it is my style that shall hold sway in this place, she thought, I will be responsible for my decisions and my way of doing things.

And so it was that Ioni met with all the servants together, at a quiet time with no one else about. She pleaded with them to be patient with her aunt, adding that Blanche had been in charge in Ronclava for most of her life.

"But you are in charge here, mistress," one of the girls said, "and it is you we must obey!" Amid a murmur of approving voices, Ioni repeated her request for patience, she asked them to promise to avoid the great lady whenever possible; to be as respectful as possible if confronted by her, no matter what the issue was. In time, she assured them, Lady Blanche would treat them more kindly. She begged them to do whatever they were told, for the moment – and to take no notice of the Lady's imperious outbursts.

It was an interesting gathering which took place in one of the rooms off the kitchen – the young lady of the house moving among her servants pleading with them to have patience, and to come to her if there were serious problems. To Ioni, all of these girls and women were more like family to her as she proceeded to hold the hand of one, embrace another, or place a comforting arm around yet another. She had, after all, grown up with the younger ones; the older ones had loved her, nursed her in illness, and had been like mothers to her, and Ioni could never forget the strength of the bond that linked her to these women. Goodwife Nell Redwood, the laundress, broke into tears as Ioni approached her, "Our poor pet, mistress, pray don't be troubled on our behalf – " at which Nell then took a deep breath, stuck out her ample chest and said, "And do not let that high an' mighty lady bully you, nor boss you, mistress – as we'll not have it. If you have trouble with her – you just come and tell us about it! Isn't that right, girls!" And there was a loud murmur of approval for Nell's words.

"I'll be alright, I think!" chuckled Ioni, with tears in her eyes. "But I thank you all for your patience in this matter, hopefully all will be well soon. I know the work gets done – and gets done well! Oh I know, too, that there are long conversations and chatting sessions during working time! However the work gets done and that is what matters! But please I pray you, when the Lady is about – please stop the chatting and get to action straightaway and work hard as if your life depended on it. Please! And then, when Lady Blanche has gone, go back to work in the usual way, but keep a wary eye out for her, mind. Make sure she is well gone before – well, before your chatting sessions begin again, please. Let's make a game of it – all hands to the work when Lady appears – then afterwards back to the way you were!"

This was greeted with laughter and a little cheer. A little deception is no harm, thought Ioni, these girls work hard and they get on well together; a little happiness goes a long way when it comes to long hours of work. Besides, she thought, so many of our men folk are away in the wars that we must keep our spirits alive for them.

* * *

Not long after these events, upon a bright and breezy afternoon, Ioni and Fleur went riding together as usual, taking the south road through the fields of the estate. When they paused to dismount and water the horses at a little stream, Ioni said to her cousin:

"Fleur, I must ask you something. It may only be my imagination, for all I know, but you do not seem to be yourself this fortnight past. You have grown quiet in yourself, or so it seems to me. Are you unwell, my dear, or is there something troubling you? You know you can tell me, whatever it is."

Fleur gave a weary little smile and sighed. The only sounds were the gusts of wind in the trees and rippling of the stream waters.

"I knew you would find out sometime, Ioni. It is something I thought I could sort out for myself without troubling you, but it seems more troublesome than I can manage on my own."

Ioni looked at her, perplexed, as she began to lead her mount away from the water.

"I must know, Fleur – I cannot have you missing meals and hiding away in your room as you have been."

Fleur patted her horse and looked back at her cousin.

"It is Blanche, Ioni, Blanche. The great Lady of Ronclava has taken it on herself to be our educator and disciplinarian, my sister Anna and me! She insists upon us attending on her every day, for lessons in deportment, courtesy and I can't think what else. I do not like it, Ioni, my mother and your mother did all that for us a long time ago. I attend every day, but Anna makes her escape to some quiet corner where even the maids cannot find her. I don't know what to do!"

"I see!" said Ioni, now walking in step with Fleur, as the horses plodded behind them. "Fleur, you must not worry, I'll sort this out!"

Fleur laughed. "But how, Ioni? Aunt Blanche is a formidable force at anytime!"

"I don't know, Fleur, but rest assured, I'll think of something."

Fleur turned to Ioni and embraced her.

"I'm sorry to burden you with this. Are you not afraid of Blanche like all of us?"

"Yes, I suppose so, Fleur. But I cannot permit her intrude upon your life like this. I cannot accept it, I will not accept it."

As the two cousins walked together it became clear from Fleur's description of things that she was having rather a difficult time at the hands of Lady Blanche. The latter frequently launched into tirades against Fleur's family; she was quite disparaging in her personal comments on both Fleur and Anna comparing both of them unfavourably with her own daughters, Eleanor and Clara. Added to this, Blanche frequently ridiculed Fleur who was at a loss for words to defend herself. When each session ended, Fleur could only run to her room and cry bitterly. Ioni was adamant in offering her support for Fleur and was determined to sort out the issue once and for all. As she had said, Ioni did not know exactly what steps she herself should take. Then there was little Anna to think of as well, the last thing she wanted was to see the child's early years made unhappy by anyone; after all, Anna had never even known her own mother, in fact Ioni herself had taken on that role for the child's sake and the bond between them was as close as it could be.

When Anna was first summoned to Lady Blanche's presence, she listened patiently to one of the lady's broadsides and solemnly refused to attend upon her ladyship again with the remark to no one in particular, "I don't like her anymore – anyway, she's not my mother." This caused Blanche to fume even more at Fleur regarding little Anna. "It will continue to grow," Blanche said referring to Anna. "To grow from what it is now – a mere village urchin – into a worthless woman, without the manners of a mere worker woman!" At times like this, Fleur felt broken in the knowledge that neither she nor Anna had the benefit of their mother's presence.

Ioni continued to listen.

Fleur spoke of Anna and how well she was coping with the unpleasant situation. Anna had attended but one of Aunt Blanche's summons but thereafter ignored the great lady. For Anna, Blanche was just another dragon in human form, to be listened to if she had to, but otherwise to be forgotten. "I don't like dragons!" she would say and find a safe place to hide away.

Fleur spoke wistfully, "Thus, our happy years at Valdelaine may be at an end if this goes on much longer."

"Hush, Fleur!" said Ioni, embracing her cousin. "I will not have anyone in this house make you unhappy. I will deal with this; let me do it for you as you have done so much for me!"

Formidable though Blanche was, Eleanor at eighteen, was her mother's daughter and quite as formidable in her own right. She could put anyone back in their own box, even her mother, if need be!

Of course the situation could be easily helped if Eleanor were in Valdelaine – but in the early summer some friends had arrived from the Ronclava country bound for Belmont to spend the summer there. When prevailed on to accompany them Eleanor needed little persuading – a summer in Belmont was the very holiday she would relish, especially as many of the young Belmont boys would be there. Mysteriously however, her sister Clara declined the invitation and preferred to stay in Valdelaine. For Ioni, Eleanor would have been the perfect go-between to settle the problems between her mother Blanche and her cousins. But there it was – it was Ioni's problem.

"But, Ioni," Fleur moaned, "I cannot drag you into this – I don't want to draw Blanche down on you too!"

Ioni placed her fingers under Fleur's chin and, looking into her eyes smiled,

"I will do it – leave it all to me!"

"But how, Ioni?"

"I don't know, something will occur to me!"

In the days that followed, when she had the leisure to do so, Ioni pondered over the situation. She was determined to find a solution to the dilemma. She knew in her heart that she did not wish to broach the subject directly with Blanche. She was afraid that Blanche, if approached could take a simple conversation and raise it to the level of a melodramatic row. Ioni would avoid this, it was her whim, it was her way. She was sure there must be an end to this disagreeable impasse. An end must be, she thought, if in my thoughts and reflections I can find my way to it. She would find it for sure or she was not her parents' daughter!

As so often might happen, it was in a moment of blank idleness that Ioni found it. Not a solution, but perhaps a strategy towards a solution. It occurred to her when she was out riding and her mind was free. It was something Fleur had said during their conversation, amusing to Ioni; Fleur had been angry and said how much she would like to punch Lady Blanche, or even stick an embroidery needle in her! Ioni smiled and pulled the horse over to a standstill at the side of the road. She remembered that sometime in their childhood she had heard a story of a great lady somewhere in the Northern Marshes whose quiet life was disturbed by the arrival of three orphaned – and very young nieces. She would use this story as a cautionary tale meant for Blanche. She would tell it carefully herself – no! She decided she would get someone else to tell it, some evening at supper when there were stories, strange stories doing the rounds of the conversation. For sure the story might, in an oblique way, give Blanche cause for thought and even persuade her to desist from her plans for Fleur and Anna – it was worth a try.

And try they did, Ioni and her accomplices. A week and more passed and as the evening meal was almost finished, relaxed with wine, Claude de Chalons, the Frankish knight began a story of a strange event that took place in a castle in his native land. It was a tale that involved the locking up for five years of a lady that had become a menace to the rest of the household. As he spoke he seemed to address his story to Clara who sat opposite him and she was enjoying his attention and his story. Gilbert's story inaugurated a goodly number of stories of strange and extraordinary events that took place in the castles of the nobility near and far. At length Ioni found her opportunity, and glancing at Uncle Robert, gave him a nod.

"Yes, there it is. So many strange tales of our no-bility – mind you, I am reminded of an interesting story which happened when I was much younger. It concerns a great and noble lady who lived in a fine castle in the Northern Marshes. It seems, with her own daughters mar-ried off and married well, by all accounts, she was sud-denly entrusted with the care of three young nieces, mind you hardly a year separating them in age. Well at first, the three young damsels were manageable enough, but that soon changed and they turned against the noble lady who had so generously agreed to be their foster mother and mentor. They grew disobedient, they grew quite im-pudent toward her. She, in turn grew more strict with them, sending them to bed early and insisting on good be-haviour from them at all times. Instead of reforming, though, they grew even more recalcitrant. Anyway to make a long story short – the upshot was that one night the three hussies cornered her ladyship and pinned her to the wall. Then they drew out tapestry needles and pressed them to the unfortunate lady's throat, swearing they would kill her if she did not allow them to do whatever they wanted. The terrified lady agreed to their demands. Imagine!"

"And what happened then, Uncle Robert?" said Ioni. Robert answered, "Well of course the lady was made of stronger stuff, I can tell you – she got rid of all three of them, marrying them off to would-be suitors whether they liked it or not – in a matter of two months, can you believe it!"

And Uncle Robert chuckled to himself, "Sometimes it is better to let young hussies have their way – they'll have time and plenty to grow up when they have children of their own!"

It was a clever ruse on Ioni's part, it was a clever tale. Ioni was impressed with Robert's telling of it – but would it be enough of a cautionary tale for the mind of Aunt Blanche, she wondered. Only time would tell. At any rate it was worth a try.

The following day passed peacefully and Ioni was pleased. Two more days followed in peace and calm, then another and another and Ioni experienced the first feelings of calm – oh blessed calm after the previous tension. By the end of a week Fleur and Anna were coming back to their own selves – again a blessed relief for Ioni. Clara was her usual placid self, more intent on enjoying more of Claude's stories than anything else. She seemed to take after her father Uncle Raymond in many ways.

A second week followed, mercifully in the same vein. But, unfortunately Lady Blanche was not one to let something go – without a fight. And be assured it was a fight, for there is no other name for what was to happen next.

The morning came when Fleur and little Anna found themselves summoned to attend on Blanche. Anna turned on her heel, ran the length of the great hall, and bolted the little door of the minstrel's gallery behind her. Even the maids could not catch her as she mounted the wooden staircase to hide out her time until this particular storm was over. Fleur, warned in advance to send for Ioni, proceeded to do just that. When Ioni arrived and heard what Fleur had to say, she sat her down and disappeared for a little while returning with an earthenware flagon and two little goblets. She poured some of the liquid for Fleur who asked:

"Whatever is this, Ioni?"

"It is a little drink to fortify you specially made to a secret recipe by the monks at Campaldo." And then Ioni proceeded to pour herself the sweet and fiery liquid for herself.

"Come on, Fleur, throw it back – I will accompany you to Aunt Blanche's apartment and I'll be waiting outside the door to ensure all is well with you."

"Oh! Thanks, Ioni. I feel I need all the support I can get. I can't believe she's up to her old tricks again, especially after the lovely weeks we've just had."

They then left and mounted the stairs to the chamber of Aunt Blanche. When Fleur entered Blanche and her ladies in waiting all stood up.

"To what do I owe this visit, Lady Blanche? I came as soon as I could."

"And so you should, my child, so you should. As to the purpose of this visit I shall be brief and to the point. I am displeased with the latest turn of events and I remain determined that you should accept a period of regulation and discipline from me – to the purpose of making you the lady you ought to be."

Fleur sighed a deep sigh, she noticed the ladies in waiting were watching her intently.

"Well then," Blanche said sitting down again in her throne-like chair. "When my daughters were disobedient I chastised them severely. Both my daughters Eleanor and Clara were soundly whipped and it did them no harm at all. In fact they turned out excellent young ladies. Do I make myself clear?"

"Of course, Lady Blanche, but you can hardly be thinking of whipping me!"

Blanche looked long at Fleur and answered,

"That is precisely what I intend to do – it is the only way to bring you to your senses!"

"Good lord! Blanche, you cannot seriously be planning to have me chastised by – whipping – whipping? Lady Blanche – why this is monstrous!" Fleur was feeling flashes of alarm and anger by turns.

"I am quite serious, my child – and your chastisement will be carried out here and now!" After a signal from Blanche two of the ladies brought forward a small table covered in tapestry and placed it on the floor in front of Fleur.

"Now, my child, my ladies will assist you to bend over the table, and also will assist you with your dress and underskirts. I myself will administer the whipping. Shall we say, ten strokes or maybe twelve."

By now Fleur's heart was pounding and her face was hot and red – by no means was she ready to submit to such a humiliation. But she calmed herself sufficiently to say,

"Blanche! This is a terrible thing you are doing. No one has the right to have me chastised except my father, Lord Robert!"

"Your father is a fool and knows nothing of bringing up young ladies."

Then with a nod to her maids the two of them made towards Fleur as Blanche stood up now holding the whip in her right hand.

Fleur could take no more and raising one side of her skirt to reveal her leg, she gave the little table as vehement a kick as she could manage. As for the table, it shot forward on the floor catching the two waiting ladies in the upper shins. This happened with such force that the two ladies collapsed in pain on the floor. Pleased with the outcome of her anger she then turned on Blanche who was taken completely by surprise by the sudden and agile movements of her niece. Fleur now tore into Blanche ripping her veil from her head, then ripping the top of her dress to the waist. Fleur then ripped the whip from her hand and then turned on the two ladies but they were still rolling on the floor nursing their shins with copious moans and tears. There had been a third lady in waiting who had been standing by the door to ensure Fleur had no escape. Already this lady had gone white in the face witnessing Fleur's devastation of the others. At first she made as though she would block Fleur, but thought better of it when Fleur produced from her skirts a long tapestry needle which she pointed at this lady's throat.

"Move away from that door," Fleur hissed like a cat. "Or, so help me God, I shall run this through your scrawny throat!"

Suddenly, silently the door swung open and Lady Ioni stood there silently framed by the threshold and lintels. Straightaway Fleur ran to Ioni and embraced her. Anger and tears were close in her heart and Fleur was now sobbing into Ioni's embrace. Soothing words were whispered and slowly Fleur recovered her calm. On Ioni's instruction Fleur waited out on the passageway, she was still panting from her exertions and still drying her eyes with her kerchief.

Slowly, and without a word Ioni entered the chamber, she strode up and down, ignoring everyone there. She gazed a long time at the whipping table. The two injured ladies were now curled up, still in pain, in chairs. Ioni stood and gave them a long, long stare, but still did not speak. She then turned her gaze at the third lady who had now moved well away from the door. Again Ioni, her eyes large, cold and fierce stared long at this woman who eventually moved to find a place to sit down. Finally Ioni, head erect, moved towards the door but turned round, her eyes now staring at Blanche – for a very long time the lady was transfixed by Ioni's eyes and icy expression. Blanche was rooted where she sat, attempted once to say something but gave up. Ioni stooped to pick up the fallen whip which she held horizontally across her person with both hands. With a sigh she then moved to the door, turning half around she said in a loud voice,

"There shall be peace in this house! That is not a request – it is a command! Let anyone breach that peace, anyone! Ever again! I will make such trouble for that person, such that she will rue the day she ever set foot here."

"How dare you threaten us!" hissed one of the waiting ladies, the one at the door.

Ioni's head turned slowly her eyes finding the speaker and fixing her with a blazing look.

"Oh, this is not a threat," she said with an icy smile, her face then losing the smile to her blackest piercing look yet. Eyes widening she said,

"It is a guarantee!"

With that Ioni turned on her heel and departed, conveying Fleur to her own chamber.

Before she closed the door Ioni had said quietly,

"Lady Blanche, ladies, for all our sakes, for sake of the good God – let us have peace in this house – I entreat you, one last time!" And then she was gone.

Poor Blanche was shattered, so much so that she remained in her chambers for some days; what she was able to eat, she had sent up from the kitchen. When Ioni asked Clara how her mother was faring, Clara replied, "I'm afraid mother is ill." Ioni thought about this for a moment and said, "I must go see her!" to which Clara replied, "I think that would be good, Ioni." Ioni visited the chambers from which she had so angrily departed four days before. When she entered, she smiled benignly at the ladies in waiting and asked to be announced to Lady Blanche – who was resting in her bed.

"Forgive my intruding, Lady Blanche," she said, "for I have been at my wits end with worry – worry about you, my Lady." Ioni was expecting something of a chilly response from the patient, but Blanche immediately sat up and said,

"I thank you, Lady Ioni, for coming to see me. I'm afraid I don't feel able to be up and about. But I daresay, I shall be well again quite soon." Blanche let her head rest against her pillow. There was a pause and Ioni said,

"Aunt Blanche, is there anything I can do for you – can I send for someone to…"

"Thank you, Niece Ioni, I'm just a bit weary these days that is all."

Ioni took a step towards the bed and knelt beside it reaching out to take Blanche's hands in hers. Then she blurted out, "Oh! Dear Aunt Blanche I pray you, take me in your arms!"

Blanche shuffled herself sideways and reached out taking Ioni in a strong embrace. Ioni began to sob a little and Blanche said,

"Now child, do not distress yourself so. All is well, Ioni, and all will be well my child. It was good – and quite a brave thing for you to come and see me!"

Ioni knelt upright, still holding her aunt's hand, with ribbons of tears still flowing down her face.

"There now, child, let's have no tears – I said you were good – and brave, I like that in a woman!" and Blanche gave Ioni a little smile.

"But I want to do something for you, Aunt." Ioni sniffled and wiped her face with the kerchief Blanche gave her. "Is there anything you would really like?"

Her head fell back on the pillow once more and Blanche was silent for a moment. Then she spoke,

"If only my Eleanor were here. I miss her now! Yet I wish her to have her time with the Belmonts."

Ioni, still kneeling had her hands joined with her forefingers pressed to her lips.

"I think we should send for Eleanor!"

"Oh but I don't wish to…"

"Aunt Blanche! It would be four weeks before she could be here – as you know Belmont is far down the Golden Plain – a week for a messenger to get there – two weeks for Eleanor to get dressed and…"

This made Blanche chuckle a little.

"It would be great comfort – my Clara is a darling but my Eleanor is – well, she gives me strength!" Thus Ioni made her peace with Blanche, though it must be said that Fleur never did.

Four weeks later Eleanor arrived back at Valdelaine. Those intervening weeks however were not weeks of dull waiting; those weeks had yet another story of their own to tell. What was it Blanche had said of Ioni – that she was "good and brave." Well in those weeks Ioni was pressed from another source to be as good and as brave as she could ever be.

It was Clara. Quiet, warm, rock of common sense Clara, nearly fifteen now – well it seemed she had quite fallen in love with Claude, the Frankish knight – and he, in love with her? Well Ioni could not be sure. More and more they were quietly slipping away to be together. Catching sight of her mistress one morning, Nell Redwood, the laundress, had come to Ioni, whispering that though it was none of her business, she felt obliged to tell Ioni. Claude and Clara had been seen many times together, and sometimes in each other's arms – and did anyone know about it? Oh God! Thought Ioni, Clara is too young, and, well her parents would not approve of a liaison with a wandering Frankish adventurer. Mind you there was nothing wrong with Claude, he was a fine man and reliable, good natured. But with Clara? No it could not be, it could not be. Ioni sighed. What do I do now?

She decided she could meet Clara first and did so in the privacy of her father's study. When Clara was seated before her she broached the subject of her time spent in Claude's company. Clara was not surprised, nor shocked, nor embarrassed and smiled and said,

"I love him, Ioni, and he is a wonderful man. Yes I love him with all my heart!"

Ioni reached out and took Clara's hands in hers, looking a while into those gentle eyes.

"But my dear Clara, your parents would never approve of what you are doing now and certainly would never approve of any thoughts of marriage to Claude!"

"Well I can wait until I am able to marry him, for that is what I want."

Ioni sighed, "But Clara, Claude may be the greatest man in the world, but he is still a wandering knight – adventurer. He has no fortune, he has no place of his own to live."

"Ioni these things don't matter, I love him and want to go wherever he goes."

"So are you going to go on meeting him as you have been? Because if you are – I shall have to tell your parents."

Clara smiled.

"Then we will just have to run away together – elope, Ioni."

Ioni's jaw dropped.

"Oh God, Clara! You cannot do such a thing – your father would have you both tracked down. You would be punished of course – but your father would have him killed. You don't want that!"

"No!" exclaimed Clara, biting her lip at the thought of Claude dead.

"Then you must break it off – go to him and tell him you cannot see him any longer!"

Clara looked thoroughly glum at this stage and a tear trickled down her face.

"Please, Ioni. I must go now!"

Perplexed and anxious, Ioni watched her cousin go.

Clara of course, did not break it off, and saw Claude as much as ever. And Ioni knew it. At the end of a week Ioni began sending Claude patrolling the estate further and further each day. At least the two lovers would be out of each other's way during the daylight hours. But of course they kept their trysting places by evening and into night! Finally Ioni sent Claude to Ron-clava with messages for the people there and to fetch various items requested by Raymond and Blanche. This little enterprise took at least a week. However the two lovers were even more together than ever. Ioni was on the point of speaking to Claude and ordering him to keep away from her cousin – when Eleanor arrived home from Belmont.

When she had time to settle back into normal life Eleanor approached Ioni. Before Ioni could say a thing Eleanor said,

"I know about my sister and Sir de Chalons – I surmised the minute I saw her. There is only one thing to do, Ioni – send him away! The two of them cannot live here day to day. I know Clara, she will not give him up – and certainly not if he stays here."

And thus it happened that Claude de Chalons was banished from Valdelaine. He rode south to join Count Michael's forces. He was gone. Clara's world was shattered, but such was her heart that she bore no grudge against Ioni. Rather did she run to Ioni and buried herself and her outpourings of grief in her cousin's embrace. Ioni cried too that day, but she was not to know then that, by her actions, albeit unwittingly, she had saved Claude's very own life.

Thus it was, by dint of sheer endeavour that Ioni gradually won mastery over herself and over the vast responsibilities which her father had placed upon her young shoulders. She was wise enough to delight in her successes and learn from her failures. She was happiest when others were happy, she had found within herself a gift she had not known was there – the gift of taking people as they were, overlooking their faults and as it were, playing them to their strengths, delighting in their achievements and consoling them in their failures. Years later her father would say of her, "Valdelaine was never better governed than during your time as mistress, you carried out your own way of ruling other people simply by seeing the best in others. Would to God, all our rulers had your gifts. And you were strong also. I have two sons, Jean and Eris and I am proud of them – but in you,

Ioni, I had a daughter who was every bit a son as either of the boys!"

The two boys were of course now in the south of Esmor, Jean riding to battle in the company of the greatest knights of the kingdom. Eris was there, too, but, unlike Jean, he was still Count Michael's squire. The count was quite fond of Eris and very protective of him. It would be some time before Eris would find himself in the line of battle, but that could wait. Already the army of Bergmond had invaded and had wrestled the country west of the Gavenne from the grasp of Esmor. Despite these early successes the Bergmondese commander, the Duke of Anflair, was hesitant to cross the Gavenne – but he had other arrows in his bow with which to torment Esmor.

Chapter V: The Fields of Battle

*T*he campaigns opened in early summer and most of the fighting took place along the Gavenne river, roughly, from north of the lakes down to the confluence of the Gavenne and the Gavette. Leaving the main body of the army, commanded by Duke Anflair, west of the river, Germaine, with his strong force of the youngest knights laid waste the country west of the Gavenne. For some weeks he encountered only token resistance until Count Michael reinforced the garrison at Holgen Fortress, which overlooked the territory between the lakes. When Germaine did not attempt to raid in this latter area, and turned south, Count Michael with his large force passed down the eastern shore of the Great Lake hoping to come round at the bottom end of the lake, then wheel north again in an attempt to catch Germaine's army. But the wily Germaine got word of the count's whereabouts and turned quickly about and swiftly attacked the interlake district, defeating the Holgen garrison and plundering and burning the castle. Count Michael was now moving up the west side of the lake believing that Germaine was now far away, resting up somewhere after the battle at Holgen. Quite the opposite was true however, as Germaine had moved south again to completely surprise and rout the count's forces as they descended from high craggy ground west of the lake. Count Michael was lucky to escape alive and, before he had time to muster a new force Germaine had taken their castle below the lake, rested and watered there, sent wounded back home and called for fresh forces from Duke Anflair who was encamped in the foothills beyond the border.

In the late summer Germaine, was ravaging and foraging in the country between the rivers, preparatory to an attack on the last two great fortresses, Rocharden to the south, and if possible, Pelaine at the confluence. He soon received information that Count Michael with a great force of knights had left the country of Deer Forest and was making its way towards Pelaine. Having called in substantial reinforcements and set upon Pelaine, taking it only a day before the count arrived, Germaine took the precaution of leaving a strong garrison there. He also sent word to Duke Anflair to begin a siege of Rocharden. With Pelaine in enemy hands, and Rocharden under siege, Count Michael decided to cross the river Gavenne at the only stone bridge he could find and having got half his force across, was fiercely attacked by Germaine's force. The fighting lasted more than two hours before the count withdrew back across the river and withdrew his force eastwards. He had considered another foray for the following day, but withdrew further east on receiving the news that Rocharden, too, had fallen. Later that autumn Germaine, with large forces was foraging and plundering further north in the Borderlands, in the marshes and even in the vicinity of Fontrue, only eighty miles from Valdelaine. But large forces protected Borderland Castle and Fontrue, so Germaine wisely kept his distance from both of these massive castles. Winter came on and he returned home to Anlac, a hero of legendary exploits.

Meanwhile back in his winter quarters Count Michael brooded on the campaign and wondered what he would have to do to stop, kill or capture this demon Germaine, who had defied him and defied the very nature of war itself. The demon had been everywhere, turning defeat into attack following up victory with victory; Germaine, he pondered, had taken the entire south Gavenne without even once involving the main body of the Bergmond army. The count began to pore over some maps and soon found the area he would attack come the next spring.

During that winter, back in the safety of Anlac, Germaine pored over his collection of heraldry parchments. He had good reason to do so, arising out of an incident during the battle for the stone bridge. Towards the end of the fight, with the bridge in sight, and large numbers of enemy troops trapped on the near side, a singular knight had rallied the other knights about him. Led by this gallant one, they had charged and charged his forces, delaying them sufficiently to allow the trapped foot soldiers to finally get across the bridge to safety. A brave knight indeed, thought Germaine, as he perused his manuscripts, a worthy enemy, brave and gallant, he had risked his life to save so many of his own men. Then Germaine stopped on a particular page, there in the candlelight on the page was a painting of a knight in the colours of the brave knight he had remembered from that day. He scanned the writing beneath the painting for the name. The purple and gold colours belonged to the House of Valdelaine. Valdelaine, he mused, a brave man, I like him already, perhaps we shall meet some day, Lord Valdelaine. Germaine smiled at the motto on the coat of arms.

Valor Veritasque – courage and truth. Interesting, Germaine thought as he closed the manuscript.

"Would that such a man were my friend rather than my enemy!" he said aloud.

Writing long after the events of this the first year of the war, many historians have faulted the Duke of Anflair for not pressing home the advantages won by the Bergmondese along the Gavenne. They point to the fact that when the Gavenne forts were taken, the duke could have taken his entire army across the river and poured onto the beautiful lush country eastward threatening the very heartland of Esmor itself.

But this view does not take into account the nature of the duke himself, nor of the internal conflicts within the Bergmondese camp. At the young age of thirty two, the Duke of Anflair was the supreme war commander of the army. Anflair was not a party to the Raven League nor was he interested in their aims. His task, the occupation of the territories west of the river, had been completed. But the league barons wanted even more and so, he permitted them to raid across the river and they did so, spearheaded by Germaine himself and supported by the league barons, Gavron, Agron, Conrad and others. The duke's unwillingness to take the entire army across and face Count Michael in open battle was based on his shrewd political skills. The top echelons of his army were the great lords and barons of the league. However the vast bulk of the Bergmondese army was made up of knights of the lesser nobility and yeomanry, who had no truck with the great barons of the league. Even if he ventured across the Gavenne and defeated Count Michael in battle, the victory would be claimed a success for the league. Of course on the other hand, if he were defeated by Count Michael, the greatest losses would occur among the lesser nobility and yeomanry – and with these classes decimated the league stood to gain even greater power in Bergmond than it hitherto held. Hundreds of small estates and large freeholds would become vacant and for sale to the highest bidders, who would of course come from the league cohorts. And Anflair was determined that the league should not prosper overmuch in this war – as we shall see from subsequent events.

Today we are inclined to think of ancient kingdoms as completely united in loyalty to king and country. This was not the case in those days however. The king of Esmor was always forced to rely on the good will of Raxtene and the people of the southern mountains, whose allegiance was not out of loyalty, but had to be bought with money, titles and favours. On the Bergmondese side the northern lands of the countess of Norland were lost to the king of Bergmond.

For reasons of her own, this independent minded lady, known popularly as the 'Witch of Norland', had refused first to embrace the Raven League and thereafter refused to enter her troops into the war. The league masters concluded that if they could first defeat Esmor, they could later deal with the witch countess and her cohorts. There was quite a difference in the approach to these problems by the two kingdoms however. Count Michael had ever and always urged his king and council to humour Raxtene and his wild mountain hordes, at least, as far as the state coffers would allow. On the other hand Bergmond's king represented by the master of the league, Baron Gavron de Laude, had very different plans for their problem region of Norland. Over time, Norland was to be infiltrated by the league and the witch countess was to be destroyed by whatever means it took, fair or foul, to achieve that objective.

*   *   *

Somewhere, as though far away at the extremities of her consciousness, Ioni first came across the word, or name, Germaine. She gave it no notice nor had she even the time to dwell on it for any length, but it seemed to echo in every overheard conversation. The name came up frequently in mealtime chatter too, but Ioni was constantly forgetting it, having plenty of important things at the forefront of her mind. In this first year of the war, as mistress of the house and its vast estates, she rarely found time to dwell on anything. Eventually, as the name persisted in every conversation, she did make a mental note to remember to ask someone what it was all about. At last the opportunity came when the name was mentioned, as the girls were chatting one evening in the embroidery chamber. Ioni raised her head from her work, put down her needles and looked across at Eleanor.

"Who is this, or what is this Germaine that everyone is speaking of?" she asked. "Do you know, Eleanor?"

Fleur, Eleanor and even Clara exchanged surprised and amused glances.

"Oh dear, Ioni!" exclaimed Eleanor, still with the look of surprise in her eyes. "Don't you listen to anything that is spoken of these days? I vow you are so caught up in running Valdelaine that you take in nothing of what is happening elsewhere!"

Ioni returned Eleanor's words with a look that said 'Spare me! I have enough on my plate for now.'

"But what is it all about?" Ioni persisted. "All the talk of this Germaine, whatever it is!"

The other girls all put down their needlework and were each about to speak, but Eleanor got there first.

"Ioni. This Germaine is the talk on everybody's lips in this war. I'm amazed you don't know. Germaine is the name of this knight that has led the armies of Bergmond against our king!"

"Oh!" said Ioni, comprehending a little and picking up her needles again. "But why is everybody talking about him?"

Eleanor gave a sigh of exasperation giving Fleur the opportunity to speak.

"It seems, Ioni," she said gently, "that he is an extraordinary knight that has won battle after battle against our armies under Count Michael. Not only that, but he has taken castle after castle in his wars, especially in the south. Even the fortress at Holgen. And no one has been able to stop him nor defeat him."

"The stories about him are so many," Eleanor interjected. "Enough to fill a book. He has become something of a hero, a legend. According to father he appears out of nowhere, and when they think he is in the south he appears in the north. He rides like the wind with his bands of knights, like some winged dragon. Some say he is some kind of fiend or the devil himself. Others say he is like one of the heroic knights of ancient times."

"Margreth was telling me only the other day," Fleur said with a smile, "that mothers call in their children before nightfall, threatening them that Germaine will get them if they don't!"

"Oh!" said Ioni with a shudder. "God grant he'll not come this way then! Fiend, flesh or whatever he may be!"

"Father says the troubadours are making rhymes about him already," Eleanor added.

"I wonder what he looks like," said Clara. "I expect he must be very handsome, although fearsome as well no doubt! And he must be very brave as well. What a shame he is not fighting on our side!"

"Of course," went on Eleanor. "And then this war would be over soon and we would all be safe in our beds!"

Ioni smiled and was thankful that all the military action was so far away and that she was not living in the

Borderlands where this strange Germaine might come charging out of the woods and pounce without warning on the folk living there, like some wolf on a flock of sheep.

"And Count Michael has not been able to stop him," mused Ioni. "It is very strange indeed. He must be something to be reckoned with, otherwise the count would have defeated him!"

"Don't you listen to anything?" Eleanor sniffed indignantly. "Germaine is like the wind. Impossible to catch! For example, Father tells me that in April last, Germaine appeared before Holgen Fortress with a large force. For some days he was content to forage and raid in the area, but at no stage did he dare besiege the castle. Then he left the area, to the relief of the people in Holgen, only to return within days to take town, castle and all. He has become a legend already, I tell you!"

And thus was Ioni acquainted with the name 'Germaine' and the horrific stories that went with that name. Of course, she thought, stories were one thing, people had to have stories; every war throws up heroes and villains, and people relish nothing better than a good story. As the days went by, however, there were still more stories coming from the war, stories with only one subject – the dreaded Germaine.

Oh well! Ioni thought, at least I know now what everyone is talking about. No more about that, I have things to do, people to see to.

In the spring of the next year, Count Michael mustered his forces near Fontrue and proceeded across the Borderlands with his great army and boldly crossed the frontier into enemy territory. Apart from the usual skirmishes, he encountered no serious resistance as he drove deeper into Bergmond hoping he would eventually draw the Duke of Anflair into a major confrontation. He had solved the problems in the south, or rather, they had been solved for him. The wild, hardy people who dwelt in the harsh valleys of the Southern Mountains had besieged and taken Pelaine and Rocharden driving out the garrisons placed there in the previous year by Germaine. In the depths of winter, these people had descended on the Gavenne region with swinging swords and war pipes and had made war against anyone who came their way. Loyal to no one but themselves, and eager to gain any advantage from any conflict, they had been happy to come to terms with Count Michael, agreeing to hold the captured forts for Esmor, having been handsomely bribed by the count to do so. Everyone knew, however, they would be more than happy to sell their prizes to the highest bidder and then high-tail it back to their mountain homes when the time came.

For this reason, the count was anxious to come to blows with the Duke of Anflair as soon as was possible and so his great army pushed from region to region across the northern plains, seeking out the duke or, even better, the duke and Germaine all at once. The lack of serious resistance was troubling to Count Michael; if he ventured too far, might he not be walking into a great trap, stretched as his resources were, and so far from home? However, the desired opportunity was closer than he had thought as he found out one evening when the scouts had come in.

He was being shadowed from distant woods by a large force to the north. Possibly Germaine, he thought. Not more than ten miles away, there was an even larger force waiting for him camped in open ground, all the banners of Bergmond, including Anflair, fluttering in the spring air. He was being walked into a large ambush if he proceeded further. He called his leading commanders and having briefed them on the situation, asked their opinions. To properly deploy his force, he would need to turn back and move south at first light and find ground suitable to make a stand. Everyone assembled recalled how, earlier that day, as the army had descended the tracks from a cluster of low hills, they had observed what looked like a great plain on the horizon, to the south. What they had seen was, in fact, the plain of Savron revealed above the tree line by great shafts of afternoon sunlight.

"All going well tomorrow," the count said to Eris, who attended him that night, "you may see a battle soon, quite soon!"

"Yes, my Lord." Eris responded, thrilled by the prospect of action after the long weeks of the march.

"Call me," the count said, "two hours before dawn. There is much to be done. And don't fail me."

"I will not, my Lord," Eris responded.

Two hours before dawn, the first scouts were sent southward to find any roads, tracks or lanes that might carry the count's army clear to the Savron plain. At the very same time, under cover of darkness, the count sent one sixth of his force forward towards Anflair which, just before noon, turned about face and back to where they had started. This would distract Germaine's force in the forests to the north, giving the count enough time and leeway to take most of his force to the relative safety of the plain. By early afternoon, the count was breathing a sigh of relief as his troops found firm high ground in the middle of Savron. Camp was set, but Count Michael looked anxiously to the north for any sign of the rearguard he had left behind. He had reason to be worried, as Germaine's force had actually shadowed the rearguard from early morning, and when that force had turned about, Germaine, baffled and suspicious had come out of the forests to give battle. When the news finally came in that evening, the count discovered that his rearguard had been badly mauled by Germaine's force. Already the stragglers were coming in from that affray. They had stood their ground well, but repeated assaults by Germaine had driven them back. Finally they had to yield ground, and the survivors had to make their way, as best they could, through unknown country to the safety of the Esmorin camp. Count Michael was pleased enough, he had brought some of his force to safety and had caused Germaine to emerge, at last, from the forest shadows. One day later, in the evening, the Duke of Anflair appeared on the plain and camped his forces a bare three miles from the count's position. As they stood on a knoll of high ground before dark, the count and his fellow commanders received word that Germaine's force had also arrived to take up position with Anflair. They would give battle, for sure, in the morning.

Eris had never witnessed anything so exciting as he watched the two armies draw up in line opposite each other. The spring morning was dry with just light southerly breezes which roused all the great banners to lift and flutter. Commanders barked orders all along the lines, men and horses strained for long awaited orders to charge. Eris knew that Jean was out there somewhere to the left up the field and he strained his eyes to catch a glimpse of the Valdelaine colours, the familiar purple and gold. But they were lost to his view amid the great cluster of lances and banners that stretched away to the south of him. He stood well to the rear, surrounded by men-at-arms who gazed out silently from under their helmets. He had his duties to attend to; as well as his own horse, there were several spare horses that he saw to. There were supplies of food and water to be maintained as well as spare arms, lances, swords and pikes. All the young squires were busy behind the lines making sure that everything was in place before the first and all important charge.

A great roar went up from the men in the line as they moved their horses forward at a walk then a trot and finally a full gallop. Even at this distance he could hear the great rumble of hooves as both armies gained full flight towards each other, and finally the noise mounted to a crescendo as both forces crashed and clattered into each other all along the line. The morning seemed to heave as horses and men met at close range and the air was filled with the first sounds of battle. The throaty shouts of men, the neighing of horses and the clash of steel all mingled on the calm morning air. He could see where the press was closest with men flailing at each other with swords, and behind them, hundreds more strained forward to get to close quarters with the enemy.

As the great melee developed, the two forces seemed to become entangled one into another and soon it was becoming impossible to distinguish friend from foe. The line of battle seemed to heave forward here, backward there, in places groups of knights still mounted found room to wheel and charge again. Here and there, armed men paused a moment to breathe and then, with great roars charged at each other again. Already some riderless horses were galloping away from the line, maddened with terror and pain. Already, there were groups and individuals lying here and there, dead or wounded as the line seemed to move hither and thither. For Eris, when he stood and watched with the other squires it was all confusion for a long time. Already wounded knights and men were being carried from the field, their curses and their cries audible above the noise of war. As the battle raged on Count Michael was unhorsed twice and Eris was kept busy running to his master with fresh mounts and lances and containers of water to slake the thirst. Twice, indeed, the count mustered his knights for fresh charges against the Bergmond line.

The chronicles of that day show that indeed Count Michael had entered battle at a disadvantage, as he had allowed two enemy forces to combine against him, that of the duke and that of Germaine. The chronicles too, recount how Germaine seemed to be everywhere in the thickest fighting, urging his knights to almost superhuman feats of valour. Once when Germaine had been unhorsed he raised sword and shield high above his head, screamed "Anlac! Anlac!" and charged on foot at the oncoming Esmorin knights. This action provoked his own knights to action and they charged forward to protect him and one of the most fiercely fought actions of the day forced the Esmorin knights back across the field. However, Count Michael had wisely left a large contingent of knights with the prince. In the early afternoon Count Michael summoned these into battle. The knights of Bergmond had mounted a great assault that was pushing the men of Esmor reeling back across the field and now they regrouped for a final charge that would bring them victory. At this, the prince raised his banner and his sword and a great shout went along the Esmorin line, group after group taking up the shout, raising lances and banners on high, for a great charge. When indeed they did crash into the Bergmond line, it wavered and then broke and Count Michael and the prince won the day. They pushed as far as they could across the plain, but the duke had men in reserve and saved the day from becoming a rout and, in general, most of his forces got away in good order. But what became known as the Battle of Savron Field was over and won and lost. Eris spent most of the evening in attendance on his master or riding with messages to other commanders. Those who had seen little action that day were sent forward in groups of troops to ensure that the Duke of Anflair did not attempt to take the plain again. Galloping to and fro, Eris passed attendants tending the wounded, and groups of men carried the dead from the field for burial. On one of these sorties he was thrilled when he at last spotted Jean, sitting up on a stone. He was exhausted and out of breath. Immediately Eris dismounted and brought him some water and was glad to see he had no serious injuries. The two brothers Valdelaine said little to each other, though they smiled and shook hands before Eris darted away on his next errand.

As he brought his great army back towards the frontier in the days that followed, Count Michael was pleased; he had scored a victory against Bergmond. However, no emissaries from there had arrived to arrange a truce between the warring countries, so the count sent messengers homeward to recruit all the replacements they could find. This war, it seemed would go on for another year at least. He also sent joyful messages to the king. The Bergmondese and their strange league of barons would be silenced for a time.

Eris had witnessed his first great battle, he had found his older brother Jean still alive after the conflict, and later had witnessed the scene as Leon Belmont and others had been knighted.

*   *   *

As anyone who has been there can tell you, the village of Elvendene is a pretty one, and like many other villages which dot the wilds of the Borderlands it nestles happily in its own oasis of fertile ground, untroubled by the wilderness all about. Ten miles north stands the walled town and fortress of Fontrue. Thirty miles to the northwest is the fortress of Borderlands whose western battlements defy any would-be invader to encroach on the land of Esmor. Elvendene is now famous in the memory of the people of Esmor for the great, if unexpected battle that was fought there in the second year of the war. The battle was indeed unexpected as it was thought that the summer battle of Savron Field of the previous year had been enough to contain Bergmond for the moment. Count Michael had brought his army through the wilds of Borderlands, and then had descended into Bergmond itself, winning the day on the plain of Savron. For the Duke of Anflair and for Bergmond, however, the defeat at Savron was not decisive; the army was intact, and recruits were joining every day. All the principal commanders of Bergmond had survived the day.

Augsad is the most westerly city of Bergmond and as such, its history tells much of the wars with Esmor, as the city so often found itself the pivotal focus of many conflicts down the years. To the east lies the great abbey, Campaldo, at the foot of the mountains and beyond, the land of Esmor. Augsad boasts a beautiful cathedral and square, it is protected by the great castle which is also known as the citadel. High in the citadel of Augsad, the duke sat in conference with other military commanders, including Gavron de Laude and Barons Agron and Conrad. Ever since the campaigns began again in the spring, the duke had been fascinated by the progress of Count Michael through the northern territories. The more he thought about it, the more the Duke became convinced that he, in turn, could repeat the march of Count Michael, in the opposite direction, and that such a march, if effected quickly, would yield much to the Bergmond cause.

"If we were to attack here in the borders and if we were to take the forts here and there – say, before December. It would give us very good reach out into Esmorin territory."

The Duke of Anflair was pointing to a large map on the table; the forts in question were those Esmorin forts of Borderlands and Fontrue. He went on,

"A quick autumn campaign might do it. To the left, the main assault forces attacking the fort. To the right the rest of the army, somewhere here near these villages of Hawksrath or Elvendene to protect us from any force the count might send to relieve the fortresses."

Beside the duke, the Barons Gavron and Agron towered over the maps in the candlelight.

"It would be a very good plan, my Lord," Gavron's voice growled approvingly. "What is more, with the borders taken, we could launch a spring campaign down into the Golden Plain, the heart of Esmor itself."

"Yes we could," said the duke. "What fortresses stand before us down there?"

Gavron squinted in the candlelight at the map.

"Here in the middle of the plain stands Belmont – that would have to be taken!"

"Any other forts nearby then?" the duke asked.

"Hmm," said Agron, "there's one here to the north and to our left, it's called –" and Agron bent his face down at the page and squinted, "It's called Val – Valdelaine. Yes. That would have to be taken also!"

The Duke looked at the others and said,

"If we take the borders we can proceed in the spring of next year – and we can cut Esmor in two. Cut in two, do you understand, gentlemen, provided we take this Belmont and that other place, what is it called again?"

"Valdelaine, my Lord," said Agron.

"Yes, this Valdelaine. In all, we take four fortresses and we cut Esmor in two. We could finish this war next year and win all the territory we want!"

The duke and the others sat down in silence for a while gazing at the maps and taking in the scale of the plan. Eventually the duke spoke.

"How soon can we send forward units to the border?"

"Germaine is ready to go any time, with four hundred young bloods. He can go tomorrow!"

"Good," the duke said. "Tell him he is to look at everything and see what's to be done – tell him not to engage the enemy until we can bring up the main forces."

"Very well, my Lord," said Gavron, "I shall see him immediately!"

"Before you go, how long before you can take a large force up there?"

"Give me a week and I'll have – say, five thousand in arms and marching!"

"Good!" the duke said. "I'll follow you in two weeks. Are we agreed then, gentlemen, that we go for the Borderlands!"

The assembly murmured assent. Many there were eager for another campaign, with memories of the loss at Savron Field still fresh in their minds.

Far away in Esmor, Count Michael had finally reached home at St. Michel, north of the city of Esmor, around mid September. He still had much to do, especially writing communications to his commanders all over Esmor, from Pelaine in the south to Borderlands in the north. When not working, the count spent his time with friends and old comrades and state officials, all of whom he would invite to St. Michel. The September sun, the good wine and the good companions were all to the count's liking, now that the threat of war had receded until the spring. And the season was full of hawking and hunting expeditions and merry music and dancing at night! It was here that the father of the Valdelaines, Lord Henry, stayed, leaving only to ride up to Esmor for the meetings of the king's council. Upon a September afternoon, when the sun was warm outside, Count Michael and Lord Henry sat in the cool hall, having wined and dined at the count's table an hour earlier. Far from talk of war, they enjoyed conversing about absent friends, the harvest, the coming round of winter festivals. Sometimes they talked of the old days, especially the troubles of the old wars which both of them saw in their youth; in this both men had a never ending store of reminiscences and stories.

Of a sudden, the two men sat upright as there was a sound of running footsteps upon the steps outside. Suddenly the doors of the hall shot open, and in came a young page in black livery; he was white as a sheet, despite his haste, and the piece of paper shivered in his hand. He opened his mouth to speak, then coughed and then blubbered out his message.

"My Lord Count! Lord Henry! The news is terrible, my Lords! Terrible – for the fiend is on the borders! The fiend is on the borders!"

The words echoed down the empty hall and Count Michael stood up slowly and stretched out his hand to receive the message from the startled boy. He read slowly, turned to Henry and said,

"It seems Germaine is on the borders. And is setting siege to Borderlands Fortress – the message is from Sir John de Graine himself."

"I see," growled Henry. "We may call the Council together for tomorrow."

"I'll have my scribes set to work now, and send messengers later. Meanwhile pray sit down, Henry, there's no more we can do now except enjoy the wine! Send for my writing man!" the count said to the page boy who was gone in an instant.

Within the week the count was riding for the Borderlands, taking with him a force of eight hundred men. All along the way he was joined by troops from southern Esmor and from the Golden Plain – the great fertile plain of mid Esmor. By the time he reached the Borderlands he was joined by contingents from northern Esmor, but even at that, he was outnumbered by the Bergmondese marauders who had gradually followed Germaine and were now besieging Borderlands Castle and Fontrue. The count's first task as he saw it, was to keep reinforcements and supplies trickling into the two fortresses. His second task was to avoid a pitched battle with the large Bergmondese force which was encamped to the south of Borderlands. He would avoid open battles until his own forces had augmented sufficiently. But the levies of troops that managed to reach him were still too small either to break the sieges or to tackle the Bergmondese in the open. After three weeks of skirmishing he realised that he might have to make a stand somewhere and even risk losing; the Bergmondese were on the move east across the Borderlands and beginning to threaten his smaller force more and more. What was he to do? Abandon the Borderlands and the two fortresses and retreat back towards the Golden Plain until he could increase his force and fight again in the late spring? Or could he make a stand somewhere here in the wilds of the borders, and against the odds, strike the Bergmondese and get them retreating back to the frontier.

His mind was made up for him. He had stumbled upon the village of Elvendene one October evening, thinking he had sidestepped the Bergmondese for a while; until he gazed across the fields at sunset and saw the banners and pavilion tops of the enemy, as they made camp for the night.

*   *   *

The broad fields north of Elvendene were covered with the frosts of the October morning; here and there, clouds of white fog trailed along the little valley which separated the two encampments. The village, too, was shrouded in its own veil of mist with only the top of the church spire visible. The opposing forces slowly began to appear out of the fog which clothed the slopes of ground on either side of the little Elven stream. Shouts, commands and all the sounds of armies on the move, came dull and muffled across the frozen fields through the wraiths of fog. The ground itself was firm and uncluttered with glistening stubble of the late harvest. Some autumn ploughing had been done but only in the fields closest to the village. High above, the sky was almost cloudless and brightening by the minute. Gradually the sun rose behind the Esmorin camp; orange and pink, it was given a magical incandescent glow by the fogs which seemed to swirl about it. The glories of the sunrise were lost on the men in the encampments as they moved among pavilions and tents. Many were finishing a breakfast; some were helping each other into cumbersome armour. Others were testing the mettle of their swords; a few meandered about in no hurry to catch up with their companies. Horses were fed and watered, the men from both armies drawing fresh water from the stream. Harnesses were checked and squires lifted riders onto their chargers and handed them their lances and shields. Finally helmets were fitted and the riders trooped slowly from the encampment across the open ground where the battle lines were being drawn up.

The long centre of the Esmorin army stretched for some hundreds of yards along a crest which dipped a little here and there and gave the appearance of a thick winding snake. At the very front, facing westwards down the little valley were the most experienced knights of Esmor, formed in two ranks. Behind them and in full armour, came rows of less experienced men and even entire rows of young squires. Sprinkled generously among the squires were veteran knights who acted as captains to the squires, who would, in turn, follow that captain when finally battle would be joined. It was here in the fifth rank from the front that Eris de Valdelaine found himself that morning. Far behind him there were older knights and even senior page boys all looking formidable in full and towering armour. Beyond the lances of the front line Eris could occasionally see Count Michael, Prince John and other commanders as they galloped before the line encouraging the men to hold firm and close.

Eris took a deep breath of the cool morning air and felt a thrill of pride as he sat on the charger with the great throng of knights all about him. Dressed in the full armour of his brother Jean he was proud of the light silken surcoat in the purple and saffron of Valdelaine. Squinting up he enjoyed the sight of the little banner of Valdelaine, fluttering on its strings below the lance-head. Beneath him and holding him up very high was Garold the great war horse, nineteen hands high and with a girth that stretched out Eris' legs to the limit. This monumental creature was the son of his father's war horse Talon – the memory of the day he had stolen Talon crossed Eris' mind, and he smiled. As he looked about him, he marvelled at the scene. The sun was up now and the fogs were disappearing under its growing heat, the scene was indeed splendid. Rising on his stirrups, he gasped at the sight all about him, rank upon rank, row upon row, grey steel helmets and lances almost to the horizon or so it seemed. He sat again and marvelled at the sight; the knights, their armour and weapons, the multitude of colours on surcoats and horse livery, on shields and on banners. So many wore the combinations of blue and red, so common in the south. The knights from northern Esmor were distinguished by their combinations of red, yellow and black. In front of him some warriors wore pale blue, or pale blue and white that were set off beautifully by the grey silver of the armour and the grey texture of the chain mail. Where these last knights were from he had no idea. A surge of delight ran through him as he beheld the scene and he felt no fear, simply a gladness that the great day had finally come.

"I'll wager there were times when you thought you would never see a day like this, my Lord!"

It was the young squire beside him who spoke these words, whose eyes and face were likewise glowing with pride and anticipation.

"Our first real battle, Eris, after all our chase-about, skirmishes, escorting wagons and running errands!"

Eris looked at him, pleased to know that his comrade, too, was running through the same gamut of emotions as himself. The young squire on Eris' left joined in the little conversation,

"This is our day at last, my friends, and I intend to make the most of it!"

Eris turned mischievous and said,

"Pray, gentlemen, it is only our first battle and by the looks of the big fellows up front of us, we won't see much fighting back here!"

Some others heard the little conversation, chuckled quietly and said nothing.

Across the valley the army of Bergmond was drawn up and for those who could see it, it looked formidable. Word came back from the front lines that the parley was about to begin as Prince John, Count Michael and two other commanders had galloped down to the banks of the little Elven to confront the Duke of Anflair and Baron Gavron, who had likewise come down from the Bergmond ranks. The duke removed his helmet and shook back his crop of blonde hair; he bowed to the prince and called out from across the stream.

"Your highness, my dear Count Michael, we meet again!"

"Greetings, your Grace!" Count Michael's voice boomed across the stream. "You look well, my Lord!"

The duke smiled. "And you, Count Michael. Gentlemen, I am instructed to bid you to withdraw from yonder hill where you stand. On behalf of His Majesty, the King of Bergmond, I am instructed to say that you have one hour's grace in which to begin your retreat. If you do not, we will go into the attack. I pray you consider this request."

Now it was Count Michael's turn to smile.

"Alas! My dear duke, it is here that we stand and you have the honour of charging us, anytime you wish. We will be ready! Otherwise you must withdraw from all Esmorin territory!"

Gavron's face had been contorted in a scowl as he had listened patiently to these preliminary pleasantries.

"We outnumber you, Count. We've taken your frontier, taken your borders and soon your forts will be ours. Why don't you just charge our lines or leave the Borderlands forever?"

Count Michael steadied his charger, sighed and said,

"Baron Gavron, you know that we Esmorins are a hospitable people and we've let you take our borders. But we are a hospitable people up to a point, my Lord. And today you have reached that point – our hospitality ends here! Here at the Elven stream! Fight, my Lord, or go!"

There was a long silence, such that one could hear the trickling water of the Elven. Somewhere up above there was the squawk of passing crows. The duke turned his horse and looked back at the Esmorins.

"God save you, Count, Prince!" he said and re-placed his helmet on his head.

"Likewise, your Grace!" the count shouted and turned his horse about to rejoin his troops, followed by the prince and the others.

From where he sat waiting, Eris listened carefully as word came back through the ranks with respect to the deployment of the enemy. A great black and white banner was seen raised before the great mass of the Berg-mond centre. "De Laude leads the centre!" came the word. Very good, but the thought in every mind was, where is Germaine? The red and blue banner of Anlac was seen on the left of the Bergmond line. "The fiend is on our right!" came the word. Eris thought of his brother Jean who was way down there on the Esmorin right wing. Finally word rolled back that Baron Agron would lead the charge against the left.

"Then God help the right – and send the fiend to hell!" someone shouted and there were cheers and some laughter.

The morning sun was up full now and the mists all cleared from Elvendene. Slowly, the Bergmondese centre descended the opposite slope at a walk and crossed the stream in good order. There they waited until they were joined on either side by the wings. For that moment, Eris could no longer see the enemy but, after an eerie silence, he could hear them as they raised the battle shout all along their line, the clamour wafted up the slope by the breeze. Eris glanced to the left and for an instant caught sight of the little spire on Elvendene church.

A roar greater than any other was followed now by the thundering sound of two thousand warhorses as the Bergmondese charged the hill. Amid the din all round him he was first able to see the tops of their banners as they came into view atop the forest of lances; then up came the helmets, the forms of the riders and finally the warhorses as the enemy gained the hilltop. The din was now almost deafening. He put down the visor over his face with his gloved hand and the two armies crashed like the crack of some unearthly thunder. The first shock of battle, from which moment all is either lost or won. Instantly, the first three ranks on either side became merged in the murder of the melee. Eris found himself a mere two horses length from the line of fight, able to see the clouds of breath and perspiration rising in the cool air from the clashes up ahead. On either side the horses of his companions pressed close awaiting the gap that might open. The clang of weapons, of steel on metal everywhere, mingled with shouts and screams of men and the whinnying of terrified horses.

Soon it will be your turn, Eris thought. Through the slit in the visor you see the first men killed or wounded and your right hand closes tight its grip on your lance. It is not long in coming, the gap opens in the line and you dig in spurs. As you spurt ahead, what happens thereafter is only partially remembered; time, space, even colour dissolve as the soul descends into that hell, and only your brain and muscles remember for you what you must do if you wish to see the light of day once more. The lance found its place. Ah! No! You had a glimpse of a chain and ball and the lance was wrestled from hand grip with force unexpected, unbelieved. Your shield is high protecting you from blows, your right hand draws sword or you are dead. Your waist now twists in the saddle as you pound that other shield with blows, forward and back swing – he cannot raise that mace again! A back swing finds a mark and he is sliding from the horse. The horse is now sideways on to the enemy, there are two lances, one you hack away, the other grazed your back. The horse has turned and you are facing your line for an instant, swing the shield behind you, before you can turn, the ground moved and your comrades sped past you and you are now in the line again almost at the rear. As if from another world a man's voice is calling your name.

"Eris! De Valdelaine, face front, boy! Face front!" You do and find yourself in a rank of comrades. Sword hanging from your hand, you wait in the line with the others. You are catching what you can of your breath, a film of sweat has broken through your body and under the metal helmet, you blink away the drops.

You sit there and wait. If the line holds, you will live to breathe a little longer. You will also live to bleed, for of this be sure, you have been hit and hit many times by weapons and parts of weapons you never even saw.

You feel you cannot wait, the blood in the veins is pumping you on to more. The gap opens and you are in the maelstrom again, lost to all sense except for the fury of the combat. You lose count now of the number of times you lunged ahead and held sway. The enemy, you have lost count of who died and who lived. All you know is that you have made it to the rear again and a pale faced young pageboy is handing you yet another lance. As you take the weapon, you see his face and you are reminded for a tiny moment of what you were before the battle began. You remember also that you have a brother, somewhere, off over there, in the same battle.

As he trotted the horse back to its place in the rear of the line he thought of Jean and wondered how things were down there. Far down to his right the Bergmondese under Germaine had flung themselves into the light cavalry of the Esmorin left. Instantly, Germaine knew there was something amiss, these were no farm boys or elderly knights, archers and slingers brought along to make up numbers on the wing. Though in light armour or mere chain mail, these men were hitters, and their blows fell sure and firm, and Germaine's charge had ground to a crunching standstill. So seeing, he wheeled his knights about and took up a second charge. As it was the first time, the Esmorins did not budge and Germaine was now losing men. He effected a third turnabout and another charge uphill but now the Esmorins were charging, bearing down on his men and inflicting even more casualties than before. He was now being driven back down towards the stream. Undeterred, he gallantly urged his men on and flung himself at the descending Esmorins, flailing a swathe through the enemy ranks, which immediately closed all about him, cutting him off from his own companions. Again undaunted he stood up on his stirrups and with his sword swinging all about him he cried out "Anlac! Anlac!" He was hit with a half dozen weapons from all sides as the Esmorin crush tightened about him, pre-preventing his men from reaching him. A lucky lance found its way inside his shield and pierced the chain mail into his arm. First he fell for-forward, for a second his eyes glimpsed the black hair of his horse's mane, and then, slithering off, he fell through the air, man and armour crashing on the ground. For an instant he saw the blue of the sky far above – for him there was nothing new in this, he had fallen thus many times in the thickest of the fight. His hand reached for his sword, in a second he would be up and fighting again, but the points of three daggers at his throat told him he would rise no more that day. His men were gone, beaten back down the hill and over the stream desperately trying to hold their line at that spot.

"Yield!" came the shout from above him. "Never!" he cried. "Yield or not, we are taking you any-way!" Ropes were quickly tied about his body and he was dragged by a mounted knight up the hill, over the crest and finally came to rest at the foot of the Esmorin pavilions. He was a prisoner, and the clamour of the fight was now far away. Men-at-arms held him down while his armour was unstrapped, finally leaving him dressed only in his tunic and hose. The knight whose horse had dragged him so far, was now kneeling above him, a long dagger in his hand. As the helmet was finally removed, Jean de Valdelaine stared in disbelief and a pang of horror stabbed his heart. His prisoner lying before him looked like a mere boy, tall, but a boy, nonetheless. The crop of sandy hair, the bright brown eyes, the boyish face and the long gangly body – all these were not the form of a leading warrior knight. Jean drew his face and his dagger close to the prisoner who was now being chained where he lay.

"Who are you?" Jean said quietly. The brown eyes looked at him.

"I am Germaine of Anlac!" came the breathless answer.

"You have worn the armour of Anlac. That does not make you Anlac! Now tell me, truly who you are, and where is the real Germaine? Tell me, or I shall have to kill you here and now."

The real Germaine was looking up at him but Jean still suspected the trick, that this boy was merely a hireling brought in to play Germaine on the battlefield, leaving the real Germaine to fight elsewhere or to escape.

"I assure you, I am the real Germaine. As truly as, by those colours of your tunic, that you are…" and he closed his eyes in desperation trying to remember "…that you are – de Valdelaine. I saw those colours last year at the Gavenne Bridge – and curious about you, I found your name."

For a long time Jean glared down at him in surprise and wonder. He remembered Gavenne Bridge and the gallant actions he had taken there.

"And you are not an impostor?"

"Not an impostor!" Germaine gasped. Again Jean looked at him for a long time.

"Very well" Jean said. "You must yield, Germaine, and I then take you prisoner!"

"I yield, de Valdelaine, I yield!" he snarled through gritted teeth.

"See to it that no harm comes to him!" Jean said to the men-at-arms, and he rose and mounted to rejoin the battle. In the centre, the battle was raging furiously, and neither side had cause to yield. But the Esmorin left wing had slowly won the upper hand against the Bergmondese under Baron Agron and gradually the conflict on that side was moving downhill towards the Elven stream. By now, Germaine's band of knights on the right was beginning to crack and they were now being pushed uphill on the far side and away from the stream. At this point at a signal the rear echelons of the Esmorin wings turned inwards to attack the now exposed flanks of the Bergmond centre. There was still almost an hour of ferocious fighting left at this part of the battle until Baron Gavron could realise that his troops were bearing the brunt of an assault that came from three sides and that at any moment his great centre might collapse. He got word of his danger via a messenger from the duke, and ordered a general retreat. Step by step, they descended down to the stream. At about the half way point, Count Michael halted his men, but only briefly, to check that they were well marshalled and close together. After that, Count Michael rushed the stream and within minutes the Bergmond centre was in full retreat and the chase was on. As soon as Gavron's men reached the hilltop with Count Michael in hot pursuit, they began to fan out in all directions, across the fields, past their pavilions and baggage wagons and out into the wilderness of bog, heath and moors. In the rough ground, the going was slow and bands of Esmorin knights were catching up with the scattering Bergmondese, and so, mile after mile, the slaughter went on. This chase across the moors went on for seven miles until the count ordered his men to halt and regroup. It was now early evening with only a few hours of October light left. Esmorin companies with experienced captains were sent ahead to further scour the gullies, bogs and the copses, rooting out groups of Bergmondese who were now exhausted and beginning to surrender. Baron Gavron, the Duke of Anflair and other commanders had made good their escape as had the young knights of Germaine's column.

The count, finding that he had reached the village of Hawksrath ordered that the entire encampment be brought forward from Elvendene to that village. The army would camp at Hawksrath for the night before making further pursuit of the enemy. Only healers, physicians, stretcher bearers, priests and monks were left behind to tend the wounded and begin burying the dead. Groups of messengers were sent to Fontrue and to Borderlands Castle where besiegers and besieged alike anxiously awaited the outcome of the day. Great shouts of joy went up from the walls of Fontrue when its defenders saw in the distance the troop of messengers in the twilight carrying aloft the royal standard of Esmor, signalling that Count Michael had won the day. The besieging troops hastily made ready and were gone within the hour fearing that some Esmorin defenders might take after them, even in the growing darkness. Much later the same scene was repeated before Borderlands castle, except in this case, the messengers assembled on the west of a hill near the fort and began to wave the royal standard in the air above their torches. And the shouts of joy from inside the fort were still echoing in the ears of the Bergmondese as they fled back towards the borders they had crossed in September.

At sunset, the village of Hawksrath was teeming with soldiers, the baggage train with food and tents had yet to arrive from Elvendene. In the last light Prince John returned from his foray on the moors and met with Count Michael in the tiny village square. From horseback the prince reached his hand across to the count who was also mounted.

"My blessings upon you, Cousin, for what you have achieved today. You have saved Esmor yet again!"

Count Michael smiled amid the myriad of torches passing to and fro.

"Well I think we have pulled the teeth of the dragon, my Lord Prince. But it may be another year before we get at the rest of him!" and the count gave one of his customary closed mouthed chuckles.

Not alone the village, but the fields beyond were lit with torches of men moving about. The baggage wagons had arrived from Elvendene and already tents and pavilions were being erected, and great fires were lit out along in the darkness of the fields. Men rested, exhausted, others searched feverishly for their companions. Eris found his brother's pavilion and returned to him his warhorse, armour and weapons. In Jean's pavilion Eris caught his first sight of the captured Germaine, all tied with ropes and chains and bundled up in a canvas tent flap. He gazed down only for a moment and then departed, there were too many comrades to look for and find if they were dead or alive. The cooks had been busy, and as men were catching their second meal of the day and drinking their first wine they began to make merry, to shout, to laugh and sing. The toing and froing went on into the night. The wounded were brought in finally and teams of healers and sawbones, even monks, set about the binding and healing that would go on into the night.

Some men went away to rest, others talked all night by the hundreds of firesides, and told many stories before they too fell asleep exhausted.

Eris turned in early in the count's pavilion, for a moment tried to recall the day, but fell asleep instantly. In that day he had crossed the divide, from boy to man, from squire to warrior.

In the week that followed bands of Esmorin knights trawled the moors all the way to the frontier. Germaine's band had stayed in the borders and continued a kind of guerrilla warfare for a time, hoping for a breakthrough that might enable them to rescue their commander, but to no avail. Both Jean and the count marvelled at this show of loyalty to their leader and speculated that there must have been a special bond between Germaine and his knights. But Germaine had been removed to the security of Fontrue for safekeeping; his chains were removed there, for there was no escape from the dungeons of the fortress. Fontrue however was deemed to be too close to the frontier and the prize prisoner would eventually be taken deeper into Esmor, beyond the reach of anyone foolhardy enough to try to rescue him.

Like a great rolling wave the news washed through the land of Esmor. The count had won a great victory near Fontrue; and the archenemy, the fiend Germaine, had been taken prisoner. Everywhere there was delight and relief – maybe now the war would be at an end. There were smiles on many faces, and the count smiled often as he made the long journey to St. Michel, and to Esmor. At the last moment he had changed his battle plan, outnumbered considerably, he had switched his best knights to the wings, who in turn, had smashed the attack of the Bergmond wings, leaving lesser troops to man the centre. When the enemy was repulsed on the wings, their centre was then at a disadvantage and finally broke. The Archangel, or the wily old schemer, had yet again drawn victory from the jaws of defeat.

The news brought about rejoicing in Valdelaine as it had done everywhere. The news also came that Jean and Eris had both fought in the battle, and that both had survived. But far away, between the Borderlands and the royal city of Esmor, negotiations carried to and fro; these negotiations and their outcome were to have the most far reaching consequences for Valdelaine, and ultimately for the outcome of the war.

Chapter VI: Germaine

*L*ife makes such strange demands of the soul.
Surely the human longing for novelty is
matched equally by the longing for familiarity. And it
came as if from nowhere, indeed, as if there was a recog-
nisable depth from which strange feelings and emotions
come. And it came to Ioni, not in some illuminative wave
of consciousness, no, it came first as only the tiniest of
whispers, which even she was not aware of for some time.
Later, she could recall the beginnings, she could remember the first day the strange little pulses began, she had
not attended to them at all, or she dismissed them from
her mind. But the pulses continued growing a little louder
each passing day, and what was thought might be tran-
sient, was soon becoming the most distinctive part of her
inner landscape; it was there to meet her soul, no matter
what else was taking place.

She was alone, if not in fact, then in feeling; everything that previously was familiar and even exciting
was now becoming hollow and strange. Not even her
long closeness to Fleur over the years, not even this was
sufficient in the face of this new inner miasma which was
creeping across her soul, as if she had gone for a walk on
a happy summer's day, blinked her eyes a few times and
now the day had turned to cloud, such that the landscape
had become dull and strange. She was beginning to forget
who she was. Surely, she asked herself, it is not normal
for a girl like me to be living this kind of life, surely other
girls have so much to think and dream about, and here am
I, alone and the absolute ruler of this domain, which I
never asked for. A queen in a land I do not even want,
going through all these motions as if I had owned them. I

never earned them, they were thrust upon me. I am the keeper of all of this and I never desired it in the first place. What kind of fool am I, that my life has been thus altered? What kind of fool am I to be locked, yes imprisoned by my life here. When did it all begin? Why was it that I was destined to be alone and in this state of things, when my life could and should have been otherwise. God in Heaven! I can see my other self now, laughing her way through these years, totally free and enjoying every moment. I am hemmed in on all sides – but who declared it should be so? Look at Fleur, look at Eleanor, look, even at Clara – they live, they live! Why was I destined...? Thus? Does anyone else ever feel as I do? I'm a fool! And there's no foreseeable way out. Oh yes! I could write to Papa and tell him I cannot manage anymore, but what evidence is there of that? I'm managing perfectly. Oh yes! Get Papa to resign his seat on the royal council and come home because his daughter – his daughter just wants to be a child and play games again. Get Papa to write to Jean asking him to leave the battlefields and come home because Jean's little sister just wants to be a little girl – for the foreseeable future. Do other people ever feel like this? I'm grown up but I don't feel grown up! And just then the wicked little elf left his perch on the great rocks of the rapids upstream and sat in the corner of the window, giggling and cackling.

"It is your destiny, Ioni, your Destiny!"

"Oh! Bother my destiny. I'm only a girl!"

She did look up at the corner of the window and there was no elf, not even one!

So that was it, the novelty of her first years as mistress had worn off. Her zest for her life in authority had waned, this zest had borne her on wings through the early days and right up to recently. What was left for her now, she wondered, dull days and humdrum chores? She gave a wry little chuckle. "It is my destiny!" she said aloud.

*   *   *

Across the wide countryside around Valdelaine, the snow lay heavy and deep, covering everything in its whiteness, from distant hills and forests to the village rooftops and right to the gates of the castle itself. Beyond, on the wide horizon, the winter sunset had already begun to change the snowy whiteness to orange and pink, with shadows of pale purple. Slowly, and ever so silently, the cavalcade of horsemen and wagons made their way along the winding, snow laden road. On steps and battlements, the castle folk wrapped themselves as warmly as they could against the cold, to watch the train of visitors drawing silently closer. Sunlight glinted on lances and helmets, the muffled sounds of horses and wagons grew more distinct as the cavalcade made its way across the bridge and then swung heavily up the causeway towards the castle gates. Ioni had chosen to remain with Raymond on the balcony which looked out high above the main door and courtyard below.

Ioni shuddered at the cold and at the recollection of the news contained in her father's letter of a week past. The king's court had decided to lodge the prize prisoner, Germaine of all people, at the castle of Valdelaine, far from the frontier borders. Her father's letter had apologised for this burden on Valdelaine, but had expressed confidence that the family would not be troubled by the presence of the prisoner, and that life would go on in the normal way. Germaine! The very name struck terror into people's hearts, but, until now, Ioni had only vaguely listened to the tales of him that had come back from the wars, tales of terrible deeds, enough to shake the stoutest hearts; they were deeds that had defeated Count Michael and her own countrymen time and time again. Poor people, escaping from the horrors of the war in the southern Gavenne had told tales of a cruel knight with almost magical powers, who could turn up anywhere to harry the king's forces, to raze castles to the ground and drive whole villages to shelter in the woods and mountains. Nothing had been able to stop him, Count Michael's actions against him had all failed. He was known to be in action in the south only to appear a week later before the border fortresses as if borne hither and thither by some evil force. In the mouths of the people he was already a demon, a minion of Satan himself, sent to wreak havoc on her beloved country.

Ioni shuddered again. She was very eager to get her first glimpse of the 'demon'; the courtyard below had filled with mounted knights, wagons; a great jostling crowd from the village were now gathered at the gate to catch a glimpse of the prisoner. At first, Ioni could not make out where he might be, but then she noticed a group of men-at-arms move to one of the wagons on top of which was a kind of makeshift wooden cage. This was duly opened and there was a gasp from the crowd when he, the demon, was dragged out into full view. Peering into the courtyard which was now in shadow, Ioni could make out that he was very tall, with an angular, gangly body and a great shock of hair of what colour she could not make out. From the waist up, his white body was naked save for swathes of bandaging about his chest and upper right arm, his left arm was held in a sling. His lower body was covered with a kilt and hose and his shackled feet were bare. With her eyes now squinting Ioni could see that part of his face and forehead were coloured as though from bruising. She was aware of a feeling of both horror, and even a little pity for this strange sight, as the guards began to move him forward – and he walked with a limp. No sooner had he moved forward, than the crowd began to cheer and jeer at him and some picked up stones to throw at him. A full volley of missiles whizzed around and past him before the guards move to stop the crowd, some guards protecting him with their shields. For one instant, as he shuffled forward, the prisoner raised his head to look up at the parapet where Ioni stood, her face still lit by the setting sun. It was an instant, no more, and the face of the prisoner seemed to change from bewilderment to momentary wonder at the face of the lady on the parapet. Next instant his head was down again, as he limped in his chains amid the guards, and Ioni lost sight of him as he disappeared within the castle. Ioni turned to leave the parapet but as she reached the door she turned and gazed out over the countryside, the sun had set. She closed her eyes for a moment and shivered at the thought 'the war has now come to my very home.'

Ioni quickly went to her chamber to sit alone feeling numb and overawed by the arrival of the strange prisoner. She felt a weariness and a kind of wave of loneliness pass through her being. Then she roused herself, changed her clothes and went down to the banquet hall to welcome the escort knights and made whispered enquiries as to the progress of the housing of the men-at-arms. Here Ioni was greeted with another surprise which was not entirely welcome. One of the four knights who had escorted Germaine, was the handsome young Leon Belmont, to whom she had been once 'betrothed'. Quite unnerved and a little embarrassed she stepped forward to greet him. Fortunately for her, he too stepped forward to greet Ioni and gallantly took her hand and bowed and kissed it.

"I did not think to see you again, Lady Valdelaine!" he said with a reassuring smile, "and more beautiful than ever, I vow."

"Thank you my lord," Ioni smiled back at him. "I did not think to see you either. But you are most welcome to our house, now as always."

The pleasantries over, the assembled knights and family members sat to eat a hearty supper. Ioni sat, cheeks still glowing from the surprise of meeting Leon. For a while her mind was buzzing with the thought of him, and frequently her eyes darted down the table to where he sat contentedly. He had grown quite a bit since she last saw him, had a fine figure now; he looked quite resplendent in his knightly garb. Yes, he was quite a man now, and it seemed to her that the self-centred nature he had as a youth had quite left him. He was now so self-assured and calm. There was quite a funny little pang in her heart as she thought 'If I had not broken off the betrothal I might be all set to marry him soon!'

Tomorrow, perhaps, she would find an opportunity to speak with him privately. God! She thought, how he has grown up! Perhaps there was a side to his nature which she had never known in their earlier years. In those times, he had quite amused her but had never captured her imagination nor indeed, her heart. She supposed that in those times she had too often compared him to her two brothers. It had seemed to her then that their qualities had far surpassed any of his. Jean was so calm and Eris was so wild, but both gave generously from the heart in everything they did. He, however, had been amusing and quite diverting, but then he had seemed somewhat proud and a little pompous at times, having certainly shown more interest in himself and in his affairs than in anything else. Quite often these latter characteristics had given her more ill humour than good. Oh dear! She thought, maybe we were both too young, bent on making artificial impressions on each other. Could I have been wrong about him? Oh dear! Her large eyes stole another peep down the table at him, as he chatted affably with the others; her thoughts and her quick glances at him were suddenly checked when she caught Fleur, looking at her and smiling gently, but knowingly at her. She smiled back at Fleur, whom she knew would never make little of her in any way, because of that, one time, attachment to Leon.

All the family were present at the evening meal, even Uncle Robert, whom Ioni had requested to attend. Family and visitors made a pleasant company at the meal. There was even music playing as conversation swung here and there about many things, most importantly, any news there might be of Jean and Eris and Raymond's two sons. The knights, and even the men-at-arms at the lower table, had plenty of news of Jean and Eris and the others; it was good news that they were all well, in good health and doing nobly in the service of the king. During a short lull in the conversation Ioni's mind strayed back to the prisoner – goose pimples ran over her body.

Earlier, as she had left the parapet, Liefing had approached her as she stood a moment with Uncle Raymond.

"My Lady, my Lord," he had announced, "the prisoner is safely secured below!"

Ioni had said to Liefing,

"Leonor the maid will bring you some bandaging for the prisoner, there are some old shirts and an old doublet and hose of Jean's. Pray take them to the prisoner.

Later, I shall find a cloak for him, I don't want him to freeze to death down below!"

"Very well, my Lady." Liefing growled, "Too good, you are, too good!"

Then again she was drawn back to the revels of the banquet hall. The knights were taking Aunt Blanche and the girls to the floor to step a dance or two with them. Uncle Robert had been quiet enough during the meal, though he had spoken knowledgeably on any subject raised.

"There it is, my child," he said down the table to Ioni. "Shall I escort you to the floor and dance a measure?" Ioni looked up at him and was forced to smile as she gazed at his handsome face and bright eyes.

"Thank you, dear Uncle Robert," she said still smiling kindly at him. "But I think I shall retire early. I'm not in a humour to dance."

When there was a lull in the revels Ioni stood up and bade her good night to all and strode down the hall to the gallant bows of the knights and the curtseys of the girls.

In her chamber, Ioni sat by the little window, gazing out at the pale glow of moonlight on the snowy countryside below. From that lofty place, she pondered and was a little troubled at the knowledge of the prisoner who was now buried in the dungeon far below. The beauty of the night was everywhere but her heart was ill at ease. His arrival under guard earlier that day, and his dishevelled and broken condition, troubled her spirit. What a cruel thing was war, she thought, that it should bring such pain and misery such as she had seen in the prisoner's condition. Though he was the most feared enemy, she could not help thinking that if the war had not come to pass, he might have been a brave and honourable man, like her brother Jean. Perhaps, he had been a good youth but had grown wicked amid the ferocities of war.

Sleepless she was, and ill at ease. She turned away from the window, and in the candlelight her eyes were drawn to the wooden chest which contained the clothing, arms and armour of the man who was now a prisoner, her prisoner. She felt drawn by a desire to see for herself the contents of his chest, of belongings which had been carried into her chambers. Moving one of the candles closer, she knelt on the floor before the chest and began to lift the lid. Then she paused a moment feeling vaguely guilty, as if she was intruding on someone else's privacy. But, curiosity got the better of her and she lifted the lid again, completely this time. She gazed in wonder at the contents, first there was the helmet which gleamed as she lifted it out into the candle light. It was simply but handsomely crafted, she thought, as she placed it on the floor. Next, she lifted out the breastplate, then the shoulder pieces, greaves and spurs, holding up each item to the light to admire and ponder on them. Then she placed each item upon the floor about her. Next she came upon his sword and releasing it from its scabbard she held its gleaming slender length in both hands. Presently she found his clothing and lifted up one of his doublets, blue in colour and flared at the hem in scarlet and at the breast an eagle emblem embroidered in cloth of gold. She found the grey hose and then the long, silk surcoat of blue and red that he would have worn over the armour. Sadly it was gashed in a number of places, she must remember to have it repaired, but how to properly repair silk? At last her hand found the heavy coat of chain mail and the padded material worn inside it, the hauberk. It was too heavy to lift out so she left it in the chest. Once again she held each item before her wondering again and again to herself what kind of man had worn these awesome things – what kind of heart had beaten beneath all this metal and cloth. She was about to place everything back when she came across his buckles and daggers; their burnished pommels gleaming in the light.

There, as she knelt on the floor in the silence of the night, surrounded by the warrior accoutrements of this terrible Germaine, she no longer felt afraid but had some strange sense that already she somehow knew this man. Oh God! Lord Germaine, she prayed, I hope your stay here may be short and you return to your homeland and to peace. Soon, soon. God speed the day when you are free and when I am your captor no more! She then smiled and promised she would cherish each item of his against the day of his freedom in his ransom. She hoped all his fine armour might really be the outer apparel of a good and noble person. As soon as was possible she would order Liefing to bring him under escort to the great hall so that she might find out for herself what manner of man had once worn this handsome and noble raiment.

Ioni then placed each item back in the chest, but, when she came to the helmet and sword again, she could not bring herself to part with them. So she placed them on top of the chest lid, where she might see them from her bed. Then she rested her head on her pillow and closed her eyes.

She sat upright in the bed. Is there no sleep for me tonight? She thought. An hour ago she had left the helmet and sword on the chest. She had placed her head on the pillow, closed her eyes to sleep. But, moments later her eyes had opened once again and there were sword and helmet, as it were, gazing at her across the room. Again, she tried for sleep only to open them to a squint seeing the metal glow in the candlelight. Eyes closed once more but this time one eye opened to scan the gleaming steel. Turn away toward the wall, she thought; but still, no slumber. She rose from the bed and blew out the candle. After moments in the dark, eyes opened again to see them both in silhouette against the moonlight, the helmet and the sword. Twist and turn to no avail, she rose and lit the candle once more. By now she was regretting her selfish whim of having the armour of Germaine of Anlac deposited in her room. She shivered a little as she sat upright in the bed, her arms folded around her knees. The armour there was like a kind of intruder. Germaine of Anlac, what a noble title she mused; and what a pathetic wounded sight he had been, earlier that day, as the men-at-arms had dragged him across the courtyard. When he had gazed up at her for an instant, as she had stood on the battlement, her fear of him had changed to pity in that one instant. While others had seen what was left of a once fearsome knight of the enemy, Ioni had seen only a boy, and an ill-used boy at that. Was it girlish foolishness that filled her with pity for him, she wondered. She shivered. As it was, he was not far away in the lowest dungeon below. Again the same haunting sense of intrusion came over her. This boy, knight, whatever he was, was the first guest she had known in her lifetime who was a prisoner. Unhappy guest, she thought. The sooner he was ransomed back to his own country the better, the sooner this horrid war was over the better. She rose from her bed and knelt on the floor joining her hands in prayer.

"God in Heaven," she whispered, "bless and forgive this Germaine of Anlac. Bring us all to peace once more. Bless me, your servant Ioni of Valdelaine." She rose and solemnly took the helmet and sword and placed them in the chest and replaced the lid. Blowing out the candle she jumped into bed, placed her head on the pillow and slept.

Towards morning, she saw her brothers Jean and Eris, in her dreams. They were dressed and mounted for a hunting party and she was imploring them to take her with them. When they agreed she was mounted on her own horse Hero, and they went galloping through the woodlands, the morning sunlight breaking the forest mists all round her. The men-at-arms are pointing and saying that the great wild boar was seen down the forest path. Away they charge, Ioni, Jean and Eris, to pursue the creature, whom they now see dashing into a thicket and out of sight. Suddenly Ioni looks around her and she is alone, Jean, Eris and Hero are all gone. She is alone, and beyond the mist and the thicket she knows the great boar is now turning as, terrified and standing there alone, she hears the creature come crashing through and charge at her. She is about to scream, but sees now that it is not the wild boar that emerges from the darkness but a man, a young man dressed in blue doublet trimmed with red. He falls to the ground at her feet and looks up at her, the face she has seen before, it is Germaine! With heart panting, she opens her eyes to find herself in her familiar bedroom, her head falls with relief back on the pillow, but beads of perspiration trickle down her temples.

*   *   *

"From what I have seen, the fellow is a complete disappointment!" chimed Aunt Blanche to those assembled at the midday meal the following day. Everyone was amused at Blanche's frank announcement when the conversation had turned to the topic of the prisoner. "I'm quite serious, my lords! I had expected to see a great and fearsome knight, this young man is no more than a boy! When I was young I had occasion to see the great Gaston himself. Now, there was a brave and bold knight as ever there was! He was tall, muscular and had this great head of black hair and a black beard to go with it. He, too, a prisoner of this realm, though not for long, I assure you. As fearsome as he was, he proved to be a great friend of this realm for the rest of his days. That was in his late majesty's time, you know." Blanche sniffed in her usual haughty manner and then proceeded to bite into another leg of chicken.

Down the table little Anna was tugging at the sleeve of her cousin Eleanor.

"But I wasn't allowed to see him," she was saying in a low voice. "And you promised you would tell me what he looks like!

"Hush Anna!" Eleanor whispered back as the conversation about Germaine continued. "Finish your food!"

"But you promised!" said Anna in a louder voice. "Anyway, whatever he looks like I think it is sad that he is all alone by himself down in the castle prison. I'm sure he's not as bad as everyone thinks! Is he handsome?"

"Hush! I said, Anna," Eleanor rasped at the child. "I'll tell you all about him – well, later!" Anna responded with a shrug of shoulders and a little pout.

"I don't feel hungry anyway," she said, and then caught Ioni's great eyes looking from across the table at her with amusement and interest. Anna knew she had said something that had pleased Ioni, though exactly what it was she did not know. She decided to keep silent and munched another morsel of food, while Ioni's attention was brought back to the gentlemen visitors. She had other things on her mind: she must meet Leon and talk to him privately about their abandoned betrothal; she must also meet the knight Ernan who seemed to know Eris so well, and who had spent some time close to the count, where Eris served.

Ioni bided her time until she could find the opportunity to meet Leon alone. When they met, he was most polite and affable.

"I must speak with you, Leon," she said looking at him cautiously, "about our betrothal. Please believe me, I meant no offence to you or indeed to your family. But I felt I had to do it at the time. We were both so young, I –"

"You can be at peace, on that matter!" he said quite gallantly. "It certainly stung me badly at the time. But, well, you see this war came along and everybody had to pull together and well, I became quite occupied with so many things, I did not dwell on it. My family too, like yours, had much to do and I don't think there is any rancour between us."

"Thank you!" Ioni said with a little smile. "You understand, I felt badly about it always, and when you appeared here again, well, it brought everything back, and I was feeling so desperate just to talk with you and, well, to apologise to you for any offence given. I do hope you forgive me from your heart!"

"I do, Lady Ioni," he said, looking at her, "though having seen you again these last few days, it brings it back to me even more what I seem to have lost. But do not be worried, having seen you again, what can I do? But to wish you well!"

"Thank you." Ioni gasped. "Thank you for such kindness. It has been wonderful to see you again, also. I would like to think of you as a friend, a very dear friend, Leon. I would like you to think of me as a friend too, if you can. I would like you to know that there is always the most kind welcome for you at Valdelaine."

Leon nodded his head and smiled, took her hand and kissed it.

"Maybe we were not meant to be husband and wife," he said. "But maybe we will make very good allies!"

"Allies!" Ioni smiled. "That is a good word, Leon. Let us be allies, my dearest Leon. Let us be good allies!!"

With that Ioni took his hand in hers and leaned forward and kissed his cheeks.

"I expect Uncle Raymond is going hunting tomorrow and will invite you and the others to join him, if he has not already done so!"

"Wonderful," said Leon. "A day's hunting would be very welcome. Will you be able to join us, Ioni? I do hope so!"

"Oh! I had not thought about it!" Ioni said. "I've been so busy looking after everything here, I think I would like a day out hunting, it would be such a change! I'll certainly think about it!" She smiled and was certainly thrilled at the prospect of a day's exercise in the saddle, even if the winter countryside was covered in snow. She had always loved hunting especially in the cold beauty of the winter time.

"Till supper time, then?" Leon said.

"Yes. But wait, Leon." Ioni said. "You might perform a small errand for me."

"Anything!" he said, wrapping his cloak around him.

"Well I would like to speak with Ernan," said Ioni. "He has been with Eris, my brother. They are both in the count's service. I just need to know how well Eris really is; he and Eris spent a lot of time together. Could you ask him to come and see me for a while."

"I can certainly do that for you," Leon said, and with a reassuring tone continued, "but you need have no worries about Eris, he is doing very well by all accounts. He certainly is quite safe where he is, serving on Count Michael's staff."

"And what of you, Leon," Ioni said with wide intent eyes, "how safe are you, dear Leon? I fear I worry for you all!"

"Very safe, I assure you, Ioni," smiled Leon. "I have the finest knights in all of Esmor around me every moment. Now if you will allow me, I take my leave of you for the moment!"

"Yes, dear Leon," Ioni said and watched him turn and stride down the great hall.

Just as he reached the door Ioni called out. "My Lord!"

Leon turned. "Yes, my Lady!"

"Be well, my Lord!" Ioni called to him. "And be safe. You are in my prayers, my most heartfelt prayers!"

She could see him smile. "In that case I am both well and safe and I thank you again!"

With that he was gone and Ioni was left standing alone in the great hall, savouring the sweet silence of the place. Thank God, she whispered to herself, we are friends again after all that has happened. Her heart happy with relief, Ioni paced up and down the hall until finally Ernan made his entrance and bowed to her.

The conversation with Ernan was easier than the previous one, especially when Ioni explained her sisterly concern for her younger brother. Ernan told here many stories of Eris; he told of the pranks that Eris would get up to; he told of how he could put a humorous twist on every adventure; he told of a young man who seemed just to enjoy everything he did and who loved nothing more than the companionship of those around him. As Ernan spoke, Ioni could picture Eris in her mind in all the situations Ernan described. She smiled. That was the real Eris, the brother she had always known and loved so much.

"And he is quite safe, my Lady," Ernan added. "Mostly he is quite near the count. He rides in the count's escort. He is sent by the count with messages for other commanders. But he would never be sent out alone if the territory is hostile."

Ioni breathed deeply and said,

"Has he, how shall I say, has he been in battle?"

"None, save for the battle of Savron Field!" said Ernan. "The count is very protective of him and others like Eris, who are young, and new to campaigning. He may have seen some light skirmishes, and them only from a very safe distance!"

"That is good to know, my Lord," breathed Ioni. "It is such a relief to know Eris is safe. My other brother Jean is also in the war, and is frequently with the count. Though I understand that, as a knight, he may always be in danger and in the thick of the fighting."

Ernan paused a moment and then looked Ioni straight in the face. "That is correct, Lady. Lord Jean is, as you say, in the thickest of the fighting, when it happens. However, he has gained a great reputation as a warrior and as a skilful fighter. The fame of Valdelaine's knights has already passed to a new generation. However, please be aware that Lord Jean is no fool and knows how to look after himself!"

Ioni's wide eyes looked at Ernan for a long time.

"I wish this war were over," she sighed. "Then my brothers and all of you could come home to us, poor weeping women, and then we need pine no more!"

"It will soon be over, my Lady," Ernan said soothingly.

"The sooner the better," mused Ioni, "and even that young man, the prisoner now in our dungeon, can go home to his people, whoever and wherever they are!"

And she shuddered.

"Well, he is your prisoner now, my Lady," Ernan said. "For the time being at least."

Ioni looked at him again.

"Well, there was something I wanted to ask – about him," Ioni said. "As you said, we Valdelaines have a great reputation in war, my Lord. But likewise, we have also had a reputation for mercy. I was wondering – well, in fact some of us were wondering, the ladies of the family in particular, we were wondering about the possibility of moving him from the dungeon to perhaps a more gentle confinement in one of the castle chambers. After all, he is nobility like ourselves…"

"Spoken like a true Valdelaine!" Ernan smiled. "Believe me, my dear and gentle lady, that he is extremely dangerous. More deadly than someone with your good heart could ever imagine." Ernan paused for a moment, "Without offence to the goodness of your heart I would not recommend the change of quarters."

"But my Lord, he is so young and is in chains every moment," Ioni blurted out. "I mean, if Jean or Eris were prisoners I would be glad if they were treated gently!"

Ernan looked at her kindly.

"My Lady, your brothers are both noble and good young men. I pray that you do not consider this Germaine in the same light. There is no comparison here. What you have in the dungeon may well be noble born and bred. But you must always consider him an animal – yes, my Lady, a savage animal! That is what he has been!"

Ioni's face paled at the words and her eyes looked at him wide with fear. He went on speaking,

"The count has allotted you eleven men-at-arms to guard him – even though he is in the dungeon. If you were to house him as you say, more gently, you would need to raise more guards for him, locally, and, at your own expense. I suppose he could be placed in one of the castle chambers, but then only in the heaviest irons, and with a constant guard day and night and only in a chamber in the most secure part of the castle. Again, I do not recommend it at all. But if you are intent on moving him, do so with the utmost caution, I have to warn you. And leave nothing, I mean nothing, to chance."

They looked at each other for a long time.

"If we did imprison him in a safe room," said Ioni eventually, "with all precaution and chains, bolts on the door, and so on, he could not escape, my Lord! He could not possibly!"

Again Ernan was silent in thought, his forehead wrinkled in a frown.

"Well," he growled, "suppose he did escape, he would not get far. The Borderlands are a long way off, not to mention the Fens of Aren and the forests beyond them. But that is not my point. My point is that if this Germaine were given half a chance he might harm you or some of the family, the guards, the servants. As I told you he is dangerous. In God's name, my Lady, whatever you do in this matter, I beg you take no foolish chances!"

Again Ioni went pale. Ernan made his excuses and left the hall. Silence and the winter darkness closing in, Ioni sat pondering for a long time.

*   *   *

Time. Time and darkness, these were his only companions now: sleep, when it would come, gave Germaine dreams in which he might see sunlit days and happier times. Waking ever to the darkness of his dungeon cell, Germaine wondered and hoped, hoped that the moment of release might come. Even one moment would suffice, just to see the sky again and feel the sun warm upon his skin, just a moment when he might breathe the scented country air and see the colours of the world once more. Exactly how much time had gone by he could not tell; his world now, in this deep cell was all darkness every hour, and day and night were lost to him. When, if ever would he see the light of day again, he asked himself, with a shudder. The awesome sense of isolation was new to him, to be so cut off from all companionship, from all warmth and light, from any possibility of gentleness and mercy. Mercy! He knew he could expect little of that, his training with Gavron of Laude had seen to it that he would be merciless himself when it came to war. Kill! Kill without mercy, Gavron had taught him. War is war and you have no place in it except to live by the sword and by that only. And he had lived by that maxim though, at times, it had troubled him, as it troubled him now. There were the towns and villages he had razed along the Gavenne, poor innocent people he had cut down in cold blood. Yes, he had been well trained to kill anything that came in his way, he had been a most useful commander to his country, doing what few others would have done, steeling his very heart against the horror of things he was caused to do. And now, with time, endless time to reflect, the events of the past year and a half had now come back to haunt him. Mercy! He thought to himself, he could expect so little of that now. Of course he had asked no mercy for himself during his days of battle. But now, the drawn out darkness of this place had a way of coming back to nag at his mind, again and again. There was one horrific incident above all that seemed to surface again and again to his mind's eye.

The incident in question had occurred during his campaigns around Holgen Fortress two years previously. Though Germaine was well outnumbered at this time, he had used surprise tactics again and again to outwit his enemy. In one action at this time, he had burst from the cover of forests with his men intent on taking an enemy contingent from the rear. As they galloped towards the enemy pavilions a group of young squires and pageboys had emerged to meet them or give warning of their approach. These youngsters had only enough time to grab some lances in their hands as, seemingly, there were no men-at-arms to guard them. Not wishing to lose the advantage of surprise Germaine and his troops descended on them, some mere pageboys, and within minutes had despatched every one of them. "Damn it. They're only boys!" Philip had cursed and shouted at Germaine when the blood lust had cooled a little. "Damn it! They should have been protected," cried Germaine. "On! On Philip, we have no time to lose!" And Germaine dug in his spurs, and followed by his men, galloped away towards the enemy.

But in times of quiet the memory of the butchering of the youngsters began to come back to him. 'An act of war' was the expression one might use to minimise the event, but to Germaine it had gradually become a personal issue. The sheer brutality of his later training with de Laude had all but obliterated the idea of chivalry that he could recall from his earlier training with the Duke of Anflair. The memory came back, and was back with him now in the darkness of his cell, he could still see the last moments of those boys, their clumsy action with lances, their shouts for mercy and the horror on their faces as they died under a hail of sword and mace blows. The action against the enemy that had followed had been bloody and thick and Germaine had scored a victory that had been lined with luck. So the memories had taken some time to come back to him and now they were with him more vivid than ever.

Over and back, he tossed the memory around his mind sometimes with one conclusion, sometimes with another. The enemy knights should have left a guard with them – on the other hand, the enemy were not expecting to be attacked from the rear, and so on, and so on. But no matter what conclusion he came to in his mind it was immediately superseded by the simple feeling of wishing he had not killed them. And that was the problem. Oh yes! Philip and the others had joined in the killing. But alas, if there had been but the tiniest moment of grace, just the tiniest, he could have had them disarmed and bound and carried on himself with the attack. But that moment of grace had not come – and he could never be sure of the number, sometimes he was sure it was only six youths, but at other times he seemed to remember eight, or even ten. In the midst of the little fray one of the page boys, a blond-headed youngster had dropped his lance and began running for his life, across the field from the pavilions. Germaine had followed him, run him down, and with one sword blow to the head, had ended his young life.

He shuddered at the thought of it, now painted vividly on his memory, his stomach tightened and beads of perspiration came through him. What mercy can one expect, he thought, in the wake of such horrors; perhaps this place, this darkness is my punishment, who can tell?

The sound of a heavy door opening somewhere above was like thunder in the silence of the dungeon; this was followed by the rattle and jingle of keys, there were footsteps of someone approaching; there was the light from a torch beginning to flicker on the walls as even that light filtered down into his dark domain. Germaine got up, crossed the floor to hold the iron bars of the cell and try to look up the passageway to ascertain who was his visitor. It was, of course, Liefing, recognizable by the sound of his harsh rasping cough. Liefing's piercing blue eyes met those of Germaine for an instant as the steward began to unlock the metal gateway to the cell.

"You're still here, I see," growled Liefing, and burst into laughter that descended into more coughing. He said nothing as he began unlocking the fetters that held the prisoner to the cell wall. Observing this, Germaine exclaimed "Where are you taking me!"

"Never mind!" said Liefing. "You'll know soon enough! Have you your best pieces of clothing on you, if you haven't, then, put them on now. And be quick about it."

"My best clothes?" Germaine said as he opened a coffer at the foot of his plank bed and lifted out a shirt and tunic. "But where am I going, in my best clothes?" He was now holding the new shirt over his head and putting his arms up into the sleeves.

"Well, seeing you are so impertinent as to ask a second time," Liefing growled, as he picked up Germaine's holding chains, "You have an invitation to meet the household. Yes, in the great hall, no less!"

"Oh, I see," said Germaine, a little relieved as he shuffled in his shackles out of the cell onto the passageway, catching his first sight of the soldier who was holding the torch.

"Oh yes! The family would like to see you!" Liefing spat as he began to mount the stone steps. Germaine followed still shuffling. "Though in God's good name I know not why," Liefing wheezed. "If it were up to me, I'd leave you down there for good and always. Come on! Step it up!" Liefing had reached the top of the stairs and was yanking on the chains pulling the prisoner upward. The soldier with the torch had a hand firmly on Germaine's back supporting his climb to the landing. Liefing opened the door that led to another candlelit passageway and then to the equally lit antechamber of the great hall.

"Now let me warn you, young man," Liefing turned about to face Germaine, "The people I serve are good, decent people, so have a care of your manners. Conduct yourself well or if not, you will have me to answer to!"

Germaine nodded, and Liefing then knocked on the door of the hall. It was opened by an armed guard, and Germaine was able to catch his first sight of the hall, its walls, its lights, ornaments and tapestries, and finally, the group of people standing at the top end who turned around towards him as he entered.

Chapter VII: In Our Midst, A Stranger

*I*oni sat behind a table in the great hall, behind her stood Lord Raymond and on either side stood Leon, Ernan and the other two knights. Winter sunlight poured through the narrow windows lighting the great tapestries that hung from the walls; and the group of men that stood waiting expectantly with Ioni near the fireplace at the end of the hall. The eyes of all were on the doors. Presently they opened to reveal Leifing the steward, followed by the figure of Germaine, who limped forward in his shackles, flanked on either side by two men-at-arms. Slowly, this little procession traversed the length of the hall and halted about ten feet from where Ioni sat. For what seemed like an age, Ioni took time to look at Germaine, appraising him from head to toe, she had to steel herself at the sight of him. A tall youth indeed, with a shock of sandy blonde hair, at first his face seemed plain, almost featureless, except for the eyes which were dark, intense, and conveyed intelligence.

Since the arrival of her prisoner, this was Ioni's first chance to study his features, if only for a moment. His face, though pale, was a strong face; every feature, high forehead, cheekbones and jutting jaw, all were strong as though chiselled from some white marble. As she studied him more closely, his face seemed to emerge in a better light. The eyes were surprising, arresting even, deep and dark, containing a luminous spark that spoke of a lively mind and a quick intelligence. He was tall, lean and lanky, as many young men can be before chest, shoulders and upper arms have time to expand; his body was thin. It was the face and burning eyes that alone betokened strength. So this was the fiend, thought Ioni, the legend of the wars, the hero of so many battles. How, she wondered, could anyone so youthful have wreaked the havoc he did on Esmor this past two years? Only time would tell.

After the darkness of the dungeon, those eyes were still blinking in the light of the hall. In spite of his wounds and shackles he held his form, all six feet of it, upright and erect and looked askance and defensively from one set of eyes gazing at him to another, as if to en-quire what was to become of him now? Lord Raymond was about to speak but Ioni raised her hand to silence him, pushed back her chair, stood up and walked around to the front of the table. Still staring at him, Ioni thought – he's not exactly handsome but... good looking in a hard kind of way... and the intensity of those dark eyes! Is this really the monster we have all heard about?

"You are..." she paused and went on, "Lord Ger-maine of Anlac?"

He looked at her, then lowered his eyes, bowed and answered. "I am, my Lady." It was the first time she heard his voice, medium deep and resonant. But Ioni's large eyes never flinched, that wide stare never faltered.

"Alas for you, Lord Anlac," she spoke loudly. "Alas for you, I say, that you have made grievous war upon our country." She paused. "Alas for you, also, that you now find yourself a prisoner in this house, indeed, my prisoner. For I am Ioni de Valdelaine, mistress of this place and, for the moment, at least, your gaoler."

Again Germaine lowered his eyes and bowed. Ioni proceeded to introduce Uncle Raymond and again Germaine bowed and raised his eyes to Ioni once more. There was a long silence as everyone stared at him trying somehow to take him in. Germaine, thinking that the interview was at an end bowed and began to shuffle around to face the door.

"Pray, tarry, my Lord," Ioni's voice echoed around the great hall. "We would speak with you more!"

Confused and embarrassed Germaine turned to face them again. This time Lord Raymond spoke.

"The Lady Ioni, my niece, has been considering your imprisonment here and, in the goodness of her heart, has wished to see you more gently housed within these walls for the duration of your time here."

Germaine's eyes moved to Ioni's.

"You are a man of rank and title," she said. "And in the tradition of my family, I wish to see you well treated, as befits a gentleman of rank, even though you are our enemy. This means you would have a room here within the castle, locked and guarded, of course, but providing you better accommodation than the dungeon chamber. All of this, provided you agree to respect the fact that you are not quite a free and welcome guest, but a prisoner here, and I believe a grievously dangerous one. You will be fed and clothed and your needs looked after as though you were one of our guests. But, of course, without your freedom."

Germaine gasped and his eyes were wide with astonishment, even a flicker of a smile appeared momentarily on his face. He gulped and was serious again. With that, he began to painfully shuffle forward to where Ioni stood. The men-at-arms swiftly sloped their lances to hold him but Ioni prevented them with a gesture of her hand. As he stood before her, for an instant their eyes met again and her eyes searched his and found what she thought was a look of gratitude there. Then, there in his shackles he lowered himself awkwardly to one knee and then to the other, raised both his hands as if to take her hand but at the last moment his shackles held his out-stretched hands firm, inches short of her hand. She looked down at him and stretched her hand into his. He took her hand gently and kissed it softly. He raised his head to peer up at her and said,

"I thank you. I thank you, my Lady, I thank all of you."

Then, bowing his head, he dragged his right leg upward intending to stand but again the chains caught his leg, as he moved, preventing him from rising, and almost toppling him over. Instinctively Ioni stepped forward and everyone gasped, as she grasped his hand and elbow and with all her strength supported him until he could stand again. He shuffled back a step and bowed to her. "Thank you!" he breathed. Everybody relaxed again as Germaine found his way between the men-at-arms to where he stood before. Ioni was dumbfounded at her action in lifting him, she had steeled herself for this interview but what a wave of compassion had come over her! And where it had come from she could not tell. She was shaking a little from the effort to lift him and when he stood before her he towered over her. Ioni's face felt red as she tried to compose herself and announce that the interview was at an end.

Two days later Germaine was escorted up great winding stairs that led to the top of the new tower of the castle. At the top of the stairs was a little stone passage-way leading to a small room with a wooden door, in it were a single slit window, chair, table, bed and candle. A gate of iron bars had been fixed by workmen into the stone at the top of the stairs for greater security. The wooden door would be locked, the gate at the top of the passage would be locked, and there would be a guard at all times. Ioni breathed a sigh of relief that this problem was solved.

Little cousin Anna was still complaining that she had never been allowed to see Germaine and, of course, Aunt Blanche continued to proclaim her disappointment at Germaine for not being quite the fiend that she had expected. Some days later, the entire family bade goodbye to Leon, Ernan and the other knights who had escorted the prisoner to Valdelaine. These good soldiers had been showered with gifts of all kinds from the family, especially foodstuffs like bread, cakes, carved hams, autumn fruits, sweetmeats and casks of Valdelaine wine. Of course, for the duration of their visit, clothes had been washed and mended, belts, buckles and armour had been repaired and polished; even some livestock, two horses and some cattle, had been donated. As the cavalcade set off across the countryside Ioni and the other girls waved goodbye cheerfully but also with a pang of regret that the men were leaving.

The winter weeks were passing now and although Ioni was kept busy with many duties, the thought of the 'fiend' in the new tower was never far from her consciousness. Curious as she was to know what he was like, and eager as she had been to speak with him in private, there simply had not been time, this in spite of the fact that the girls had frequently appealed to her to bring him down to the banqueting hall so that everyone might meet him. However the opportunity to do so came along unexpectedly. Word had reached Valdelaine that Sir Lionel, a close aide to Count Michael was approaching with a small retinue of knights. Amid the flurry of arranging accommodation and cleaning and furnishing chambers, Ioni had time to advise Liefing that, as Sir Lionel and his men would be meeting the family in the great hall, it would be as good a time as any to introduce the prisoner to the family and to the visitors. There would be a banquet of sorts afterwards, there would be plenty of armed men present and Germaine could be presented and allowed to mingle, unarmed of course, but free of his shackles. The request met with Liefing's approval though he would take the precaution of posting the men-at-arms close by, should there be any trouble. Ioni smiled at Liefing but was thinking maybe she might get a moment to talk to the 'fiend' herself.

When Sir Lionel and his little entourage arrived and were introduced to the family, Ioni was called aside as all the others were trooping in together to be shown to their chambers and to prepare for the evening meal. Sir Lionel was young, handsome but not of great stature. A courtier more than a cavalier, Ioni thought, as she looked into his eyes enquiringly.

"You wished to speak with me, Sir Lionel," she said politely.

"Yes, Lady Valdelaine," he said. "I wish to acquaint you with the reason for our visit. The count bids me to report to him on the condition and disposition of your very important prisoner. The count also wishes me to advise you on the manner of his maintenance here. But more of that later – I trust that he is well and in good condition?"

"Be assured of that, my Lord!" Ioni said. "You will see for yourself as he will be summoned to our evening banquet."

"Very good, my Lady," Lionel was twitching his thin moustache. "You see, in the early days of his captivity, there were only thoughts of punishing him, thoughts of revenge. But Count Michael wishes me to acquaint you of the fact that he is a most valuable prisoner. Valuable in many ways that even I am not aware of. There is the possibility of a very large ransom for him, of course. But equally important to us and to our cause is the fact that he has been taken out of the war. Beyond that, Count Michael wishes him securely guarded of course, but well looked after!"

Ioni breathed a sigh of relief that she had done the right thing by the prisoner.

"I think you will find he is well, my Lord," she said, "and securely guarded as well!"

"Excellent, my Lady," Lionel said. "And it may be possible for me to speak with him – tomorrow perhaps?"

"Certainly, my Lord," Ioni nodded.

"I thank you," Lionel said. "We have brought a wagonload of supplies for him, clothes, letters and money all from his own family and countrymen."

"Very good, my Lord," Ioni said.

"By the way, my Lady," Lionel was frowning a little now. "I'll not delay you a moment longer but may I ask what do you make of him, the prisoner?"

Ioni drew a breath, "Why, my Lord, I have formed no opinion of him whatever. You understand, my duties here have left me no time to make his acquaintance, and given the extraordinary tales which preceded his arrival here, I thought it wise simply to house him and leave him. So pardon me, my Lord, but I have no opinion of him, good or bad!"

"Very well, then," said Lionel and with a bow, "Pray excuse me while I change out of this armour into something more becoming." Ioni smiled graciously, and bowed watching him pace down the hall to be attended to his lodgings. Ioni whipped round to the first maid she could find telling her to seek out Liefing, and insist that

Germaine would be wearing the finest apparel possible when he was being removed from his chamber for his entrance at the banquet. She didn't wish to present a shabby prisoner to Count Michael's elegant courtier.

At the evening meal there was complete silence as the family sat down to eat. All eyes were on Germaine as he took his place at the table. The children at the lower end were straining necks to get a glimpse of him as he sat with the older family members. At first, there was uneasy silence while everyone was seated. Ioni was about to lean across and say "Eat well, my Lord," and Lord Raymond was about to say "Welcome to our table, my Lord," but unfortunately it was Blanche who got in first.

"Pray tell me, young man," she said, in her shrill voice, "why is it that your Duke of Anflair insists on making continued war on us, when we have done him no wrong, no wrong whatever."

Ioni could have kicked Blanche under the table but it would be unladylike! Germaine looked across at Blanche, and was about to say something when Lord Raymond intervened,

"I'm sure, my dear," he said in an authoritative voice, "that young Lord Germaine, who after all is our guest at table tonight, would rather not talk of war and politics this evening."

"But I was only asking," Blanche sniffed and began to munch her oatcakes.

Germaine spoke, "In truth, my Lady, I know little of the reasons for this war. I'm afraid I was just a soldier and never thought much about the reasons for it."

"Oh! I see!" said Blanche.

"And furthermore, my Lady," he said calmly, "I look forward to the day when we can all go home, who have partaken in this war, and live in peace together again."

Ioni was now enjoying the way Germaine was taking the heat out of Blanche's questions.

"But you yourself, my Lord," Blanche said, not easily put off, "have made ferocious war on our troops, proving to be our king's most serious adversary!"

Again Ioni wanted to reach Blanche's foot with her own but it took all her control to refrain from doing so.

"Sadly, that is true, my Lady," Germaine said again with calm. "I have made ferocious war on your people. But as a soldier I had no choice, it was my duty." Then Germaine's eyes looked about at all the company present. "As I said, sadly it is true and it saddens me even more when I realise that I made war also on all the fine knights and beautiful ladies here present tonight. Your good self above all!"

There was a murmur of approval, and Ioni permitted herself a smile. Germaine went on,

"If I had known what beautiful ladies were here at Valdelaine, I should, of course, have completely refused ever to make war, especially on such beauty! I would have remained at home playing chess!"

There was an 'ooing' sound from the girls, and a hearty chuckle from the men folk which caused the conversation to divert into the usual evening subjects. Ioni was smiling with inner relief that Germaine's first introduction to the evening meal had gone well. Blanche was taking it all in good part too. He certainly has the gift of charm, thought Ioni to herself. Further down the table Eleanor and the girls were busy discussing his good looks, especially when he smiled. That was true, the young man looked rather plain until his face broadened in a smile and when his eyes sparkled with joy.

"I think he is very handsome," said Anna loudly during a momentary silence. Everyone heard her say it and there was a burst of laughter. Germaine's neck craned forward as he looked down the table at Anna.

"Why thank you, Lady Anna," he said, his eyes and mouth smiling and everyone laughed again and cheered.

Ioni was gazing across the table at him; charm he has, in some degree at least.

"Here at Valdelaine, we have much interest in this war. My two brothers are in the field with Count Michael," she said.

"I am aware of this, my Lady," he said. "I have met your brother Jean and have made his acquaintance at Fontrue. We spent much time in each other's company."

"Imagine! You know Jean! I wonder, my Lord Raymond and Lady Blanche," she said looking around her, "if it might be possible to invite Lord Anlac to sup with us again sometime."

Raymond looked from Ioni to Germaine, and his voice boomed, "Why of course, Ioni, why not invite him to supper every evening with us." Everyone agreed, even Blanche was enthusiastic!

As they made their way from the table, their eyes, Ioni's and Germaine's, met for an instant. I am so pleased that you can get on well with my family, Ioni thought. If I must be his master and controller, it is good that the others can befriend him. And master him I will, she thought; to the others he can be a friend, to me he will always be my prisoner, and my vigilance in his regard will never falter. Of that I am sure. They were still looking at each other. What I said was true, Germaine thought, since coming here I have regretted making war on such beauty, regret and a little shame, especially when those large piercing eyes seem to look through me as they do right now.

"Lady?" he said.

"You are welcome to join the others by the fire, if you wish," she said.

"Thank you," he said, "but may I not be intruding on your family?"

"Intruding, my Lord?" Ioni said, eyes widening a little. "No. You are most welcome."

Germaine gave a little bow. "Thank you," he said. "I will join the family by the fire."

Germaine proceeded to walk past her out to the antechamber at the end of the hall. Ioni called after him, "Good night, my Lord!"

Germaine stopped and swung about to look at her.

"Good night?" he said questioningly. "You will not be joining us in there?"

Ioni pressed her lips in a simper, not a smile.

"Why no, my Lord," she said. "I have things to attend to. Good night!" and there was a swirl and swish of dress material as she turned on her heel and strode away from him.

"Good night, Lady," he said with a little bow.

*   *   *

Germaine found himself summoned to Lady Valdelaine's presence; this interview took place in her father's study where she stood waiting behind the polished table. For a moment he took in his surroundings: a compact room with an oriental carpet on the floor; on the wall tapestries and shelves of books and scrolled parchments;

on the table before him more parchments, quills and a container of ink, plus two lighted candles. In a friendly voice he said,

"So this is where you rule your castle and estates, my Lady."

She did not smile and her wide eyes transfixed him with a cold stare.

"I have not asked you here to admire the décor of my father's study, my Lord. You may sit, if it is your wish."

Germaine sat in the chair before the table. Ioni did not sit down but paced up and down the small chamber. Then she stood behind her own chair, leaning her arms on the back of its decorated oak. She looked at him seriously.

"I have asked you here to inform you of a number of things, my Lord. Firstly it would seem that, so far, there has been no communication from your countrymen in the matter of a ransom for you, at least none that I am aware of. That is the first issue, my Lord. The second is this – it seems that my countrymen are disposed to keeping you here, indefinitely, and could refuse any ransom offer that might be made for your release."

Ioni paused to allow her words to sink in while Germaine sat there impassively gazing at the table.

"I see," he said eventually. "And have you any knowledge as to why – why no ransom offers have been made? And then, why Esmor wishes to keep me regardless of the ransom? As you can imagine, my Lady, this news comes as a surprise to me, and a disappointment also as I had always assumed my countrymen would make every haste to secure my release. I had thought, a few months and I would be back in Bergmond again!"

"I regret your disappointment, my Lord," Ioni said, dispassionately observing his reaction to this news. "You must know also that I would not be, shall we say, consulted on these matters, from either side of this war. I am merely your gaoler and as such, not entrusted with the truth behind your situation. But I can tell you my opinion – which is that my countrymen of Esmor are reluctant to release you back to Bergmond – only to have you back in the saddle again and savaging our borders as you did so well before! It is reason enough to keep you here, don't you think?

He looked up at her and said,

"I daresay it is – reason enough, my Lady."

Ioni moved from behind her chair and stood at the table looking over him.

"The burden of what I have been saying is that you may be confined here for, shall we say, a long, long time. Unless of course they transferred you to another castle elsewhere in Esmor, in which case I would be relieved of the burden of keeping watch over you!"

He looked up at her for a while and said,

"I regret I bring myself a burden to your house, my Lady. I shall try in all possible ways, not to be a burden of – of any kind."

She gave him, not a smile, but a simper.

"Well that remains to be seen, my Lord, or should I say, your Grace!"

At this, Germaine looked up at her and said,

"'My Lord', 'Your Grace'. I'm your prisoner, Lady Ioni, you may call me Germaine!"

Another simper and Ioni said,

"To call you by your Christian name, my Lord, would betoken a degree of familiarity, even friendship between us, which I'm afraid there is not, my Lord."

Germaine stood up and looked at her, in a brief moment he took her in, once more the face, eyes, gestures, her mind and traits of character, her authority and sense of power, her charm; all of these shot through with the vital, elemental erotic alchemy of her womanhood. The adorable, irresistible attraction of her, pulling all of his being towards her – and all at the same time the forbidden in her – a cold crystal chasm between them, he dared not ever cross. God in Heaven, what a creature. He had not known women, so this was new, all of it was new and he was mystified by it and challenged in a way that nothing had challenged him before. A woman, powerful, beautiful and erotic!

"Is there anything else, my Lady?" he almost stammered. This time she gave him a little smile.

"No, my Lord, you have my permission to be gone!"

With that he let himself out, grateful for the cool air of the passageway.

As usual, when dinner was over Ioni made her way up the stone steps that led from the upper hall, across the covered passage that took her to the turret on the south rampart. She turned left under the arch of the turret and suddenly she stopped in her tracks. He was there, standing on the rampart, looking pensively out on the scene below.

"You are here!" she exclaimed.

Not knowing she was standing there, he almost jumped with surprise and turned towards her.

"Yes!" he also exclaimed and then was momentarily lost for words. She stared at him wide eyed but not amused.

"How did you get here?" she said, coolly.

"Why…" he struggled to remember so surprised was he by her presence there.

"Well, when I left the hall after dinner the door-way to the stairs was open – I made my way up the stairs and across the passageway and then out here. I just – followed my nose, I'm afraid."

She stared at him for some moments.

"I see… followed your nose," was all she said, her eyes fixed on him with a coolness that he suddenly found a little disconcerting. She moved toward him on the parapet and wafted silently past him like some daylight ghost. A few yards further and she turned, placed her hands on the crenellations, gazed outward to the southern horizon and sighed. He was watching her intently, conscious inwardly now that he may have done wrong by coming up here without having told anyone. Still looking outward, she said,

"And you did not think to mention it to anyone?

"I'm afraid not, my Lady." His mind was groping for words, excuses or reasons, but no words would come. She remained there, silent. Firstly unnerved and annoyed with himself, no verbal expression came to him. What was it, he wondered. Why was it that in the presence of this lady he would become tongue tied, without fail? His mind was spinning with the same question. How was it that he could find no words when confronted with this, this 'girl empress', now standing but a few yards away. The words 'girl empress' and 'empress girl' spun round quite merrily inside his head, but words like these were not those that could be spoken, in a circumstance like this. Eventually he did struggle to say. "I regret," he said with a sigh. "I regret not saying to anyone – I just…" and his voice trailed away.

She never moved nor turned her head from the cool contemplation of the scene – the river, the village, the woods and the long wide horizon of the Golden Plain. Though she did not smile, inwardly she was pleased to have him at somewhat of a disadvantage, and, also, to have him here on the south rampart, which was her chosen place at this time of day.

"I come up her often," she said, "at this time of day. I love it here, it is quiet and I can enjoy the peace and the sunshine here!"

"Oh!" he said. "I regret having intruded on you, then!"

She finally turned her head towards him and said,

"It is no matter. Are you well, my Lord? You look well and strong – much better than you did the day you first came to us."

"I am well, my Lady, and I feel so much stronger again."

There was another long silence as she gazed outward once more. Presently she said,

"Those wounds you bore upon your face and body that day you were brought here – they were not wounds of battle, my Lord, were they?"

"No, my Lady," was all he said adding no more.

"Tell me, how did they happen, then?"

"On the journey here from Fontrue some of the soldiery became drunk one night and for sport took me out of the cage and lay into me with sticks and clubs!"

"How awful for you," she interrupted looking at him now with a certain compassion.

"Well, in a way, I had expected some maltreatment at some stage of my capture, but until then I had been treated very well, so I felt lucky to have been unscathed so far. And ever since, of course, I have been lucky too. Though I daresay I did not know what to expect once I arrived here. I certainly never expected to be treated so well as you have treated me – I am grateful."

She gave him a half smile.

"I am glad you look so well," was all she said before she approached him and stood but a foot or two away, looking upwards at his strong frame and coolly appraising him.

"Sometimes I wonder who you are, my Lord Anlac," she said, her eyes serious and now fixed upon his. "I wonder who you really are!"

He paused, and sighed deeply and then said,

"I'm not sure who I am, not sure at all. Here in the company of normal people I am finding something of who I am. But before Valdelaine, before the war, I was simply the commander of the Young Ravens of the league. It was all and everything I was reared to be – and I was content with that."

"Were you not lonely, simply being a commander and that, at a very young age for such an office!"

"I had wonderful friends and companions among the Young Ravens. They were my – family as it were. I had no need of human companionship in those days. Of course, cut off from them, as I was after Elvendene, yes I began to feel – alone. In Fontrue, your brother, Lord Jean and I were very much in one another's company. His conversations enthralled me. And he was so at ease, so interested in so many things, so many dreams yet to achieve, so interested in life. By contrast, there was I, a kind of replica of my league masters – a replication, mind you – and nothing else. Not knowing then that there was so much to life that I had never known. My league masters ensured that I would become a kind of fighting machine – and nothing else. I became all they wanted, and for myself, I wanted for nothing!"

Ioni looked up at him steadily.

"A strange upbringing for a young man – my, a fighting machine and nothing else, my Lord. I hear from my cousin Eleanor that you are quite enjoying the family life here."

"Yes, my Lady," Germaine smiled at her. "It is truly wonderful."

"I am glad," she said matter-of-factly. "It is good that you find some diversion to ease the tedium of your captivity. Now, pray excuse me, I must go. I thank you for our little conversation. It was, shall we say, a little enlightening. Though, in truth I doubt if I shall ever know you as you really are, my Lord. Good day!"

He bowed as she swept past him, hastened to the turret. Before she turned from view she said, looking back at him,

"Pray do not become too fond of the view from here, my Lord, for it is mine! Good day again!"

Again he bowed and she was gone. He closed his eyes for a moment, almost in a kind of prayer he said to himself,

"God! Such a woman. I certainly do not wish to get on the wrong side of her. My place here is precarious enough without her forming a bad opinion of me!"

*   *   *

The spring days were lengthening now and the first buds were coming out on the trees with the warmer air. Ioni took advantage of the brighter evenings to take her own horse Legend out through the fields for a good canter. Usually, she had Eleanor and Clara for company, but when they were not inclined, she rode out alone, walking the horse along the lane and on through some woodlands, then cutting out of the woods to the fallow land to enjoy a hearty gallop which brought her back under the walls of Valdelaine again. After the stable boys took Legend she went straight to her chamber where the maids had left the water pitcher and bowl. She loved the feel of the cool water on her skin after the flush and heat of the ride. After some quiet time to herself, she was ready for anything the evening might bring. And this particular evening brought her face to face at the bottom of the stairs with – Germaine!

"My Lord!" she gasped as she stood on the second last step. Her cheeks were quite red and her eyes seemed to glisten as she tried to catch her breath. She was annoyed to see him there alone, seemingly unguarded, and supper not yet called. She glared at him and looked him up and down.

"I was released from my chamber a little early," he said, with a near smile at the sudden meeting. "I thought I would wait here until I'm called for evening meal."

"I see," Ioni said, still panting and stepping down the last two steps, shaking her head and pinning her hair in place. "Is there no one else around?"

Germaine pointed a hand down the passage.

"My guard is at the end of the passage," he added. "I'll not get far with him at close hand!" he meant to joke.

Ioni's face changed from half-smile to frown as she pushed back her hair again, and looked at him with seriousness. They were now both standing a few feet apart on the landing, the diffused light coming through the slit window upon both of them. Eventually she spoke.

"I trust you will never get far while you are our prisoner here." she said solemnly. "And when you do go far, I hope it will be peacefully and in your ransom."

"Yes, my Lady!" said Germaine deferentially, taken aback that the lady was not in a mood for jesting. She folded her arms across her breast and leaned back against the wall and looked at him in the eye.

"As far as I am concerned," she said, "for all our sakes, and for your sake too, the sooner the better, don't you think, my Lord?"

Germaine nodded his head and said,

"Of course, my Lady!" He bowed, and stretched out his hand in the direction of the passage to mean that he would escort her further. But she remained against the wall unmoved.

"Tarry, Lord!" she said coolly, and placed her hands behind her back. "I have some more to say to you on the matter of any escape from here – if you ever get so tempted."

He was now looking at her seriously.

"I'm sure, my Lady, I have no intention of..." he said quietly but she interrupted,

"Have a great care. Have a great care that you do not attempt to escape from here. Valdelaine is well guarded."

"That is true, my..." he attempted to speak.

"Pray listen to what I have to say, Lord Anlac! And interrupt me no more!" she said insistently, as she walked across the landing past him placing her hand on the slit window and attempting to peer out.

"You would be hunted down, you know," she said. "There are many between here and the Borderlands who would hunt you to death, for the sport of it, if nothing else." Ioni craned her neck forward into the slit frame as if trying to peer at some point on the horizon. Germaine stood still and silent, gazing at her, the light framing her head.

"There are bandits on the Fens of Aren, who would be more than happy to rob you of anything you might have, and then kill you in a trice! And then where would we be," she turned from the window to stare at him, her eyes wide and fierce. "My Lord?" she added.

Germaine was not sure what to say but his head was moving from side to side. Before he could form any words she was speaking again.

"Do you have any idea what would happen to me, for instance, if you were to get away clear from this region?" The great eyes were still wide and blazing and waiting for an answer. He was about to remonstrate with her, and assure her he would never attempt an escape, when he thought better of it, and said simply, "No, my Lady!" Her face lost its blaze as she placed her hands behind her stepping to where he stood. She raised a finger towards him.

"If you were to escape, and not be captured, why then I would be, shall we say, severely punished. Yes, punished, my Lord. My father, loving and just as he is in all things, would have no hesitation in having me tied to the post in the courtyard below – and having the very skin whipped off my back!"

Germaine was standing there, eyes wide and mouth agape, trying to avoid her gaze.

"No hesitation whatsoever in giving me the whipping of my life!" She said, her lips and tongue rasping out the words as she spoke. She paused to let her words sink in. Now she brought a bitter smile to her lips.

"And, my punishment would not end there," she said, and continued with a bitter laugh. "The whipping would be the painless part. That, I would endure as though it were nothing, for my crime in losing you. No, a far worse fate would await me, I'm afraid. I would be taken from this place, my home, never to see it again, to be placed in some nunnery as far away as possible from here. I would then have the rest of my life, the rest of my life, do you hear, to grieve for my foolishness." She paused, the only sound on the landing was their breathing.

"You may attempt the Fens of Aren, and be killed there." she rasped. "But you take my life too, in a way, shut up from the world forever, and far from here, to be forgotten, unnamed and unspoken of for all my days!"

They were now gazing at each other, Germaine daren't even shuffle his feet, and Ioni was standing before him as if she were ready to pounce on him, or upon whatever words he might chance to utter.

"Escape, Anlac! And you murder me!" she whispered her eyes widening at the word murder. Outside the evening light was fading from the spring day, somewhere down the hall the sound of voices and preparations for supper.

"Your escape," she went on, her finger tapping at his broad chest, "my death. Believe me, Lord, I have, shall we say, much cause to see that you can never escape from here. I stand within your danger, Lord Anlac, every bit as much as you stand within mine. Remember that! But go ahead, and escape and die on the Fens for all I care, but remember, yours will be an easy death compared with mine! I have reason to see you always well secured within this place!"

Then Ioni picked up her skirts with an angry swish, and stormed down the passageway to the great hall. Germaine stood, rooted to the floor, as it were, for quite some time. He felt like a bold schoolboy who had a

tongue lashing from an older girl! After some time standing there, he could only shrug his shoulders, shake his
head and trudge a little warily towards the hall.

As time passed, of course, Ioni's sense of the presence of Germaine had grown and grown. She had been
thinking about him for some time now. During some
quiet moment in the day she would muse in her heart
about him, and wonder above all what was he really like,
what manner of person lay within him. She was pleased
that the freedom he enjoyed about the castle and its envi-
rons, had all worked well, at least so far. But her curiosity
about him left her with an even greater longing to know
him. But it was proving tantalisingly difficult to know
Germaine of Anlac. She sometimes saw to it that they
would meet together at some time in the day, as if by accident. On those occasions he was most deferential to her
and polite, but maddeningly so, as she was never any
wiser about him afterwards. As well as this, he seemed to
be avoiding her at times. Did he not like her presence,
she asked herself, or is he in some kind of awe of me, a
mistress of the house? Some days past, he was coming
from the fields and walking in her direction, but when he
saw her he simply turned to walk another way. And then
there was yesterday, when he was about to enter the bailey area, having been on one of his walks. The girls had
just emerged from the castle and stopped in a bunch on
the steps to greet him.

"Good day, my Lord," they had all piped up, some
of them giggling. "Good day, Ladies," he had answered
cheerfully. "But please, you may call me Germaine!"
And a chorus of girlish voices answered "Germaine!"
Then little Anna stepped forward from the girlish cluster,
and cheered happily "Germaine! And you may call me
Anna! That's my name!" Anna always had a flower

somewhere on her person and so presented Germaine with a pair of daisies. "For you!" she laughed. Everybody was laughing, even Germaine, who knelt down, took the proffered daisies, and said to Anna, "I shall keep these treasures forever, Anna!" Everybody cheered and laughed. Ioni had observed the entire little drama from inside the main doors of the castle where she was tying up her hair. The girls then asked Germaine if he would walk a little with them, and Ioni, as she descended the steps to join them, heard him agree to accompany them. But as Ioni joined the group Germaine had made profuse apologies, promising to walk with them another day and ran up the steps disappearing into the interior of the castle. Ioni had been a little bemused at Germaine's sudden change of mind but at the time was only looking forward to a bracing little walk in the spring air for herself. Later though, when she had thought about it, the incident irked her a little especially when she remembered Eleanor murmuring in her ear on their return from the walk.

"He seems to be afraid of you!"

"Who does, Eleanor?" Ioni said through gritted and slightly irritated teeth.

"Why, Lord Anlac, of course! He wouldn't walk with us when you arrived!" said Eleanor, looking sideways at Ioni, and emphasising the word 'you'.

"Why, bother Lord Anlac!" Ioni said, teeth still gritted, and looking nonchalantly past Eleanor back at the trees. "He may do as he pleases! You go and walk with him tomorrow, if you like, and entertain yourself with him. I'm sure he'll be charmed with your company. Come. I've more things to busy me now, but we'll all meet up again at supper!"

"Yes," said Eleanor slyly smiling, "and you can talk with him then!"

"Eleanor!" Ioni's wide eyes were rolling to heaven. "Don't bother me!" The other girls had gone clambering up to the solar, and Ioni was pacing away to the hall when Eleanor called after her.

"Are you in love with him?"

Ioni stopped in her tracks, eyes wide as she gasped. She turned about to face her cousin, her eyes flashing beneath her great dark eyelashes, and she waited until Eleanor had come abreast with her. She forced a mirthless laugh, and said,

"Eleanor, you are my dearest cousin, but you are capable sometimes of the wildest imaginings!"

"It was only a thought!" Eleanor murmured with a pout, and a little question still in the look she gave Ioni, who merely gasped, shrugged and said,

"Are you in love with him, then?"

Eleanor sniffed and lifted her eyes with a glance at Ioni. "Not exactly," she said looking away again, "but he is not exactly beyond the bounds of fancy!"

Ioni tossed her head, and gave her cousin a long, expressionless stare.

"You cannot even think of it, you know," she said with a little shake of her head. "But if you do entertain amorous notions about him, pray remember your position, and his, in this house. There are plenty of fine Esmorin knights to warm your heart and to think about!"

Eleanor then gave a long sigh and walked away. "Still, it's nice to dream. Isn't that so, Ioni?"

"Dream away, then," Ioni spoke to her cousin's back, "I'll live in the real world for both of us!"

"Don't be silly, Ioni," Eleanor said. "I was only teasing – why, let me assure you that when I first see the man I wish to marry – I shall simply make him marry me!"

"Oh Eleanor!" said Ioni laughing.

But suddenly, Ioni was running down the hall and up the stairs after her cousin; something had flashed across her mind and surely, it was time to talk with Eleanor alone.

"What do I make of him?" exclaimed Eleanor. "What do I make of whom, Ioni! Of whom do you speak?"

"Why, I speak of Germaine, of course!" Ioni answered. She had sought out the company of Eleanor with some deliberation, and with some burning question in her mind.

"Germaine, of course!" repeated Eleanor with some surprise. "Well – what can I tell you that I know? Let's see. I think he is a fine young gentleman – in spite of the fact that we knew him first as the fiend from Bergmond. No, he is very polite. He likes company – especially female company. Though it is easy to tell he has not, until now, been accustomed to women – I doubt he's ever known the company of women."

A shrewd observation, thought Ioni, from the ever effusive but insightful Eleanor; she was already glad she had sought her cousin's opinion of him. Was there any more, she thought.

"Is there anything else about him," Ioni said.

"Well, let us see," murmured Eleanor. "Well it is just an impression that I have, how true I am not sure. But at times he seems a little lost, as though his mind were elsewhere. Having said that, it may only be natural for a young man, a prisoner in a strange place, to be somewhat confused whilst his mind is elsewhere, on battlefields and such like. But, certainly he is somewhat lost!"

"I see," said Ioni quietly.

"You have not been aware of all this?" Eleanor questioned.

"No. I rarely get to speak to him. But I wish I knew what he was really like, what he thinks about!"

Eleanor's eyes widened a little.

"But why? Ioni. You are fond of him then!"

Ioni smiled gently at her cousin.

"Fondness is not the source of my curiosity, Eleanor. No. You see I have, shall we say, control over him here in Valdelaine, but, if I knew him better I feel I would have even better control over him."

"Control. But why? You are not still afraid of him attempting to escape, are you?

"No. I am a little more at ease on that point – for the moment. I just want to know him so that his life here is better, that life here does not render him tedious, especially to himself!"

Eleanor chuckled a little.

"I assure you, Ioni, his life here is not tedious. He seems to love all the company he has here. I swear it. He even gets on well with Mama. Mama, mind! He seems to be fascinated with – with the life of the family, Ioni, this family – as if it were his own family. He has told me this more than once. From Mama down to Cousin Anna – he is simply fascinated by everyone!"

"Is he – fascinated by me?" Ioni exclaimed.

"Well no, Ioni. With you it is different. He, well, he is possibly in awe of you –"

"I see – he is in awe of my position here, not in awe of me!"

"No, Ioni. He is in awe of you – and of how you manage everything here. You see he is not accustomed to woman, and to taking his orders from a woman. It is strange for him that his captain and commander is not a man – but a young woman. I think he finds that part of it difficult!"

"I see," Ioni said quietly. "Anything else you can think of!"

"Nothing at present, Cousin."

"I'm grateful to you, Eleanor."

"You are welcome, but then what are cousins for!"

"It is more than that, Eleanor. I'm grateful to you for everything. You said a long time ago that you would be a help to me here. I am grateful that you have been true to that promise!"

Eleanor placed her hand on Ioni's arm.

"Again you are welcome. I know that we may never be close friends, and that you have Cousin Fleur as your confidante. But I do respect you and I am fond of you in my own way!"

"Thank you, Eleanor. I am – not your closest friend, but I do respect you more and more as time goes by and, well, I was afraid we would be hostile towards each other. With your beauty and your charm, well, shall we say, I feared I might be horribly jealous of you – but no! Oh, I have my moments of – jealousy – but they quickly pass."

Eleanor looked, head sideward, and smiling at Ioni.

"I don't understand it, Ioni, you have nought to be jealous of in me. For instance, I could let myself be jealous of how capable you are, how strong, and how wisely you govern here – oh I have my moments too! But my opinion is that no two women should have been better friends than you and I. But it didn't happen, and I accept that. Maybe someday!"

Ioni smiled, gratified and a little mystified by her cousin's words.

"Again, thank you, Eleanor. Maybe someday! But thank you for taking me in your stride. It means a lot!"

Eleanor shook her head and her treasure of golden curls and said,

"Again, Cousin. You are welcome!" And Ioni smiled happily at her.

"Is there anything I can do for you, dear Eleanor?"

"You can continue giving me the benefit of any doubt that might lurk in your mind regarding me!"

Ioni chuckled.

"I shall do that, dear Cousin!"

The little interview was over and Eleanor rose to make her departure when Ioni said to her,

"Before you go, Eleanor. Are you fond of him?"

Eleanor drew herself up to her full height, and addressed Ioni with a manner of mock disdain.

"As you should well know, Lady Valdelaine, I am fond of anything that is capable of wearing chain mail!"

Ioni laughed and Eleanor departed with a flourish.

Ioni did find him one evening on the battlement. She knew he went there frequently to walk up and down, to pause and gaze out at the countryside. She had donned her cloak and wore her veil, the spring evenings were cool. He stood there with his hands on the wall gazing into the distance. He looked at her sideways and then looked at her again. He was always impressed with how well she looked, and how beautiful. She was smiling gently.

"May I talk with you, my Lord!" Ioni said, her smile quite sweet.

"Of course, my Lady," he said turning to face her. They were now standing face to face, her eyes and lips smiling up at him. There was silence as he looked a little askance at her. But she turned her glance away over the battlement.

"What was it you wished to talk to me about, my Lady," he asked, watching her gaze. She turned to him.

"Oh!" she said, "I just wanted to talk, you know, just converse with you."

"Oh!" he said leaning against the parapet. "Was there any particular thing you wished to converse about?"

"No! No particular subject," she said, "I just wanted to talk with someone – with you!"

Germaine was silent for some moments, then turned to rest his back against the stonework and looked sideways at her.

"But, may I ask, why do you wish to talk to me?" he said quietly.

She turned enthusiastically towards him and said, "Oh no big reason, I think I wanted to talk with you and maybe get to know you a little better, my Lord."

He frowned and his head shook a little.

"But, my Lady, why do you wish to know me," he said, "I am just Germaine of Anlac, formerly knight and now – well, now prisoner of this realm."

Ioni felt some of her warmth ebb a little, maybe getting to know Germaine was not going to be easy.

"Well, yes my Lord, of course," she said holding her veil in the breeze that had blown up the great wall and over the parapet. "But I think what I meant was that I would like – well just to get to know you, the person you are."

A faint frown again on Germaine's brow as he said,

"But surely you already know me – as a person!"

Her good form was ebbing a bit more now but Ioni stood before him again as he stood back to the wall.

"Well!" her eyes were blinking and her face was bobbing a little from side to side, "I suppose I was curious about you and wanted to know you better, that's all." And she added with a smile, "We women are very curious – about everyone, I suppose!"

He looked at her gently but with a wry smile.

"Well, I don't think there's much to know in me at all, my Lady," he said with a grimace, "and we both of us know that my presence here is not a game!"

She looked at him uncomprehending,

"A game, my Lord? I don't understand," she said.

He took his time trying to think of his next words.

"Forgive me," he said folding his arms, "but I am your prisoner here and you are my lady and mistress and – how can I say it, my coming and going are all in your hands, as it were."

She was looking at the cords on his jerkin, her mouth slightly open, still not understanding.

"Yes, of course. You are a prisoner here," she said, "but, my Lord, surely this does not prevent us from knowing each other – at least, I thought it would help, if we did know each other."

He was looking down at her now and struggling to find words that might explain his mind to her. He didn't wish to deliberately offend but what else could he say but the truth.

"But isn't it enough for you," he said, "that you have mastery of me and of all I do. How will it help either of us, as we are, just to get to know me. I don't understand. Don't you have enough of me as things stand?"

She shot a little look of disappointment into his eyes and then continued staring at his jerkin cord, taken aback, certainly, and at a loss for comprehension.

"I just thought..." she stammered.

"My lady," he interrupted. "You command – you command, and I obey. That is all there is to know – my Lady."

"Oh!" she said looking at him from one shoulder to another and then up into his eyes. "I see. I see, my Lord." She looked away for a moment before she began to walk slowly to the parapet steps and door, some bitter sour feeling inside. She paused at the steps, gathered her cloak about her, turned around to look back at him and smiled bravely in the wind.

"I – I think I just longed to get to know you, my Lord," she said sadly, "I also thought it might help me, that it might help me to be, well, shall we say, a better governor to you. But maybe you are right, given our circumstances. Good night, my good Lord!" And she hopped lightly down the steps and was gone.

Oh... God! Thought Germaine, I must have offended her. But women don't understand things, he mused. She was really so likeable and so beautiful, especially that last moment when she stood above the parapet steps and turned to him, her dress blowing in the breeze, that face of hers so beautifully framed by the cowl of her cloak. But there it was, the moment was gone and a vague feeling of unease came over him, a feeling that was very familiar to him in certain situations; indeed there were so many things in life, simple things, perhaps, for which he could not find words. They were never his stock-in-trade were they, he thought, words? Just when the knowledge or emotion emerged inside, the mind was flailing about for words, for the right words but they would never come; more often than not, the words that came to hand were insufficient or wrong. I'm a dumb ox, perhaps, and at times I do envy the men who can make talk. In the saddle, with sword or lance in hand, I seem to fly, but once my feet touch ground again, the awkwardness begins again.

She sat up in the bed with the drapes of the canopy drawn, feeling a little weepy and a little angry. Great knight indeed, great Lord of many battles; great churl more likely.

"Isn't it enough for you that you have mastery over me." Yes Anlac, it is enough, and for now I have enough of you, she fumed to herself.

Germaine was seated in the antechamber outside the great hall waiting for the evening meal. A few feet away his guard stood by a window, whistling some tune to himself. There was a little commotion of female voices at the far end of the passageway. The commotion in question was the little Lady Anna, Lord Robert's daughter, and one of the maids, both of whom were scolding each other for some unknown reason. When they approached the antechamber and saw Germaine they both suddenly hushed into silence. However Anna gave Germaine one of her most charming smiles and said with a little curtsey,

"I bid you good evening, Lord Germaine!"

"A good evening to you, Lady Anna!" responded Germaine, a little amused at Anna's efforts to be grown up in her salutations

"What are you doing here?" Anna blurted out, a childish curiosity getting the better of adult mannerisms. Anna was now standing directly before him, though her maid was hissing at her to come away, and leave the knight alone.

"I've been escorted from my chamber a little early," Germaine explained, "and I am awaiting the evening meal."

"Oh!" said Anna, noticing the guard standing near the window.

"As you can see, Lady Anna," Germaine went on, "the guard must stay with me until everyone else comes to the hall."

"Hmm," murmured Anna, now standing next to his knee. The maid remonstrated with Anna once more to come away and leave Germaine in peace, but Germaine made a sign to her that Anna's presence was not a problem for him.

"In case you would escape!" Anna went on.

"Yes, quite so, Anna," Germaine said as she came even closer, resting her arms upon his thigh and looking up into his face.

"I don't want you to escape," Anna said up to him. "I want you to stay – with us, with me."

"Very well," Germaine said with a smile.

"Promise you'll stay with us," Anna said patting her fist against his thigh. "I don't want you to go away! I…" And she lost her train of thought but reached up her arms to his neck. Whereupon he gathered her up and perched her on his knee.

"You would like me to stay then!" he said.

"Yes, stay!" Anna said nestling her head against his great chest. "Stay!" she commanded, clutching the cloth of his tunic in her little fist.

"But Anna, you know that it's not up to me!" Germaine was about to say more, but was stopped when Anna shot her little palm up to his face and pressed it over his mouth.

He made an effort to speak but Anna giggled as she held his lips shut and lifted her face to his so that her eyes were but an inch from his.

"Promise, promise, promise!" she said. "I command you to promise!"

Again the maid wanted to intervene, but again, Germaine signalled her not to. Anna was looking solemnly into his eyes now and Germaine was trying to keep a straight face. When Anna withdrew her hand from his lips he said,

"Well," he said, "I promise you, Anna, that maybe…"

The little hand shot up to his lips again and, unable to control himself Germaine burst out "I promise" followed by hearty laughter. Anna laughed a little too and then sat solemnly looking at him again.

"I want you to stay because," she took a deep breath and searched for words, "because, because I like you and we can be friends!"

Again she was looking at him seriously and she opened her hands and with a shrug of her shoulder said,

"I have no friends. Everyone else has friends." Again, she lifted herself up to eyeball him again and pull his ears.

"But not me!" she said, comically wagging her head, and even more comically, pressing her nose against his. There was more laughter from him and she sat there amused and pleased that she had made him laugh at all.

"After all that, I think I shall stay, Anna," he said and chuckled again.

She looked at him, her face was imp all over.

"I rather thought you'd say that!" she said and she jumped off her perch on his knee to rejoin her maid. The maid took her little hand promptly to march her away, but not before Anna turned her face back to Germaine to give him as solemn and as comical a look as he had ever seen in any face. "Do not fail me now!" Anna seemed to be saying!

*   *   *

In the mid afternoon, Eleanor just remembered something. After dinner, she had left Germaine sitting on a stool by the fire – he had been left to chat to the Lady Blanche, her mother! She had seen no trace of him since and now wondered if he was still trapped there listening to the Lady, who could easily find plenty to talk on about, especially when she had a polite captive audience like Germaine. I'd best go and rescue him, she thought, and found the two of them, still by the fire wrapt in conversation. The fact was that Germaine was enjoying Blanche's endless stories of this and that. He must be a good listener, she thought, as she swept in towards them.

"Mother!" she said, "I think Lord Germaine has things to do before the day comes to an end. Let me borrow him now, and you can continue your conversations tomorrow!"

Blanche thanked Germaine, who politely took his leave of her and accompanied Eleanor out on to the passageway.

"You must be very privileged," she whispered sideways at him. "Very privilege indeed! It is not every-one my mother would have time for – she seems to like you!"

"I don't really mind," Germaine whispered back. "Stories about families fascinate me, as I never had any family myself."

"Still, you must be very different!" Eleanor could speak louder now as they had matched step for step along the corridor. "Yes, I suppose it must be all very different from anything you have known,"

Germaine stopped and turned to face Eleanor.

"Yes, different and new to me." Germaine said smiling. "I love meeting all the various people; various ages, various stages in life."

"Mmn," she murmured, with a shake of her head and a hand to her golden hair, brushing it back. "You do seem to have time for everyone – from the oldest to the youngest. I mean, you have just spent nigh on two hours chatting to Mama – or rather, listening patiently to Mama chatting about herself and probably telling you all her old stories – does it not drive you to distraction?"

Germaine took a breath and said, "No, not at all, I seem to like listening to people's stories!"

"Yes – and from Mama all the way down to my little cousin Anna! A few minutes is all I could take from that child, mind you. But you, well if you don't mind me saying so, you are almost like a second father to her now. Perhaps there is a father lost somewhere inside you!"

Germaine smiled again, "Yes, it is amazing that here, in my captivity, I find everything interesting in a family – well, in a family like this one, at any rate!"

They were now standing together looking out a window. Eleanor spoke, breaking the silence.

"Let me ask you, Germaine, how do I stand in your opinion?"

"Oh!" Germaine said chuckling, and then a little bashful. "Your company, Eleanor, is always welcome. You are charming, intelligent, you have great wit. When things are in danger of becoming dull, you bring us all back alive! You keep us all going. Whenever there is excitement, you are there right in the midst of it!"

Eleanor nodded and smiled, a smile with a little mischief in her eyes.

"Your compliments are most welcome, Germaine," she said. "However I notice that the word 'beautiful' was missing from your list of my accomplishments!"

"Oh dear!" Germaine said with a little laugh. "I thought, in your case, the word went without saying!"

She looked at him and patted his sleeve.

"For a woman, the word beautiful never goes without saying!"

He laughed, she smiled indulgently. Then they both laughed together and he took her hand in his.

"I shall remember that forever!" he said. "And, well yes of course – beautiful, Eleanor; of course, very beautiful!"

They both smiled and sighed and then there was another silence between them as they both turned to look out the window again until, at length, Eleanor spoke again.

"Tell me something, Germaine, how does it fare betwixt your good self and that other lady – my Lady Valdelaine?"

Germaine stood for a long time in silence staring out the window – now there was a question, he thought, a look of puzzlement on his face. He was still holding her hand, though now he felt he was doing it out of some far off sense of the need for support.

"I am never sure, actually," he said frowning deeply. Then he turned his eyes to meet hers. "I think that I do not know the lady at all. No, I'm sure of it, I do not know her at all, though I meet her every day, just like I meet all of you, there is what seems like a wall of glass standing between us. A wall such that, though I see her, I can never pass through to her, nor she to me. A veritable pathway of ice stands between us. I do not know her nor understand her at all."

"I see," was all that Eleanor said.

"I'm not complaining, Eleanor. Every one of this household has made my captivity here most gentle and indeed, most charming."

"But for Ioni."

"But for Lady Ioni. I just want to be friendly with her, you know, a little laughter, smiles, a little banter now and then!" His speech was quite animated now. "Just to show her that I appreciate her, that I like her, that I want to make her feel at ease with me."

"Flirtation?" Eleanor quizzed, eyes mischievous.

"Well, not quite that, Eleanor, not that for sure! I'm her captive and I want to respect that fact, and respect her too! Think of it like this, that it is like a challenge for me, a kind of giddy challenge – but a challenge I cannot win, in the circumstances. What to do, I do not know. The lady is encased in crystal!"

"And your natural charm cannot melt this crystal?"

"It seems not." He smiled at her, grateful for her understanding.

"My cousin Ioni has much to do and has many things on her mind," Eleanor said solemnly. "Not least of which is your presence here – and she fears the possibility of an attempt by you to escape from here. Please bear in mind that she has given you scope in your living here; that is her nature. As to her character, there are few that I know who are better than her. I say this, even though she and I are not close cousins, as she and Fleur are. I can tell you that her heart is warm though it seems cold to you. Yes, warm of heart, generous, strong. All of us Valdelaines seem to be strong minded, but she has some inner strength that surpasses anything we can understand. Bear it in mind, Germaine, she is a loving person."

"I see," Germaine breathed. "And I thank you, Eleanor, for telling me this. I shall leave you now to ponder what you have said." And with that they parted company.

Chapter VIII: Ribbons of Black, White

F rère Benedict was about to depart the castle after conducting some business for Lord Raymond, when he was approached by one of the maids, who announced that two very devout looking monks had reached the castle after a long journey, and had begged to stay the night. They were now having some well earned supper in a room off the kitchen area. Frère Benedict smiled, thanked the maid and set off for the kitchen area pleased at the prospect of meeting some monastic guests, and, of course, enjoying a little ecclesiastical news, gossip and chatter. Eventually, he found the two monks eating supper in the candlelit chamber.

His face broadened with a beaming smile as he entered the chamber. "Ah! My dear good men and holy!" Benedict boomed. "Welcome to Valdelaine! What a surprise!" The two cowled figures arose from their places as the frère paced forward to embrace them. *"Beati sunt qui venit in Nomine Domini!"* ("Blessed are those who come in the name of the Lord!") The two monks only grunted something unintelligible, and received his embrace rather awkwardly.

Face all abeam, Frère Benedict sat with them, hastily helping himself to some wine, and beginning his long litany of questions, comments and chatter on churchly matters. The two monks had come all the way from Bergmond. They were mendicant and begging for funds for their friary. They also wished to visit the Lord of Anlac, enquire as to his spiritual and general welfare, and to report back to their superiors on their return journey. 'Good', Benedict thought, a mission of mercy indeed.

When he left them, however, Frère Benedict paused a while. He was troubled, deeply troubled. His questions on matters ecclesiastical had been politely avoided, on the grounds that these monks led lives well separated from both civil and church affairs. Goodness me, he thought, as he paced away down the corridor, not one, but two monks, coming all that distance, and not so much as a scrap of gossip between them. What was Mother Church coming to at all! Something was wrong here. He could not quite pin it down; their awkwardness in the holy embrace, commonly used by all churchmen; their most unusual (for monks, that is) ignorance of church matters; their appalling lack of good church news was all quite mysterious indeed. If they were monks, then there was no problem, however out of touch they were. If they were not monks then – Oh my God! He thought, could they have come all the way from Bergmond to see Germaine, and spring him to freedom!

"Strange, I know, my Lady!" he said to Ioni when he had told her. "I may be wrong about these two, but they seem rather strange characters to me!"

"I suppose we can't refuse them," Ioni was pale and staring at him. "If they are monks then, refusing them would cause offence!"

Some time later, Germaine was escorted from his chamber to the dining hall, where she told him of his visitors but told him nothing of her suspicions. If this was to be his moment of escape, then she would pretend nothing to him, but she would have the men-at-arms waiting out of sight, beyond the doors of the great hall.

The two monks stood demurely inside the door. Germaine sat perched against the high table, arms on the table rim and legs crossed. Ioni made the introductions, and then made her way down the hall. As the two monks processed downward to meet Germaine, she slammed the door shut from the inside and disappeared unseen into the shadowy corner at the end of the hall. From here, behind a pillar of the minstrels' gallery, she would hear and observe the escape of Germaine of Anlac, only to foil it! Every door and gate that led from Valdelaine had been locked and guarded less than an hour previously.

Before anyone could take it in, suddenly there was a flash of steel in the outstretched hand of one of the monks. With lighting speed, Germaine evaded his attacker and with a ferocious kick he sent a chair crashing into him causing him to stumble forward. With equal speed, Germaine picked up another chair and brought it down with full force on the monk's back sending him sprawling forward to the floor.

Ioni screamed, "Germaine!"

With a second to spare, Germaine turned to tackle the other monk who, like the first, had drawn a dagger! Germaine grabbed the man's wrist and began pushing him backward, toppling over one of the tables until he had pinned him against one of the tapestries on the wall. The monk squirmed, struggled to break his dagger hand free of Germaine's grip, but he could not. Germaine opened his free fist and brought the lower part of his palm crashing upward against his assailant's nose, causing him to crash the back of his head against the stone wall behind the tapestry. There was a gush of blood from the man's face as he slithered helplessly to the floor. The dagger was now in Germaine's hand as he bounded over a table to the first attacker, who was vainly trying to lift himself from under the chair that had brought him down. In the melee, the men-at-arms had burst into the hall, alarmed by Ioni's screams. Germaine was dragging the monk, or whatever he was, by the cowl. He soon had the two of them dragged together where they writhed helplessly in pain. The men-at-arms held Germaine by his arms, and others began dragging the would-be assassins away. Raymond had them placed in the dungeon, one was unconscious and the other was being questioned with torture.

"Will we take the prisoner to his chamber now, my Lady?" came the question from the men-at-arms.

"No!" Ioni was still in some shock, and struggled for control of herself. "Leave us now and wait outside!" When they were gone, Ioni walked down the hall to where Germaine was standing.

"Pray be seated, my Lord," she gasped, and reached for a chair for herself. Germaine perched himself once more against the edge of the high table. He looked at her for an instant as she sat there, her eyes cast down, her face deathly pale. He noticed her hands were trembling.

At length, she looked up as though to speak but could not; in the candle light she looked about and saw the tapestried walls, the arched windows, the candles themselves. And then she saw him there at the high table dressed in his blue tunic and doublet gazing at the floor.

"Pray, will you take some wine, my Lord," she said nervously, taking a goblet from the tray that had been delivered in the aftermath of the night's horror. "Thank you, no, my Lady," he said still staring at the floor and adding, "but you partake of some, you appear as though you could do with it." Hands shaking she raised the goblet to her lips and drank deeply of the wine savouring the warmth of it as it went down into her, and gradually becoming calm with its steadying effect. She glanced at him again, and again looked away.

Finally he looked at her, half smiled and then said, "On second thoughts, I think I will have some wine." She took the goblet from its tray stood up and brought it to him. He took it and began to drink the contents.

"I feel I must ask your forgiveness," she said, her eyes wide with pleading, "for this, for what happened – I never – suspected..."

He finished the drink and looked at her and spoke, "There is nothing to forgive, Lady Ioni. I think we, neither of us, understand what has happened. You least of all. May I go on?"

"Please do," she said, her ever wide eyes now little wells of tears. "Pray be seated again then," she said. "No, not out there – close to the table where you can rest you arms." He had lifted himself from his perch and gone round the table to sit opposite her, just the candles between them. The two looked across at each other and he began to speak.

How long they remained there Ioni could not tell. Certainly it was late into the night. In the end they both climbed the staircase to his chamber where the guard saluted them. They bade each other a good night and the men-at-arms escorted Ioni to her room. Ioni had locked the door of Germaine's room and the key was in a pocket in the folds of her gown.

She remembered little enough of their conversation that night. What she did recall, however, was that, at one stage he had suddenly began to shudder and lift his hands from the table to cover his face, while he shook his head almost violently and inhaled great gasps of air.

"Do you wish to retire to your chamber, my Lord!" she said soothingly from across the table.

"No!" he said suddenly, and then more quietly, taking his hands from his head and looking at her, "No.

No. I would like to remain here, please, for some time, if that is alright."

"Shall I withdraw now, my Lord?" she said ever so gently.

"Er... I would like if you could stay," he said. "A little more, if you could."

"Very well. I'll stay as long as you wish, Lord Germaine," she said. She could see his hands were trembling a little.

"Thank you," he said, "I don't wish to be alone, for now. It is not every day that one kills a man!" Ioni looked with a frown.

"But you haven't... I mean the two are both alive..." she said.

"No. Please, my Lady," he stammered, "I've killed one of them... I know... he may not be dead now... but I know he will not live. I know that."

"I see," she murmured as the horror dawned on her, gazing across at his face in the candlelight. So many things flashed across her mind about him – what was Germaine? A knight, a hero, a demon, a fiend... but now in this light at this hour he was more like something else – he was more like a child, she thought. A child coming out of a horrid dream and needing nothing else but human company.

"I will stay with you for as long as you wish," she said again. "All night if you like. Will you take some bread and some more wine."

"Yes, thank you," he said almost cheerfully. She stood and took the tray and moved it across the table towards him. She poured the wine and cut the bread for him. He ate and drank gladly and in the light he even looked at her with a momentary smile.

"My country, not yours, is one that has fallen into the hands of evil people," he had said.

"I am now obliged to be your protector as well as your gaoler," she had said.

The two were not monks, as Lord Raymond found out, but hired and paid assassins. Who had paid them to do so, he never found out. The one that he had examined, and had tortured, gave nothing else away, and eventually Raymond had him hanged. The other never regained consciousness and died the same day. It had been in someone's interests that Germaine would die, while in custody at Valdelaine, someone on the Bergmond side of the present conflict, but who that person or persons were, remained a mystery.

The following day, everyone was somewhat on edge at the events of the previous night. Ioni, of course, was troubled, Raymond was busy to and from the dungeon, and Germaine, sitting alone in his locked chamber wished he could arm himself with some weapons, a dagger at least. Would I had my mail and weapons, he thought, but, here in Valdelaine, while I am a prisoner, perhaps that cannot be. Then he smiled and thought perhaps I will have to leave all matters of my safety in the gentle hands of the Lady of Valdelaine!

* * *

On a spring morning there was a kind of pandemonium in the kitchens, it was one of those tantrum mornings when Margreth was on the warpath as it were, screaming at the maids and scolding, in particular, the ones who seemed sluggish in their work. The unfortunate maids who had been on the receiving end of Margreth's angry tongue knew only too well that her bad moods could last for the whole day if something didn't happen to sweeten her day. On this particular day, they were lucky, as, at midmorning Clothilde arrived from the village with a big basket of herbs, a gift for Margreth.

"Oh! Mother Clothilde! You are welcome," shouted Margreth, her mood changed to sweetness at the sight of her friend.

"I came as quickly as I could," puffed Clothilde as she removed her cloak and placed her plump figure on one of the kitchen chairs.

"You brought herbs I see!" chirped Margreth. "A whole basket full!"

"Yes!" said Clothilde, her face still red. "I brought them by way of thanking you for the two pieces of material you gave me!"

Margreth remembered well, the two pieces of material in question were the monks' habits, the ones which were worn by the two strangers who had attacked the prisoner Germaine some weeks earlier. Margreth had pondered on what to do with the habits – for her, the cloth was tainted by the act of murder intended by their former wearers and she was determined they should not remain within the house. She had thought of having them burned, but the material was so good she decided to give them to Clothilde. They would make good material for the husband or son to wear. The material was warm and would wear for many a winter to come.

"Alice!" screamed Margreth as she sat down beside Clothilde. "Shake yourself up a bit and bring a goblet of wine for Mother Clothilde! And be quick about it!" Not all of the fury had left Margreth, for all the joy of meeting Clothilde!

When the wine arrived Clothilde drank quickly and deeply and then the two matrons began to converse, chatter and gossip about everything and everyone. Margreth even ordered a cup of wine for herself. A long hour of chatter passed and, when finally there was a lull in the conversation, Clothilde gazed about and even got up to the door to ensure there was no one else about. Looking back at Margreth she raised her fingers to her lips to indicate silence and with a conspiratorial wink at Margreth she sat her full weight down again.

"There was something else I came to tell you!" said Clothilde with a hush.

"What was that?" queried Margreth, mystified.

"Well!" whispered Clothilde. "As you know, I cut up the robes you gave me to make various things, winter jerkins for my husband and for young Andrew, caps and even a pair of trews. Well whatever do you think happened when I undid the hems of both robes?"

"Whatever happened indeed, Clothilde! Tell me!" gasped Margreth, completely mystified.

"Well, as I was cutting away the old hem stitches," went on Clothilde, "whatever look I gave down on the floor when I was shaking out the first hem – there on the floor in front of my eyes was a beautiful length of ribbon!"

"Ribbon! Clothilde?" exclaimed Margreth. "Ribbon? What was it doing there sewn into the hem!"

"I don't know, Margreth," said Clothilde. "But a lovely length of ribbon in two colours, black and white, with silver embroidery on the black. And when I snipped the stitches away from the other hem, out fell another ribbon of the very same colour."

"And what did you do with the ribbons?" Margreth exclaimed.

"Well first I was tempted to keep them myself," Clothilde went on. "They are fine material but then afterwards I began to be afraid they belonged to some noble person and I was afraid to keep them any longer."

"And what did you do with them!" Margreth quizzed.

"I brought them here, this morning," Clothilde said as she placed her hand in the folds at her breast. Her fingers drew out the long pieces of material, in black and white, with the silver embroidery against the black. Both women gazed at them, filled with admiration and puzzlement. Margreth picked them up, held them to the light, and then peered closely at the silvery embroidery.

"I think it depicts a hand holding a dagger!" whispered Clothilde.

"I will bring them to my mistress," whispered Margreth. "She will know what they are and what they mean."

When the two women embraced and parted Margreth placed the ribbons in a big pocket within her own dress folds and then it dawned on her. Of course! In times past she had heard tales of lowly servants of great nobility who sewed the colours of their noble masters into their own clothing. This was done if they were sent on a difficult or dangerous mission and in the event of capture, or danger of death they could show their masters' colours. This might not save them but usually it could save them from death if they persuaded their captors of a possible ransom, however small. As well as this, the captors might not be in any position to incur the wrath of the nobility involved, by killing their servants.

Margreth would meet her mistress immediately. The ribbons in her pocket might be the clue which would reveal the noble personage who had sent the assassins in the first place. Puffing and panting she began climbing the stairs that lead upwards from the kitchen area.

"Has any of you seen the Lady Ioni?" she asked of the maids in the great hall who were preparing the place for the midday meal.

"No! Mistress!" they chimed in unison as they went about their tasks.

"I've been looking for her ladyship," puffed Margreth as she bumped, literally into another maid at the top of more stairs. "Do you know where she is, girls!" The maid thought a moment and said,

"Sometimes she's in her father's study at this time!"

"Ah!" puffed Margreth and at length knocked loudly on the study door.

"Enter!" came the sound of Ioni's voice from within.

Moments later Margreth sat with Ioni staring at the ribbons as they lay strewn on top of the table in Lord Henry's study. At length Margreth spoke, "Mind you, I never told Clothilde where those two robes came from. But luckily she found these pieces of cloth, and, more luckily, she brought them back to me!" Then after another silence Margreth said, "Do you think they are important, Lady?"

"Of course, Margreth!" Ioni said. "It would take me hours to go through father's heraldry parchments to search for the owner of these colours. And even at that, if these colours are those of a new noble, we may not have them in our parchments at all. No, there is only one thing to do."

"What's that, my Lady?" said Margreth.

"Tonight after supper I shall present them to Lord Germaine, and he may know of their owners."

"If he does, then, will he know who sent these assassins?" Margreth whispered.

"I think he may, Margreth. I think he may!"

Ioni shuddered. "I'm cold and hungry. Are we
ready to eat yet, Margreth?"

"I should think everything's about ready now, my
Lady," Margreth chuckled and went.

Ioni waited a while holding the ribbons in her
hands.

Germaine jumped as he heard the guard knock
loudly on the door, and he then stood waiting as the key
was turned in the door. The guard leaned inward as he
opened the door and said, "The lady Valdelaine wishes to
see you!"

Night had fallen and Germaine was surprised to be
summoned by the mistress, or by anyone else, at this hour.

"Oh! Do you know why she wishes to see me?"
Germaine asked, pulling on his tunic, and trying to adjust
his eyes to the light of the guard's torch.

"How should I know?" the guard grunted and then
spat on the floor. "I only know that I'm to escort you to a
chamber in the old tower. So make haste!"

Germaine followed the guard along the little passage to the stairs, and then down along the spiral steps
right to the ground floor. Their way then led through a
variety of passages and antechambers, through the great
hall, down some more steps, and eventually into the lower
regions of the old tower. Uncle Robert lived up there
somewhere, Germaine remembered. Then the guard
tapped lightly on a door and as he opened it, Germaine
could see Ioni standing at a table inside in a chamber that
was lit by candles and had a fire in its small hearth. Germaine stepped in, and noticed that Ioni was smiling gently

at him. The door closed behind him. Ioni was standing before the fire with her hands together in front of her. The red dress with golden braid at the neck and on the wide sleeves seemed to glow in the firelight.

"You sent for me, my Lady," Germaine said.

"Your pardon for bringing you here at this hour, my Lord," Ioni said. "Pray bring yourself closer to the fire. It is chilly tonight. Forgive me, I should explain. I come here sometimes at night just to rest, just to be alone for a while, before retiring. After a long day, this place is my little sanctuary!"

"I see!" Germaine said moving towards the fire. "But what am I doing here at this hour, in your sanctuary, as you call it?"

Ioni did not speak but looked at him for a while. Then she took a deep breath and said,

"My Lord, today we discovered that the monkish robes of your would-be assassins – well, when the seams were opened they contained, shall we say ribbons?"

"Ribbons, Lady," said Germaine, puzzled. "What ribbons?"

"Ribbons, my Lord," Ioni went on. "Ribbons, favours, tokens that had been sewn into the assassins' clothing."

Germaine's face was blank for a moment but then, the meaning of Ioni's words dawned on him. He gasped.

"They may be colours of the sponsor of the attack," Ioni went on.

"Do you know whose the colours are?" he blurted. "Where are they, may I see them?"

"I don't know whose colours they are, my Lord," Ioni said calmly, "but if you wish to see them – why they are in that little cloth pouch on the table!"

Germaine's eyes moved to the table, and there he saw the little purple velvet pouch.

"May I open it?" he asked, as he moved toward the table.

"Please do, my Lord," said Ioni watching him as he picked up the pouch and began to pull open the drawstrings. She continued watching him, as his fingers rummaged inside, and as they began to pull one of the ribbons. His face was a study in concentration as he drew first the white end of the length of ribbon, but as the first of the black end emerged, she could see the look of horror that came over him. He held the ribbon up before his eyes. Even in the candlelight, she could see him go pale, as he clutched the ribbon in his fist.

"Good God!" he gasped, "De Laude, it is de Laude!"

Ioni move towards him and said, "Pray, be seated, my Lord! You look unwell. Be seated I beg you!"

Germaine sat, as he was bidden, but his eyes were on the ribbon, stretched between his taut fists. "Oh God!" he said again, as he found the little cloth of silver dagger embroidered in the black fabric. "It is de Laude!" His eyes looked straight ahead now into space. Ioni quickly took a seat and sat close to him.

"Can you tell me, my Lord," she said gently, "can you tell me about these ribbons, whose they are, and what is this de Laude you speak of?"

Gradually he looked at her and placed the ribbon on the table.

"I spent my younger years in the service of one of the most powerful lords in my country," Germaine said. "And these are his colours. These are the colours of the knight who trained me; his name is Gavron of Laude. And these colours, found on my attackers, would seem to say, that my tutor and mentor would wish me dead! My God! I cannot believe it!"

"Can this be true, my Lord?" Ioni said after a moment or two had passed.

"That night, after the attack," Germaine went on, the ribbon still trailing across the palm of his hand, "I told you that my country is being held by men who will do anything to take all power into their own hands. They have banded themselves together into a kind of league – a league which is intended to improve our country, but as time goes on, this league seeks nothing but the destruction of everything that stands in its way. Gavron of Laude is a leading force in the league, I know, but I never thought even he would seek my death. Unless, of course, if he thought my death here in Valdelaine would prosper his own cause!"

"And there is nothing we can do here?" Ioni asked. Germaine gave a wry smile.

"Nothing, I think," said Germaine. "But at least I know my enemies at home, if nothing else! My father, the Duke of Anlac…"

"Your father is a duke!" exclaimed Ioni. "Oh, I had forgotten…"

"Why, yes, my Lady," Germaine smiled. "My father never held with the league, nor ever gave it his approval. But as a boy, I was placed in the service of de Laude, perhaps to ensure my loyalty to the league. De Laude was, I think, a most cruel and ruthless man, though to be honest, I didn't know any better for much of the time I was with him. In those days, and even now, de Laude, along with other barons of the league, took in scores of youngsters, sons of prominent knights, to train them. My father had warned me that de Laude and the others were brutes. I had no choice but to follow his instructions, and I did become what they wanted – a young hero, not for my country, but for the league."

Germaine was silent for a time before she spoke again. "But why would this man want you dead, my Lord?"

"It would solve a lot of problems, I suppose! A political assassination," Germaine said grimly. "My death would be blamed on Esmor and on you, Valdelaines. The death of a hero in a foreign prison would help to rally support for the war. And, of course, as I happen to be an only son, there would no longer be a future Duke of Anlac, a thorn in the side of the league. One stab of a dagger could achieve more than a thousand swords on a battlefield."

"My God!" whispered Ioni, and she gazed away from him at the fireplace, her mind racing to make sense of all that Germaine had said.

"It is all so strange," she said as she looked back at him. "What am I to do with you, my lord Anlac, to keep you alive and safe!"

Germaine's eyes and smile turned gentle towards her as he spoke again.

"As to my safe guarding," he said, "I accept your judgement in whatever way you wish me held here. You may send me back to the dungeon…"

"No, my Lord," she gasped, reaching out her hand to touch his arm. "You need not fear, I will not send you down there – ever!"

Germaine paused a moment, took a deep breath and said, "It seems, then, that my life and safety are in your hands. I regret that I bring you any trouble, my Lady Valdelaine. But there is nothing between my danger and me – except your good judgement – and, well, your kindness!"

Her eyes were now wide as ever, and beautiful, so beautiful, he thought. She sighed and swallowed hard.

"In that case," she whispered, "you shall have kindness, in abundance, in abundance my Lord, from me." A log crackled in the fire behind her.

"I thank you," he said politely.

"Before I let you go, my Lord," she said, "may I ask you again if you are sure these ribbons of black and white bear the colours of this man you knew?"

"Quite sure," he said. "See here this image of a silver dagger, it is one of the emblems of this league I spoke of. Black and white the colours of Laude, the silver dagger of the league. It can be no other, who sought to take my life!"

*   *   *

The early spring was now over, the weather growing warmer and mild, the evenings beginning to lengthen. In the forests about Valdelaine the trees were putting forth their first buds and every glade echoed with the sound of birdsong, all the harsh gales of winter forgotten in the happy burgeoning of the springtime. Ioni too, seemed to find new energies within herself and the change of seasons sent many lovely tokens that lifted and warmed her heart. She had taken time to reflect on the situation of Germaine; he was the prisoner, of course, taken by her countrymen in the wars and brought to Valdelaine to spend such time there as it would take for him to be ransomed by his own people. So far, there had been not a hint of ransom for him, no diplomatic inquiries to the king, no approaches to Count Michael, who was in the field, as always, with the army. There were occasional letters and messages from Ioni's father, Lord Henry, who was serving in Esmor with the king's council; but even in these missives there was not a mention of any ransom bid for Germaine. Ioni had begun to conclude that maybe Germaine of Anlac would be staying on as a prisoner in Valdelaine for much longer than she had imagined. Then, of course, there was the matter of the attempt on his life. So far, not alone was there no ransom bid for Germaine, but some of his own people wanted him dead. It had all turned out so strange, Ioni thought. He had been brought to Valdelaine, hated, feared and despised by everyone. She could remember his earliest days at Valdelaine when she could think of him only as some kind of demon that had been cast on Valdelaine in the uneasy fortunes of war. Later, she had permitted him the luxury of a chamber at the top of the new tower; later again she had permitted him a place with the family at supper. But it was the attempt on his life that had finally changed her attitude towards him. In the weeks before the attempt, she had been obsessed with the fear that he might attempt an escape. She had thought that the armed bogus monks sent to kill him, were in fact there to set him free. Now, though, her mind was different regarding Germaine, he was no longer the demon he had seemed to be, far from it. He was now, to her, a mere boy with a price on his life. Her womanly instincts wanted to see him safe and protected from any possible harm.

She thought of him as he passed long days alone imprisoned in the chamber high in the new tower, released only to join the family for a brief period in the evenings. The days must be long and dull for him, she thought, and the assassination attempt and other things may play upon his mind. Maybe it would be possible to have him released from his cell for a number of times a day, under guard, of course, just to break up the tedium of his confinement. Yes, it would be better for his mind, if he had more time away from his solitude in the tower. She would consult Uncle Raymond and Uncle Robert on the matter; perhaps they might not mind spending time with him in men's type conversations. She smiled to herself as she thought that Aunt Blanche and all the girls would be more than happy to entertain him, at any time in the day. She sighed; I will put it to them all, she thought, and see what they think.

She smiled again, cousin Eleanor will be especially pleased, given how well she and Germaine get on at the supper table. Eleanor had also taken to detaining Germaine in conversation, usually for quite a long time after supper. Frequently Fleur and Clara joined in as well, and sometimes even little Anna, when she was not too tired to go to bed. But, for the most part, it was just Eleanor and Germaine who enjoyed these nightly conversations. With her outgoing temperament she could easily engage even a foreign knight in conversation about anything; with all her gifts, Eleanor could hold his attention easily, with her especially vivacious, charming manner that could keep a man interested and entranced for a long, long time. I don't seem to have such charm, Ioni told herself, I must be dull company compared with hers. Of course, Eleanor took after her mother Blanche in so many ways, not least in her gift of the most beautiful long blonde hair. I don't begrudge either of them each other's company, she thought, but I do feel a little jealous from time to time when I see them together. They do look well together, she thought. The handsome young knight from far away, and the tall, blonde and enchanting young lady, Eleanor. It is well that they can be happy in each other's company, she thought, it is good for both of them; Eleanor could do with the presence of a man and Germaine cannot but enjoy her presence likewise.

Ah me! Ioni sighed, for I am not Eleanor, but dull old Ioni, I speak my mind too much, and even my very eyes give my mind away when I do not speak. Long ago as children, she remembered, how Eris would shriek with laughter at seeing Ioni's reaction to things, expressed only in her eyes; my eyes give me all away, alas, alas! Her mother used to say if she had been born with no speech, Ioni's eyes would have said everything. "God gave you the deepest, darkest, widest, most penetrating eyes I've ever seen in any child, Ioni," she had often said. "They are so beautiful to look at, my child, but equally they seem to look right into the soul of the person looking at you!" Eyes or no eyes, she thought, I must set about bringing Germaine out of his chamber for longer periods in the day.

Ioni had been thinking to herself as she watched the sunset out through a slit window on the first landing atop the spiral steps. Her mind had meandered quite a bit, as she had beheld the drama of the glorious spring sunset far off to the west. Over there, somewhere beyond the frontier, her two brothers Jean and Eris were, even now, in the service of Count Michael in the great war against Bergmond. Every time she thought of them, she whispered a prayer for their safe return. Her sunset reverie was broken by the sound of laughter echoing up from the great hall. It was Germaine, Eleanor and the girls, in yet another after-supper revel, sometimes they chatted and laughed, sometimes the girls took musical instruments and played merry tunes. There they were striking up even now, and the sweet notes were audible where Ioni stood on the landing. She smiled, she was grateful for the sound of laughter and music wafting up to her in her darkening solitude, as she watched for the first stars to appear.

Lord Henry de Valdelaine returned home for a brief period of a few weeks, during that autumn, partly to survey the condition of his estates, and partly to escape the king's court and council for a brief time. Overall, he was pleased that Ioni had done so well, in her stewardship of Valdelaine. He was pleased, and was quite proud that his daughter had coped with the task he had set her. As well as this, he knew from Ioni's letters, how well she had managed the prize prisoner, Germaine, who had been placed into her care the previous winter. He agreed with the amount of freedom she had given him.

"At first," he told Ioni, "we were inclined to be cautious about him, here. But then we were given valuable information about him, to the extent that, he should be well treated. That was why Lord Lionel was sent to you shortly after Germaine arrived. The politics of the situation are delicate and complicated!"

"Well, to be honest," she answered, "I did what I did with him out of concern for his own welfare. I knew nothing of the politics!"

"Well to put it simply, Ioni. This Germaine is the son of the Duke d'Anlac who is more loyal to his king and country than he is to this informal Raven League of theirs. In the future he, Germaine may prove a good friend to us, and bring this war to an end! We shall have to wait and see!"

"I see, Papa! I am glad that my intuition about him coincides with the politics of the situation!"

Lord Henry laughed and hugged his daughter. Three weeks later, he departed once more leaving Valdelaine in the charge of Ioni. As the autumn turned to winter Germaine continued happily with his work 'about the place.' Ioni had granted him his request that he be allowed work – wood chopping, blacksmithing, anything that allowed his muscles to stretch. When the weather was foul he fre-quently spent time with Frère Benedict who was teaching him to read and write; as there were many books stored in Valdelaine, Germaine spent many the winter nights pe-rusing these tomes. Stories about knights and heroes intrigued him, he liked the 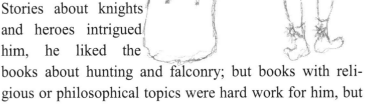 books about hunting and falconry; but books with religious or philosophical topics were hard work for him, but he determined to persevere.

It was at this time, that the news came about Eris, and about how he had fallen into enemy hands, in far off Bergmond. The letters that bore the news came from Jean, but he did assure Ioni that her brother was safe and well, and that very soon Ioni would hear from Eris himself. In another letter Jean went on to say that negotiations for Eris' ransom would soon begin. But Jean was careful to point out that, with the turmoil created by the war itself, it might be some time before Eris could be returned.

The Valdelaine family, of course, were shocked at the news and the womenfolk were in tears, that one of their own family was now in enemy hands, and alone and far from home. When the first shock of the news faded and Ioni became calm again she retired to her room to reflect. Her heart could not but go out to her beloved Eris, her favourite brother, and childhood companion. But she reminded herself that this was a time of war and these sort of things did happen. At least he was safe and well, according to Jean, whose letters she read again, and which were calm, matter of fact in tone. She prayed that Eris would be well treated, even as she had treated her Bergmondese prisoner, Germaine.

Germaine! She must send for him soon and talk it over with him! Yes that would help, and maybe he could shed more light on Eris' whereabouts and what his captors were like.

And so the late spring passed into summer and Ioni continued her work of managing the Valdelaine estates. Things were changing greatly for her prisoner Germaine who was now given more freedom than ever. He spurned the idea of living as a carefree knight however and instead threw himself into all kinds of work. Apart from being allowed to maintain his military skills with sword lance and mace, he was given the freedom of the stables where he fed, groomed and exercised the horses. With the workmen he lifted bales and carried wine barrels to the cellars. All the hours that he could, he worked and worked and was intensely happy to do so. Gradually he earned the respect of everyone he encountered, hearth knights, stable hands and workmen, and he was accepted by them without fear or suspicion. He loved it all, because for him, it was a holiday from the responsibilities and politics of his class. He was no longer cooped up indoors and simply revelled in all kinds of physical activity. He ate well, he slept well and was content. At the end of each day he paid a courtesy visit to Ioni, and the two young people both enjoyed these end of day conversations.

Gradually, over this time, Ioni became more and more at ease within herself about the presence of her prisoner. What she could see for herself of him, and what others reported to her of him was all good, and this relaxed any anxiety she might have in his regard. And from the evening conversations they had, she would see for herself how pleased and contented he was. Everybody seemed to like him. Lord Raymond her uncle had long ago taken to him, and he was no fool. In fact, Raymond frequently consulted Germaine on one topic or another. Frequently Raymond took Germaine with him when touring round the vast estate, when dealing with manor lords, village elders and peasant leaders. Maybe it was all meant to be, Ioni mused when she thought of Germaine; maybe it was part of my own destiny to have the care of such a man. The reason I was saved from the waters of the Gavenne all that time ago!

Chapter IX: The Fool's Errand

*B*e careful up that country! Watch out for the witch, the count had said. This was the territory into which Eris de Valdelaine was now riding. His mission was to deliver a message to the garrison holding Alorin bridge and fort and then to return as soon as possible. As he rode onward Eris, glad he had orders to return, was quite spooked by the quaint and uncanny nature of the countryside. Here and there great forests streamed down from low conical hills, here and there were large ponds reflecting giant towering crags; even the tilled land, pastures and villages seemed set against strange rocky ridges. A different and lonely kind of place this Norland, and as he rode along in search of Alorin fort, he shuddered as he thought 'A fit country for a witch to rule!'

"Be careful up that country," said Count Michael with a laugh. "Watch out for the witch!" Earlier the count had sent a force to take Alorin. He judged this to be a tactical move, hoping to persuade the 'Witch of Norland', as the countess was called, to enter the war on the Esmorin side.

Eris was never to make it to Alorin Fort. The winding road took him into a deep forest, laden with colours of autumn. After about a mile or so the road dipped into a deep dell and Eris slowed his horse down to a walk, as the road descended. He stopped and dismounted where the stream opened into a wide pond. There, he took some food, dried meat, and drank some wine from his leather flask. The horse was glad of the rest too and drank deeply from the pure water of the pond. All the time, Eris kept a wary eye up and down the dell, even though the place was quiet and beautiful, with autumn leaves and the shy reflecting stream.

Refreshed, Eris took the horse's reins and trudged up the far slope of the dell to the top, where he found the road again, which by now was little more than a forest track. He mounted Strang and was about to dig in his spurs when the whirring sound of an arrow passed above his head. A second arrow crashed into his helmet with a pinging sound knocking the helmet away. Within seconds and with heart pounding, both he and Strang were thundering forward along the forest path. Eris leaned forward on Strang desperately digging his spurs into the warhorse. His mail cowl was blown back on his shoulders and his golden hair flew in the breeze. Eris reached down low and lifted up his shield from its mooring on the horse's flank. When the shield was safely on his arm he looked behind and there, a hundred yards or so behind him were the dark figures of mounted knights in hot pursuit. The path wound this way and that, and every now and then, Eris would look backward to glimpse his pursuers. But Strang was holding his own, and moving well. Eris smiled and urged him on with slaps on his neck, and shouts of encouragement. A long straight lane came into view and Eris' whoops of joy changed to gasps of horror as, ahead of him, heavily armoured knights calmly emerged from the forest on either side of the lane. As he galloped forward, Eris searched the sides of the lane for a gap in which to wheel Strang and hopefully, plunge into the depths of the forest.

Eris smiled and whooped as he thought he saw such a gap on the left, what Eris did not see however, as it hurtled towards him was the dark form of a crossbow bolt. There was a crashing sound as the bolt caught Strang right in the chest, sending the great horse plunging to the dusty ground, and sending Eris flying through the air to crash into the dust, some yards ahead. Eris was stunned and the world seemed to go quiet as he clung to the ground beneath him. After what seemed an age he lifted his head, his face covered with dust and sweat. He was not sure anymore if he was waking or dreaming, but as he blinked to clear his eyes he saw a knight on a great black charger, casually walking towards him. The knight wore silver plated armour and blue surcoat and held a long lance before him, the point of the lance moving towards him, close to the ground. From his prone position on the ground Eris tried to move, but could not. He blinked and managed to move his gauntleted hand to clear his eyes. When he did so, the point of the lance was but inches from his face. With great effort Eris turned a little on his side and stared up the full length of the lance, to the great black warhorse, and to the silver armour of its rider.

"Do not move, young man with golden hair! Or I shall have to kill you."

Eris, breathless, lowered his head and lay as still as he could. In the dust of the road, prone, in front of this strange knight, with his heart still pounding from the chase and the fall, his mind seemed to be drifting in and out of clarity. The words 'do not move, young man with golden hair, or I shall have to kill you' seemed to be bounding around inside his head like the strains of some kind of unearthly music, not just words but the voice too. Yes, the voice too was ringing some-where inside his brain, but not a harsh voice, no, a soft clear dulcet voice, a musical voice, the voice of a young woman. 'Good God!' he thought, 'It is the witch!' Eris abandoned his search for comprehension and his head fell forward on his arm.

There was a splashing of cold water on his face and Eris awoke to find himself sitting with his back to a tree, a little way from where he had fallen on the lane. There were knights and horses standing about the road and the grassy verge. Straight in front of him, kneeling in the grass on one knee was the knight of the silver armour, but above the armour was the face of the most beautiful woman he had ever seen. The dark eyes were piercing and the face was framed in a great shock of flowing black hair. Kneeling beside him was a trooper who was placing a goblet of water to his mouth. Eris drank deeply, still staring at the apparition in silver armour in front of him. Finally the apparition began to speak, the same dulcet voice.

"What a pity, what a shame," the voice said, "that you were sent on a fool's errand."

Eris continued to drink and stare. The voice went on. "I took Alorin Fort two days ago. Your Count Mi-chael had a cheek to take it from me in the first place. But now all is well. Alorin is now back with its rightful owner!"

Eris' eyes began to blur a little and in the face of the lady in armour before him he seemed to see a face that he remembered.

"Mother!" he called out, as he thought he was go-ing to faint yet again but the musical laughter of the lady revived him.

"No. My dear boy with golden hair," she said, "I am not your mother!" She paused, picked up a stalk of grass, chewing on it, her lovely eyes glancing here and there.

"My name is Beatrice d'Erkindhal," she said quickly, "Countess of Norland."

At this Eris shook his head as if to clear it.

"But you are supposed to be a witch!" he blurted out. The countess laughed a high piping laughter and when her mirth subsided, she looked at him curiously with head to one side.

"And you," she said, "boy with golden hair, who are you and what is your name, if you can remember it."

"My name is Eris," he said. "Eris de Valdelaine."

She stopped chewing the stalk of grass, and looked at him a long time as if searching his face with some kind of memory of him from some other time. Eris wasn't sure, but he thought she blinked a tear from her eye.

As he mounted the horse that was provided for him, Eris took a long rueful look back at the forest road that he had galloped with Strang and hour earlier. He smiled grimly, as he thought how lucky he had been, until now, that is. In his short military career he had witnessed battles, skirmishes, foraging trips and countless courier journeys. Now all of that had come to an end in, literally, this neck of the woods. It had all been going so well, and had been so full of excitement. Now all of that was over as he joined the long troop of the witch's soldiers just behind the countess and her group of commanders. Where he was bound for he did not know, and what kind of existence lay before him now, he could not even hazard a guess. Typically, Eris just shrugged his shoulders and hoped for the best.

Three days' journey brought the countess and her force into what Eris considered to be a wild and beautiful country. Tall mountains lifted their snow laden peaks to the skies, high above a beautiful district of shimmering lakes. Eris thought the contrast could not be greater, as he recalled the lush gentle countryside of his own Valdelaine, now so very far away. It would not be long before news of his capture would reach Valdelaine and he hoped that sorry news would not distress his folk there, as he felt well and strong. Indeed, he had already begun to feel that his captivity was a new adventure as was everything else in his life. On the journey, the countess had not spoken to him, though she had frequently sent one of her lieutenants to enquire after his wellbeing. When in the saddle, however, the countess had frequently turned around to look at him, sometimes even smiling at him. Intrigued by this, Eris had hoped that it would prove a good omen for him. On the third day of the march as the road rose and then fell again among high rocks, Eris got his first breathtaking view of the Castle of Broudenlac, to give it its full name, as it was frequently called simply Broude. It was truly magnificent, its ramparts and turrets rising from a high promontory that stretched halfway into the lake. The wind had died down and the lake was still, reflecting the rock of the promontory, the castle itself and the magnificent mountains beyond. The castle of the witch, he thought, as he surveyed the awesome splendour of the place; a place fitting for a witch.

Once inside the stony bawn of Broude, Eris dismounted. He was allowed to wash at a huge trough that stood in front of the stables. His guards chattered away among themselves, but kept a watchful eye on him nonetheless. Eris smiled as he drained a bucket of icy water over his body, it was a welcome sensation after the days and nights he had travelled with the countess' men. All about him were the sounds of welcome for the homecoming troops and a pretty young maid with a basket of fruit and oatcakes even reached in her basket and presented him with an apple and a cake which he hungrily devoured. Munching away amid the throng, he raised his eyes upwards to survey the high walls of Broude, and he knew that whatever might befall him here, escape was not a possibility. In a moment he felt an arm on his shoulder, it was the captain who had escorted him for much of his journey.

"The countess would see you now, my friend," he shouted above the clamour. "Let me take you there now."

Eris was ushered through the crowd and under the portals of the castle itself, down some steps and through the doorway of the great hall. At the centre of a large group of knights and ladies stood the countess herself who had ungirded her armour and stood elegant in a long blue dress. The group made way, as Eris and the captain approached and the countess raised her cup of wine and smiled.

"My friends," she spoke. "Let me present to you our prisoner, who is called Eris and is young Lord of a place called Valdelaine."

There was a murmur from the group and the countess continued,

"As you know, we took back our fort at Alorin from Count Michael but we also collected this young man as our prisoner."

Someone placed a cup of wine in Eris' hand and the countess spoke again,

"Let us all drink a toast to our little victory at Alorin, to our safe return to family and friends!"

There was a loud hearty cheer and everyone Eris included drank to the toast. Yet another toast came from one of the knights,

"To the countess!"

There was an even louder cheer this time and a lot of laughter. When the noise subsided the countess looked at Eris.

"And now, master Eris," she called cheerfully to him, "what are we to do with you!" And before she could answer herself one of the knights piped up,

"Throw him in the deepest dungeon!"

And there was another burst of laughter which puzzled Eris but which the merry company had found amusing.

"I am at you service, Ma'am," Eris spoke for the first time.

"Good, my young Lord," the countess beamed. "Captain-at-arms! Pray find this young man lodging, if you can and then bring him back here. We will dine, and dine well I assure you all, in one hour!"

There was another cheer and Eris was escorted away to his lodgings; he was pleased to note that the quest led him up the steps to some quarter of the castle and not downwards to any dungeons. After much climbing the captain opened a door to a simple room which contained a bed, a clothing chest and a very old piece of tapestry hanging against the wall. On a tiny table there were candles. The captain murmured,

"I take it this will be comfortable for you, young man!"

"Very comfortable indeed," responded Eris who leaned far out on the triangular window ledge to catch a glimpse of the outside world. His head jerked back and he took in a sharp breath as he saw how high he was and when he saw the waters of the lake lapping below. "Oh. You'll get used to the height of this room," said the captain observing Eris. "This castle does not have dungeons, you see, we give our prisoners the highest rooms instead!"

The captain stepped through the entrance back out on to the stone landing leaving the door ajar. Eris said, "Aren't you going to lock me in?"

The captain's armour clinked as he laughed and turned back to look at Eris.

"There's no need to lock you in, young laddie," he said. "There's no danger from you. Every man, woman and child in Broude carry daggers somewhere on them and besides, this tower is cut off from the rest of the building, from here you have no access to the rest of Broudenlac except by passing the guards at the bottom of the stairs on the ground floor. If I were you I'd light a candle and then get busy dressing yourself – there's some clothes in the casket there. See you at supper then!"

With that, the captain clanked down the stairs and was lost in the deepening darkness, it was now twilight outside.

*   *   *

Hundreds of candles lit the great hall and the noise of chatter and cheer was high as Eris took his place at a trestle near the farthest end of the room. Amid the din he found himself seated opposite two very gruff looking midgets who quickly introduced themselves.

"I'm Sastro and he's Janus," one of the little fellows called across the table.

"I'm Genius and he's Disastro, more like!" bellowed the other and they both laughed. Eris smiled across at them, and though he did not know it then, Eris himself looked quite handsome in the glowing candlelight, dressed as he was now in a fine velvet tunic and with his blond pageboy tresses curling inward under his chin. Janus leaned forward on the table as only his stature would allow and called Eris,

"And what brings you to Broude, young master Golden Locks?" Eris cupped his hands to his mouth,

"I'm a prisoner!" he called loudly. The little men looked at each other in mock amazement and shouted to each other,

"He's a prisoner!" and they both laughed.

"Well, eat your supper, prisoner Golden Locks."

Eris did eat and drink. He was famished but as his hunger and thirst were slowly sated, he spoke again asking Sastro and Janus what they were doing in Broude. Sastro, in response, drew himself to his full comical height and informed Eris that both of them were honoured guests in the countess' household. Janus only smiled.

"We entertain the family, we do tricks, we accompany the children," Janus said, "and we make everyone laugh."

The bright blue eyes of Eris wandered up the length of the teeming hall where just about everyone of the distinguished throng were eating, shouting and especially – laughing.

"You are honourable guests here then!" he said.

"Of course, silly boy," said Sastro, "and that's a lot better than being a prisoner like you!"

Eris only smiled and again looked up the hall. The two likely little men opposite him began to fill him in on the names of the people at the top table who dined with the countess. To the left of the countess sat a lady who was a mirror image of the countess but a little more plump, and whose facial features were a little more rounded and kindly than those of the countess – her sister Elaine. To the right sat Lord Helven, the close confidante and possibly also the lover of the countess.

*   *   *

Eris rested well that night; the bed was good and the sound of the wind around the walls outside his high cell, and the sound of the lapping waters of the lake below served to lull him into heavy sleep. When he awoke in the morning light he found no guard at the door; when he descended the stairs, no one accosted him. He was free it seemed to come and go as he pleased. A friendly, fresh faced maid bade him to come and partake of breakfast in the dining hall, which he did eagerly. As he ate he was joined by the two dwarfs from the night before and the three of them made merry company as they ate and drank.

Afterwards Eris spent most of the morning ensconced in a special chamber with the family scribe. It seemed the countess was eager that messages be drafted right away, pertaining to his capture. These messages would be taken and sent to Count Michael. As well, Eris was requested to dictate any messages he might have, to be taken to his family. Eris complied happily and dictated letters to his brother Jean, to his father, Lord Henry, and one other to his sister Ioni. There was yet another letter to be dictated and written; it was the letter to Count Michael detailing not only the story of his capture, but also giving assurances of his wellbeing and safety.

"Do you know," Eris asked the old man when all the despatches were completed, "how long I will be kept here?" After a long pause the scribe joined his fingers and stared with his grey eyes into some imaginary distance.

"Difficult to say," the man said. "It takes time for despatches to come and go. It may depend on the willingness of your countrymen and family to come to speedy negotiations on your behalf. But I do not really know. And then, the countess may have other plans for you."

With that the scribe arose, bade Eris good day, and left the chamber with the bundle of scrolls under his arm.

*   *   *

"You do not look like a witch!" Eris said smiling at the countess. "At least, not like any witch I've ever heard of!"

The countess looked at Eris and laughed heartily, brushing back her raven hair with her gloved hand. That morning, the countess had invited Eris to come riding with her. They had left the castle grounds together and ridden their horses into the craggy country west of the lake. The area was rugged with very small fields of arable land, confined between the many outcrops of rock; clusters of pine trees grew here and there but otherwise the countryside was bleak. It intrigued Eris that he was allowed to be even alone with the countess; but he was thoroughly enjoying the day, the riding and the conversation of this strong, beautiful woman. They broke off their ride at the verge of a pond to rest and to water the horses. The day was sunny and the wind over the crags was bracing and fresh. Leaving the horses, they walked along the narrow goat tracks together.

"Well, I am a witch in a way!" the countess laughed. "I am a witch in many ways!"

"How can that be? I understand there was only one way to be a witch!" Eris said, amused. The countess stopped and looked out at the wide countryside and the mountains beyond.

"When our ancestors came to Norland," the countess said, "they did not conquer, so much as were married into the place. The ladies married the local chiefs. And my ancestors the Erkindhals, eventually married the last queen of Norland. We have the titles earl and countess of course, but the people here do not call me countess, they call me queen; they still use the old titles, even to this day. They called my husband, the king; well, my two husbands, in fact, when they were alive. Now our ancestors, descended from the knights of King Arthur of the Britons, well they were Christian of course. But the people here live by a convenient mixture of the old gods and the Christian faith. They are still faithful to the old customs, as are we. So, it is not surprising that, beyond our frontiers we are regarded as half heathen anyway!"

The countess paused for breath and looked at Eris to see how he was taking all of her story so far.

"I see. So you are – shall we say – regarded as half heathen," Eris said smiling. "You look too beautiful to be heathen or witch! In what other way are you a witch?"

The countess thought and then smiled again at Eris.

"I have been declared a witch, Eris!" she said. "By the king and his council in Bergmond. I nearly married one husband but he died before the ceremony. I actually did marry two other husbands, and they too died – after the nuptials, let me say. It was unfortunate that neither of them could stay alive – for my sake. If a woman like me loses two and a half husbands, the verdict comes down on the woman – it is usually either murder or witch-craft. And for a woman in my situation to lose so many husbands by natural causes – well it is not regarded as natural. However, while murder was mooted at the time, the real nature of their demise was far less exciting."

The countess laughed at her own telling of the story. Eris was smiling at her, enchanted by the power, the strength and the humorous energy exuded by this woman. If she was not an enchantress, she possessed a living energy that was difficult to resist even out here on the craggy heath, with wind and sunlight dancing about her. She stopped in her tracks and looked back at him.

"Are there any other ways to be a witch?" he called to her. She held out her hand to him and, as he came to her she held his hand in hers, a gesture that was natural for her, perhaps, but for Eris it was a gesture of great confidence and trust. Eris was touched by such majesty and informality. Agile as a mountain ram, she began climbing a crag, all the time holding his hand, like a mother with a child. It was steep and hard going, the upward climb, but all the time she went up ahead of him, reaching back each time to take his hand and guide and even pull him to the top. Inwardly, Eris was fascinated more and more by this extraordinary creature, who ranged in her gestures from girl to giant in each passing moment.

When they both gained the top of the crag the countess gazed over the wide wild landscape. Far away to the east was her fortress standing proudly by the lake, while on three sides about them were the mountains rising sharply from the plain. The countess spoke,

"Eris, my young friend, there is yet another way for me to be a witch. It is political, you scc. In this part of the world we are slow to change anything, and so, nei-ther the nobility nor the people here ever accepted the Raven League, nor its ideas. If the royal line in Bergmond was weakening over the years, and God knows, this present king has been the weakest of all and has no heir, we still could not see how a league of barons would save the royal family. When my grandfather rejected the league it was not received well in Bergmond and, over time things went from bad to worse. My father and my uncles paid the price for refusing the league any sway in Norland, and they were beheaded in the Cathedral Square in Bergmond. My mother also died, but differently. Alorin, where she was living and hiding was finally taken by Gavron de Laude. My poor mother was driven out into the forest in the snows and wandered about for days before she died of exhaustion."

Eris was looking at her, amazed at this horrific story.

"And what of you, Countess," he said. "How did you come to escape the fate of your family?"

The countess looked at him, her dark hair blowing wild in the breeze.

"I did not escape, Eris!" she breathed. "I was already imprisoned in the White Tower of Bergmond. I was only fifteen at the time. I saw my father and uncles leave for their execution. Later I heard of my mother's death. After a few months, a sufficient number of my countrymen had secretly got within the walls of Bergmond and one night they sprang me free. And after a long journey I finally reached home again – since then I have done nothing with my life except fight the league. I have caused them much damage, Eris... until your Count Michael came along and I had to see him off too!"

She laughed again and then her eyes narrowed.

"I think it is well known what Gavron de Laude said of me, as I went from strength to strength and troubled his league at every opportunity."

"What did he say, Countess?"

"He said 'I should have cut that bitch's little white throat when I had her a girl prisoner!'"

"I see."

"I hope so, Eris. Up here in this wild part of the world, we have to fight to survive. The royal council has declared me not only witch, but also traitor and outlaw! The archbishop of Bergmond refuses to declare me a witch without my standing trial there first. But I'm not likely to set foot in Bergmond with such other prices on my head!"

The countess laughed again, turned to Eris and said, "Now let's ride homeward to a good warm supper!"

A half mile out from the castle the countess galloped ahead having challenged Eris to a race home. Eris' horse bounded forward and was catching up on the countess, but Eris failed to catch up with her. As she veered in and dismounted in the yard she was laughing again.

"Silly boy, but very gallant of you to let me win!" she called to Eris as his mount clattered into the yard.

"Never!" cried Eris to her. "You won fair and square, Countess!"

"Silly boy, but gallant too! You are riding the best horse in my stable. Maybe even the best horse in Norland!"

*   *   *

As time went by, Eris settled well into his confinement in Broude. He was not the type to waste his time fretting over his change of fortune. In fact, he seemed to revel in his new life and his natural charm won him great affection from all sides. Whether in the company of the doughty Norland chiefs who visited the countess, or in the company of the maidservants and milkmaids, he was quite at home enchanting all by his ready wit and kindly nature. Even the daughter of the countess, Catherine, spent her happiest hours in his company, relishing his many stories and enjoying his hearty and humorous approach to life. With Eris for company, Catherine never failed to emerge from a certain shyness, and when she was with him, even the mere comical twinkle in his eye brought forth from her the most hearty laughter. And Eris enjoyed this response as though he considered it his mission in life to raise the spirits of all the women folk he met!

Only one issue about Broude puzzled Eris at this time, and the more he observed it and reflected upon it, the less he seemed to understand it. The issue in question was the man who was the chief steward to the countess, Lord Maiklin. It was none of his business, he knew, but it caused him no little wonder at how Maiklin had ever made his way into the affections of the Lady Beatrice. Eris had disliked him from the beginning. Behind Lord Maiklin's bushy eyebrows and beard, Eris beheld a cruel face and sly eyes that moved too quickly for his taste. Unlike the other Norland chiefs who cursed, spat and drank themselves to sleep, Maiklin's manners were smooth as a diplomat's while those eyes were ever watchful – watchful of everything. Eris did not consider him good for the countess, whose own manner was so honest, brave, and hearty. In the presence of the countess, Maiklin put on airs that were meant to be charming, but which seemed to Eris to be ridiculously fawning and obsequious.

To his own contempt, Eris had found that the man could be arrogant and harsh when his lady was not about. Not that Maiklin was ever troublesome to Eris, of course, he was too clever for that; in fact Maiklin carried the same greasy, fawning manner to everyone he knew was in good favour with the countess. At banquet or meeting, his eyes were everywhere as though his mind was never at rest. Not endeared to the man from the beginning, Eris found that, with the passage of time, he liked him less and less. He was the exception among Norland chiefs, Eris mused, he did not curse and swear, he did not spit, and most certainly he may have drank others to sleep, but never himself!

With the passage of time, Eris continued to be puzzled and intrigued by Lord Maiklin and by his curious relationship with Countess Beatrice; though he was careful not to mention his concerns to anyone. But, eventually there did come a day when Eris' casual curiosity deepened into suspicion of the man. In an after dinner conversation with Eris, Maiklin was somewhat boastfully elaborating on the many people of status that he knew, from knights to bishops to diplomats, and on the many places he had visited or knew about.

"And I believe, my Lord Eris," he went on, "that your own Valdelaine is a very beautiful place, and indeed the castle itself is one of the finest, is it not?" Eris was nodding his head, pretending to be gratified by these comments. Then, warming to the subject of his great knowledge of things, Maiklin went on,

"And of course, what a coincidence that you should be from Valdelaine of all places, as that is where the great Germaine d'Anlac now resides as prisoner!"

"That is correct, Lord Maiklin." Eris, masking his surprise, simply nodded his head and smiled in agreement.

Maiklin's eyes flashed at Eris for a second as he realised his faux pas but relaxed as Eris showed no surprise at all at Maiklin's knowledge of Anlac's whereabouts, and continued smiling and sipping his mead contentedly.

"Agreed, Lord Maiklin," Eris said. "A most extraordinary coincidence of fate or fortune. I'm not sure which! But of course time will tell – why it is possible that I may even be exchanged myself for the great Lord Anlac. My family of course would be very happy if this were to happen, although I'm sure I'm not as valuable a prisoner as Germaine is to his countrymen!"

"Yes!" was all that Maiklin could say, his eyes searching those of Eris for any sign there of recognition of his blunder. But there was none, as Eris finished his jug of mead and stared wistfully into the distance as if he were already seeing the towers of his home in Valdelaine.

But, in truth, behind the mask of wistful smiling, Eris' brain was teaming with suspicious questions. How was it possible that this minor lord of this remote and backward region, could know of the precise location of Anlac's confinement? Eris himself had never mentioned it, of course; the knowledge was not exactly totally secret, but there were only a trusted few on all sides of the war who, for diplomatic reasons, were acquainted with Germaine's place of imprisonment. Interesting, Eris thought, as Maiklin rose and took his leave. Very interesting that Maiklin would know about a secret shared only by the highest echelons of the two warring states. Very, very interesting indeed. And how exactly had Maiklin come by this knowledge, Eris wondered. Maybe he was fishing for information, but if he was, why would a Norlander be even bothered by the fortunes of Germaine d'Anlac, a Bergmondese leaguer, and, as such, not exactly endeared to the people of Norland. They themselves refused to take sides in the present war and until now, under the banner of the countess had continued to fight the Raven League. Eris watched the figure of Lord Maiklyn as he left the hall.

I have liked you not, he mused, but now I like you even less! He gulped back the dregs of the mead and left in a hurry. Already Eris was late for a trysting dalliance with one of the ladies, or one of the milkmaids, or one of the kitchen girls! He racked his brain to remember which one. "Strong Mead!" he said aloud, clearing his throat, shaking his head and buttoning up his tunic.

"Never!" Eris exclaimed later as he stared down from the balcony to the empty gallery below. His eyes widened in horror and waltzed across the front of his face to meet those of Tarina, the milkmaid he had promised to meet. Little musical peals of laughter came from her and she looked fondly at him. She had just now declared that she had seen him in amorous embraces with many other girls. With mock intensity he looked at her and declared, "But they do not kiss like you do!" Again Tarina laughed.

"So, you do kiss them, Master Eris," she chuckled. "And you have never been kissed by me, so, how could you know what mine are like!"

"One look at you and I can tell!" Eris whispered. When, after yet more banter passed between them, and when they finally did kiss, Tarina drew back suddenly, slapped Eris' face and said,

"You call that a kiss, Master Eris! I vow that you're thinking of some other little miss while you did it.

But you are a dear boy! Now, I am away, and see that you kiss better next time!" And she tripped down the stairs.

"I will pine and die!" Eris called after her.

She laughed, turned and blew him a kiss.

"You have this to survive on!" she chirped and was gone.

'Damn!' thought Eris. My mind was elsewhere and girls can tell, though it was not on another girl, sadly!

*   *   *

And so, Eris was to pass that winter in the company of Countess Beatrice and her people at Broude. In that time he was to see much of Norland, from the Bergmond frontier to the south, all the way up to the spectacular mountains to the north. Likewise, he came to know so much about the people of that remote part of the world and their strange ways. The Norland folk were rough and ready; uncouth perhaps, by the formal standards of Bergmond and Esmor, but above all they were warmhearted and merry. This endeared them to Eris, and just about everyone he met there, Lord Maiklin excepted, had taken him to their hearts, they had loved his blond good looks and his ever present humour and sense of wildness. Far from being reduced in spirit by his captivity, Eris was enjoying it all with a kind of boyish sense of adventure, as though every experience was to be received with welcome into his consciousness and there to be treasured for all of his life to come. Thus it was with fascination that he had watched the great ceremony of 'The Bond' which had taken place on the Linkl Rock, a high promontory of crags to the north. Sometimes called 'The Marriage', the ceremony took place out in the open air on Midwinter Night and was the highest feast in the Norland calendar.

Amid thousands of her people, and in the light of hundreds of fires, the countess made her way on to Linkl Rock on horseback. There amid the throng she dismounted and her cloaks and dress were removed, leaving her with nothing to protect her but a white dress of flimsy material and a wreath of holly to bind her hair. Escorted by the chiefs as far as the base of the crag, she then proceeded to climb the great rock alone, while the crowd watched her every move in silent expectation. Having gained the spot high above where she could stand upright, she then stepped forward carefully and with arms outstretched to balance her, tiptoed barefoot forward until she finally gained the foremost high peak. There she stood with the winds whipping at her white dress while, above her, white clouds scurried across the face of the moon. The crowd was hushed by the sight of her, her form diminished by the gigantic crag, which seemed to raise her upwards into the very moonlit sky itself. Slowly raising her arms above her, she began to cry out on the stormy air the Oath of Bond to her people; she did so shrieking in some ancient forgotten language which for Eris, as he watched, sent shivers down his spine. The crowd remained silent after the last words of oath. She still stood facing outward, as one of the chiefs of Norland approached her on the crag and placed the Great Sword of Norland in her upheld hands; the hilt in one hand, the blade in the other above her head. She now shuffled her feet a little to move and face the four points in turn. Then from her lofty height she turned to look down on the throng again. A little silence and then she raised a cry which seemed to pierce the night around her, and as she did so, the crowd launched a thunderous roar and all of

Norland went wild with joy. For another year at least, the queen and the people were married once more.

Eris could only gasp in wonder where he stood, some distance from the crag. All about him the people continued to cheer and cheer, their faces lit by the hundreds of fires that littered the place. And soon, the sound of cheering was mingling with the sounds of drums, pipes and tambourines, as the celebration was getting under way. When he looked back at the cragtop, the countess was being taken down from the crag on the shoulders of some burly chiefs.

"What if she fell from the crag?" Eris gasped aloud. The man beside him laughed and shouted back at him with a hefty nudge,

"If she fell from Linkl Rock, she would not be our queen, would she? No she would not!"

The festivities continued into the night and the morning; later in the day the crowds began to disperse as people began their homeward journey. Eris met the countess briefly. She too had enjoyed the festival, and was none the worse for her experience on the high rock. She gave him a smiling, knowing look and said, "I'll wager you have not seen anything like that before! Not the least like your fancy coronations in Esmor, I imagine!" And indeed, as he rode homeward to Broude, in the countess retinue, Eris could say to himself that he had not witnessed the likes of it ever before. But, at least, he knew now how powerful was the bond between Beatrice and her people, she celebrated and laughed with them, and when the need arose she rode before them into battle.

*   *   *

Within a month the league made its first overtures to the countess to secure the handover of Eris de Valdelaine into Bergmondese hands. The first letters arrived, including one from Gavron de Laude; these were arrogant in tone, and they demanded, without conditions, the immediate surrender of the countess' prisoner. Beatrice merely dismissed these first letters with a laugh, writing a reply to Gavron, merely to state that the young Valdelaine had been taken in Norland territory and that she was well within her rights to ransom him directly back to his countrymen, if they were interested. When, a month later again, there was a second letter from Gavron, this time more placatory in tone, to the effect that he wished to negotiate the release of the prisoner, the countess was happy to reply that she would make a bargain with the league, and with Gavron. She was amused to add that the price of the boy would be very high. At that time, she had no fears of invasion of Norland by Gavron's forces, as such a move would deplete the Bergmondese forces, badly needed to keep Count Michael and his marauding Esmorins at bay. Though she viewed him as a nuisance at first, it was now her opinion that Count Michael's recent forays in the regions south of Norland had been a blessing, as they had kept Gavron and his hordes well pinned down beyond her frontier. For the moment, at any rate, Norland was safe. But of course, that could all change quickly if the main fighting moved to another region, so the countess was determined to keep her advantage and to keep Gavron's interest in Eris truly alive.

The countess need not have been too troubled, as Gavron responded quickly to her letters and demanded to know the price of the ransom. Sensing that Gavron was very keen to have Eris delivered, the countess suggested a direct meeting with him, face to face, over a bargaining table at some mutually available venue. Though exasperated at Countess Beatrice's demands, Gavron wrote to say that a meeting would be acceptable and that representatives from both sides could decide on when and where the meeting would take place.

"You are a most valuable prisoner!" the countess chirped when she next met Eris. "It seems the league will go to any lengths to get you!"

"Will my price be very high!" Eris quipped.

"Higher than you can know, dear Eris!" she said, "and higher than Gavron can imagine! But no more of that now! All will be revealed in due time!"

*   *   *

"Master Valdelaine!" came the shout from the landing beyond the door of Eris' chamber. It was late in the January afternoon, and the shout was accompanied by a loud thumping on the door. Eris sat upright on his bed and shouted, "Yes? Enter!" The door opened to reveal the form of Lord Maiklin who was accompanied by three of his troopers. There was a scowl on Maiklin's face and Eris knew that there was some trouble brewing. He stood up as a steward swaggered into the room.

"I have some words for you, Master Valdelaine," Maiklin said. "Serious words! In fact I have some serious questions to ask about your behaviour! And I expect answers, mind you, or I am more than happy to hand this business over to her ladyship, the countess!"

Eris was now wide awake with astonishment and answered,

"What is the trouble, my Lord?"

Maiklin was looking up at him, grim faced, and two of the troopers had entered the room, one on either side of the doorway.

"It is the matter of documents, Valdelaine, important documents!"

"Documents!" said Eris, bewildered. "What documents!" Maiklin was patting his left palm with a scroll that he held in his right hand.

"Documents of great importance to this house, and to the countess!" There was a pause. "Documents which you, Sir, may or may not have removed from her ladyship's library!"

On hearing this, Eris felt himself between laughter and outrage, and he fell backward to a seated position on the side of the bed. He gulped a breath of air, gasped and then said quietly,

"I know nothing of documents, my Lord!" He could see that Maiklin was serious, and eyeing the troopers by the door he could see that the intrusion was no comedy. Maiklin stared down at him with a downward curl on his lips.

"Are you saying that you have not stolen certain letters from the countess?" There was a pause.

"I know nothing of letters of the countess!" Eris blurted angrily. Lord Maiklin paced up and down a little, hands now behind him and still twiddling with the scroll.

"Are you saying you know nothing of the letters that were stolen from the countess?" More bewildered than ever Eris said,

"I know nothing of this!"

"Do you have letters of any kind here in your chamber?"

"I have letters, of course! But they are from members of my family and from my master, Count Michael!"

"You do?" Maiklin paused. "Where are they these letters of yours?"

Eris looked across at the clothes chest on the floor by the wall. He made to get up but said, "They are in the chest, over there!"

"I see!" Maiklin said. "And are these family letters the only ones you have here?"

"Of course!"

Maiklin bent his face down close to Eris. "Then you will have no objection if we take a look, will you!"

Eris could feel the anger rise inside him and hissed, "Look all you wish!"

Maiklin nodded to one of the troopers, who stepped over to the chest and opened it, then reaching down to search among the clothes. Eventually the trooper's arm came up out of the chest and in his hand he held a roll of documents. Even in the half light, Eris could see across the room from where he sat and his heart began to chill, as he knew that the roll in the soldier's hand was more than twice the thickness of all the letters he had received in his life. The trooper handed the roll to Lord Maiklin who unrolled one document and held it before Eris' eyes.

"Is this yours?" Maiklin demanded.

Eris felt his heart sink as he said wearily, "No!"

And the realisation sank in, that he was being tricked into a trap.

"I have never seen those before," he said with an angry scowl at Maiklin.

"And I have no knowledge of what could be in them – nor did I steal them from the countess."

As he was escorted by the troopers and marched down the stairs to face the countess, who was waiting in the great hall, Eris felt himself grow calm with the movement and his head cleared as the shock of his astonishment waned. It could be anyone that was laying a plot against him, and then again it might only be Maiklin. It might be in the latter's interest to drive a wedge between himself and the great goodwill he had hitherto enjoyed in Broude. By the time he was placed standing before the countess, he had fully recovered his wits and his courage. After all, he thought, I'm actually a prisoner here, not a privileged guest – and he smiled inwardly for a moment. His mind sank into a restful state behind his face as he watched as Maiklin's little comedy was now taking place. The countess was surprised, not shocked; it was difficult to shock this lady. Her face was serious, though, and her eyes were open wide as she quizzed him on the so called theft of the papers. He felt a momentary wave of sorrow for her as the weight of his 'crime' sank in; another wave of shame that anyone, especially the countess, could think him even capable of such a vile act. If you are a good man, then the reproach of a good woman, even if you are innocent, does carry a certain sting. But he held his ground. At length he played the only card available to him.

"I did not steal these papers," he said, calmly looking from the countess to Lord Maiklin, "and I did not place them in my room. The door of that room is unlocked at all times, as you know; anyone could have placed these things there!"

There was indeed a good pause, at this point, and no one said anything. Then the silence was broken as Maiklin said,

"But you were seen! You were seen taking these to your chamber! You were seen by one of my guards! Isn't that right!"

"That is right, my Lord," came the growled response from the trooper who stood behind the group. Eris looked around at the guard, then looked back at the countess.

"Upon the honour of the Valdelaine's and upon my own honour, I say that I have not done such a thing of which I am accused." Eris then turned towards Lord Maiklin. "But I thank your Lordship!"

"What do you mean by that!" Maiklin hissed at him.

"I thank your Lordship for questioning me first – about these papers. Especially if you say you already knew they were in my chamber!"

There was a silence as the countess glanced through the parchments and tapped on the table with her finger tips. For a moment, she looked as if she would say something, then she glanced sideways at the casement window and finally she simply nodded to Lord Maiklin. Eris was promptly taken by the guards and was pushed out of the hall and up the winding stairs to his own chamber. He listened in silence as the door was locked. When all sounds from outside had faded, he simply shrugged his shoulders and sat on the bedside for a moment. Then he stretched out on the bed and thought about the events of the past hour. Though night had fallen, he was not in complete darkness as his chamber candle had been lit.

It must be in someone's interest to have me thus discredited with the countess, he thought, but there was nothing he could do about it. At least he was in his chamber with the candlelight, it could easily have been otherwise, he could now be somewhere uncomfortable in the dark! For the present, the carefree days in which he had revelled until now were over and done with. He would miss a great many things, not least the goodwill and merry company of the countess herself and, of course, he would miss his never ending courtship of the girls here in Broude. However, he comforted himself with the thought that as experiences of imprisonment might go, his had been wonderful until now. An hour or so of musings passed for Eris; at that stage his thoughts had begun to centre, with some self-pity, on his family and on his far off home. It was then that he thought again of the letters from home that he kept in the clothes chest. These would be so comforting to read at a time like this – if they were still there. With a start, he sat upright at the thought that these letters may have been removed in reprisal for the theft of the countess' documents. In a flash, he was kneeling by the chest, opening it, and with both hands was fumbling downward through the layers of clothing to know if they were there. He almost did not see it happen, such was his haste, but as he searched, a single scroll did pop out of the clothing and fell to the floor. He gave it no heed, as his hands found the roll of his own letters at the bottom of the chest. Relieved and, greedily almost, he pressed those letters to his heart and took them back to the bedside and the candlelight. Reading and writing had never been strong points with Eris! He could read a word or two, a letter or two. But that did not matter now, as he knew each letter by the imprint on the wax seals, which in turn he held up to the light. As he unrolled the pages, there was the Valdelaine seal on Ioni's letter, there was the St. Michel seal on Count Michael's, and so on. And he smiled to see every one of them. He even sighed with joy as he completed his deciphering every one of them down to the last. Then with another sigh he placed the last letter on the bed beside him. It was then that he saw and remembered the scroll on the floor by the clothing chest.

With a start, he jumped up, crossed the room and picked up the fallen scroll – it must have been one which the guard had failed to remove. Eris picked it up from the floor and walked across the room to hold the seal up to the candle light. In doing so, Eris was in for yet another shock. The seal on the scroll was that of – Gavron de Laude! Eris had no trouble recognising it – how often had he seen it on letters to his master, Count Michael. Even though they were bitter enemies and on opposing sides, Gavron and the count had to correspond with each other, even in the midst of the war.

But why, Eris asked of himself, was Gavron in private correspondence with Maiklin – he knew well, by now, that all of Gavron's letters were addressed to the countess herself. Try as he would, Eris could make no sense of it, as he read the letter down the page, as best he could. What a pity, he thought, that he did not learn his Latin better as a boy, under the tutelage of his own Uncle Robert. And then he stopped suddenly – and his heart almost stopped too – there was a sentence about the countess, followed shortly by the words "puer Valdelensis." Good God! It was about himself – the 'Valdelaine boy'.

*   *   *

"You released me!" Eris exclaimed when he met the countess.

"Yes, of course. It was Lord Maiklin who suggested it. He said it would do no good to keep you locked up. Besides I do declare that I have never seen all the girls in such foul humour. Especially in the past week or so. You seem to cast a spell on all of them. They begged and even demanded your release. I've never seen the like before."

They were standing on a little promontory on the lake where the countess liked to walk on fine afternoons and enjoy the view of Broude Castle and the mountains, all reflected in the lapping waters.

"You have been good to me," Eris said, tossing a little stone across the water. "I wondered often why you have treated me so well – I mean it has been like being at home here!"

She was gazing at the lake, arms folded, lost in her thoughts. Then she looked at him and her face began to beam with a gentle smile.

"There are many reasons, I suppose. But I think there is no harm telling you the little hidden truth about you, that I have kept a secret all this time. The day I first saw you, you were lying in the dust of the forest road and, in spite of the dramatic nature of your arrival in Norland, my heart was suddenly enchanted as I saw you there. Your helmet had come off and so I could see your hair, your golden hair!"

"What has my hair – my golden hair to do with anything?"

The countess smiled and then laughed a little reaching out her arm to touch his cheek and his hair. The she sighed.

"My dear Eris, we are a superstitious people here. We set great store by signs and portents of all kinds. As I have told you, I spent my childhood in a state of war, never knowing when life might end, never knowing where I would rest my head for the night. However, during that time my mother used to tell us that she had this dream, this recurring dream. She told us so often, mind you, that I can almost see the dream myself. My mother said that she could see all the people of Norland, travelling like a great flock and, leading them to safety was a golden haired boy!"

The countess sat down on a boulder – both she and Eris were silent. Far out on the lake a fisherman's oars splashed, breaking the quiet of the water.

"When I first saw you, I was moved to remember my mother and her dream!"

Eris stood silently now as the countess gazed out upon the scene before them and he knew that she was in tears. A long time passed in that silence and then the countess gathered her cloak about her, stood up and took Eris' hand.

"So much for dreams and omens," she said, as the sorrow passed. "But it was a good dream, Eris, my dearest boy, it was a good dream!" And she wiped her eyes. They walked the promontory, away from the lake and took the little pathway back towards Broude. As they walked Eris found himself suddenly alone and turned about to find that the countess had stopped walking some way back. She stood there, her black hair moved by the breeze, all the beauty of the wild place about her, she was smiling at him, though she looked so strong and yet so frail. She walked to him smiling.

"You don't have to fulfil my mother's dream, silly boy!"

"No?"

Then she walked up to where he stood.

"I was fond of you for yourself, silly fellow!" And she linked her arm in his and they walked homeward like old friends.

"It is good to have dreams, Eris," she said. "God in Heaven, it is good to have dreams! The day is long when you have no dreams!"

Chapter X: The Second Spring

*W*hile all this adventure was happening to Eris in his captivity, life had been anything but quiet at the castle of Valdelaine. Messengers came to and fro; soldiers, knights and courtiers had stayed, some going outbound for the battlefields, others making the return journey. At times, great processions carrying supplies with horses, cattle and wheat wagons had paused there for rest, filling the castle, the courtyard, the stables and the fields. Gradually, Ioni, as mistress of Valdelaine, had become the steward of all the comings and goings – organising, delegating, dispensing orders – placing all her energies in the service of each new task. Uncle Robert and Uncle Raymond were in charge only in a nominal way; Ioni had seen to that, gradually drawing to herself all the control of everything that happened in Valdelaine. For Ioni, the presence of Germaine, strange as it was in the early days, had become an essential part of the scheme of things. He had thrown himself heartily into every task and, had become a part of the family, liked by everyone, young and old. And he had been a tower of strength to Ioni, someone to turn to in every crisis, and Ioni herself felt the thorn taken out of every problem, knowing that she could rely on Germaine's common sense and on his willingness to give everything his utmost best. Ioni was pleased and grateful. She had taken the awesome risk of giving Germaine his freedom in the castle and its surrounding countryside. And he had honoured her confidence in him; in fact, to all the family he had become like a brother or favoured cousin. Ioni shuddered at the thought of him spending all that time, bound below in the darkness of the dungeon. How it would have crushed his spirit and darkened his young mind. But now, he was strong and happy, and her intuition about him had proved right. The many quarrels such as they had had in the early days were only very sporadic now and most of those were her fault, she felt. Strange, she thought, and lovely was the bond of trust and confidence that had grown between them. Even though they were captive knight and captor lady, so to speak, they were in fact, simply two young people, coping with all the whirling happenings of a time of war, coping, for instance, with statesmen and soldiers twice their age or more. And cope well too. Why, Ioni asked herself, did fate destine Germaine to be an enemy in this awful time, and how was it that the fortunes of war had cast them both into each other's care, trust and confidence? For, indeed, Ioni now relied on him for so much – simply his being there at all seemed to sweeten the long days. She had lost her mother in death, she had lost her father to the service of the king's court, she had lost her brothers Jean and Eris to the wars. And now had come this gallant young soldier of the enemy into her care, under her rule, and most of all filling her life, her mind and heart with a strange new peacefulness. It was as if God had given him to her as a blessing and a comfort.

For Ioni, the thought of Germaine was so awesome, and yet fascinating at the same time. Here was the son of some foreign household, a hero of his country at nineteen, who had inflicted countless defeats on her own countrymen, who had been so brave in defeat and capture, and he was now, as it were, always at her disposal, her prisoner and responsibility. If ever she might have fears that he might attempt an escape and destroy her trust, she had only to see him engaged in some task and know the sheer goodness that seemed to shine through his being.

Weary of so many things in life, Ioni's heart was glad that he was there.

And he was there, standing in the doorway at the end of the great hall looking so lovely and comical, she thought, in the peasant clothes he wore each working day.

"I think I'm done for the day – my Lady!" he called to her. She had been sitting at the end of the banqueting table, lost in her own thoughts. Recently, he had taken to calling her 'My Lady!' in a kind of teasing fashion. "May I come in?"

"You may come in – Sir!" she replied, smiling down at him. "And you may call me Ioni, my first name – after all, we are equals by birth and rank!"

He looked at her for a long moment as he sat at the end of the table; her hair, her face and her long wine-red dress were caught in the evening light from the window. He removed his gloves and walked from the door, lifted a chair from his end of the table, threw himself onto it and turned his head towards her.

"Are you well, Ioni!" he asked, suddenly. She gazed down the length of the table at him. Somewhere inside herself she felt suddenly, a kind of weariness which surprised herself. Her eyes widened and she sighed.

"Am I well, Germaine?" she sighed again, some unsought cloud coming over her spirit. "Am I well? What a question!"

"What a question!" she repeated in a louder quivering voice. She looked at him again and he in turn was looking at her intently. She sighed again.

"A short time ago," she went on, "I was just a little girl – a little girl, Germaine. And sitting at this very table were my father, my mother, my brothers, cousins and all I ever loved. Such a short time ago, Germaine, I was a little girl – the darling of my family, surrounded by love and strength – and… and I miss them, and all that life now."

The tears were now welling in her eyes and she paused. Germaine was silent.

"Don't you ever think about things, Germaine?" she cried. "How… how is it that everything has changed? How is it that nothing is left? What is to become of us, Germaine?"

She paused again and let the tears flow down her face then bending her head forward and sobbing quietly into the palms of her hands. Germaine had worked long that day and felt a little weary himself, but seeing Ioni weeping there, he knew he was seeing part of her which he had not seen before. He did not move. Eventually she raised her head, more calm now and, recovering her loss of composure, spoke again.

"Everything is so fine for you. You can come and go, do as you please. You have no burden of responsibility – in fact, you are my responsibility. When you sit there," her voice trembled again, "when you sit there like you do now – do you know what I see, Germaine? I see the time when that table was surrounded by all I knew and loved – and now…"

"And now," he spoke for the first time, "there is only me, only you and me!"

"Yes!" she cried angrily, looking fiercely down at him.

"You wonder what has happened," he said, "to take everything away from you. Everything that was familiar and – beloved. What has happened that you are left with just me – a total stranger, sitting at your table."

"Yes!" she cried, suddenly realising that he seemed to understand. Amazed, too, that she had allowed herself to be so vulnerable in his presence.

"I don't know how this has happened, Ioni," he said. In his heart he wanted to run down to her, to pick her up like the wounded child she was now, to comfort her.

"I don't know," he said quietly, humble in the face of her grief. Briefly, it crossed his mind that he could easily fight in battle but could not, with such ease, comfort the manifest grief of this lovely girl. He could hear her breathe; her hands went to her face to wipe the tears away and to toss aside the hair that had fallen across her face. Still, he stayed where he was, not daring to tamper with this passionate grief.

"Sometimes, sometimes I wonder about it all – sometimes it all seems too much, too much to understand, too much…" Her voice trailed off again. She was silent for a moment and then turned to look at him.

"I want to know," she panted. "I want to know who in all this world decreed that I should lose so much of all that made me happy? Can you tell me, Germaine? Who decreed, for instance, that I should be left here alone, alone with you, this very evening?"

She was standing now and shaking her hands angrily.

"Why was it," she went on passionately, "that I should grow up so soon? I don't feel grown up, I feel like a child! I don't know if anything I am doing is right! God in Heaven! I don't know what I am doing from one moment to the next. And here I am, eighteen years of age, playing lady of the house, and not knowing what may happen next! I took all the risks for you – setting you free. If I have lost so much so far, what is there to hold you here, nothing! Not iron bars, not walls – you can escape at any time, anytime, it's as simple as that!"

She glared down at him, seated as he still was. In the evening, beyond the silence of the room, there were distant sounds, somewhere distant voices, somewhere the lowing of a cow, the barking of a dog, even the song of an evening blackbird.

Germaine gazed down at his hands and removed the ring from his finger tossing it bouncing bumpedy-bump down the length of the table towards her. Ioni jerked suddenly and caught the ring in the palm of her hand, her eyes wide with astonishment.

"Take it," he said steadily. "And hold it in your care. It is our family ring, my father's. Hold it; hold it as a token, Ioni. Let it be some kind of token of – shall we say – trust, between us."

She held the ring in her hands, looking down at it and looking up at him by turns.

"Please," he went on, "hold it, and if you can, then trust me. Yes. Hold it, Ioni, until someday all this war is over and we are free again – free to be ordinary people. Free to be the people we ought to have been in the first place, before all this happened."

He stood up and said, "Good night, Ioni." He turned and left her there to sit, for how many hours she did not know, until the light faded, until the darkness en-folded her and until, finally, Margreth arrived from the kitchen with the lamp.

Sometime in the mid-morning of the following day, he caught sight of her as he trudged from the stables, her form framed by the doorway. He looked again and she was looking at him. When their eyes met, she raised her hand in a little wave of greeting. He smiled and her face lit up with another smile. He stood at the bottom of the step, looking up at her.

"Forgive me for last night," she said to him. "I had not meant to burden you!"

"No burden!" he answered.

"I thank you, Germaine," she chirped. "What I had meant to say was, that we shall have some visitors, it seems. A prince of some kind from far away, with a retinue of knights. They are but two days away now. Will we be ready?"

"I think so," he answered. "We'll be ready!"

"I wonder," she continued. "So many people. How will we entertain them?"

"We'll think of something," he chuckled.

"Thank you, Germaine," she said warmly. "I must go now!"

*   *   *

Ioni was up early. In just another hour the maids and Margreth would be up to her room to formally dress her. She had long since dispensed with this practice, except for Sundays and special days, preferring to dress and undress on her own. Her life, she felt, had become too busy for niceties, such as being dressed each day, but this would be a special day, being the day on which the Spanish knights were expected.

She had also another reason to rise so early. She was not good with wearing what the maids might choose for her. In fact, clothes in general were a bit of a bother for her. Normally, she wore plain gowns of red or maroon, her favourite colours. On special occasions, however, Margreth or the maids chose what they deemed most suitable and, generally, their choices brought out the worst in Ioni.

"No!" Ioni had often shouted when one particular offering was prescribed – an old gown of Aunt Blanche's.

"What's wrong with it, Mistress?" Margreth would demand. "It's beautiful."

"I don't know," Ioni would cringe at the sight. "It has just got too much material. I will look like a ship under sail!"

"The cream dress?"

"No! I'll look like a goose!"

Headdress was another difficulty for Ioni; as she was now a young lady she was expected to don one of the fashionable headdresses of that time. She loved her long, dark-auburn hair; she usually placed a gold coloured band around her head, tying back the bulk of her hair in a net. That style keeps everything neat and simple, she thought.

Though she could just about tolerate a plain linen butterfly – she loathed the great steeple hennin, with its streamer ribbons flying from the top. If she had to wear them, then only the smallest butterfly or hennin would she wear. She was a tall girl and did not wish to appear any taller. The older fashioned headdress was her favourite which was the plain wimple and coif combination topped with a light veil, held in place by a little tiara. It formed her face beautifully and made her look like a nun, or like the Holy Virgin in paintings.

As for the dress she had already chosen it. The plain blue dress would be lovely, topped by the wimple and veil – and girded with a white slanting girdle. The bodice of the dress was close fitting enough and the skirt fell away in folds to the ground.

Later, when the maids would come, she would reject each item with a pout or a foot-stamp, until eventually, when the blue dress was presented, she would give it the most cautious, mock consideration. With sighs of mock exasperation, she would agree to be placed into it, and receive the maids' words of adulation with the most carefully contrived nonchalance.

"Huh!" she would gasp, "if I have to wear something, it might as well be this!"

However, if the soul had a mouth, then Ioni's soul would be grinning from ear to ear, happy to have won a woman's first battle of the day.

"Well," she said to Margreth, "let the sun shine fair on this day!"

"Amen to that," said Margreth.

*   *   *

Ioni permitted herself a glance down at the end of the hall – Germaine and the Spanish knights were deeply engrossed in conversation, at times very serious and at times there were bursts of boisterous manly laughter.

Men, thought Ioni, when they get together they talk of war, make fun of it, and lighten it all with laughter. As she gazed, she realised it was Germaine who was regaling the Spanish with humorous stories, and she realised that the Spanish had warmed to him and had taken a liking to him. Strangely too, all through the meal, Germaine had sat with little Anna by his side, was able to pause in conversation and address her too, teasing her from time to time about the handsome Spanish knights, and asking her which of them she fancied. Little Anna was well able for him, announcing to them all that she fancied only the prince, and would one day be married to him! This announcement was greeted with a loud cheer and much laughter.

What kind of man is he, Ioni pondered. He can entertain a band of foreign knights, never having met them before, and at the same time bring little six year old Anna into the conversation also.

"I have very good news for our guests and for our people here!" Ioni was standing now at the top of the table when the meal was over. "Our Spanish friends have agreed to give us a day of entertainment and jousting. It would be wonderful to have a day of celebration. We need some time to organise everything – shall we say, your Highness, in four days?"

"Four days it is, my Lady," the prince bowed to her.

Everybody cheered, Ioni was conscious of the fact that it had been some long time since cheers so loud had been heard in that great dining hall.

Though the days that followed were busy, they were days full of celebration too, the Spanish entertained the family every evening with music. Ioni joined them on the lute as did the other women too. The Spanish turned out to be excellent dancers, and the female cousins, aunts and Ioni herself found no shortage of partners as the musicians struck up notes of galliard or gavotte. It was indeed the merriest time in Valdelaine for many a long day. The prince gallantly danced with Ioni many times. But even in the merriest dance, and no matter who her dancing host was, her eyes always searched and found Germaine. He was usually in some corner, drinking wine and engaged conversational banter with the Spanish knights. On the first night, towards the end of the evening she accosted him between dances. Her cheeks glowed and her eyes sparkled as, quietly she called to him.

"Why are you not dancing, Germaine?"

"I am keeping an eye on things – making sure there's enough wine and sweetmeats," he answered.

"And can you do that, and entertain our guests at the same time?" her eyes sparkled and face glowed in excitement of the dance and in the light of the candles.

"So far I am doing quite well," he answered smiling.

She caught his smile in the candlelight and felt a glow of warmth and gratitude. A rock of strength, she thought.

"Besides, there are plenty of dancing partners for all you ladies. Now excuse me, I must see about more wine!" And he was gone.

Every day the men and women of the village came to help with the building of the pavilions, and the construction of the wooden gallery which would house and seat the spectators. In return, knights would entertain the villagers with feats of horsemanship and swordplay. They also enthralled the people with feats of wrestling, archery and spear throwing. To top off the display, they would engage in an extraordinary feat, never before witnessed by the people. Six of the biggest knights would link arms and form a circle, on top of this base five knights would climb up on their shoulders and stand erect linking arms; four more knights would then climb the growing human tower. At this stage the strongest village men were called on to come to the original six on the ground and press against them with all their strength supporting the base. Three knights then ascended linking arms at the top. These were then followed by two knights and people could now see how high the human tower was becoming. Finally, one knight climbed the human tower and, for just a moment, stood on the shoulders of the two below, balanced himself, and waved to the crowd. A cheer erupted from the crowd; they had never witnessed such an athletic feat. Immediately, the tower began to come down as the knight descended followed by the next two, all climbing down the backs of their companions, until one by one, all the human layers had come down, to terra firma again. Once again a great whoop of a cheer went up from the villagers.

Beer and wine were then distributed to one and all to wash down the mountains of oatbreads and meats which would be eaten by knights and villagers alike, signalling the end of the day's work and play.

During one such athletic performance Ioni found Germaine enthralled at the spectacle and she pulled at his sleeve.

"I've been looking for you all day," she said.

"What is it?"

"I want to know something," she said, comically reaching out her hands and turning his face towards her, away from his viewing of the human tower.

"What is it you want to know?" asked Germaine amused that her hands were still keeping his head towards her.

"I want to know, will you dance a step with me tonight?" she whispered. "I've never danced with you. I would like to."

"I suppose we could," he answered unenthusiastically. "But you have plenty to dance with you – handsome Spanish knights…"

"Listen you!" Ioni hissed in mock anger. "You will dance with me tonight, or else!!" Her eyes smiled at him, "…or else I may… think of something terrible to do to you!!"

Germaine gave her an amused look.

"You could have me locked in the dungeon again."

Ioni's face changed now to mock haughtiness.

"What a very good idea, Señor Germaine!"

"I'll do my best," Germaine said.

"Oh good!" chirped Ioni, happy that was settled.

"I'll do my best – to see if I can dance with you!" gulped Germaine.

Ioni gave a sigh of mock exasperation and her lovely eyes were glaring with mock anger.

"Germaine of Anlac, humour me in this, or the consequences will be..."

"Terrible," he interjected.

"Quite terrible, my Lord," she smiled.

They both smiled and she was gone.

She had an important errand to perform – that was to find out if the herald she had sent out this morning had returned. She had dispatched him at first light to ride to all the nearby villages, to proclaim a fair day in the castle grounds in three days, and to invite all to a spectacle of jousting – a tourney of Spanish knights. This would bring the people, with their produce of the soil and cattle and poultry, to sell. It would bring tinsmiths, blacksmiths and candle makers; it would bring hawkers, and alert travelling groups of players, musicians and, even, gypsy dancers.

The herald had not arrived back, in fact, he did not return until an hour before midnight. Ioni had already begun to retire for the day but she got word of his late return, pleased that he must have covered much ground in that one day.

The following evening, after the meal, the musicians began to play, and knights and ladies stepped across the floor of the hall to the rhythm of the tunes. Germaine sat in the corner with some of the knights but, by the third round of dances, he could feel Ioni's eyes upon him from across the hall, beckoning him to step forward. He gallantly rose to his feet and strode across to where Ioni stood.

"May I have the honour of this dance, my Lady," he asked of her, with a smile and twinkle in his eye.

"Most surely, my Lord," Ioni's eyes twinkled too. "Only on condition that you dance most superbly!"

"That, I shall endeavour to do, Lady," he answered.

The notes struck up and everyone took partners. Like a little army the dancers moved down the hall, with mincing steps, moving to the tune. Step by step, and pace for pace, one, two, three and a skip, one, two, three and skip, and so on. Ioni felt her hands in Germaine's, moving to the poetry of the movement and music, she smiled with exhilaration. Her sidelong glances found Germaine's eyes; they were smiling too, as he seemed to glide effortlessly with her down the hall, pausing at the end to allow her to trip to the music around him. He turned perfectly in time to take her hands again and begin the step all over again moving up the hall. Eyes and glances met again in the glowing candlelight and Ioni felt a thrill of excitement run through her, a sheer and simple happiness at moving so gracefully, with Germaine at her side. Up and down the hall they went, and it seemed to last forever, the delight and the movement. Such happiness welled up in her, she felt as though she and Germaine were the only two people there, all the other dancers quite forgotten, they seemed to be sailing on the very air. Gradually the music slowed and stopped but, for Ioni, as she stood facing him on the crowded floor, it seemed they were both still sailing – together. For a long moment, she was breathing deeply and gazing at him, her eyes calm, but her heart racing. The words "Thank you, my Lord!" which came from her lips were paltry compared to the sheer affectionate love she felt for him.

"Thank you, Germaine," she breathed. "You dance – shall we say, most superbly!"

"Thank you, my Lady," smiled Germaine. "So do you!"

"Come, Germaine, let's sit awhile," Ioni said leading him to some empty chairs at the top of the hall near the fireplace.

They sat in silence for some moments, while the next dance was called. Their eyes met and they both knew they would not dance again together that night. So far, their friendship was a matter of short chance meetings, amid hectic days. They both understood that this friendship must always be kept, somehow, under discreet wraps. Ioni was the mistress of the house; Germaine was the prisoner guest. She desperately wanted to dance again with him.

"Would you dance with me again?" she asked.

"I doubt it," he answered, knowing that if they were seen too much together, if they were both observed in unabashed enjoyment of each other's company, people would suspect there was more between them than met the eye. This would compromise her and there would be demands for his imprisonment to be more confining.

"Why not," she smiled gravely.

"We both know why not," he answered.

Yes, thought Ioni, her fondness for Germaine could never be known. She loved being in his company, but God! It was so difficult to be so fond – and never be able to express it. But she was getting good at keeping her feelings a secret and hidden away from everybody – but, it was difficult.

*   *   *

"You wished to see me?" Ioni raised her head from the embroidery frame. Embroidery was a rare pleasure for her these days.

"Yes! Ioni," said Germaine, almost out of breath. He had run the spiral staircase, two steps at a time.

"On what business?" she said, coolly appraising her work.

"Well, Ioni, it is the tourney, the jousts," Germaine said eagerly.

"What of the tourney, Germaine?" Ioni bent forward to examine closely her last stitches.

"Why, I'm to take part in the tourney!" Germaine chirped. "But I thought I'd better ask you first."

Ioni's eyes appeared over the top of the frame.

"Ask me, is it?" she said coolly. "Do you think it wise to take part? And suppose I refuse you permission to take part?"

"But, Ioni," Germaine went on, "the knights expect me to take part, even the prince…"

"Oh, the prince, the prince," cooed Ioni, holding some green thread up to the light. "It is all the prince with you, these days. I swear, to look at the two of you together, one would think you were brothers in arms from the very cradle!"

"He is a magnificent gentleman," Germaine chimed in.

"And I'm glad you like him!"

Ioni stood up once more from the frame, her wimpled face now staring coldly at him. It was a mock coldness though; inwardly she was in a giddy mood.

"If I could stop you taking part in the tourney, I probably would. You are a prisoner here – and besides I could not bear it if you were injured," she said, her eyes momentarily widening to emphasise some of her words. Germaine was at his full height, looking at her, as he said,

"I won't be injured, Ioni. And I know what I'm doing."

"Yes?" said Ioni. She sighed. There was a long pause.

"I will need my armour!" Germaine blurted.

Ioni's head was bent close to the embroidery again. She was in fact hiding her grinning face. Germaine could not see her.

"And why will you need armour, my Lord!" came the unbelievable question from behind the frame. Germaine stifled a laugh.

"I cannot fight a tourney, my Lady," he answered, "without my armour and weapons – any more than you could embroider a beautiful picture, without... threads and needles."

Ioni's veil and eyes appeared over the frame again. "My! Thank Heaven you will be using only wooden swords. Otherwise I fear you might suffer some grievous injury." They were looking at each other, eyes full of humour.

"The swords we use are not wooden, my Lady" Germaine said. "They are bone of whale!"

"Bone of whale or bone of spider, it matters not if you are hurt! You may count it comical," she said. "But spare a thought for lesser mortals than yourself; I shall be, shall we say, less than happy if anything ill befalls you. I have you in my care – in the care of my – heart!"

Ioni took a sharp intake of breath. They both looked at each other a moment, searching each other's eyes. Ioni spoke to cover her little blunder.

"Naturally, after all this time my Lord, I should grieve if you were hurt!" she said. "But, of course, maybe

I should not care at all. There now! Maybe I shall be just as happy to see you threshed to pieces by the prince or one of his men!"

Germaine smiled – for the first time since he had known her, Ioni had mentioned her heart and himself, in the one breath.

He paused, and said, "I shall take great care, then!"

And amused he added, "Care of yourself and care of your heart!"

The eyes that met Germaine were no longer eyes but veritable daggers that glared at him from beneath her brow. Slowly the daggers went back to her embroidery.

"The casket with your things will be outside your door in the morning," she said solemnly.

"Oh, thanks Ioni," chirped Germaine. "You know, I long to wear that armour again after all this time!"

Ioni looked at him a long time and then, smiled gently at him.

"I think even I too, will be glad," she said, "to see you in armour – remember, I have never seen you in armour, in all this time!"

Germaine was smiling broadly, so boyish, she thought. "I take my leave of you then!" he said and turned to the door. She smiled after him.

"You will be careful!" she called after him.

He turned and was about to speak, but his forehead frowned as though there was something he could not explain to her. She will see for herself! He thought.

"I will," he called. "I will be careful!"

*   *   *

With all the womenfolk and children, Ioni stepped out of the hall and into the sunlight. Cousin Eleanor was to her right, and Aunt Blanche was on her left, as they descended the stone steps. Ioni had spotted the little group of knights, chatting in the shadows of the archway, but she took little notice, Eleanor was chatting away unceasingly. And then, Oh God above! She saw him! He had stepped into the sunlight – there he was, one hand on the hilt of his sword, his helmet in his other arm as he chatted away to the others. He looked magnificent. Try as she might, Ioni could not look away, though she kept pace with the others, who were now calling and waving to him. He turned and waved back. He was smiling, the head mail thrown behind his neck like a monk's cowl, the imprint of his magnificent arms and legs showing through the heavy chain mail. From below his neck to down almost to his feet, the bright red and blue of the surcoat, edged in gold at the neck, hem and sleeves. The helmet in his arms crowned in red and blue plume. Glancing sidelong as she walked, Ioni recalled that night long ago when first she had set eyes on that armour. The night she had first wondered what manner of man might wear such things. And now she knew, now she was gazing at him as she passed, she was gazing at the armour and the man. He had come into her life that far off night as a prisoner taken in the wars. And now, she thought, how beautiful he was. The cortege of women passed out on the lawns, Eleanor was still chattering.

"Ioni," she exclaimed. "Your face is quite red!"

"Don't be silly, Eleanor!" chided Ioni. "My face is always red when I walk in the sunlight!"

As head of the household, Ioni was seated in the centre with her female cousins and her aunts around her. On either side of this womanly cluster sat her uncles and other men of importance. The canopy overhead flittered in the light breeze. A mighty roar erupted from the crowd, as the prince and knights, mounted, made their appearance, riding three or four abreast. They were a marvellous spectacle, as they rode into the arena. Lances and armour shone in the sunlight and their surcoats and horse covers made a colourful show. Many of them wore red and yellow, but some wore black, pale blue and other colours. The prince was in red and yellow and another great roar went up as he lowered the long lance towards Ioni, who gracefully placed her maroon scarf upon the lance. Deftly the prince raised the lance again and caught Ioni's scarf, riding onwards to place it in his helmet. The other knights followed and the other ladies followed Ioni's example placing the coloured scarves upon each outstretched lance.

Amid all the excitement Ioni was now seated again, she looked quickly beyond at the prince, and saw her scarf proudly billowing from atop his helmet. But immediately, she cast her eyes in the other direction from where Germaine was approaching. She pulled her veil against her face, against an imaginary breeze, and her eyes feasted sidelong on him as he approached. God! He looked so wonderful, she thought, her heart beating. With all the ease in the world Germaine wheeled in his horse, lowered his lance deftly until it found Ioni's little cousin Anna. "Germaine!" Anna cheered loudly, as she clambered forward and tied a gold coloured piece of cloth to the point of the lance; there was laughter, and a good humoured cheer from the crowd and Germaine spurred forward. Ioni laughed too, relieved of the spell which the sight of Germaine had placed on her. Everyone then sat back comfortably to wait for the first joust to be announced.

Presently, the fanfare was blown and the crowd grew silent, as the lists were called. The entire number of knights was twenty six and included the Spanish lords, Germaine, and five knights of the Valdelaine household. There was an excited hush as the first pair of knights charged, gradually lowering the long lances towards each other until they clashed midway down the fence. There were gasps and cheers as both riders smashed their lances but managed to remain in their saddles. Cheers went up again as both men swung their horses about and charged at each other again, this time swinging their swords. One knight was unhorsed in the impact and the other dismounted to continue the duel on foot, at which they fought fiercely for some time until one was forced to yield. And so, the jousts went on, to the merriment of the crowd, who were enjoying every moment of the spectacle. Ioni, seated in the pavilion with the womenfolk, was beginning to relax and enjoy the entertainment, but she tensed again somewhat when Germaine's name was called. She permitted herself a glance upfield to the right to catch a glimpse of him, astride the horse and resplendent, as the afternoon sun glinted on his armour. Another glance and Germaine was drawing down the visor of his helmet, covering his face. Ioni clasped her hands tightly together upon her lap. 'Oh God!' she thought, 'I hope all will be well with him!' The shout to change was given, and she looked sidelong upward again. Great God! From the moment of the spur, Germaine's mount seemed in full gallop, thundering down the field; horse and knight were like some awesome dragon bearing down on its quarry. She shut her eyes at the last moment, and her heart pounded, as she heard the crash of arms. The crowd gasped, and someone shouted "Germaine is down!" Before she could open her eyes another shouted "They're both down!" She opened her eyes to see Germaine rise, reach for his sword and, like a flash, he was vaulting over the fence and bearing down on his opponent who had not even time to rise before Germaine's sword was pointing at his throat. Ioni was relieved for Germaine's victory, but was also in awe of him, as she was sure she had never seen a jousting knight ride so fast, nor move with such effortless speed. The crowd cheered him again, now, as, with one arm he was lifting up his defeated opponent to his feet.

And so the joust went on, and again, Germaine thrilled the beholders there with such skill and speed, as they had never witnessed before. Time and again he was cheered by the crowd and, time and again the Spanish knights went to congratulate him with outstretched hands and embraces. As the afternoon passed on, Ioni pondered and realised, as never before, why Germaine had become the hero of his country. It was happening before her very eyes – there were many feats of bravery that day, but none were so daring, nor as lightning quick, as the actions of Germaine. Whether mounted or unhorsed, he moved and fought like a man on fire.

The Spanish prince acquitted himself splendidly that afternoon also, and outclassed every opponent until finally the lists called upon the prince and upon Germaine to enter against each other. It was certain to be a fitting climax to an afternoon of wonderful skill and entertainment. The sight was indeed magnificent. At one end, Germaine in blue and red, struggled to steady his excited charger. At the other end the prince in black armour and in the surcoat with its red and yellow stripes, calmly waited for the charge to be called. Visors were lowered, the shout was given, and Germaine and the prince were launched into a full blown thundering attack towards each other. There was almost symmetry as their lances came down together, pointed straight at each other; and on they rode, their speed increasing with every stride until finally they clashed with a hideous noise. Both lances snapped with a crack, and shot upward. The prince's horse reared and screamed while Germaine's mount stumbled and careered forward, crashing into the ground, sending Germaine somersaulting outward until he, too, hit the soft ground with a dull thud. The prince struggled to bring his mount about, and drew his sword, but Germaine did not move from where he had fallen, face downward. Ioni, as she watched, clasped her palms to her face in shock, she could not bear to look. His mount now under control, the prince trotted down his side of the fence, coming to a stop opposite where Germaine had fallen. He raised his visor, and dismounted and bent under the plank of the fence. He knelt down on one knee over his fallen adversary.

Gently, he took Germaine's shoulders and turned him face upwards, lifted his visor and felt for a pulse at his throat. By now a small crowd of men had joined him.

"Bring water!" shouted the prince. "He's stunned, but alive!" And the prince's words ran through the throng, finally reaching Ioni's ears, where she sat with one hand over her eyes. "Thank God!" she whispered to herself. The prince was removing Germaine's helmet, as the crowd now milled about, and he began emptying the contents of a water pail over Germaine's face. The splash of cool water was enough; Germaine opened his eyes, and blinked.

"Ah! Good!" the prince smiled down at him. "You are alive, Germaine, by the grace of God!"

"And you, Prince," he said, "by the grace of God – are dangerous!"

The prince laughed heartily, and with one arm, pulled Germaine to his feet.

Once the crowds were ushered back to their place and the field was cleared, the knights called for the traditional melee as an end to the proceedings of the afternoon. Ioni, watching from the pavilion, had had enough excitement for one day. She moved down the aisle of benches to where Uncle Raymond sat, and asked him if she could prevent Germaine taking part in any further horseplay. Raymond replied by drawing Ioni's attention, across the green, to where Germaine and the prince were absorbed in conversation. The prince was calling for a lance and, having obtained it, handed it to Germaine who took it in his left hand. When Germaine transferred the weapon to his right hand, he was unable to grasp it as his fingers, in the mailed gauntlet, refused to close around the handle; and so, the tip of the lance fell to the ground. The prince then drew his sword, and handed it to Germaine, who failed to hold that weapon either. Finally, the prince removed Germaine's gauntlet, and this revealed a wrist swollen largely, sprained, or broken outright. In vain, Germaine struggled to force his fingers to move, but they would not. Germaine looked at the prince and said,

"I'll have to be content, and use my left hand for the melee!"

But the prince was adamant Germaine should not do so.

"Nay, Germaine!" he said. "You have fought well enough for one day. Your hand needs rest now. Do you recall how it happened?"

Germaine shook his head ruefully, now holding the damaged limb in his left forearm.

"It may have happened," Germaine said tensely, "when my lance shot upward after our impact."

"Well then, my friend:" the prince said, "go now, and see that it is attended to. There is no disgrace in leaving the field. Today you have earned much honour. Go now, I entreat you!"

With heavy heart, and sore wrist, Germaine ambled down to the enclosure, behind the pavilions, the reins of his horse trailing over his shoulder. As he was about to disappear from view, a loud cheer went up from all present. He stopped for a moment, turned, and bowed to the crowd, then he continued on out of view, his horse plodding behind him.

"Broken wrist, I think," Uncle Raymond said to Ioni.

"Very well then," Ioni said. "I must go to him, as soon as the final melee is over and done with."

Three days later, the Spanish knights were ready to depart. In the morning, there had been a flurry of farewells – from the men of the household strong hearty goodbyes, from the women promises of kindly remembrance, from the girls there had been not a few stolen kisses. Ioni bade farewell to the prince in private, she curtseyed low before him and he, in turn, gently took her hand and kissed it. Shortly after, the courtyard was thronged to see the knights kneel for Frère Benedict's blessing. Then there was the sound of hoof beats on the cobblestones as the cavalcade made its way under the portcullis and through the gateway. As the excitement died down and people went about their tasks, Ioni, who stood with Fleur, Eleanor and Clara, began to look about for Germaine – but there was no sign of him, neither in the courtyard nor the bawn. She frowned and asked the girls to accompany her down to the portcullis. From there she was most surprised to see him way below, standing in the middle of the bridge staring down river, seemingly lost in his own thoughts.

"Perhaps he is missing them already," said Eleanor.

"Perhaps he is wishing he could be going with them," said Fleur. "Back to warlike ways!"

"Let's go down and capture him," said Eleanor. "And bring him back from whatever his thoughts may be."

Ioni sighed, "No, cousins, let me go to him alone, if you please. It is my wish."

The girls looked at each other a little surprised, a little amused, and turned back, allowing Ioni to descend the causeway to the bridge and have her own private moment with Germaine.

"You seem lost!" Ioni said as she stepped onto the bridge.

Suddenly he was shaken out of his reverie by the sight of her there. He was surprised but happy to see her there at all.

"Come," she said kindly. "Walk with me a while."

He obeyed and they began to stroll together parallel to the riverbank.

"Your wrist," she said. "Does it feel better?"

"Much better, my Lady, I must have good healing strength."

"Tush!" she chuckled. "You had the most excellent care Valdelaine could give you!"

Seated upon the stone, Ioni looked at Germaine with slightly smiling eyes. No matter how she tried to deal with it, the same old curiosity seemed to well up inside her. What did Germaine really think of it all, she wondered; could he ever be really truthful about his innermost feelings, given that there was no escaping the fact that, at best, he was a prisoner here, and not even a guest. How could he say anything genuine about anything when he was in captivity here. And I am his gaoler, Ioni thought.

"What do you think of us?" she said.

"What do I think of who?" he said, puzzled and turning to look at her eye to eye.

"What do you make of us? Valdelaines!" she said, head a little to one side and looking at him with a smiling, curious look.

"Oh!" he said, comprehending, and looked away for some time. "Well, you are all certainly very interesting, I'll say that."

"Interesting! Is that all you can say about us!" exclaimed Ioni with a little pout and a roll of the eyes on high. Germaine frowned thoughtfully.

"Well, how shall I say? You are not what I expected."

"Oh!" said Ioni with mock hauteur. "And pray, tell me, my Lord, what did you expect of us then?"

"I really thought I would be given a bad time here." Germaine said. "I never expected any kindness or favour, and that's true. But now, well, it's like being part of the family. You know, you Valdelaines are high nobility, but you are warm and welcoming. There's not a day goes by that there's not laughter, and plenty of it!"

Ioni gazed at him, her face expressionless.

"Do you look down on us?"

"Good God in Heaven, no!" he exclaimed and then said gently, "No!"

Ioni gave him one of her simpers. Again she gazed at him.

"We are good friends, Germaine, are we not?" she said.

"Good friends we are, Ioni," he answered.

"That is good then!" she said, standing up and pushing her hair back and tossing her head. Germaine felt a little more reassurance was needed and he said,

"No! You are good people with a lot of special traits. Certainly I am thankful that I am here, and not a prisoner somewhere else. You yourself, and all the Valdelaines have made life very good for me here, beyond anything I might hope for."

"Let us walk, together, a little," said Ioni, joining her hands and stepping forward ahead of him. "Tell me then, what do you like about us?" she said, as they began to walk.

"Well, many things," said Germaine, as a boy does, who is searching for the correct words in response to a girl's questions. "As I said, you are warm hearted, and you laugh a great deal. Many a noble house there is where laughter is never heard, and where only an atmosphere of grimness prevails. So I have been lucky to be here!" Ioni was thinking for a while about what he said and then finally stopped in her tracks, and with one foot placed in front of the other, looked up at him, her great eyes full of magical mischief.

"You think we're funny, then, I take it," she said, blinking her eyes and adding "My Lord!"

Germaine stopped with her and sighed. How to pay a compliment, he thought, a compliment that could be found fault free! Before he could speak Ioni went on,

"While you're gathering your thoughts on that subject," Ioni said, looking again at him, from under her eyelashes, "yes, I suppose, to you, we must seem funny, rather like the actors in one of the comical mystery plays that sometimes come to the village. Is that the way we are?"

Germaine took a deep breath, rubbed his forehead and eyes with his hand. Yes, he thought, Ioni herself could be so funny, especially when she started a conversation so seriously and yet could, in her expressions, dart here or there for the fun of it! She was challenging him by gentle teasing. He could think of no more to say, he turned towards her, stood to his full height, heaved a sigh, and said,

"Mistress of Valdelaine!"

The head went sideways, her great eyes looked up with admirable innocence.

"My Lord?" the eyes blinked.

"I lose my thoughts and words," he said.

"Why, indeed you do, my Lord," she said in mock reassurance. And then with a frown of mock seriousness she added, "I do find it exceeding strange that you think us funny, my Lord."

And Germaine finally laughed.

Ioni pursed her lips a moment to keep her face straight.

"And now, forgive me, my Lord," she said, "but with so much to do I cannot stay all day speaking idly with you. Pray excuse me."

*   *   *

"My Lord!" Ioni exclaimed, as Germaine's frame appeared in the doorway of the embroidery chamber.

"I thought you might be here," he said, still at the doorway. "I just wished to bid you good evening. I am retiring now!" Ioni's face smiled, the mouth and also the eyes. She was inwardly pleased at his routine of coming to see her when he wanted to do something.

"That is good of you, my Lord," she said, standing up. She enjoyed the earnestness of his manner.

"You wish to bid me 'good evening,' but not just yet I pray you. Stay a while and speak to me!"

Germaine stepped into the chamber and stood facing Ioni near the fire. "Speak to you, Lady?" Germaine glanced at her. "Pray, about what, my Lady?"

Ioni pursed her lips and frowned a little and then said, "Yes, you may speak about anything at all," she said, lifting off her veil and tossing her hair back.

"Yes, you choose the subject, my Lord!"

Germaine took a breath and then clapped his hand to his mouth to suppress a laugh. Lately he had begun to recognise this manner of Ioni's as a prelude to humorously teasing banter that he could never win, let alone stay serious for long. However he liked her for it and was thankful for the trust that humour brings. Ioni was lighting some more candles but eventually, she looked back at him over her shoulder.

"You haven't said anything yet that I can disagree with, my Lord!" she said with reproving seriousness.

"I haven't said anything at all, Lady," he said biting his lip to prevent his laughter and looking away toward the window. Then he turned to face her and said,

"Now that I can think of it I do have a question to ask if I may!"

"Pray, ask it, my Lord," said Ioni coolly, "and if it is within my power to answer I shall do so."

"Some time ago," he went on, "you asked me what I thought of you Valdelaines. What I wished to ask was – what do you think of me?"

Ioni's eyes were cool and wide, almost unblinking as she looked at him first and then sideways at the fireplace.

"Well, little Cousin Anna thinks you are wonderful, something out of a romantic fairy tale." Ioni paused and then went on, "All the girls like you, and even Aunt Blanche is not exactly immune to your charm – whatever that happens to be, I'm not quite sure, my Lord!"

Germaine was now smiling at her.

"What I really meant was 'What do you, Lady Valdelaine, think of me'!"

Ioni breathed, looked sideways again and said, "From what one can observe, my Lord, to outward appearance, you seem to be – shall we say – good!"

"Good!" repeated Germaine.

"Yes, good!" repeated Ioni, "Though what is inside your heart one cannot know. But I hope you are as good in your heart as you are in your outward demeanour! Beyond that, I don't think I can say." And she was looking straight at him, eyes unmoving.

He was silent and thoughtful.

"Well, I suppose 'good' is something," he said slowly, "and a long way better than 'bad' or 'evil'. Which, as you will remember, was the reputation I brought with me to this place."

"I don't think of you as evil, Germaine," she said. "I don't think of you as bad neither!"

He was silent for a time and then smiled gently.

"Thank you. I am glad."

"I think that you have, shall we say, earned good trust of me."

His heart warmed to hear these words; he was touched by them and said eventually,

"Those words, well, they mean a great deal to me."

The chamber was silent save for the crackling of a log in the fire, which was, with the candles, gaining strength of light as the darkness was falling outside.

"Good evening then, Germaine," she said, "and a peaceful night to you." He stole one last glance at her standing in the firelight as he strode towards the door and bade her good night.

Chapter XI: Golden Hair

*O*f all the strange encounters of those years, and there were many, none was more strange and unexpected than that which took place between Baron Gavron de Laude and Countess Beatrice of Norland. Early spring sunshine illumined the great field where the territories of Bergmond and Norland met. Ranged to the north were a hundred of the countess' knights, to the south an equal number of the Raven League. In midfield stood a long table and on a given signal the two parties approached and were seated, Gavron and his advisers on one side, the countess and her aides on the other.

"Well now, Countess," Gavron's voice rumbled on the still air. "We finally meet again."

"We do indeed, Baron, after all these years," she said, keeping her eyes straight on him, a faint smile on her lips.

"The years have been good to you, Lady Erkindhal. You look as beautiful as ever. I had expected you to age – but you haven't, Madam! No!"

"Thank you, my Lord. But we are not here to trade compliments – we are here for another kind of barter, are we not?"

Gavron smiled a rear smile, looked around at his companions and nodded his head.

"That is well put, my Lady," he said. "Barter it is indeed. Let us come to the point straight away then. You, my Lady, have this young man. And of course, we want him – and want him ransomed home to Esmor. Pray let me caution you, Countess, yes caution you, to be modest in the price you ask for him. As you know well, we are at war."

She was still eyeing him firmly across the table and nodded her head a little at each point of his little speech. How close we are, she reflected, only the thrust of a dagger apart, we could kill each other at this distance, except for the fact that we are, by protocol, unarmed. She shook herself free of her thoughts and concentrated anew on his words.

"There is a costly war," he was saying, "and the coffers of the state are not quite as full as they might be. There can only be so much worth this Valdelaine youth can have for you. I must impress on you, Countess, there are limits to our monies…"

"My Lord," she interrupted quietly, "I want none of Bergmond, its monies nor its coffers. In truth, golden coins are not in the price which I am about to ask."

Gavron stopped in his tracks and his facial expression morphed several times from amazement to puzzlement and finally ended in a scowl. He looked at his aides on either side, they only shrugged in equal puzzlement and looked back at the countess.

"Not money, Countess, not money?" Gavron growled suspiciously. "What else is there to barter with?"

"Documents, my Lord," Beatrice said evenly. "Valuable documents, valuable to me, that is."

The scowl of Gavron's face deepened, if that were possible as his brain filled even more with suspicion. He studied her for a moment then he released an exasperated gasp and said, "What do you want then?" His eyes narrowing as he searched her face for meaning.

"I want only what is mine, only what was taken from me a long time ago."

Again his eyes narrowed. "Meaning?" he bellowed.

The countess shifted a little on her seat and placing her chin in one hand, she looked away and began drumming the surface of the table with the fingers of the other hand. After a long pause she said,

"There is the matter of my title, I want the full reinstatement of my title in writing – from the king himself!"

There was silence from the Bergmond delegation seated along the table and staring at the countess with surprise. The only sound was the morning breeze among distant trees. Gavron sat back in his chair, sighed, and gave himself a moment for her words to sink in.

"That, Lady Erkindhal, is an entirely different matter. You are and you have been, for the past fifteen years an outlaw to the state –"

"The title, Baron," she interrupted, "and all the documents of restoration of all my Norland estates."

Gavron paused for thought, this was a sting indeed. Money was only money, but the title of the countess was political and possibly dangerous to him, if her demands were conceded.

"Say for a moment, this title is restored – you will be obliged in loyalty to Bergmond – and to Bergmond only – obliged not to give succour to the enemies of Bergmond."

"I have given none till now and I do not wish to do so in the future. As you know well, I had to take pains to prize Alorin from Count Michael and drive his troops from Norland. And will do so again if need be."

"Countess, permit us to withdraw for a while that we may consider this…"

"No, Baron, do not withdraw, for there is more for you to consider – from the Archbishop of Bergmond, in writing, a full revocation of the declaration of witchcraft against me. If the archbishop will not do it, then write to the pope for it. Either way I will have it or you will not have Eris de Valdelaine!"

"These revocations which you demand, they will take some time to arrange, weeks, maybe months…"

"Do not worry, Lord Gavron, I can wait for I am in no hurry. Besides, the youth you seek is strong and well, and he is not likely to fade away to nothing."

As the meeting broke up to give time for consideration to both sides, the countess stood up and left the table; she took to walking up and down with her advisers, her arms folded about her. Gavron remained at the table pondering. The revocations would cost nothing, mere documents – this was good. But even better from Gavron's point of view, though fatal for the countess, the documents of reinstatement would mean nothing. Once we had Eris, the life of Beatrice d'Erkindhal would count for nothing, once Gavron's plans for eliminating her came to their grisly fruition. He would have Eris – by whom he would ransom Germaine home and he would have Norland in his grasp for all time.

With that he called for the meeting to resume. He then indicated to the countess that he would accept her demands – it would not take the scribes long to draft copies of their agreement. As they did so Gavron pressed a question to the countess.

"Will you accept the Raven League in your newly restored dominions?" To which the countess answered,

"The men of Norland do not hold with the league, Grand Master, nor could I force them to do so!"

"Very well then, let us agree that we have a bargain as it is."

Soon the papers were ready and Gavron and the countess duly signed them.

"It may be some months, Countess," Gavron left the table with his papers tucked into a satchel. At long last there was peace between Bergmond and Norland and all she had lost years ago would be restored to the countess. Gavron would have the means to exchange prisoners and bring Germaine home to fight once more by his side. By so doing he would have the speedy end to the war with Esmor to this own satisfaction.

Of little importance in the great scheme of things, or so it might seem, was the fact that messengers were despatched to all quarters with the news of the day's doings. One messenger alone, of all the others, would carry the news to a destination which would change everything. The news would have to reach Germaine far off in Valdelaine, alerting him to his impending freedom. How little could anyone have known that evening, as the despatch rider galloped eastward towards Esmor, the far reaching consequences of this news. How it would burst in upon the life of Germaine, on the life of Ioni, on subsequent events! Within a week or so the letters would arrive at Valdelaine, one for Germaine, one for Ioni. They would read – and their lives would change forever.

The countess and her troops set out northwards to Alorin, from there she would travel on to Broude, there to await the word that all the documents of restoration were signed and ready to be handed over in exchange for her 'golden boy' Eris. Gavron and his troops set off southward and back to the business of war.

*   *   *

By now the eldest daughter of the countess, the Lady Catherine had been possessed of a great affection for Eris. They were now in the habit of meeting each other at secret trysting places. Eris had been greatly taken with the young lady and, more and more, was enjoying the pleasure of her company. By now the tête-à-têtes were not mere conversation pieces, they had passed that stage and were wont to share a kiss and an embrace.

"Oh Eris," the lady was saying at their most recent tryst. "You're kisses are delightful – they are as sweet as honey!"

"That's interesting," said Eris. "I partook of some honey for my breakfast!"

Lady Catherine giggled and said, "Do be serious, Eris, I was speaking of the honey of love!" and gently she slapped his hand.

"Love?" queried Eris, "I love love, don't you?"

"Of course, silly boy. But we have to be careful not to be seen together. If Mama found out I'd be locked away in my room!"

"So would I!" Eris quipped. "And not for the first time either. I assure you, Catherine, I love being with you and maybe someday I'll be free again and I'll come back to you and we can be together all the time."

Catherine looked at him with raised eyebrows.

"Not so fast, Eris. Be real, the future is a long way off – anyway I doubt mother would marry me off to a stranger – even to a very handsome stranger, I grant you," she sighed. "I'll probably be married off to some Norland chief – then where would you be?"

"Well let's enjoy what we have now," and Eris swept her up in his arms and kissed her."

"As good as honey?" he asked when they were unclasped.

"Better!" she laughed. "Much better."

"When you are married off to some Norland chief I shall come back in shining armour to rescue you!"

"Very well then, Eris," she chuckled. "You go ahead and do that – I shall be waiting impatiently!"

When Catherine was gone Eris had some weightier things to think of. He roused himself at once and went down to meet the two dwarves, Janus and Sastro, if he could find them. Ever since he had read the awesome contents of Gavron's letter to Maiklin, he had been at pains to think of some way to get into the secretary's chamber unseen, and search, and hopefully find further proof of Maiklin's complicity and double dealing with Gavron de Laude. The latter had been the most implacable foe of the countess for nearly a generation now. The question for Eris was to find out more, and thus to find if the life of the countess was truly in danger as he feared it might, especially when he, Eris, would be handed over to Gavron's troop for ransom. He knew he needed help from some quarter to effect the plans he had in mind. But where to find that help in a castle full of intrigue and maybe treachery. Finally he had settled on seeking help from a most unlikely quarter, the dwarf jesters Janus and Sastro. If he could persuade them of the countess' danger, then they would surely help.

"Greetings, Goldenhair," Janus said as Eris approached them, comfortably ensconced, as they were, by the fire in the main hall. Fortunately there was no one else about. Eris sat on a stool before the fire and looked from one to another.

"What can we do for you, then," Sastro asked.

Eris sighed and said, "I need your help."

"He needs our help," the two said in unison shrugging and then giggling.

Janus spoke. "Well, Goldenhair, we serve the rena by making her merry with jokes, jests and japes and acrobatic tricks as well, but the rena does not pay us to do so – if we have to make you laugh, then you must pay!" And together they giggled. "And pay well too, Goldenhair, for I do declare you look right morose this morning!" And more laughter followed from the two merry dwarves.

"I need your help to do something – something important for the countess – but it has to be secret – just between the three of us! Can you keep a secret? Can I ask you to swear to secrecy before I tell you what I want?"

They looked at him in silence for a moment. "We only swear oaths to the rena," Janus said, "and to magistrates of course! But I doubt if I could, say, besmirch my very fine conscience by swearing an oath to a mere squire like you!"

"Me neither," Sastro interjected. "Mine is shall we say, a conscience by far too fragile for an oath of secrecy!"

Eris looked away, took a deep breath of exasperation and said, "When I am gone from here and ransomed home, the very life of the rena, the very safety of Norland may be in grave danger. I have very strong reasons to be-

lieve this – and so I had best leave you to your fine consciences – especially if the enemies of the countess are
successful in destroying her and Norland together. See
how you feel then when your combined consciences hin-
dered you from saving her!"

The two little bearded men looked at each other
and raised their eyebrows quizzically and in unison.

"I see!" they both said together. "What makes you
think the rena is in danger?"

Eris eyed the two of them sternly and said, "I will
give you near enough to proof – but you must give me
promise of secrecy."

"Very well, I give you my word," Janus said.
"You seem to be serious about whatever is bothering
you."

"I give you my word," said Sastro. "But why
come to us with this mystery? Why did you not go to
someone in authority – even to the rena herself, if you
have suspicions of her being in danger!"

Eris sighed. "I am an outsider here and who could
I trust? As for the rena I did not wish to alarm her now
because she is not in danger yet. But I tell you, she will
be in danger when I am gone!"

The dwarfs looked at him seriously.

"Very well then," said Janus. "Tell us how we can
help you. But first show us your proof of all this."

"Very well then," said Eris, taking a chair and sitting with them. He took from his doublet the letter of
Gavron de Laude to Lord Maiklin. He explained how he
knew who it was from and then in whispers began to
translate its text for them. He read the dreaded line concerning the 'disposal of the countess' at some stage after
the 'puer Valdelensis' was safely handed over in ransom.

His two diminutive hearers were shocked, gone was their frivolous giggling.

"The letter from Gavron, the countess' arch foe, was addressed to – Lord Maiklin... our own Lord Maiklin, a favourite of the countess."

The two were silent a long time and then Janus said, "What do you want us to do?"

"A feat of daring!" Eris smiled.

Eris reached into his doublet and produced the letter showing them first the seal of Gavron de Laude, then proceeding in a low voice to read the letter to the two dwarves, translating each sentence as he went along. When he finished, his two companions were looking at him though neither said a word.

"You see what it means," said Eris. "Lord Maiklin is corresponding directly with the enemy of the countess. Surely he does this without the countess' knowledge?"

"True!" said Janus. "The countess writes all her own correspondence. Her secretary of course advises her on some matters, but in the end she writes her own letters."

"You are sure about this?" Eris asked.

"Quite sure!" both of them said in unison.

"Well it may be that Maiklin is betraying the countess all the time. And he is keeping Gavron well informed of all that passes here in Broude. Methinks the countess is in danger, my friends."

"True," said Janus. "It would appear so."

"Think about it," Eris continued. "It means that Gavron has not forgotten that the countess has bested him all these years. And it means that Gavron has some designs on the countess and on Norland. At any rate, while I am still in Norland the countess is safe – but when I am ransomed, the countess is in danger from a traitor in her own house. You heard the reference to myself, the 'Valdelaine boy'. You heard the words which followed. After the boy is restored to us – 'it will be time to find a way to dispose of the countess and bring Norland finally into our control.'"

The two dwarves nodded their heads and were silent again. Sastro spoke at length.

"Why did you bring this news to us, Goldenhair? Surely there are plenty people here whom you could tell of this."

"I thought about it quite a bit," Eris said. "I do not know anyone here in Broude. Whom could I confide in? How are we to know that Maiklin is alone in his treachery in Broude. How are we to know?"

"I had thought every Norlander loyal to the countess," said Janus. "Yes, loyal to the point of death. Now you tell us Maiklin is a traitor, in league with Gavron!"

"As for now, things are safe for the countess but when I am gone she is in danger – a knife, a planned accident, poison – anything is possible. But the question is, what do we do?"

"We can make more certain by searching Maiklin's chambers for further evidence – not an easy task, but I think it can be done."

Some days later Lord Maiklin left his chamber and strode down the passageway. Suddenly from around the corner Janus and Sastro came running at speed and crashed into the knight sending him sprawling backwards along the passageway floor. The two dwarves crashed on top of him heavily, pinning him down.

"My curse on the two of you buffoons," Lord Maiklin roared. "How dare you little ruffians knock me down!"

"A thousand apologies, my Lord."

"A million apologies, my Lord. We were making haste to fetch a message for the countess.

Maiklin was now flailing about with both fists at the two little men who were making heavy weather of rolling off him and away from him."

"There! There! Take that and that! You miserable little ogres!" Maiklin panted as he tried to hit Janus on his left.

"And you too, take that!" He gasped. "I'll have you both reported and whipped." He was throwing swipes at Sastro now.

Janus was lying face down, howling from the blows. But underneath him he had gripped Lord Maiklin's key and was busy pressing its imprint upon a lump of warm wax. This done he rolled away out of Maiklin's reach.

"Let me help you up, my Lord."

"Get away from me you misbegotten whelps!"

Janus and Sastro were now standing and stepping cautiously back from Maiklin who was lifting himself up slowly.

"I'll make an example of the two of you that you won't forget," he panted as he finally found his feet and stood up. He was about to pour out another torrent of abuse at the two little miscreants but his words never came. They were gone, vanished, melted into thin air.

A week passed and Janus and Sastro lay low, keeping out of Lord Maiklin's way, keeping out of everyone's way. To anyone who met them and questioned their absence they replied simply that they had to work on new tricks for the rena's amusement and needed time and a quiet place to practise and concentrate. They had approached the blacksmith with the wax imprint of the key to Lord Maiklin's door. The blacksmith was easily persuaded to make the key when presented with a purse of Eris' money.

At the end of the week Eris, Janus and Sastro finally got the opportunity they were waiting for. With numbers of other knights Lord Maiklin had ridden out for a day's hunting and they would not return until sunset. While the two dwarves gave a performance of new tricks in the great hall for the amusement of all present, Eris slipped away. Up the many flights of steps until he stood in the passageway outside Lord Maiklin's chamber. Checking once more that there was no one about he reached inside his doublet for the forged key and smiled when he felt its steely hardness. Taking it out, he looked at it in the palm of his hand. With a deep breath he placed the key into the lock, and to his relief it slid in perfectly. So far, so good, he thought. Another deep breath and slowly and gently he began to turn the key and it went beautifully, catching the metal inside the lock and moving it sweetly. He was almost there but suddenly at three quarter turn the key would go no further. Eris' heart began to beat fast. He loosed the key back and then tried again. Again it blocked at three quarter turn. Eris was dumbfounded – was it the right key that his friends had copied – was it a mistake on the part of the blacksmith? Now he began to work the key further in and turned but there was no yield. Drops of sweat were trickling down his face, especially at the thought of those documents inside the room and he, at the last, could not get at. He stood up and sighed, placing his hands on his hips. On the point of giving up he decided on a last try, with one hand whipping the key round again and again when suddenly the key slipped through a complete rotation and the door was unlocked. Eris gasped with relief and wiped the

sweat from his face and pushed the door inward, its creaking and whining sound like music in his ears. He was inside and locking the door from inside. Now he began his
search. There was a bed, a table and a clothing chest. He
scanned the many parchments on the shelves but found
none with the seal of Gavron de Laude. Inch by inch he
began a methodical search of everything there. Nothing.
He opened a number of satchels. Nothing. He opened the
clothes chest and reached his hand down searching the
bottom of the chest. Again nothing. Where could they
be, he was screaming inside of himself. Where could they
be? He began to search the garments. First there was a
fine cloak lined with ermine fur. He searched pockets,
cuffs and then at the collar his fingers pressed against
something strong inside the lining. He pressed again – it
was paper, parchment for sure. There was a tiny aperture
where the collar lining began, he eased his fingers inside
and felt the unmistakeable touch of rolled parchment!

Half an hour later he had wormed all the documents out of the collar and placed them neatly on the table. He was thrilled, for they all without exception carried the same seal – that of Gavron de Laude.

Now with the aid of a candle he perused them over
and over again. He strained to decipher the Latin but jot-
ted down the bits he could understand and more especially
everything mentioning the countess. At length he sat
back and pondered – one thing was clear, the countess and
her movements and doings were being well monitored by
Maiklin, as Gavron's letters confirmed. Gavron knew
everything the countess was doing.

He then continued to draft down every quotation
referring to the countess, even when he did not fully understand the meaning of the Latin text. As he worked, his
heart pumped with shock as some passages, read over and

over again, finally dawned their meaning within his mind. Like when he read Gavron speak of 'amici tu in Norlandia', your friends in Norland. So there it was in black and white before him, Maiklin was not alone in his enterprise against the countess. He had accomplices, whoever they might be. Who could I trust now, Eris thought grimly. Further on Eris found the passage that turned his blood cold, 'Quomodo la Contesa moriatur, totus hic labor in manibus tuis est' – how is the countess to die, all this task is in your hands.

Eris placed his head in his hands feeling his temples pounding. He had seen enough. Time to return the parchments to their hiding place and get away from this evil chamber, this den of murder. Quickly he left, locking the door and stuffing his parchments of quotations into his doublet. He was back in the great hall in no time where the dwarves were still performing their tricks. A large crowd had gathered to watch their antics. Presently Janus made a couple of spectacular somersaults which brought him face to face with Eris. "Murder," Eris whispered in the dwarf's ear. "We shall meet tonight."

"Tonight it is then," Janus whispered back and bounded away with more cartwheels and somersaults.

*   *   *

The countess and her forces were now far down the lakeside on the first leg of their journey to Alorin. From there, as agreed, the countess would ride south, meet the emissaries from Bergmond and exchange Eris for those precious documents, restoring her to her full rights; documents she had bargained for, and for which she had longed these past fifteen years. She would now no longer be the Witch of Norland, she would be recognised by all as countess in name and in fact.

Raising himself in his saddle, Eris took one last look backward. Bathed in the glow of the breaking dawn and reflected in the morning stillness of the water, the fortress of Broudenlac looked quite beautiful. He sat back in his saddle and smiled at the countess. He wondered if he would ever see the splendour of it all ever again. The time he had spent there was truly wondrous, but best of all wonders had been the countess herself, larger than life and locked in permanent conflict with the league forces of Bergmond. There was somewhat of a twinge in his heart too for the daughter of the countess, the Lady Catherine, with whom he had fallen in love. If life should give me the chance, he thought, I will return for her one day. I thought I was charming her, he mused, but all the time she was stealing my heart away! But I must leave her now and wait until this confounded war is over – but then, he was promising himself, I will tear down everything in my path to return to Broudenlac and hold her in my arms again!

He felt within him yet another twinge, this time a deeply terrifying one – once he was ransomed to Gavron de Laude – the life of Beatrice d'Erkindhal, Countess of Norland, was in mortal danger.

The journey to Alorin took some days and was uneventful, except for the fact that all along the way they were joined by more knights and sword-wielding footsoldiers. It was sufficient that the countess was on the move, to bring to her side escorts from all of Norland, far and wide, no matter what the purpose of her journey. Of course, word had long since gone out that she was ransoming the Valdelaine youth for the rights and freedoms of Norland, such that, by the time of her approach to Alorin, her forces had swelled to thousands.

On the final approach to Alorin, Lord Maiklin left his place in the cavalcade, and cantered up beside the column stopping beside the countess.

"Why, Lord Maiklin!" the countess smiled benignly at him. "You have come forward to join me. Will you do me the honour of escorting me over the last mile of our trek to Alorin, or have you joined me regarding another matter?"

Maiklin cleared his throat and said, "I have a serious request to make of you, Ma'am."

"Go on," said the countess.

"Ma'am, if you will permit me to escort you closely for the rest of our time here in the south, I shall be most honoured!"

"But we are in no danger, my Lord!" she said.

"Even so, my Lady, I fear the treachery of the Bergmondese, I fear the wiles of Gavron de Laude. It would be peace of mind for me to see you safe at all times. Let me, I pray you, give myself as your personal steward."

The countess looked at him and smiled.

"I grant you this request, my Lord, and will be happy, knowing you will be close by at all times."

Thus it was that Lord Maiklin succeeded in making himself the closest to the countess.

There was still a long way to go to the border to trade Eris for the countess' demands, but Maiklin's evil plans were made easier for him, a hundredfold now, by being always close to her whom he intended to kill. The traitor was happy, all was going well.

Eris had observed Maiklin's move and had overheard most of the conversation. When some time had elapsed, he wheeled his horse about, galloped back to the wagon train, and found Sastro and Janus. At a nod from Eris, Sastro leaped from the wagon and seated himself neatly behind Eris.

"Maiklin has made his first move," Eris said in a low voice turning his head sideways, so that Sastro would hear him all the better.

"What move is that?" Sastro whispered in Eris' ear.

"Maiklin has just ridden up to the countess and gracefully offered to be her steward for the duration of her stay in Alorin."

"Mmn, that is interesting – I'll wager you'll not get near her, while he's in charge!"

"Correct, but I will get access to Lord Tancred and Lady Alice without him knowing. I will alert them to her danger. What is your plan of action then?"

"First, we have to find a way of getting one of us into the quarters where the countess will sleep. Distract the maids, anything – we're tricksters, as you know!"

"What then?" asked Eris.

Sastro chuckled, "You do your part, Goldenhair, and we'll do ours. Don't worry. Now, let me leap back to the wagon and you ride up to where you belong!"

Sastro leaped, and Eris trotted his horse up to where he had been. The tall outlines of Alorin Castle were now looming close in the evening light.

*   *   *

At last the day of days arrived, when the countess rode south to meet the delegation from Bergmond. By an agreed protocol, both sides met some fifteen miles south of Alorin, each side accompanied by a retinue of twenty five knights. Lord Maiklin rode beside the countess, and Eris rode some paces behind. When they reached the meeting place, the Bergmondese produced a group of Esmorin prisoners who positively identified the countess' prisoner as Eris de Valdelaine. Curiously Baron Gavron was not present, but had sent Baron Conrad in his place. The abbot of Fontroyal, Maelruain, and the other monks stepped forward, and opened the satchel containing the documents which the countess had demanded, months before. The kindly abbot read each document to the countess, translating them from Latin into French. One by one, the countess took each one from the abbot. Each one was perfectly satisfactory. The revocation of witchcraft against her, the revocation of outlawry against her, the declaration of reinstatement as the lawful Countess of Norland – they were all there. The countess had them placed carefully in her leather pannier bags that were then strapped to the trappings of her own horse. Eris said his farewell to the countess and strode across to the waiting group of Esmorin prisoners, greeting each one personally, as he knew many of them. Finally, the countess knelt before Abbot Maelruain and received his blessing "Benedicat te Omnipotaris Deus…" to which the countess answered clearly "Amen."

Both Eris and the countess then mounted their horses and the two delegations withdrew – the countess northward to Alorin, Eris and his captors southward to Baron Gavron's encampment, wherever it might be. Both he and the countess took one last look at each other, and waved farewell.

On the journey southward, Eris had many thoughts and memories – but uppermost in his mind was the plot he had hatched with the dwarves Janus and Sastro. The safety of the countess was now in their hands, and of course, in the hands of the lord of Alorin, Lord Tancred.

He was right about one thing – when he did reach Gavron's encampment, he found it well hidden, and containing a very large force. He was welcomed by Lord Gavron and shown his quarters among a well guarded group of tents, which housed the Esmorin prisoners. Gavron was pleased – he had Eris in his power, he could trade him and the others for Germaine. But before this could happen he would wait for Maiklin to destroy the countess. Then a quick dash north to Alorin with his assembled troops would be the first move in his annexation of Norland. The severed head of the countess would be delivered to him within a day or two. With Norland subdued, he would then resume the conflict with Esmor with even more confidence and force, especially with Germaine back on Bergmondese soil.

For the present, however, as the countess rode back towards Alorin, she was happy, and she felt a sense of relief and safety. She had given Eris away, but she had won back all that was taken from her so long ago – there, in the panniers, were the guarantees of safety for herself. there, too, was the return of safety for all of her dominions. Norland was now safe and at peace with the king and the church. She smiled to herself as she remembered her mother's dreams of a golden haired youth who would one day come and rescue Norland from all its woes.

The countess retired early, and stretched out on the large bed. Her sleeping companion, the eldest of Lord Tancred's daughters, lay beside her and for a while their voices could be heard by the guards outside. They chatted for a time, before turning over and falling asleep. There were only two guards posted outside the door of the chamber – Lord Maiklin had insisted on dispensing with the maids who would normally sleep on pallets outside the door.

From his perch on the stairs beyond the chamber, Janus sat and waited patiently hoping and praying that his ally, Sastro, had not fallen asleep, in his particular bundle of cushions underneath the countess' bed. Both dwarves had their own bag of juggling clubs strapped around them. It is important to remember that Janus and Sastro were expert jugglers – normally, as entertainment at feasts and festivals, they could toss clubs at each other with incredible speed. They could loft clubs into the rafters, do several cartwheels and catch the falling clubs, without so much as batting an eyelid. They could even do more such feats with their eyes blindfolded.

The hours passed infinitely slowly – and then, two hours after midnight the faint sound of footsteps could be heard climbing the stairs from below. There was a light also as someone approaching was carrying a candle. Janus took a cautious look around the corner, the two guards were looking the other way as Lord Maiklin and another knight tiptoed towards them, along the passageway. For a long moment, Maiklin waited, listening for any sound inside the countess' chamber. Then he took a deep breath, nodded to the others and as with one movement they all drew their swords.

Janus' heart was now pounding, as he hoped and prayed again that Sastro was ready and waiting within the chamber. Slowly and silently, Maiklin turned the key, and the door gently swung open. In the light of the candle he could make out the bed and hear the sleep-breathing of the two women. What he could not see, however was Sastro standing low beyond the bed. Suddenly, Maiklin was hit centre forehead by a flying object; before he could react, he was hit again by another, and still again by another. Before his knights could react, they too were being hit front face by flying juggling clubs, and all four men were beginning to reel backward from the door as the flying clubs had been drilled and weighted with lead filling. Now it was Janus' turn to act. He had taken from his bag a wheel of steel and reeds, lit it and sent it hurling through the air down the passageway until it reached the stairs and clattered downward. This was the signal for Lord Tancred's men to move, and move they did, up the stairs and along the passageway where they found Lord Maiklin and his accomplices, stunned, reeling and falling, from the barrage of missiles Sastro had thrown at them with such accuracy.

Lord Tancred was first at the scene, and while his men disarmed and bound the four assassins, he himself entered the chamber where the countess was now wide awake sitting up and about to rise from the bed. Lord Tancred spoke.

"Pardon our intrusion, my Lady – but we have just intercepted an attempt on your life! Lord Maiklin, and three accomplices attempted to enter your chamber with swords drawn!"

"My God!" the countess exclaimed. "Maiklin? Maiklin of all people! But why?"

"It seems he has been colluding with Baron de Laude for your destruction – for quite some time it seems. He is a traitor, my Lady!"

And so, the conversation continued for some time. Meanwhile, Lady Alice and her maids arrived with mulled wine for the countess, bringing to her their own comforting company.

Lord Tancred took it upon himself with some of his troops, to guard the chamber for the rest of the night. For a time, the countess was restless, but gradually sank back into sleep, surrounded by Lady Alice and her ladies. It would be morning before the countess would learn of the part played by Eris, Janus and Sastro, in saving her life.

The following day, under torture, Lord Maiklin and his two associates revealed the names of a number of others implicated in the plot against the countess. Interestingly, none of these latter had joined her in her hosting of troops at Alorin. They had stayed behind in the safety of their castles, to await word of the countess' overthrow and begin to assist Maiklin and Gavron with the Bergmondese overthrow of Norland. One by one, over the next few days they were all rounded up, and imprisoned to await trial for their treachery. Maiklin and his two accomplices were promptly beheaded.

The following day three Norland knights found the whereabouts of Gavron's encampment and were challenged by his guards about a mile or so distant.

"Who are you," the guards demanded. "Identify yourselves and state your business here!"

"We are friends!" the leading knight answered, "And we bear a message to be delivered to Lord Gavron de Laude!"

With that, the knight unloosed a bag from the trappings of his horse and tossed it to the ground at the feet of the guards. Then, as with one movement the three Norland knights wheeled their horses about and rode away.

Within a short time, the guards delivered the bag to Lord Gavron. He smiled, knowing that this would be the signal for his march to Alorin.

Upon opening the bag, however, his face grew red with anger and horror. The bag, which was to have contained the severed head of Beatrice d'Erkindhal, contained instead the grizly head of Lord Maiklin. As he looked with horror Gavron knew then that his plot for Norland had failed. In his rage, he wanted to kill Eris and the other Esmorin hostages – but by now they were miles away, imprisoned in a castle close to the frontier with Esmor.

In the bag, there was a letter, a scroll written by the Countess Beatrice.

"Look well, Gavron," it read. "Thus befalls the fate of traitors. Look well and be warned, for it will be your fate one day. Beatrice d'Erkindhal, Countess of Norland."

Chapter XII: Threshold of the Heart

*I*t was evening, almost night, and Germaine sat in his room reading a book. To be more correct, Germaine was struggling with the text in the effort to make sense of the story. True enough, he was slow at reading; and this little volume, a romance which Ioni had given him, was proving tough going despite its romantic content. There was a knock on the door.

"Who could this be at this early hour?" he wondered.

"Enter!" he called.

The door swung open and there stood Ioni. He was surprised but greatly pleased. Ioni closed the door behind her, and Germaine stood up to embrace her.

"What brings you at this hour alone?" he asked. "Someone could have seen you. What about the prying eyes of Valdelaine?"

Ioni smiled and chuckled.

"I had a perfect excuse to come to you!" she said cheerily. "Even if all of Valdelaine were prying it does not matter this time!"

"What is special about this time?" he asked.

Ioni took a breath and said,

"You have a visitor it seems. He's waiting for you in the great hall and Lord Raymond is seeing to his needs."

"But, Ioni, who is he? Do you know?" Germaine frowned.

"This is the other reason I had to come and see you alone," Ioni said. "It is another – well shall we say, another monk, this time. So I have to be careful of you.

His name, he says, is Father Roland, a monk of Campaldo. Do you know him, or of him?"

Germaine's face relapsed.

"Yes, I know this Father Roland," said Germaine now smiling.

"My father and he are old friends."

"Good!" Ioni smiled. "Let's go and meet him, but, let's take our time and chat on the way! We can walk around at our leisure as he is dining with Uncle Raymond at present. There's no hurry!"

*   *   *

When Ioni entered the great hall she got her first glimpse of Father Roland of the great Abbey of Campaldo. As she approached the priest she could see this was no wan or world weary monk; in fact his eyes shone brightly from a ruddy well fed face that contrasted most handsomely with the white hair of his beard and tonsure. He exuded strength, health and indeed, merriment.

Uncle Robert spoke.

"Ioni, this is Father Roland of Campaldo. He is by birth a countryman of Germaine and wishes to meet him and tend to his spiritual welfare. Father, this is my niece, the Lady Ioni, mistress of Valdelaine."

"Kindest greetings and welcome," said Ioni as she knelt at the monk's feet and kissed his ring.

"Rise, my child," said Father Roland kindly. "I wish to have your permission to see the prisoner on behalf of his spiritual welfare. The monastery of Campaldo houses men of many countries. I am a countryman of the young Lord of Anlac and have received permissions to visit him."

"You shall see him, dear Father," said Ioni, now standing, "and we hope you shall be our guest for as long as you require. But first, will you eat and drink?"

"Your uncle, my Lord Robert has already seen to my needs, my child," spoke Father Roland, "and I really would prefer to meet him before the household retires for the night. Thank you and God's blessings on you for all your kindnesses."

"You will meet him presently," said Ioni. "I take it you may have known him and his family?"

"We have known each other for a life time, my child – I mean I have known the young lord's father for a life time. I have not known Lord Germaine."

Soon Germaine and Father Roland were closeted in a candlelit chamber. The holy father paced up and down the room, Germaine sat with his arms resting on a table. Father spoke in a rambling kind of way sometimes enthusiastically and by turns hesitant; he spoke of news of family, home, country. Even so, he still continued to pace up and down. By now Germaine knew he had something to say, but seemed reluctant to say it. Finally after another long silence Germaine said,

"Will you shrive me then, Father?"

Father Roland stood still, turned his face towards Germaine and said,

"As a priest, of course, the salvation of your immortal soul is of the utmost importance to me but – not at this very moment, not in this very place." Father Roland's face grew serious. "Germaine of Anlac, it is not your soul that I have come about."

Germaine sat looking at him, mystified. He said, "What then, Father, is the purpose of your coming here?"

Father Roland placed himself in a comfortable chair, admired his chubby fingers awhile and then said,

"The purpose of my coming is – communion!"

"Communion, Father," Germaine, more mystified than ever repeated bleakly.

"Yes, communion," Father repeated. "A wonderful word you know, Germaine. Ah yes, communion. What wonderful layers of meaning are contained in such a word. Meanings like – trust, unity, combination and so on, wonderful meanings, Germaine."

Germaine was shaking his head.

"Forgive me, Father, I am a soldier not a scholar – I have no notion of what you speak of. Please I pray you come to the point."

"Very well," said Father Roland, his eyes searching Germaine's face. "Let me come to the point – the point is this. I think it safe to say that I know where you stand regarding the league."

Germaine looked into Father's eyes then away again. Indeed, he thought, Father Roland's thoughts are far from spiritual matters; he is here on some political quest.

"Let us say then, Father," Germaine said, "that your opinion of my opinion of the league of barons, sometimes known as the Dark League, might be rather accurate."

Slowly Father Roland's lips widened into a smile. "You might well be a scholar someday with clever talk like that, young Anlac! But I said that communion was about a bond of trust. Now I will trust in you, for... although I am a worldly monk, as many think – yet I have no fear. I love my own country and would do a great deal to ensure her peace. And peace, my son, is what she needs now, more than anything."

Germaine spoke, "Father, I am a prisoner here, I have no means of doing anything to ensure the peace of our country."

"All things are possible to God, my son!" Father continued. "But, first of all, let me recount the true state of things. Our country is now in the gravest peril, my son. The war with Esmor may drag on for years but that is not the problem. The problem is the league of barons, or the Dark League as you called it. The barons now plunder our country with the greatest savagery. Anyone who dares question them is slaughtered. And with such plunder they can afford to prolong this conflict for many many years. Already towns, castles, villages in our country are ruined just to pay for the latest exploits of the league. They behave like demons of hell towards everyone."

Germaine was dumbfounded. The league of barons had been founded to protect their ageing king. But now they were promoting a war to protect their own interests. He looked at father intently.

"Are the rumours true," he asked, "that they even engage the assistance of Satan himself to further their own ends?"

Father Roland looked away. "The barons have now so immersed themselves in evil, that I doubt if they need any assistance from that particular quarter. Let me ask you, Germaine, how long have you been held a prisoner here?"

"Nigh on two years, Father," Germaine replied.

"And soon you are to be exchanged for one of their prisoners, I believe," the priest said.

"Do you know how soon it will happen, Father?" Germaine asked.

"I'm not sure," said Father.

"There are what seem to be negotiations taking place between the league and the Countess of Norland. If the league wants him, the countess it seems, will drive a hard bargain."

"So it may yet be some time then, Father," Germaine said.

"That is correct," Father said.

"You know that your good father was never a leaguer. I understand that you yourself never took the oath of the Raven League. From the first day your father never held with the barons – for your father it was an encroachment on the king's legal powers.

"That's right," said Germaine.

"What's more," Father continued, "your father was right. The barons have taken what was not theirs. They have weakened the king's position to nothing.

"And now Germaine, now we have no law, no leader no right or wrong – we have only the league. And God knows the evil deeds they have done at home, not to mention this horrible war! Why? I have not been able to mention the awful nature of their crimes against our people, Germaine, against our own people!"

There was a long pause, a silence. Father had closed his eyes for a while, joined his hands just below his lips and Germaine observed him beginning to mutter and mumble words to himself as though he was in some kind of trance. After some more of the mumbling Germaine realised that Father Roland was rendering some kind of prayer to God.

"Mumble... mumble... have mercy Oh God on the plight of thy people... mumble... mumble... who Oh Lord will save us from this wickedness?" And so it went on for a while until it abruptly stopped and Father shook himself out of his trance, looked at Germaine and smiled.

"I... I will do anything I can, Father," Germaine muttered, "but I don't see what I can do here, a prisoner in a far off land."

Father Roland's eyes were smiling.

"Be of good heart, my son," he said. "There are many like you who would now strike a blow against the league, let me assure you. And this is the meaning of my word communion – there are many like us, we are hidden, I know, but we are strong in trust and faith. We have a bond, and you are just one of many!"

"But who could dare oppose the league, Father," Germaine cried. "They have everything!"

"You know, my son, that I could never reveal to you the names of others in this bond, anymore than I could reveal your name to anyone. But, as you know, we are a very holy Abbey of Campaldo – but having said that, there is not a mortal sin or the sting of a bee that we do not hear about. From where we stand in Campaldo we reach out to a sea of souls who would save our good land! And that, my dear boy, is the truth!"

Germaine was quiet for a moment and then said,

"I am with you, Father. I am with Campaldo!"

The two men, priest and knight, were now standing face to face. Father Roland reached out his hands and took Germaine's arms.

"God bless you now and always," Father said. "But I must acquaint you with further danger. I must beg you to kneel before me and swear that you will reveal none of what you are about to hear."

Germaine knelt and said, "I swear before you, Father, and before God that what you say to me, will remain with me."

Father helped him to his feet.

"How shall I put this!" he muttered then turning again to face Germaine he said,

"There is no safety in any of this situation, Germaine. Your father is not safe, but then anyone not sworn to the league is not safe. When you return to us after you are released from here, even you will not be safe. Yes even you – who gave such service to the league and the war in recent years. Having said that, Germaine, neither am I safe. The league has already burned two abbeys and killed devout monks – they would not hesitate to destroy Campaldo, for all its fame and glory, if it got in their way!"

Father Roland saw the look of horror on Germaine's face.

"Save your dread, my son," said Father. "You and I and even Campaldo are as nothing – as nothing, Germaine."

"I don't follow you, Father," Germaine breathed.

Father Roland raised his right hand and made the sign of the cross over him.

"My son, even the king and the royal line may be in danger."

*   *   *

"Hmm," was all that Father Roland said as he joined his hands against his lips and closed his eyes. Before him Germaine was kneeling having made his confession. There were sins of anger, resentment, impatience and lustful desires of the flesh. But there was more. Germaine had told Father of his feelings for Ioni.

"And you truly love her," Father had pressed.

"More than anything in life," Germaine had answered.

"Does she love you?"

"This I do not know, Father," Germaine whispered, "but she has always treated me with a special affection."

"Do you intend to tell her?"

"Yes, Father. But I don't know how. I am – afraid the circumstances of our situation here are – complicated."

"But you do love her."

"More than anything."

Father was lost in thought for yet another while and then said,

"If this girl loves you, I believe her love will be made manifest in time."

"But how, Father?"

"That I do not know, my son, but love finds its way from one heart to another."

"You do not disapprove, then, Father," Germaine had said. That was when Father had murmured 'Hmm!' and closed his eyes. Finally he said,

"Yes, it's all quite complicated I'm afraid. You cannot declare your love to the world. Not with a war like this and the two of you on opposite sides, it would ruin you both."

"Yes, Father," breathed Germaine.

"Well then," said Father. "There are two things I would have to ask of you – those two things – one, patience, the other, total secrecy. You have fought wars with courage, my son, but now you are locked in a conflict of the heart. You will need all your courage – but even more I must ask you to be patient and discreet."

"Yes, Father," said Germaine.

"You will not be ransomed, Germaine, the league does not want you. But there are other circumstances at work which, in time, will cause your release, believe that. Besides, it may someday work out for the best – in fact, if you and this girl are in love then it may work the better in the cause I spoke of the other night."

"I don't know what you mean, Father."

"Believe me, my son, you will find that a man in love is a good man to have in any cause. When you do come back to our country, you will be fighting a cause with love glowing in your heart. Much better a man with the love of a good and beautiful woman in his soul than a man with no love at all."

Father paused and Germaine smiled.

"But how can you know this, Father." He asked.

"We were not born monks, my son." said Father. "I too loved in my youth but lost my love. She lies in a quiet and lovely grave. Knowing that I could love no other caused me to become a monk. In doing so, I could serve love itself and see it grow in the world. You see love did abide in me for the rest of my days and it still does."

Germaine raised his head and looked into Father Roland's eyes. There, he found no bitterness or hatred only it seemed joy and thankfulness.

"Germaine of Anlac," he said. "In the grace of God I abjure you to be patient, silent – and brave."

"I will, Father." Germaine breathed.

Benedicat te Omnipotens Deus, in nomine Patris…

Just as Father Roland reached the door Germaine exclaimed, "But my release, Father. When will it happen?"

Father looked back at Germaine, smiling, his hand on the door.

"You have much time now, my son, for prayer and for reflection!"

With that Father Roland closed the door behind him and was gone.

*   *   *

The dining hall was quite empty when Germaine burst through the door; he had hoped to find her here at his hour, as he so often did at the end of a day. Now, seemingly, she was nowhere to be found. The messenger had arrived less than an hour before; he and Uncle Robert had been in the courtyard when the horse and rider had clattered in. On reading the message Uncle Robert's face had broadened with a beaming smile and he handed Germaine the happy news. As soon as the necessary arrangements could be made, Germaine was to be set free. The joy of the news had gone through Germaine like a shock; Uncle Robert had shook his hands and embraced him. But Germaine knew he must find Ioni and had already begun searching for her.

He was just on the point of abandoning the dining hall when he noticed that the door leading to the south rampart was wide open. Could she be up there, he thought, as he ran the hall's length with the piece of parchment clutched in his hand. He paused to look out the open door to where the stone steps led upwards and there, above, stood Ioni looking dreamily out over the rampart to the wide countryside below. She seemed lost in her own thoughts. He could see that she too, was holding some parchment in her hands. Perchance, two messages had come that evening.

"Ioni!" he whispered, as he leaped up the steps and stood looking at her, the moonlight streaming down her hair and down the outlines of her dress. She stood there in silhouette with the aura of the silvery moonlight about her. Like a saint, he thought.

"Germaine." she answered quietly.

"Ioni!" he gasped, breathless. "I have received news. Good news!"

She lifted her parchment towards him, almost wearily.

"I also have received this news, my friend," her voice seemed strangely sad. "Good news, indeed, my dear Germaine!"

But something in her voice and manner was quite strange; he could not quite fathom it.

"You are to be ransomed, at last," her voice was wavering, she took a deep breath. "You are to go back to your homeland," she continued. "Imagine, Germaine, you are free. I am so happy for you!" Her voice did not betoken happiness, Germaine was sure of that. They were standing on the rampart looking at each other.

"Yes, Ioni," Germaine panted, he knew something was amiss but could not determine what it was.

"Yes! I am free, Ioni, I am free!" He was almost jumping for joy, then stopped. "How can I repay you, Ioni, for all the..." his voice now trailed away. What was she saying? She had used the word 'ransomed'.

"No Ioni," he stammered. "No! Not ransomed! Don't you understand? There is to be an exchange of prisoners."

She did not seem to comprehend nor even to want to. "I received the word, earlier in the evening," she said, "that you were to be set free! I meant to bring you the news myself, but now you know. You are free!" Germaine was about to speak but he paused again and realised that the message in Ioni's hand was not quite the same as the message in his.

"No, Ioni," he blurted. "You don't understand – I am not to be ransomed – I am to be exchanged for one of your countrymen, a prisoner in my land!"

"That is good, Germaine," she stammered and turned her head away.

"It is better than good, Ioni," he stepped forward, placed his hands on her upper arms, and turned her towards him. "Ioni, didn't your message tell you?"

"Tell me what? Germaine," she said wearily.

"Why! I am to be exchanged for your own brother Eris," he said elatedly. "For Eris, Ioni. Eris is free!"

For a long and endless moment she looked at him as he stood there, face to the moonlight. Her eyes by turn, fluttered open and shut, she wavered for an instant, and then collapsed slowly, falling first to her knees, and then sideways so that her pale hand clutched at the cold stone of the crenellation.

"Oh! God!" she cried aloud. "Oh God!"

She leaned her head against the stone, bursting into a convulsion of weeping.

Germaine stood dumbfounded for a moment, he could never fathom this beautiful girl, nor know at any given time, what his own expectations of her should be. He stepped towards her, knelt by her, and taking her hands in his, lifted her sobbing frame. She wept and wept, silently in his arms for a long time. Then, suddenly, she released herself from his embrace and stood back from him, a pace or two.

"No, no." she cleared her throat. "I am calm now and I am well grown up and strong. I pray you forgive me, my Lord! I had not meant to trouble you!" She burst into tears again. He took hold of her again.

"Ioni," he gasped, "for the love of Heaven, what is it? Why do you weep so! How have I offended you? What is it, Ioni? What have I done?"

Once more she tore herself from his arms. Panting heavily, she looked at him, reaching her hand out for support to the stone wall.

"What is it?" she cried bitterly, wept again and ran her fingers through her long hair. "What is it you ask. Why? I am angry," she gasped, searching for words. "I am angry!"

"But why angry," he gasped. "I thought you would be glad! I thought..."

"Because," she breathed, her face and body quivering with grief and rage. "Because I love you! God forgive me, but I love you!"

"I love you!" she wailed again and again as she hurried away and, hand over hand she held each stone merlon of the rampart. She stopped where the rampart met the castle wall and hissed at him.

"I love you so much! I have loved you for so long, Germaine! I cannot help loving you, and now I do not want to lose you! And lose you I must," she breathed, "to save my own brother! To save Eris! God in Heaven, am I to have nothing of my own in this world!"

She stood awhile, breathing in gasps, and then eventually stepped forward to him, quivering.

"Forgive me, Germaine, but I love you!" she whispered and ran into his embrace.

Germaine held her there for a long time. She raised her head to him, still quivering, she looked into his eyes, and said, "Please, forgive me, my Lord. I think I did not realise till now, how much I loved you! If I had known, I probably would never have told you." She paused for breath. "But now, now I have told you and it is true. I love you," she paused again, "I love you more than anything in this world." She lowered her head, placing her forehead against his chest. "I have told you this now, and under these circumstances. However," she looked up at him again. "My love for you places no obligation on you. I have loved you for yourself, but, even so, my love places no requirement that you love me in return. My love was freely given. But it changes nothing!"

Germaine held her close to him and whispered, "Ioni, it changes everything!"

She loves me, he reflected, holding her in his embrace. She loves me, he thought again, after all the times they had known together, after all the quarrels they had had, after all the strain of being captor and captive. She had held him like a butterfly in the palms of her hands, and it was she, now, who was wounded and helpless in his arms. He was filled with a sense of such powerfulness now, combined with a sense of unbearable tenderness towards her. This is Ioni in my arms! I am the one she loves! An hour ago he was an ordinary man. Now, this night had taken wings of its own and swept them both beyond everything that was ordinary. There, with her in his arms, a thousand years might have passed them by and he would not care, time was dissolved in the moonlight, and in the magical delight he now felt. He was now no longer alone, she was there like a candle that was lit in his heart, and whose flame was growing, melting him away, so that he knew nothing, nor had he even existed – until now. A far off star on the northern horizon caught his eye, and to him it looked more beautiful, happier than the dancing midday sun!

Maybe a thousand years did come and go, but eventually she lifted her head towards him.

"Ioni," he said, at last breaking the silence. "We must talk. We have so much to talk about!" And yet Germaine feared that, even if he so much as blinked an eye, she might disappear like an elf in a story, and he might find himself alone on the battlement.

"Yes!" she whispered solemnly, wiping her eyes. "I will fetch my cloak, and lock your room and mine. Germaine, you go straight to the third stable. "Wait by the door – in the shadows. In about an hour I will meet you there. Wait for me! Go now!" And she was gone.

An hour later Germaine stood in the shadows, by the door of the third stable. He breathed in the sweet air of the night. Above him, across the courtyard, the tower keep gleamed white in the moonlight. *And she is somewhere up there*, he smiled. *What an evening*, he pondered, *and what a night of delirious emotions.* He knew, he had known nothing in all his life compared with all that had happened this past hour.

He waited, it seemed, an endless age, bewildered by joy and love. *Could it be real*, he pondered, *an hour ago he had beheld Ioni collapse on the rampart at the news of the exchange of prisoners.* Then had come Ioni's passionate confession of her love to him, carrying them both beyond anything they had ever known.

In an instant, he knew she was approaching. Strange, he had always known her presence, the touch of her slippers on the ground, the swirl and rustle of her skirts, until she stood before him.

"Did you think I would not come!" she whispered.

"I knew you would!" he whispered.

"Thank you for waiting for me!" she whispered again. "There were matters I had to see to."

"I'm glad you're here, now," he whispered. She bade him open the stable door, and on entering the darkness within, she took his hand and placed it against the stable wall. In the darkness, he felt the coolness of a great stone.

"That stone is loose, it can be removed," she whispered. "See if you can move it free of the wall." Germaine reached forward both hands, with his fingers he pulled at the top of the stone, it loosened and fell to the ground.

"Now what happens?" he whispered.

"Reach inside and you should find a metal bar," she whispered. "Prise it forward, further into the wall."

Germaine reached in, found the metal bar and began to push it as Ioni had instructed. Immediately, there was a strange creaking sound underfoot and Ioni gave a little giggle. "Now!" she said, "the stone beneath our feet has been released. It acts like a trap door and can be lifted up. Can you lift it?" Germaine was kneeling now in the darkness, and his hands scanned the floor for a catchment space between the floorstones; he found it, and his fingers searched downwards until he could begin to lift. With an effort, the floorstone began to lift. "What is down there?" he gasped, raising the stone away from its space.

"A kind of tunnel, a passageway," whispered Ioni excitedly. "A passageway runs under the stables – under the castle curtain wall, and under the front field." Germaine raised himself panting.

"A secret passageway?" he breathed.

"Of course," chirped Ioni, her voice had already gone downward. "Reach down your hand, Germaine," she chimed, "and find my hand, take hold of it?"

Guided by her hand, he began to descend a set of steps, which led him ever downward until his feet eventually found some terra firma. She was standing beside him but he could not see her for the darkness.

"It is a passageway," she repeated, "to the outside! And don't worry, I know every step down here. I often came here with Eris, when we were children! Let me take your arm and you can walk with me, I know every step, I will guide you!"

As he placed one foot past another in the darkness of the passageway he felt her hands take him by the arm first, and then, her arms were placed around him, her happy voice coaxing, and encouraging him, step for step. Once again, he was her prisoner, he thought happily as he found ground beneath his feet, as she guided him. She was so cheerful now – strong, knowing and self assured.

"I'm not afraid, are you?" she chuckled. "I'm not afraid down here when I'm with you! We can stop for a moment if you like. It's not much further anyway." Her voice carried with an echo along the cool, earthy air of the passage.

He was thinking, an hour ago, she was helpless with grief back on the castle rampart, now she was almost recklessly happy, as if it had been a dream. She only felt the happiness of holding him in her arms, in this long darkness, with only their voices and whispers between them. What was all of life? Nothing she felt, compared to the worth of being with him at this hour.

"Imagine," her voice came again, "we are here to-gether." He smiled in the darkness sensing the gladness in her voice, in the tug of her arms and in the soft presence of her body. "All the times I walked this passage, how little did I ever think, I would walk it with you!" Again, the joy, as her arms tugged him tightly. He did not answer, but gently pressed his arm to her shoulder, it was as if, some wonder moment, promised all through life, had finally come to pass. Where it was gone, the last day he had lived, he could not tell; where tomorrow might be, he could not say.

Soon a glow of light appeared up ahead.

"There is a grate," said Ioni. "It is large, but I think you will be able to lift it open. Then we will be out of the passageway, and on the riverbank."

When they approached, Germaine was able to lift the iron grate, and they both passed out into the moonlight. They stood for a moment in the lea of the high bank, below them the river sparkled here and there in the moonlight. Soon they were walking arm in arm across open field, talking quietly. Then they reached the wooden stile that led on to the woodland pathway. Germaine assisted Ioni over the stile.

"I think I can manage this," Ioni whispered, as she trod the wooden steps supported by his outstretched hand.

"I crossed this stile so often, but never had such a fine gentleman like you, Germaine, to assist me!"

"I've never had such a fine lady, to escort," he quipped. They crossed another small field and then found a grove of trees. Inside the grove lay a great fallen tree trunk, Ioni jumped up on the trunk, sat there and gathered her knees in her arms.

"Germaine," she said, "back upon the battlement, an hour past, I told you that I love you. And it is so, Germaine, I love you, more than anything I can think of. But, I pray you forgive me, for, it was not meant to happen – no, never!" She stood up again and walked a little way from him.

"As my love grew and grew inside me," she continued, "with every passing day, as God is my witness, I struggled against it. I fought it, thinking it would go away. But to no avail, Germaine, as every day I loved you even more. Yes, you can believe me, that I have loved you so much, all this time. Oh yes! My task was to hold you and keep you safe here in Valdelaine till you were ransomed. I beg your forgiveness, my Lord, I had never meant to burden you with the knowledge of what my heart held for you."

She paused for breath, and placed her hands to her head.

"And finally, tonight, with the news of you and Eris, I could hold it in my heart no more! You see, the thought of losing you – well, it was too much for me. You came into my house, into my life, and into my heart, and try as I would I could not repel you from my heart. Do you believe me, Germaine? What am I to do, my Lord, I have no right to claim your love in return – that love can only be given freely and from your own heart!"

She turned away from him again and stepped further into the grove of trees and in and out of the moonlight.

"I am spurred to ask you if you have any feelings for me, at all, my Lord?" She took a very deep breath as she turned to face him again, across the grove.

"Do you – shall we say, have – any – any…" and her voice trailed away as a surge of emotion welled up inside and she was in tears again. She turned away from him, and buried her face in her hands. Presently, Germaine began to speak gently across the space that divided them.

"I first saw you, the day I came here to Valdelaine. You were standing up on the little parapet above the main doors. Your face was lit by the winter sunset. I looked up for a moment, and you looked so beautiful there. For an instant there was a pang of regret that I had made such war on Esmor, on its knights and people and above all I had made war on that beauty that was now looking down upon me. I knew that I could expect little mercy or kindness from that beautiful face. And yet what I received from you was mercy and kindness, not in paltry helpings, but in abundance. Even beyond that, I was given a kind of redemption. Yes, the redemption of being able to have feelings again, feelings of affection, compassion and joy. Feelings, not to be banished as they refreshed my heart, and made me know there was more to this life than simply being a soldier – brute and unfeeling. Before that, the harshness of my life had stolen all that away, but here with you my own heart seemed to live again. Some years ago, when I was a page, I asked the Duke of Anflair what was the most important quality for being a great knight. The answer he gave me, was one word. "Love!" he said. And I had not the least idea of what he meant. But now I think I grasp his meaning. From the first, I admired you, respected and trusted you, and all of that simply turned into love. Yes, love, for I would do anything, dare anything for you, Ioni. Anything! To gain the love of your heart."

At this, her hands dropped from her face, she drew up her skirts and began to run to him, across through the light and dark of the grove, finally stretching out her arms to embrace him and hold him with all her strength. In that moment, their two hearts, so long repressed, were eased of all pain. And heart sang to heart in happy silence.

"Forgive me, dear Germaine!" she sobbed. "I am weeping with – sheer happiness. I've never felt..."

He sat beside her, on the fallen tree trunk, placed his arms round her and she buried her head against his chest. There were some more tears, of happiness, love, gratitude.

"You have saved my life," he murmured in her ear. "You found me first, a prisoner and rescued me.

And after that you gave me such a life here, and all the time, Ioni, I was being drawn to you."

"And you never told me?" Ioni wiped tears from her eyes.

"But how could I tell you," he chided gently. "You were the lady of the house. I was your prisoner! But I have loved all our time here. I loved your company – but could not tell you!"

"You loved my company?" she quizzed. "Even with all the quarrels we had!!" And she laughed.

There, in each other's arms, with the darkness and the moonlight all about, their hearts had crossed the threshold from coolness into warming love; droplets of happiness continued to fill them like rain on parched ground – and Oh! The sensation as the heart received such love coursing through its veins. Pulsating and glowing by turns the heart was relieved to know such warmth, warmth glowing again and again into happiness, and even tears of happiness, over and over again. And when those two hearts had filled unto the brain, they overflowed into each other's and into a bond of eternity, and the moon and stars, the earth and all the universe enfolded the two lovers in its wide embrace.

The following evening they met again. After the long day of many tasks Ioni's heart could not wait for the moment she would meet him. Her heart might burst with longing to be near him as she had thought of nothing else through every moment of the day. She made her excuses to the others that she was tired and wished to retire early. Germaine had disappeared early also, only to keep his tryst, waiting for her in the shadows by the third stable. His heart too was pounding with anticipation. Would she appear at the appointed hour? Would he hear her little footsteps as she made her way from the keep? Suppose something happened to delay her, how long would he wait there in the shadows. Suppose she could not keep their rendezvous, could his heart bear not seeing her this night? The day had been an endless delay to this one moment of delight. He looked to the sky and breathed the sweet cool air of the night, every moment his entire being quivering with longing just to see her. What a thing is love, he thought, that I ache with desire to be with her.

Ah! Relief! As he heard those beloved footsteps approaching in the darkness and saw her frame in silhouette cross the courtyard. He stepped from the shadows to greet her with the whisper,

"Ioni!"

"Germaine!" she whispered on the night air and they were flung into each other's arms for a long long moment, savouring every second of being together again after such a long day's delay. They could have been there forever for all they knew. At last they were together again, all the aches of longing forgotten in that embrace.

Once again they trod the depths of the passageway until it gave out on the river bank now in floods of moonlight. Their cluster of trees once attained, they sat together on the fallen trunk as they had done the night before. And then the hours passed, the happiest hours that Germaine and Ioni had ever known. There were long animated conversations and long silences, tiny phrases and laughter. There were blissful silences in just being there.

After one such silence Ioni lifted her head to Germaine's and said,

"There was always something I wished to ask you but never could." Ioni was looking at him smiling.

"What was that?" Germaine said stretching his arms out and back over his head.

"Well," Ioni hesitated, "I always wondered about something about you."

"You did," said Germaine. "What was it that you wondered about me – had I loved some other maiden before I met you –"

"No, silly boy!" Ioni laughed. "I've no interest in any maiden you may have met before me!"

"What, then," said Germaine sitting upright. "What was it you wanted to ask me?"

"Why, Germaine," said Ioni, "it's your name. I always wondered about it –"

"Ah yes, my name," interjected Germaine. "My name. Amazing you never asked before –"

"It's a girl's name," blurted Ioni.

"And you wondered what is a great knight doing with a girl's name."

"Well," smiled Ioni, "I like your name, I love it, but –"

"The name or names that I carry," said Germaine thoughtfully, "are a testament to my mother's devotions when I was born."

Ioni paused a moment looking at him quizzically.

"You have other names?" her eyes were wide even in the moonlight.

"Yes, Ioni," Germaine said solemnly. "I have exactly three names."

"Three names!" gasped Ioni. "What are they, tell me! Three names! Well, I know one of them – Germaine."

Germaine looked at her smiling now.

"There are two others," Germaine paused, "but I shall not tell them to you for many years yet!"

Ioni reached out her hand gently taking his hand, she moved so that she was kneeling before him smiling up at him.

"You shall tell me your other names now, Germaine or else, I shall die tonight on this very spot!" Ioni laughed.

"Very well," he snapped with mock seriousness. "I cannot have you dying on this spot."

"No," she chimed with anticipation.

"Very well then," he said smiling down at her.

"I am —" he paused. "I am Hugh, Christian. Yes, Hugh, Christian de St. Germaine?"

The words were to Ioni like the sweetest tones of a church bell. For a long moment they simply gazed at one another. Germaine broke the silence.

"Ioni, my full name is Hugh Christian de St. Germaine."

Ioni said nothing and as though spellbound she lifted up her arms to him placed them round his neck whispering over and over.

"Hugh Christian, Hugh Christian."

Then drawing herself up to him she kissed him saying,

"Oh! Hugh Christian, I love you. I love you." And she clasped him together for a long time, kissing him and whispering his name.

Another long and sweet silence passed between then, as Ioni nestled in his arms, her head cradled against his chest. At length she looked up at him and said,

"I too have a confession to make to you."

"Oh yes?" he mused. "Then tell me all."

She paused awhile and rested her head in his chest again.

"Ioni is not my real name," she said.

"Good Lord!" he said in mock horror. "Have I been loving a total stranger, then. Who are you then, my little changeling?"

"I'm not a changeling," she laughed, "and my name is not Ioni."

"Not Ioni," he said. "What then? I must know – or I shall die on this spot!"

"The name Ioni is a testament as you call it, to my brother Jean when he was small and I was his baby sister. He could not pronounce my real name and would get cross if anyone called me anything but Ioni."

"And what was the real name, your real name," Germaine pressed.

"You must promise not to laugh," said Ioni chuckling, "or if you do, you will die on this spot."

"I promise," said Germaine. "I am the soul of seriousness."

"Well," said Ioni, "I am – my name is Leonine."

There was silence as Ioni looked into Germaine's face.

"You are Leonine?" he said. "Leonine, Leonine."

There was a pause and Germaine said,

"Leonine?"

"Yes, Hugh Christian."

"Leonine of Valdelaine, I love you Leonine!"

"And I, Leonine, love you, Hugh Christian!"

And they kissed each other again. After some time Ioni spoke again,

"Amazing isn't it," she said, "that we have come such a long journey in both our lives before anyone called us by our real names."

"Leonine," was all he said.

"And I'm so glad you were the first to call me by my real name!" she said.

"Now," said Germaine, "we have our real names back again and I'm glad you were the first to use mine. It is something special between us."

"Yes," mused Ioni.

"And the moon," said Germaine.

"The moon?" quizzed Ioni.

"Yes the moon, Ioni," said Germaine. "That moon is ours, Ioni. It shines for us. It waxed knowing it would find us together. Strange isn't it, the good moon has waxed and waned for thousands of years since God made the world. And now, Ioni, it waxes and shines just for you and me. It is our moon.

"Hmm! That's true, Germaine. It is our moon!" repeated Ioni. Presently she spoke again.

"There's another question, Germaine."

"Oh no. What a night for questions!" said Germaine.

"It's a very important question, though," pressed Ioni.

"Very well," said Germaine. "Out with it. What is your question?"

Ioni paused and said,

"Did you love any other maidens before you met me!"

Germaine fell back over the tree trunk with laughter and Ioni tumbled with him.

And the two lovers were happy in the moonlight; they were silent in their happiness and happy to be silent.

*   *   *

How these two young people managed to stay awake in the blissful days that followed was nothing short of miraculous, given that their moonlit nightly trysts stole so much of normal sleeping time. But when considered, the young heart in the flower of first love is surely a winged thing, and strange new energies are released into the spirit which are not available in normal life. Ioni might steal an hour or so in the afternoon curled up on top of her bed. Germaine often dozed a while, hidden amid the straw of the stables. Waking in the morning or in the afternoon they would both open their eyes to a world of happiness never before experienced by either of them. During the long day they would seldom catch a glimpse of each other, and if they did, it was only for a fleeting moment of loving glance, smiling eyes and even laughter, though no words could be spoken.

*   *   *

For Germaine too, these were days of wonder. To think of Ioni, even to see her for a moment was spellbinding; to be in her presence for any length of time was enough to drive him giddy. And yet, all feelings had to be hidden, all emotions held in taut control. Her voice too, was a challenge as it hung on the air for him to hear, especially at mealtimes or when they both found themselves in company with others. This was, he thought, this was the girl who has kept the keys of my freedom, who has held the scales of justice over me, the girl on whom I live or die; this was she that had scolded, cajoled and counselled me all this time; this is she that now, well, that now loves me, in whose heart there is a flame of love so great that it meets and matches the very fire in my own heart. And if there were any doubt of the matter, then remember how this very morning she swept past me in the hall with her head in the air and on reaching the doorway and see-

374

ing no one about, had swirled around, ran to hold me and kissed me with a whisper, "Be well, my love, till soon we meet – soon my love, or I will die." She had then turned away in the direction she had been going, straightened her hair, cleared her throat with a cough, opened the door and given him a last divine look as she disappeared. He could still see her eyes, long after she had gone, blinking at him from the doorway! He thought, when I see you, Ioni, I go mad, but then if I see you not I will go mad likewise. There are things of which I am certain, he mused as he lay on top of his bed. Around me now is this chamber with its familiar walls; through the slit window the sky is now blue; it is the evening of this day; my name is Germaine of Anlac and I own no other. And I know that I love Ioni to my heart, blood and bones; this love is as certain as anything that I have ever known. If I have ever known anything as a certainty, this is it. This knowledge, when one has pause to let it sink in, is the most powerful force that I have ever known. If she walks, speaks or sings, she no longer does so outside myself – she walks, speaks and sings within me. Like a little genie, she dwells in my heart. How, he thought, could I have been so lucky? I would not have it any other way, whatever fortune holds in store for me in this life, it is nothing compared with this love I have. Now I am no longer what I was, for now, in this love I surge above, beyond everything I ever knew, I tower above my former self. How often indeed, have I heard stories of love and thought I understood something of them only to know it all now. I know it, I feel it and I live it now. I could never have known then what I feel now, that I would do anything, risk anything, risk every-thing for her, and not be afraid of anything. Only now do I know that this feeling could exist in the human heart at all, I am glad I lived long enough to know it and now I can live again. And here, of all places, to find this love where I only expected harshness, reproach and hostility. Who could have thought, the day I first came here to begin a life of bitter imprisonment, that I would find here something so wonderful, something to live or die for, something that would change my life so much. With that, Germaine rolled over the side of the bed, leapt high in the air, let out a great shout and almost touched the rafters of the ceiling above him. When his legs hit the floor again they crumpled under him and he fell heavily. But he just rolled over, looked at the ceiling and laughed for sheer joy.

A few days later, in the midst of some similar ponderings as he sat alone in the hall, he again leapt high in the air only to grasp at the antlers of a stuffed stag's head that hung on the wall. Germaine and the antlers, stag and all, came crashing down on one of the trestles, and then crashed to the floor where he rolled about with loud whoops and laughter. He sighed happily still clutching the stag's head and then his eyes met hers as she stood mouth agape in the doorway. He was about to say something to Ioni when she gathered up her skirts and barged onward past where he lay.

"My Lord Anlac, pray take your high spirits somewhere else other than the dining hall! We will need what is left of it for the evening meal!" A swirl of skirts and she was gone!

"Oh God!" gasped Germaine as he looked sideways and saw that even the stag's eyes looked reprovingly at him. And he didn't care.

*   *   *

Not all of the meetings between Ioni and Germaine took place at their secret bower among the trees that lay beyond the fields. Long hours beneath the moon had devastated their precious sleeping time; and so, Ioni had to find some suitable places within the castle walls where shorter trysts might be held, places which could be quiet and isolated and safe from all possible intrusion. As a woman, and more especially as a woman in love, Ioni was more than adept at finding the best locations and at communicating to Germaine the location of the next trysting place. She managed to do this each day when discretion allowed her even the shortest moment in the company of her beloved Germaine. Having successfully tried a number of places here and there, they both agreed that a chamber at the base of the old tower was best of all. All that was needed was a simple candle, two chairs and a table and, of course, a length of cloth to place against the base of the door to prevent any passerby from seeing the light of the candle in the tiny space between the door and the ground. There they could meet, whisper, even talk aloud and laugh. They could be there together, for a few hours before midnight and then, parting silently they could make their long journey separately to their respective quarters in the new tower. Uncle Robert was usually the only one in the old tower, but he lived way up at the very top of it well out of earshot, and anyway he never came down at night preferring his solitude above. Sometimes, of course when they were making their way back to their quarters, Ioni, who always went first, would encounter someone or some group of people, family or servants. With complete coolness Ioni would greet them, converse with them and spin any number of plausible yarns to explain her being up and about. Germaine, listening in the darkness from a good way behind would often be forced to chuckle and smile at Ioni's calm manner. Invariably she would urge family members to their bedchambers, or send the servants upon some errand, clearing the coast as it were, until Germaine himself could reach his chamber unnoticed. There was no guard now at Germaine's room, it was not deemed necessary for quite some time past.

These secret assignations in the early part of the night were the most precious times they had, Ioni and Germaine. Frequently these were times for the two of them merely to converse. Frequently also they were times for them to tell stories of their lives and experiences. Sometimes there was much laughter between them and sometimes there were long loving silences. Most times they sat with the table and candle between them, but at times they were silent in the comfort of each other's arms and whispering as they had cause to.

Over these times, Ioni gradually explained many of her difficulties to Germaine, the difficulties of being a woman in love, secretly, in the midst of so many people. For instance she had to be formal and yet friendly towards him when they were in company. At such times she could not let her eyes linger upon him for too long, "Or my heart would beat and my face would go red, and then people would notice me – and you!" For Ioni, Eleanor was especially the problem, being very sharp in her ob-servations and possessing such quick intuition that she could tell at an instant what Ioni was thinking. The other girls were sharp too, but, for Ioni, Eleanor was the one that missed nothing of any situation. Always, Ioni had to be on her guard and quick witted whenever she was about. Germaine was learning quickly, and in situations where he found himself in the company of both these ladies he executed a most affable banter with Eleanor while maintaining a deferential kindliness towards Ioni, as if he hardly knew her.

"Ah! The ladies of Valdelaine, I vow!" he had exclaimed once on meeting them both together.

"My Lord, Germaine!" the two of them cooed. Eleanor went on, "Are you well, my Lord?"

"Well. Of course, I am well," Germaine cleared his throat with a little bow. "Nothing makes me well like the sunlight on golden hair like yours, Eleanor!"

"Why! My Lord, you flatter," Eleanor was chiding but pleased nonetheless.

"Flattery, is it?" Germaine went on with a funny glance at Ioni. "Eleanor, how can you possibly doubt my – well, my utter sincerity in this matter! Lady Ioni, pray come to my assistance in this matter, what say you?"

"I'm afraid I'm with my cousin Eleanor in this," said Ioni, keeping a straight face. "Eleanor is beautiful in every way but you do flatter, my Lord!"

"Thank you, Ioni," said Eleanor drawing Ioni close to her. "It is of course flattery and you have paid no compliment to my cousin, Lady Ioni. Is she not worthy of compliment!"

Germaine took a deep breath, stole a glance at Ioni and then said to Eleanor.

"Well, you Eleanor, with that golden hair, you are the very sunlight. Whereas, dear Lady Ioni is more, shall we say – for the moonlight!"

Ioni had a sharp intake of breath at the word moonlight and her eyes flashed at Germaine.

"Oh! How quaintly put, my Lord," Eleanor went on. "Sunshine and moonlight – indeed!"

Germaine was smiling at Eleanor but he could feel Ioni's fierce glances at him.

"Thank you, my Lord." Ioni said sweetly. "You compliment us both, quite handsomely too! I must remember that one – I am moonlight!"

On many a night in their trysting place Ioni and Germaine had plenty to tease and banter about, especially the occasions in other's company when in their speech they could only be formal. Now, in their together time they were free souls, free in each other's company as they were this night. Germaine had seen many things this past day, but now in these most precious of moments, his eyes were filled with the sight of her. All day long he had wanted to see her, and now, in the chamber with the candlelight and the silence of the night all about them she was there before him, her face close to his. He sat with his chin in his hand leaning on the table, simply gazing at her as she spoke. She was in cheerful and chatty form tonight and he continued gazing at her, as her expressions changed from thought to thought he was merely happy to be lost in the spell that she cast. Ioni talked on and on while Germaine sat wrapt in a kind of magic; she could be talking about anything at all, for all he cared. As long as she was there, as long as that beautiful face was before him, he merely sat in his silent adoration. Suddenly she stopped and looked at him, her face serious, her mouth open a little.

"You're not listening to a word I say!" she snapped.

Germaine laughed heartily as his erstwhile trance was broken and he was found out, even Ioni gradually gave a little smile. He bowed his head down into his hand and was still chuckling at his own surprise. Ioni straightened herself upright where she sat and looked about her with a long sigh.

"What is the matter with you, Anlac?" she said, looking again at him. "Don't you realise I have told more lies to get you and me to this place this very day, more than I've told in my whole life!"

One hand still covered his smiling face, and he tried to reach across the table to her with the other.

"What is the matter with you," she said again drawing back her hand. "I have all these things to tell you now! Things I have treasured up all day to tell you. And you sit there, not listening to a word I say, lost in a world of your own. I swear I don't know what to make of you sometimes."

Again he put his head in his hands and laughed. Meanwhile she twisted in her hair and began to tap the table loudly with her fingers. Quickly, he reached out and took her hand in his.

"Forgive me, Ioni," he said, "I am lost, I am lost as you say. But, I think I am just lost being here and looking at you." He paused for a moment and then added, "And loving you, Ioni, loving you and every moment being with you!"

Gently she took her hand from his and, as she sat there, folded her arms together protectively in front of her.

"Oh!" she whispered, comprehending, "I see!" her breathing was audible on the silent air as she placed both her white hands just below her throat. She looked away from his gaze but gradually she brought her eyes back to look at him, and her eyes stared at him for a long, long time.

"I, too, am lost with love for you," she gasped at last. "I am – melting, as it were – just with love for you." Her breathing was even quicker now as she went on. "But someone of us has to do the talking. Talking, I mean when we are here, here alone. We have to talk about something! God! Else, I do not know what might become of us – when we are here alone!"

Her head was tilted back a little allowing her to breathe more easily but she kept her eye fixed on him.

"I!" she gasped, "I love you so much!"

He looked at her longingly for a moment and shuffled back his chair to stand up.

"Let me hold you," he said.

"Nay!" she exclaimed with a look of alarm on her face. She turned sideways placing the palms of her hands on her chair. "Nay! I mean, pray do not touch me, my Lord. I am – helpless with love for you and if you but touch me now I will lose all control," and then she added pleadingly, "I beg you!"

He resumed his seat and placed one hand on the table. Looking at her there in the candlelight he began to understand. As she fumbled with the collar of her dress, her hand was trembling, as she looked back at him, her breathing was heavier. The skin of her erstwhile white face was now glowing red, and her eyes stared at him, dilated and without focus, empty and serious and with a longing he had not seen before. She swallowed hard from time to time as though her mouth had gone dry and now and then there was even a little shade in her head. And still she could only gaze at him, unspeaking, her breath almost loud and shivering on the night air.

He looked at the candle, at the table, then at the floor and sighed. He disengaged himself from his chair, stood up and paced slowly over to the door. There he turned about and rested his back against the stone of the doorframe. He looked at her across the room as she sat there looking so small and alone, her eyes cast downward. At last she spoke with a nervous manner.

"Forgive me, Germaine. Right now I have such feelings for you. Feelings that I've never had before, feelings for you, Germaine. Feelings that I know... feelings." And her voice trailed off and she turned away from him burying her head in her hands. A long, long silence passed between them and at length he said,

"All I long to do right now is to run to you. To take you up in my arms and hold you. Just to run away with you – to run away with you to any place where no one could ever find us!"

She raised her head from her hands but still did not look at him.

"But alas, Germaine, it cannot be!" she wailed. "You see, don't you, that, as we are – as we are, Germaine, it cannot be. Our love for one another cannot be fulfilled. Oh God!" And her face was in her hands again. Yet another silence filled the room, a little eternity of love, pain and confusion.

"Our love cannot be fulfilled," Germaine said quietly. "As we are. As we are, mind. But fulfilled or no, I will always love you, Ioni – as I love you now!"

Slowly she lifted her head from her hands and looked around at him. She arose from the table and ran across to him, her arms outstretched to hold him, and when they held each other they were comforted in each other's arms with no space nor distance between them.

"As God is my judge, Ioni," he whispered, "I love you and adore you now and will always. I beg you to believe this. I beg you to believe also that no longings of mine will I ever allow to cloud my love and care for you. My love, if you are not safe within my arms then my love is nothing, my life is nothing. No love of mine will ever harm you. I swear that to you!"

For a long time she held to him as though for dear life. Then she lifted her head to look into his eyes a moment. Then she rested her head sideways against his chest.

"You are brave, you know. Good and brave," she whispered, hugging and tugging him. "Brave, good and strong. I am a woman, Germaine, and when a woman gives her heart, well, she gives everything – do you understand this, Germaine? I beg you to forgive me that I love you so much. I beg you to forgive me that I have allowed myself to give you my heart – but I have not given you everything that goes with my heart." Her last few words were a little whine and she wept into his chest, but he, in turn, only held her ever closer and gently ran his fingers soothingly through her hair.

"Don't be afraid of our love, Ioni!" he whispered. "There is nothing to forgive. I understand. You too are brave, good and strong!"

At length her breathing was becoming steadier and as they stood there in each other's arms her sobbing subsided. He could feel the tension ease out of her and felt the calm descend. She even reached into her gown for a kerchief, blew her nose loudly and they both laughed.

"Oh God! Germaine I love you, but what kind of fools are we at all." And she laughed again. He took a deep breath and said solemnly,

"Big fools, Ioni. Big fools! Probably the biggest in the world!" And they were both laughing again. "In fact," he went on, "can you imagine some day it will be carved on our tombstones. Germaine and Ioni. Two big fools!" They were laughing at nothing and everything now and embraced for sheer joy.

"Oh my Lord!" she said at last. "You have cheered me up. Thank God I have known you, Germaine. Thank God I have loved you!"

"When I came first to Valdelaine," he answered, "I came here, wounded in my body. But on my heart and mind there was a cloud, a cloud so great I had no reason nor wit, nor care for anything anymore and I knew not why I was there at all. And now you have given me everything, my life, my heart, everything."

She smiled and said, "We must leave now, Germaine. But let me give you a kiss. A kiss to send you sweet dreams and sleep!" When she turned to open the door he whispered after her. "A kiss like that could keep me awake all night!" She paused at the door until they were both serious again. "Be silent, my Lord. And don't forget to take the candle with you when you leave!"

There were days when Ioni and Germaine did meet each other in broad daylight and in full view of anyone who might happen to see them. They met deliberately and by prior arrangement; they could be sure that no one, even by a far stretch of the imagination, and seeing them together, could even faintly guess at the fervent passion that possessed each one for the other. Having been together so much in the past, people would have no surprise at seeing them together now. Ioni had agreed to meet him that evening as he was walking one of the horses from the fields to the stables. That they would meet and converse would be a surprise to no one. He stopped and held the horse by the reins as she approached. They seemed to talk a while, in casual fashion, and then he turned about with the horse to walk beside her. They paused again a little further on.

"Have you thought about, well…" she said, turning her gaze away back towards the castle. "What I'm trying to say is – have you thought about the future?"

"The future, Ioni?" he quizzed also looking away. "What about the future?"

"The time when you leave Valdelaine," she said reaching out and picking a blade of grass from the bank.

"As you know, Germaine, you must leave all of this, Valdelaine – and me!"

He breathed hard and coughed. "That is something I don't want to think of," he said frowning and fidgeting with the horse's throat lash. "At least I try not to think about it. I know it's there, ahead of us but I refuse to think of it!"

"But we must think of it," blurted Ioni, suddenly turning and looking straight at him, but he started walking again the horse beside him. She trotted after him and keeping pace with him said,

"We must think about it, Germaine. What are we going to do when you are gone from here. Oh God! Germaine, I don't want you to leave!" He stopped again and turned to look at her, her face flushed and already a tear welling in her eye. Even as he wanted to, he could not reach out to her.

"Ioni, I think about this too," he said calmly, "and I don't want to leave you. Look, you have been very brave. But neither of us knows what our future will hold."

She paused, looking at him with a weary curious look. She placed her napkin to her mouth and spoke.

"What's to become of us when we part," but she could say no more and stepped forward into his embrace. Germaine held her to him and with his free hand deftly moved the horse around so that they could not be properly seen from the castle. Presently she looked up at him.

"I will be faithful to you," she said. "As surely as I love you this minute."

"And I will be faithful to you," he tried to soothe her with his voice. "I have never known nor loved anyone like you."

But Ioni tore herself from his embrace and ran to a tree beside the lane. This conversation had gone all wrong for her, she had wanted his love and his reassurance but when her ears heard what she was saying, she had felt sudden fear and panic at the thought that he would soon be taken from her, how soon she did not know. She had raised the subject with him here out in the open, not realising what convulsive emotions of loss and terror would ensue. She was now standing under the tree, trying to keep out of view, and he was standing with the horse in the laneway trying to peer at her through the leaves.

"Forgive me, Germaine!" she called. "I did not realise I would be so upset."

"I forgive you," Germaine called back. "But you had better come out from there. There are people approaching us on the lane."

"Oh God," cried Ioni, jumping out from under the tree, straightening her face, her dress, herself. She was just in time to glance down the lane and see approaching them where they stood a large group of workmen making their way homeward with horses and carts. Even at a distance they were a merry crew talking boisterously on the evening air, laughing and breaking into song. As they approached the spot where Germaine and Ioni stood, the noise of banter and song died down and their red faces beamed into smiles as they recognised the lady of the castle. Hats were doffed and Ioni was greeted with a hearty "God save your Ladyship!" by one and all. Ioni smiled and even gave a little bow. "God save you men!" she cheered. The cortege trundled past the two lovers until the last of the lads called out a final "God save your Ladyship!" Slowly as the men and carts made their way away from the couple toward the bridge the banter and the songs were resumed again causing both Ioni and Germaine to smile. God bless them, in their simple happiness, thought Ioni.

"Forgive me," Ioni spoke at last as they both made their way toward the castle, the horse plodding between them.

"Let's not talk about it now," said Germaine. "Let's talk about happy things!"

"Yes," said Ioni. "Let's talk about happy things!"

"I think men are wonderful."

"You do?"

"Yes, when I ponder on all the heroes of the great stories of the olden times my heart is so filled with wonder at how great and heroic they were."

He was silent for a time and then said,

"Yes, there were so many heroic men and women in the great legends. But I think rather that perhaps they, too, were ordinary people like ourselves. The times they lived in called for heroes and heroines, else there would be no legends, there would have been no one to stand up to the evil times they lived in."

"So you think they may have been very ordinary folk who became heroes in their appointed time?"

"I think so," he said.

"And do you think we live in such times like in the legends?"

"Perhaps we do. Only time will tell!"

*   *   *

There was a long silence between them.

She was very different in her manner tonight, Germaine thought. The usual effusive outpouring of conversation was replaced by an occasional remark about nothing in particular. She seemed to be in a distant world, and in her manner and few words it seemed as though an invisible glass case had descended upon her keeping her remote and far from her usual warmth. They were seated at the table in the little chamber on the ground floor of the old tower – the chamber which had been their casual trysting place for so long. Germaine was certain that he detected an uncharacteristic barb in some of Ioni's remarks and comments. The change of mood was so vast that the usual Ioni had vanished and in her place was someone new and strange. Germaine was at pains to recognise any of the usual in his loved one. After a long silence Ioni said, "Let me put it to you, Germaine, that soon you will have to depart from Valdelaine."

Germaine thought about her words for a moment and said, "Yes Ioni, that is true!"

"I wish you didn't have to go!" she said without expression, pulling her shawl about her, then resting her chin on the palm of her hand, and looking away.

"You know that I must leave, Ioni," he said gently. "You know there are many things I have to do in Bergmond. But it will not be forever. When everything is settled in Bergmond, I shall come back for you, with all speed!

She turned in the chair and looked at him and said, "I doubt that, Germaine!"

Germaine could not believe what he was hearing and he clutched both sides of the table in his strong hands.

"How can you – how can you possibly say that. You know I love you, Ioni, and would do anything for you!"

She looked sadly at him, her lips in a simper.

"I'm afraid, Germaine, that you have loved me simply because I was there, I was available."

Germaine struggled to speak.

"You loved your time here," she said, "and you loved me because you were a captive. But now you will be free – free to love every fair maiden in Bergmond. I softened and sweetened your time here, but what you felt for me was a kind of loving, Germaine. You were grateful, Germaine, but you did not really love me."

Aghast and angry, perplexed and surprised, Germaine spluttered and stammered but could not find words. Finally he threw back his chair angrily, stood up and towered over Ioni, leaning on his hands on the table.

"My God, Ioni, I love you now and will always. What do you think I was doing these past months – playing at love? Pretending? For God's sake, Ioni, believe me. I don't give my heart away lightly!" and he pounded his fist angrily on the table. But Ioni only swung away from him in the chair.

"Honestly, Ioni, I cannot believe you are speaking like this – what has happened to change you, to change everything?"

She turned about in the chair, stood up as he had done allowing the chair to fall with a crash behind her.

"Nothing has changed!" she said loudly. "But we have to face it, you fool!" She began banging on the table with every word, hurting her fist as she did so. "We are neither of us in a fairytale!"

Germaine took a step backward from the on-slaught of her anger. Baffled beyond understanding he said angrily,

"What do you mean – what has fairytale got to do with you and me!"

She turned away, picked up the fallen chair and sat in it facing away from him, her hands clenched together before her.

"We have to face it, we have to be realists and mature. When you go back to Bergmond and Anlac, you will forget me because it is all so far away and God in Heaven knows how long this war will last." She sighed a moment and then went on, "My father had designs for me in Belmont. Ye Gods! Why did I not listen to him then! This very night I could have been Lady Belmont – and not meshed in a love that has no way forward! There is not a future for us, Germaine." With that her head began bobbing up and down, she was lost in convulsions of weeping.

And then suddenly there was the sound of the door ring rattling. The two stared wide eyed as the door swung open to reveal the gaunt figure of Uncle Robert, smiling mouth and eyes wide with amazement.

"Oh! My children!" he blinked at both of them. If the situation had not been so tragic it would be comical. Or at least Uncle Robert's strange appearance and presence would have been comical. "What to do! What to do! And what are the two of you doing here at this strange hour!"

Germaine had lost the power of speech but Ioni answered calmly,

"My Lord Anlac and I had business to discuss, Uncle!" she said and moved down the room looking out the window.

"Oh! What to do!" he moaned, shiftily looking at them both and wrapping his cloak tightly around him. "I thought I heard voices down here. I thought I heard quarrelling! What to do! There it is!"

"Well, Uncle Robert, we were quarrelling," said Ioni looking round at him. "But it is all right now. I've said everything I want to Lord Anlac!"

"Oh! Good," said Uncle Robert, shrugging his shoulders. "Quarrelling over. Quarrelling over. Good! What to do indeed!"

Germaine shifted uncomfortably in his seat while Ioni paced down the room and placed her arms about Uncle Robert's shoulders.

"There's nothing to worry about, Uncle Robert," she said to the old man. "We have finished speaking to each other. And you may go back to bed! Everything is fine now!"

Uncle Robert nodded and made to go to the door but turned around to them, his face widening into a mischievous grin. His eyes twinkled from one to another.

"There it is!" he chuckled. "But there is a very good wine. Yes. What to do! A very good wine!" And taking his hand from beneath his cloak he pointed a crooked forefinger upward and his twinkling eye followed the direction indicated from his finger all the way up to the ceiling. "Up there. A very good wine just matured. There it is! You both must come up and taste it with me. The Bible," he chuckled, "says it is not good for man to be alone! But I say it is not good for a man to drink wine alone!"

Germaine and Ioni were standing now not knowing whether to laugh or cry when Uncle Robert turned their way again and gave them a conspiratorial wink.

"Oil on troubled waters, they say," he said. "But I say 'Good wine on troubled spirits.' There it is! Come with me, my children. Come with me!" He was gone out the door and up the stairs giggling as he went. Germaine and Ioni looked at each other with strained eyes and strained hearts, neither spirit over the shock of their quarrel.

"I will go up to him," said Ioni, coolly gathering up her cloak. "But I doubt there's any wine in this world this night to soothe me! Will you come?"

"He is your kith and kin!" said Germaine bitterly. "You go if it pleases you!"

"Very well." said Ioni with equal bitterness. "I can see your guilt has got the better of you."

He turned from the door and looked at her coldly.

"Not guilt!" he spat at her. "Just more than enough Valdelaines for one night!"

She wrapped the cloak about her.

"Coward!" she hissed back. "You could not bring yourself to do this much even for me! Go to bed and sleep, Anlac!"

With that she stormed out the door past him and began to step up the stairs.

"Go to bed and sleep, Anlac!" she called to him as she disappeared round the spiral.

"Damn!" was all Germaine could say and he trudged angrily up the stairs. What a night, he thought, first a row with Ioni and now, and now, a night of tasting wines with mad old Uncle Robert. When he reached the door of Robert's quarters he saw Ioni divest herself of her cloak and step around his table to make him comfortable in his seat.

"And where is this wonderful wine you have made, Uncle?" Ioni was saying as though full of wonder and interest.

"Patience, my child," Robert said solemnly and joined his hands. He spotted Germaine at the door. "Be seated, my Lord. And you, Lady Ioni, pray fetch three pewter mugs from the shelf behind you."

Germaine sat. Ioni fetched the mugs, placed them on the table. Robert now placed his hands on the table and looked from one to another.

"The wine, my children," he said peering at them both solemnly. "Pray pour the wine, my child."

Ioni reached for the pewter jug and began pouring the red liquid, a measure to each mug, while Germaine looked on in gloomy discontent.

"I do believe," said Robert, "that you are about to taste the divine liquid such as you have never tasted before."

They were about to reach for the mugs when the raven on the stand gave a great squawking cough, spread its wings and sailed across the room to perch on Robert's shoulder. He was unperturbed by this event but neither of the other two could suppress their amusement. Robert merely turned his eyes sideways to the great creature.

"Ah! You black hearted old scarecrow," Robert smiled. "You've come to taste the wine have you? Taste away but remember your manners, we have guests present," and he held up the mug for the raven's inspection. The raven dipped its beak in the wine and then lifted its head to sip back some of the concoction and, not finding it quite to his liking, again squawked and coughed his disapproval. Turning about on Robert's shoulder he flew back to his perch by the wall, his great wings gave a loud fluttering sound as he steadied himself.

"And what, may I ask, do you think of that for impudent behaviour?" chirped Robert winking at the two young people.

Ioni could not contain her laughter and even Germaine smiled with amusement. Robert joined his hands on the table, looked up to heaven and said,

"This is no time for giddiness, my children. There is some serious drinking to be done!" And he held his mug before him.

They drank deeply as Robert chatted on. It was good wine. Hearts were lightened and the two lovers stole smiling glances at each other, their faces gleaming in the candlelight. As they chatted, and especially listened to Robert and his stories and witticisms, Germaine began to realise the fact that Robert was no longer stammering or repeating himself in his speech. Was it the wine, or was it the company? At any rate Robert was totally lucid, relaxed and happy. At the end of the little festivity Robert raised his mug and said,

"To what shall we drink, then, before we part? To what else, my children, but to friendship and to happy love."

Germaine and Ioni stretched out their mugs in toast and said in chorus,

"To friendship and to happy love."

Before they left his room Robert said,

"Now, my children, don't let me down! Be up and about early in the morning. And remember! Never a word to anyone. This little wine fest of ours never happened! I pray you never reveal to anyone the secret of our conviviality, especially to my brother Raymond! You see, Raymond actually thinks that I am mad!" and he nearly fell over the table with his own laughter. "And not a word to Frère Benedict – not a word mind you. That old religious windbag thinks that I am both a heretic and mad!" Again he was in convulsions of laughter at his own humour. "And you, Ioni. Not a word of this to Raymond's wife Blanche – a very worthy and beautiful woman, grant you – but as formidable a she dragon as ever breathed fire!" Uproarious laughter again and even the wolfhound began to howl.

Ioni and Germaine descended the winding stairs to the sound of laughter, the squawking of a raven, and the howls of Brach the wolfhound.

When they reached the great hall there was silence. Ioni turned to Germaine.

"How are you feeling?" he asked in a whisper. She stood here before him shaking a little.

"I feel I need your forgiveness!"

He held her. "You have it," he whispered. "I need yours."

"Oh God, Germaine!" she sobbed. "I pray that never again such bitterness pass between us." Amen.

Chapter XIII: When All Is Said and Done

*I*t was a large crowd that had gathered about the steps and courtyards of Valdelaine that autumn morning. Hearth knights and stablemen mingled with villagers and tradesmen as if it were a festival day, all keen to get a last look at Germaine of Anlac before his departure from Valdelaine. Though the sun shone brightly and the sky was blue, the very air had lost the sap and sweetness of the summer time and was scentless, dry and cool. Even now, Germaine, dressed in full armour and regalia, was moving among the crowd, saying his farewells to one, then to another. At the furthest edge of the throng stood Lady Blanche, Eleanor and the other girls. Already, little Anna was in his arms, clinging to him with all her strength and trying her best not to weep. At the gates stood the baggage wagons and ponies, and just beyond these, Raymond and other men stood with the warhorses which would carry Germaine and his company away from Valdelaine, away to his own country.

Ioni had stood apart from the crowd at the top of the steps beneath the awning of the main door. From there, above the crowd, she could observe him as he moved here and there, and then, at last, as he mounted the warhorse. Only now did full realisation of what was happening sink in, and, in her heart there was a pang of panic, a quickening of heartbeat followed by a longing which screamed inside her. Just to run through that crowd, to tear her way through that crowd and reach him. To pull him from the warhorse and not let him go; to keep him for herself no matter what the consequences would be. But, across the gathering, the farewells and laughter and banter continued. He raised his hand as the horse began to move, he was in shadow for a moment passing beneath the archway and then, for an instant, his lovely form was caught by the autumn light. Then he was gone! She turned and stepped within the house and was glad to be there and alone; the world and all it held seemed to dissolve to nothing as she breathed a deep sigh, thankful that this moment was over and that she was still alive though the sight of her eyes was clouded by rising tears.

These were moments Germaine would not forget, ever. Later, far down on their journey, when they had paused to rest and he was glad to stretch his legs by a stream where the horses were being watered. There, he had time to recollect the last moments in Valdelaine and the last moment with Ioni. He could remember striding along the passageway, his armour clanking all about him, the helmet in his left hand. There she had stood in the hallway inside the main doorway dressed in a long blue gown. She was looking intently at him as he approached, a cheerful little smile on her face. As he stood before her, she stole one last glance at his eyes and then curtseyed before him with the simple words, "Farewell, my Lord. God speed you on your journey!"

She had then reached out and placed a little cloth pocket in his hand and he knew it contained his father's ring. He bent low, took her hand and kissed it with the words.

"Farewell, my Lady!"

For the tiniest instant he stood and looked into her face, but her eyes remained downcast as then she took his arm to lead him to the steps, to the sunlight and to the crowd. Even there he felt it as she removed her hand from his arm for the last time and already he was lost in the sea of people that thronged the steps to see him.

*　　*　　*

And so, days passed into weeks, and then into months and, for Ioni, there was hardly a waking moment that she did not think of him. How could she be otherwise? Every scene and view that met her eyes by daylight was the familiar background to their time together, every nook and cranny held memories of him, every stone and bush could tell some story or other of happenings and conversations that took place in that strange and blessed time. Sometimes at night she let grief have its sway as she wept for him, she wept for every cherished moment of the time he had been here, her prisoner, her friend, and finally her loved one. When she thought about it now, it seemed a time extraordinary beyond any other she had ever known. A time when life itself was somehow taken upwards and when one's very existence was swept above the air to another sphere of being. And now, with Germaine gone, so too was the wonder of that time, and she longed and longed for it to come back again.

As a woman, she had always known somewhere inside that there was a powerful loving force within, but only now did she realise how fully powerful that force could be, tearing her heart to pieces, tossing her about like a shipwreck in a storm. She was no longer present to herself but lost in some other world that no longer was there. If anyone had been able to notice, Ioni could be frequently seen standing forlorn and gazing into some distant time and invisible place, and only with some gust of wind or sudden sound would she recollect herself, gather her cloak about her and then step forward to her next task. She was longing to see him, perhaps for just an instant; she was longing to hear his voice once more, longing just to hold him to her heart. Without him Valdelaine was empty now. And he, of course gone far into a world of war, so distant that she begrudged every road and river, every field and mountain that now lay between them. Sometimes, her heart would jump at the sound of footsteps only to realise it was someone else. She did see him, of course, but only in the consolation of dreams just before dawn, only to wake in the winter morning knowing he was gone.

The passing of time had not allayed her love nor her grief. If anything her energies seemed to flag. She spent long hours in her room alone, sometimes she just stood staring out of windows. Even on winter evenings with cloak wrapped about her, she often stood on the battlements gazing at the countryside below.

Even so, she thought, I am not a fool. I've heard the stories of girls and women who pined for a lost love but who eventually came to laugh at it all and live their lives again. But, when I think of it, I am lost. I have no one with whom to share my grief and my stories of love. My love for him must be, and must remain, a secret. No one must know. Before God and before myself I am lost, as I am now. I cannot even remember the time before him, she thought. I cannot even recall what life was like. The path of my life was lost to me the day he came here, and now, I am so lost I cannot retrace my steps within myself even to find the woman I was then. Oh God! She sighed. Who am I now? Oh God, Anlac! You have stolen me from myself! If only I could fathom why it all had to happen like it did. And at the end of it all, I can still do nothing but only love you, Germaine. Only love you.

Ioni was thinking about herself. Amid her distress, an image flitted across the tapestry of her imagination; it was an image of herself as a child, a girl running across a meadow in the golden glow of a summer day. The image was so sudden that, involuntarily Ioni reached out to that child, that loving and lovable child, that golden hearted darling, that dashing darling child. Then all at once, a love and rage and melting grief burned her heart and broke her into hot tears. Who was she, that golden love of a girl, she asked herself. What kind of dislocation had taken place that that golden happy child was – no more? What trick had life played upon her, she sobbed, that that child was no longer within her? How would she ever find that girl again? "Ioni, Ioni," she called out. "How I have lost you!" She fell upon the floor and then bent doubled over as though struck by an arrow. She cried and cried until finally weeping had brought relief.

When she finally arose to her knees she said, "The sad gates of sorrow and distress – I pass through you now. Though you close in upon me to tear me down, yet ye shall not do so, unhappy gates! For this I swear that you had better break me to death, because if you do not, then I swear as a Valdelaine, that I shall break ye – yes, I shall break ye!"

She knelt there a long time and the 'gates of sorrow' did not come to break her, and as the moments passed she again lay upon the floor – and slept.

Gradually, without her knowing it, people around her had become aware of her loss of spirit. They themselves, of course, had no idea of the cause of her weariness but unknowingly they brought moments of light to her heart. And some of this light came from unexpected quarters. Above all, children have this divine sense of the tempests and emotions raging in the hearts of grown-ups. Little Anna, Ioni's cousin, in her childlike way, had sensed the loss in Ioni. At some time every day Anna would approach Ioni with some loving token to please her. At first it had been bunches of flowers, artlessly arranged by Anna herself; then, with the autumn, little posies of berries and wry, and by winter collections of pine cones in pine fronds.

One evening Anna entered Ioni's room to present her with the day's treasure and, jumping up into Ioni's arms, kissed her and declared,

"I love you so much, Ioni!"

Ioni felt her heart lifted from the drudgery of the day and she hugged her little cousin.

"Why, I love you too, Anna!" Ioni laughed. Anna thought for a moment and said,

"But I love you – specially!"

"Oh that's beautiful, Anna," Ioni said cheerily. "And it makes me so happy!" And it did, these daily meetings with Cousin Anna made her heart feel warm, made her laugh and lifted her spirits so much. Anna went on,

"I think I love just about everyone, Ioni!"

"Why, that's good, Anna. Pray tell me, who do you love?" said Ioni gazing into Anna's bright eyes.

"Well," said Anna, "there's you of course, and I love Papa so much. I love Uncle Raymond and Aunt Blanche. I love sister Fleur of course. Cousin Eleanor, Cousin Clara too. Cousin Jean and Cousin Eris."

Anna paused for breath and Ioni asked,

"Anyone else you love, then?" Anna sat up and thought for a moment, took a deep breath and said, solemnly,

"I love Germaine!"

Ioni's heart missed a little beat, her face lit up at the sound of his name; her eyes opened wide as she peered at Anna and said,

"You love Germaine, Anna?" Ioni said in mock surprise as she recovered from her little loss of composure.

"Of course!" said Anna, matter of fact. "I love Germaine and miss him very much!" With this, she gave a little sigh. Ioni felt thrilled and amused at the child's proclamation of love. She was speechless for a moment. Here before her was little Anna talking to her about the very love of her own heart and soul.

"I expect Germaine misses me too!" chattered Anna placing her flowers into Ioni's hands. "And some day you know, Germaine will come back and see us all again!" Her eyes wide with amusement, Ioni's heart was racing with emotion. Anna made herself more comfortable and rested her heart on Ioni's breast.

"Don't you miss him, Ioni?" she asked. Ioni got a little fit of coughing and didn't know whether to laugh or cry. Anna's face turned upward to look at her for an answer but Ioni could only burst into laughter. Anna waited calmly for an answer looking up at Ioni's eyes.

"Don't you miss him, Ioni?" she repeated.

"Well of course I do!" gasped Ioni. "Of course I miss him." She looked into Anna's eyes – if only dear Anna knew how much I miss him, she thought.

"Did you love him too?" said Anna.

"Well, of course!" Ioni was coughing again. "He was a fine gentleman and – I liked him very much!"

"Well, he loved me," Anna went on, "and now he is gone away to be a soldier in the wars. But he will come back some day to see me."

"Well, would you like to know what I think?" asked Anna, looking comically grave.

"What do you think, Cousin Anna?" said Ioni looking at her with a little smile of curiosity.

"Your problem, Ioni, was that you loved Germaine too, like the rest of us, it is just that you didn't know it at the time!"

Ioni's upper body shot forward, coughing, spluttering and laughing heartily into her sleeve. Presently Anna reached across and held her cousin's arm; she gave a little chuckle too, amused by Ioni's mirth. Then she said,

"Aw! Come on, Ioni! What I said wasn't that funny! Not really! Honestly Ioni, I don't know what's come over you this evening!"

Gradually Ioni's hysterics subsided somewhat, though her laughter continued to erupt for a little while as Anna's words continued to swim back into her mind.

Then she was calm again.

Ioni's heart was full and she hugged Anna so tight. She gazed out the casement window into the twilight. Out there, beyond Valdelaine was all of God's universe, so great and so wide. And somewhere out there was a tiny part of the universe that was Germaine, who shone like a star in her heart, a heart that had known her heart, a brave soul that had loved her. A tiny piece of the universe that had come to her heart and had told her just how loved she was.

"Ioni, what are you looking at?" Anna asked. Ioni directed Anna's gaze towards the casement and to the afterglow beyond.

"Perhaps, Anna," she said, "Germaine is away out there somewhere, somewhere far away. And perhaps he is even now thinking of us here in Valdelaine. Thinking of you, Anna, and maybe, even thinking of me too." There was a long silence as they gazed out the casement, a silence filled with wonder.

"Maybe he will come back to us one day," Ioni murmured.

"Hmm!" murmured Anna and sitting upright she turned her face earnestly to Ioni. "And when he does – I shall certainly marry him!"

At this, Ioni laughed again holding Anna to her bosom. Ah! My little Anna, she thought, if only you knew how much he means to both of us, if only you knew!

*   *   *

Gradually as time moved on Ioni began to spend time again with Aunt Blanche, with Eleanor and Clara, with Fleur and Anna. It took her mind away from her grief to some extent. She also spent time with Eleanor and Fleur who were both closer to her own age. Their conversation and their musical gifts were especially welcome as a diversion for her mind. Fleur, the quieter of the two, had a great gift for interesting conversation spiced here and there with quietly witty observations that brought tears of laughter to Ioni's eyes. Eleanor tended to be more wild and more imaginative especially in the telling of the most ordinary stories of her daily life, in which she seemed to find humour in the simplest happenings. Ioni was to spend many a happy hour with these two cousins, their company inevitably bringing sweet relief to her troubled soul.

"Oh yes!" chirped Eleanor. "You'll never guess what happened to me last night. It is only now that I remembered it. I said I would sit up awhile with mother in her room, she had been feeling poorly. Before she fell asleep she took a potion to make her sleep. She did sleep and sleep soundly. And I said I would make myself comfortable in the chair and have a little doze myself. Well I was doing nicely until suddenly mother began coughing and choking in her sleep. I jumped up with the candle in my hand. What do you think it was? Only the maid had forgotten to remove her pearls and they had ridden up under the bedclothes and into Mama's mouth – which was wide open. There was nothing for it but to put my fingers in her mouth and pull out the pearls. Jesu! Thank God they're held together with a chain or Mama would have swallowed them all!"

Ioni and Fleur were laughing.

"And did Aunt Blanche wake up?" giggled Fleur.

"Not a hope of it!" piped Eleanor. "Her sleeping potions are the best in the world!"

"And what did you do then!" quizzed Ioni.

"Oh! I said I'd enjoy my dozing again," continued Eleanor. "So I sat down, put my feet up and prayed there would be no more alarms for that night. So I did doze until finally Papa came in to go to bed!"

"What did you say to the maid?" asked Fleur when their laughter subsided.

"I said, 'You nearly choked my mother!'"

"And what did she say?"

"Why, nothing, she was sound asleep, too! Oh dear, what a night for sleepers!"

*   *   *

Besides Anna, others had noticed the mysterious loss in Ioni's spirit. Margreth, too, had sensed something was amiss – this was not the same Ioni that she had nursed from birth; the bonds formed between her and Ioni over so many years spoke loudly within Margreth's heart. She was sure that all was not well with her mistress and though she tried to think about it Margreth could not fathom the reason for Ioni's changed disposition. Sometimes at Ioni's bedtime she would pass some remark in the hope of finding the source of Ioni's pain.

"You seem tired and listless of late," she had said on one occasion. "Is there something that ails thee, or, is there something troubling your mind?"

"No, dear Margreth," Ioni smiled weakly. "I'm just tired, I think!"

As time went on this conversation was repeated, and one night as Ioni sat gazing into the fire, Margreth came bustling up the stairs and placed herself in the other chair.

"My Mistress," Margreth began. "Permit me to speak to you, child."

"What is it, Margreth," Ioni mumbled still lost in her gazing at the fire.

"What it is, my Lady," Margreth said, "is that you appear so changed of late as if some trouble had afflicted you."

"I'm alright, Margreth," Ioni said gently straightening up in her chair. "I just think..." and her voice trailed away as her thoughts were lost again.

After a little pause Margreth continued gently. "My dear Lady, I have known you all your life, I nursed you – and now I can tell something has changed inside you, for the worse, I fear. I love you as my own child.

Are you grieving for someone, Ioni, are you grieving for your mother, perhaps?"

Ioni was wide awake now and her eyes looked across at Margreth and they were filling with tears. In her heart Ioni longed to tell Margreth of her love of Germaine, but instead she broke into sobs of grief. The two women arose and embraced.

"Your mother," whispered Margreth, "is in Heaven, looking down on you and on all of us, praying for us and protecting us."

"Yes!" was all Ioni could say as she wept for Marie, her mother, but wept even more for the loss of Germaine and all he had been to her.

Margreth gradually calmed her tears and ushered her with whispered words of comfort to the bed chamber.

From moment to moment Ioni wished to stop there and then, to stop Margreth's whispers and blurt out to her nurse the whole story of herself and Germaine; to tell the whole story out straight into the heart of this woman who was a second mother to her. Every time she was stopped by the memory of Germaine and the thought of how horrified Margreth would be at the revelation. Her love story must remain secret until the day came, if ever, when Germaine would return.

Ioni slept well that night. Some weeks later, after a particularly wearing day Ioni had left the company of the others early and traipsed away to her room falling into a sleep on top of the bed. Later in the night when Margreth came to the hall to find her, there was no one there. She checked the dining hall also, again to no avail. Holding the lamp above her head Margreth climbed the spiral staircase to find Ioni's room door wide open. She stood a moment in the doorway and then her attention was arrested by the faint sound of sobbing and weeping coming from where Ioni lay, still clothed in her maroon gown. Margreth stepped forward towards the bed and was about to whisper some word of comfort when she stopped still in disbelief. Holding the lamp over Ioni's head she realised to her horror that her mistress was weeping uncontrollably – in her sleep. Margreth gazed motionless as Ioni would stop for a while, sob and turn her head a little and begin crying all over again. In God's name, Margreth thought, what could so trouble my child's heart that she weeps even in her sleep? Quietly Margreth took a wooden stool and sat by the bed whispering little words of comfort to the sleeping girl, she gently stroked Ioni's hand and tear stained face. Gradually, after what seemed an age the young girl's grieving began to subside, as if some inner storm was slowly passing away. Eventually Ioni was silent in her sleep and the only sound was her breathing. Margreth stood up and gently covered her mistress with a quilt, taking the lamp she moved across the room towards the door. She stopped again suddenly when Ioni turned her sleeping body towards the wall and cried out again. Margreth froze as she heard the words,

"Germaine, Oh God, Germaine!"

Margreth stood where she was for a long time, staring wide-eyed at the form of her mistress. When it seemed to her that Ioni had gone into a deeper sleep, Margreth moved to the chamber door and shut it silently. Now she knew everything that troubled her poor mistress.

"Germaine, Oh God, Germaine!"

When she had taken a good deep breath and allowed the full truth to sink in to her heart only then did she descend the stairs. As she went she was reminded of a day in summer, on an evening rather, when she had seen the two of them – yes, Germaine and Ioni together. They had been seated on the steps in front of the great door, at times deep in conversation and at times deep in silence together. She had smiled as she watched them together, how well they looked together, how beautiful they were together now, at this moment, like a pair of friends, or lovers. Such a pity, she had thought, that they could never be lovers as things were, but if circumstances had been otherwise, she mused, they would have been perfect for each other. She remembered thinking, well, whatever, friends or lovers, she had better get them in from the front steps. It would be cold soon and if they wanted to talk, Margreth had determined it would not be out there where anyone could see them. The kitchen was quite empty and they could talk away in there, far from any possible prying eyes.

"What are you both doing out here," she had chided them. "Come inside to the kitchen. It is nice and quiet there. The two of you can chat away over a cup of wine with no one to bother you! I'll see to that!"

The two, Germaine and Ioni, had got up, a little red faced. They smiled at each other and followed Margreth to the kitchen where they were seated at the table, a cup of wine each before them. Margreth had left. She now smiled and tears came to her eyes at the memory. The two of them had been in love and now she knew it.

There was little sleep for Margreth that night, but towards morning she had formed some plan of action to help soothe Ioni's heart. She had racked her brain for some time with one possible solution or another. Now, at cockcrow she decided to opt for one scheme she had rejected earlier in the night. Discreetly she would go to the abbey and see the Reverend Abbess. She would not reveal anything of Ioni's real trouble but merely confide to the abbess Ioni's state of weariness and her need for a change of people and surroundings. She would urge the abbess to write to Ioni expressing the desire of the sisters to see the Lady of Valdelaine again, and to avail of her company for some time, if she would deign to visit with the sisters for a while.

In the days that followed Margreth accomplished all her plan and within a short time Ioni received a letter from the Mother Abbess.

"What to do, Margreth!" sighed Ioni when they met. "I've been invited to the abbey for a time. You know, I would love to go there, in fact. But there is so much to do here.

"Silly girl!" chided Margreth. "You could do with a good rest, my dear. And you could do well with a change from Valdelaine!"

"Yes I could!" sighed Ioni longingly. "But how can I leave here with so much to do!"

"Well let me put it this way," said Margreth folding her arms. "If anything goes wrong here we will send for you straight away. Just go away, Ioni, child, we'll manage here, for a while at least."

Ioni took a little more persuading, and after speaking with Uncle Raymond and Blanche, also with Uncle Robert, she was assured that all would be well in her absence. She could go, stay at the abbey with a light heart.

And she did.

*   *   *

For Ioni the first few days at the abbey contained a mixture of impressions and emotions. Though she had not visited the place since her mother's death she recalled every nook and cranny as she went about her daily routine. There was a familiarity too with the sisters whom she had met there before, and she relished meeting them again. She felt a sense of refreshment in this female haven and in the encounter with each sister and the stories they had to tell. As ever, of course, in the sisters there was this eternal sense of the other world mingled with warm femininity. Though they had nothing of the comforts of her life at Valdelaine, each one seemed to glow from within with a quality Ioni could not quite define. Perhaps it was sheer peacefulness, Ioni reflected. They truly believe, she mused, they truly hope and love. The rest seems to follow from this. If only I could be like this, she reproached herself, if only I could be so completely at peace and trust totally and completely in the providence of the Divinity. Of course no one, not even the mother abbess knew of her inner torment of recent months, but the conversations with the sisters, the sense of compassion and the sense of humour of these women, provided the first balm to her soul that Ioni was to experience here.

She accompanied the nuns to most prayers, to meals, and to recreation times, but otherwise she was left to her own devices. It was in the times of solitude however that old fears and griefs seemed to assail her. The strange atmosphere of the abbey during the hours of silence was so difficult. It was in these hours that she felt the strangeness of being so different from the nuns, a feeling so strong at times that she felt quite lost and unworthy. She could not fathom why she felt this way. If Germaine were to appear out of nowhere at the abbey gate she would just run to him and be so happy. Germaine! God! Would the longing for him ever leave her, she cried inside her soul. Here I am in this holy place, and all I can think of is him, Hugo Christian de St. Germaine.

Save for Ioni, the little chapel was empty; she had come to like this time of evening just before nightfall, when candles had been lit and the singing of the nuns echoed along the dark stone corridors. The only other sound was that of the wind, gusting outside around the abbey towers, but within all was calm and peaceful and the inner silence of the chapel was sweet and comforting. Some time had passed and Ioni simply sat and savoured the quietness of the atmosphere; there was no longing to leave this holy place, only the reverse, the longing to stay in this sweet silence forever listening to sounds and watching the winking of the lamps and the flickering light they cast on pillars, walls and rafters. Gradually her attention was brought to a bookstand near the altar and she rose and approached it to find a book perched atop the stand, opened. In the available light she found it was a psalmody book, and in the light of a nearby candle she stood and began to read.

Benedicite Dominum anima mea. "Bless the lord, Oh my soul." Ioni peered closer and squinted to read on. "And all that is within me bless his holy name." Ioni read on intrigued by the beautiful words. "Who redeemeth thy life from destruction, who crowneth thee with loving kindness and tender mercies." Line by line she read the illumined text, breathless now with its beauty. "As far as the east is from the west, so far hath he removed our transgressions." Word by gentle word, the psalm seemed to sink into her own soul. She read the text again and again, savouring every word and every nuance of its meaning. She repeated parts of it. "All that is within me, bless his holy name."

All my being! All my being, she thought.

Tears began to flow gently as she thought about all her being. Every tiny iota of me, every pulse of blood, every thought of my heart, every impulse of passion, every emotion I have ever known – bless his holy name.

All the losses, all the pains, all the giddy joys she had known; all the state of confusion and perplexity, all of it was in her and it was praising God. Ioni was now breathless with excitement – somehow God had been there within her through every tiny moment of her life, the eternal silent witness of all her griefs, her mistakes and her terrors. I have redeemed your life, Ioni, from destruction. I have crowned you, Ioni, with loving kindness and compassion. She was standing at the lectern holding it with both hands, shedding silent tears and almost out of breath. "All my being," she gasped, "bless his holy name." All the crazy whirlwind of my life, she thought, all the love and the loss, all the...

"All, all, all my being!" she cried out loud.

Her heart full, she ran to the steps of the altar and threw herself there, again tears, but this time tears of joy that all of her life had been lived, for better or worse, that all her life had meaning. She lay there on the steps, breathing the words, even laughing with joy and with the feeling that all her life as it had all happened had been meant to happen. It was all part of some plan. In spite of all, all was well.

She continued to lie a long while there breathing heavily with excitement until gradually she became calm, and an eerie wonderful gratitude seemed to slip gently into her soul. At length she raised herself to her knees, kissed the stone altar step and returned to her seat. There she lived a long silence, a happy heart, a soul refreshed. "All my being, bless his holy name," her mind no longer spoke these words, they just sang somewhere in her merry soul. Over and over again she mulled the lines that she could remember. "He remembers that we are dust," and "As far as the east is from the west, so far from us He has put our transgressions!" The night time had come and a sweet darkness had enveloped her while, on the altar candles flickered in the happy gloom. Ioni had no desire to leave the holy place, but soon the sisters would file in for matins. She rose from her place and went out into the cool air of the cloister, the precious words from the Holy Book seemed to follow her. "He has redeemed your life from destruction, He has crowned you with loving kindness and compassion." As she strolled the cloister paths she thought – yes, now I know that, perhaps it was all meant to be. Strange as it all was, it was all meant to happen, for whatever reason I do not know. But now, I think, I would have it all no other way. Certainly I have been crushed by it all, by the loneliness and by the longing for Germaine. But my soul has known such wonder and delight, such sheer entrancement in the experience of finding Germaine in my little life. And how that life was lifted away beyond anything I had known just by knowing him. Without him I would not have known such joy was even possible. No wonder the poets and troubadours wrote and sang about it. Now I have known it, I miss it all with terrible pain. But I know that it is not the end, it is part of the life and destiny of the person that I am. It is the destiny of souls that are blessed, for sure. "He has redeemed your life from destruction, He has crowned you with loving kindness and compassion!"

*   *   *

During the course of a busy day it had crossed Ioni's mind that, having finally returned to Valdelaine after her sojourn at the convent, she had not been up to see Uncle Robert. With her heart now much more at peace than it had been of late she was rather excited at the prospect of calling to see him again. That night, by candlelight, she climbed the stairs of the old tower. Halfway up the climb she heard Brach's deep barking and the great hound trundled down the steps to greet her. She petted and spoke to him and he turned about and bounded happily up the stairs before her. As she reached the open door the raven too was squawking from inside the candlelit chamber. Coming in the doorway she beheld Uncle Robert standing by his table, one of his hands was on top of his head and the other was placed on his heart. He seemed distraught about something, though he smiled at her as she entered.

"My child!" he chirped, as she reached out to embrace him. But she saw his eyes were reddish and there were tears on his face.

"Uncle Robert!" she exclaimed. "What's amiss with you. You have been weeping! What troubles you!" But his face simply beamed with a smile.

"Why, nothing's amiss, Ioni, child." He held her by the arms, "Nothing's amiss, dear child. All is well."

"But why have you been weeping then," Ioni cried.

"Oh! Yes! There it is. Weeping!" he said. "I have been weeping haven't I?" He thought for a moment frowning. "Ah! Yes. I have it now!" he said. "My tears are tears of joy and gratitude!"

"Gratitude?" Ioni took him to the chair and seated him. "Gratitude to whom and for what?"

Robert's eyes turned slowly to a little shelf on the wall where Ioni could see a crucifix standing next to a little icon of the Holy Virgin. She had never seen either of them before. He looked back at her.

"Gratitude to God, Ioni!" he said as if in a mystical trance. "For all his great goodness. For all his great favours to me – to me, Ioni." Ioni was very conscious of her own recent spiritual experiences and felt a familiarity now with anyone else in a similar state of devotion. She smiled gently at him as she held his hands and nodded her head.

"Gratitude to God, Uncle Robert," she said soothingly.

"Yes Ioni. God has recently blessed me –" he searched for words, "has blessed me with his great favour. Before you came in I was – on my knees, Ioni. To thank Him, you understand – to thank Him for His great gift to me!"

"Very good, Uncle Robert," she said. "I'm glad you were – praying to God."

"Of course I was, my child," he smiled back.

"So you have come back to the Lord!" she said cheerfully, still holding his hands. His face grew serious for a moment as he said looking at her,

"Well, of course, I was never very far from Him – you know."

"Of course, not, Uncle Robert," she said glancing first at the display of religious devotion on the shelf and then looking back into his eyes.

"So you are well, then!" she cried.

"Never better, my child, never better," he chuckled. "And you, dear child, have you been well? I have not seen you for some time, but I have been very busy, you see."

"No – I mean yes! I have been well," she said turning in her chair, in towards the table, placing her hands on it. "I have been away for some time. I went to stay at the abbey with the nuns!"

"With them old hags!" he exclaimed. "Did they treat you well!"

Ioni couldn't help laughing. "Yes, Uncle, they were very good to me," she said, "and I was happy there. But now I'm back to Valdelaine again."

Eyes wide open as if in wonder he gazed at her for a long, long moment and then drew his face close to hers and whispered in her ear.

"And not a moment too soon!" She was wide eyed now with curiosity, but he placed his finger over his mouth, indicating silence to her, got out of his chair, went to a cupboard by the wall, opened the door and took out a casket which he placed before her on the table. He then opened the casket to reveal two silver goblets that gleamed in the candlelight when he placed them on the table before her. Though mystified she said nothing, thinking the goblets looked like church chalices and might have something to do with his sudden religious 'conversion'. He reached out and placed one goblet before her, then he turned away and reached up to a topmost shelf, taking down a silver decanter and placing it on the table between them. He was looking at her, eyes shining with a kind of triumphant joy.

"This is it, Ioni," he said. "This is the gift of God," and he uncovered the decanter. "What you see before you is a decanter of wine. It is the wine, Ioni – it is the wine of Cana in Galilee!"

Oh God! Thought Ioni, poor Uncle Robert, he has really gone mad after all, and a tear rolled down her face. But Uncle Robert simply sat down across the table from her.

"Don't be afraid, Ioni," he said gently. "After all these years I have finally blended it. It is what every true wine maker dreams of and works for – the perfect wine above all others. We call it the wine of Cana in Galilee. We call it this, in humility and gratitude. Because it is the nearest we humans will ever come to the holy wine of Cana. And you don't have to take my word for it. You can taste if for yourself, my dear child Ioni."

He reached out and poured the red sparkling liquid into her goblet. Then he poured into his own.

"Taste, Ioni," he said. "Taste and see that the Lord is good!"

Quite unnerved now and almost in a daze she reached out and lifted the goblet to her lips – all the while he gazed at her smiling and intent. It was good wine, as good as any she had ever tasted. But that was as far as it went, or so she thought.

"Close your eyes!" he bade her. "And drink some more."

Meekly she obeyed. Nothing. She was about to open her eyes again when it slowly began to sink in. She became aware of a warm glow inside her heart, she became aware of the room around her, she became aware of the world outside the room, she became aware of everything that existed. She floated on a kind of cloud and saw all of God's universe. Every creature and every person. She felt nothing but a sense of total peace and boundless love for everything. Love, love bonding everything in existence, love in her heart and her heart somewhere at the centre of everything. Tears rolled down her cheeks, tears of lovingness, tears of heartfelt thanks for everything, tears that, after all there was in life, there was something loving holding everything there was. Of Cana in Galilee. Tears. Of Cana in Galilee. Uncle Robert, her father, her mother... and Germaine, tears of thankfulness for them all.

Whatever eternity passed in those moments she could not tell.

Her eyes opened. Uncle Robert – dear, funny, mad Uncle Robert was still there smiling at her. He came around to her, and lifting her gently, took her to a pallet by the wall and laid her upon it. Her eyes closed again, in Cana of Galilee.

"And what shall you do, Uncle Robert?"

"I shall continue, my child, to be quite mad!" he said. "Not more mad, not less mad, just simply quite mad!"

"God bless you, Uncle Robert."

And he kissed her forehead.

*   *   *

The silence of the woodlands. The crackling of logs on the camp fire. As he turned to sleep Germaine thought of Ioni and wondered what she might be doing or thinking at this hour. It was strange to be lying on the forest floor, the magic of the night all about him, but his thoughts far away to Valdelaine and its ordered life and time. His companions still gathered at the fire, the conversation and laughter rising and falling. In the darkness he could see her face and form as though it were a vision before him; he was glad and comforted that he could see her before him in his mind's eye, her many traits had long ago enchanted him. He recalled how her head used to shake ever so slightly when she was addressed in conversation as though she wanted to look at something else first and then look at the speaker, all within the tiniest second. He smiled to himself at the memory and continued to gaze at her as though she had just come to visit him across the night. At one stage he shook with silent laughter as he remembered how, during a silence in the conversation, her head would move gently from side to side as she carefully examined the backs of her hands, almost as if they had not been there before. He had often meant to comment on this gesture in the past but had never got around to it. God! What memories came back to him on his journey homeward, especially in the precious moments before sleep came, and plunged him to the morning of the next day. There was another gesture that he recalled now with a grim little pang of longing, a gesture that betokened the mercy he had found in her existence, a gesture of reassurance also. How she would place her left hand to the pendant at her throat and reach out her right hand to the other person.

Once, in the early days of his captivity, she was reproaching him angrily about something. In those days he was wary of displeasing her and feared that he might be returned to the darkness of the dungeon far below.

"If it please you, my Lady," he had said, "should I return to the dungeon, if that is what you wish."

"Oh! No! My Lord," she had exclaimed, with a look of alarm followed quickly by a look of such kindness towards him that he never forgot it. "No, my Lord. Of course not." and the left hand went to her throat and her right hand had reached out towards him. Mercy, kindness, reassurance.

Germaine turned on his side and smiled to himself again. There, next to him and sound asleep was the ever faithful Philip, wrapped in a cloak. The ever faithful Philip lying in his own dreams, the light from the fire flickering on his face. On leaving Valdelaine, Germaine had been escorted across the wide Borderlands to Cevon, where Count Michael was encamped. Having spent some days as guest of the count, Germaine had eagerly awaited the arrival of an escort from the Bergmond side which would deliver Eris de Valdelaine to the count, and which,

in turn, would fetch Germaine home. Three days of waiting had passed when the escort finally arrived. And what
an escort it had been! It comprised three of Germaine's
closest friends – Philip himself, with both Edgar and Romain for company. It had taken some time for the joy of
such a reunion to die down, but Germaine had been determined to meet and present himself to young Eris de
Valdelaine, considering two particular reasons. Firstly, he
wished to shake the hand of the young man who was being handed over in exchange for his own freedom. Sec-
ondly Germaine dearly wished to meet the younger
brother of the girl he loved back in Valdelaine. As Germaine embraced Philip and the others, a crowd of cheering knights had surrounded Eris who was dismounting
and presenting himself before the tall figure of Count Michael. As Eris bowed before the count another great
cheer went up. On the edge of the crowd Germaine bade
his friends to wait and made his way through the throng to
greet Eris reaching out his arms to embrace the young
Valdelaine. Another great cheer went up as the two freed
hostages from both sides stood face to face in greeting.
Amid the pleasantries and the noise of the throng Germaine's eyes had searched the face of Eris for any trace of
family similarity with Ioni. The face of Eris was as different from the dark Ioni as could be, but there somewhere in the shake of the head or the glance of the eye,
Germaine had found for a split second the similarity of
manner which, despite the surrounding crowd, betokened
without doubt the Valdelaine in Eris, which was also the
Valdelaine in his beloved Ioni. And Germaine's heart had
skipped a beat.

Germaine also presented Eris with a satchel of
gifts for Valdelaine, among which had been sealed letters
to Ioni. Germaine had turned to bid farewell to the count

and then rejoined Philip and the others. They mounted and rode together the little road that stretched across the plain to Bergmond, to Anlac and home.

And so, this happy company had ridden onwards pausing for rest in dingy wayside taverns or upon the forest floor, drawing happily ever closer to Germaine's beloved fortress Anlac. Germaine glanced once more at the sleeping face of Philip and his heart warmed at the sight. The autumn half moon was up now and its light searched among the branches for the face of his friend. Philip, the faithful friend of his youthful years, who with Edgar and Romain had come to escort him safely home. How safe he was, now that he was on his native soil, Germaine had no way of knowing. He had not yet confided to Philip that Gavron de Laude had wished him dead. Yes, Gavron of Laude and his crony members of the league which now governed the country in place of its king. Germaine took some comfort from the thought that once he reached the safety of Anlac he could then plan what his next move would be to enable him steer clear of the clutches of de Laude and the league. One thing was urgent, Germaine must somehow make contact with Father Roland at the monastery at Campaldo, and by so doing place himself in contact with those who wished to overthrow the league and its evil power within their country. At any rate things had gone well so far; with the help of Philip and the others, he had avoided any contact with any of the barons of the league. Two more days and they would be in Anlac.

As he studied the face of the sleeping Philip, Germaine was glad. Since they had first met at thirteen years of age they had been close friends, though what good Philip saw in him, Germaine could never tell. Always Philip had been there, Philip the beloved one, the piercing dark eyes beneath the shock of shining jet black hair. For

Germaine, Philip had been his joy, his wisdom and his conscience. Indeed, if ever an evil impulse arose within his heart, Germaine had only to remember Philip and be restored to innocence. As he mused on, Germaine found that now Philip was in good company within his heart. If ever an evil impulse arose within his heart, there was Philip of course, and now too there was Ioni. Now too there was little Anna, looking up at him, her eyes squinting in the sunshine, and there too were the spring flowers that he had seen bloom around Valdelaine.

On the long journey westwards towards home, Germaine had wondered secretly as to the private opinions of his companions, especially regarding the league, the war, and the political machinations of de Laude and the other barons. Did they, he wondered, entertain any suspicions of the people who now ruled the kingdom? Germaine longed to speak openly with them. If he could not trust them, who could he trust in all the kingdom. Time and again, in conversations with them, Germaine attempted to touch lightly on the sensitive topics of the league, the monarchy and the shift in the balance of power within the kingdom. During the intervening years since they had last been together, had any of them thought to question the state of the kingdom, its transition to war and its transition to rule by a particular class of the nobility? Had any of them thought especially to question the devious and evil means by which all of this transition was accomplished? Sadly for Germaine his companions gave him no clues as to any possible questions they might have regarding the state of affairs within the kingdom. Romain was as bland as ever, Edgar seemingly cared about nothing save soldiering and the girls he loved, and Philip, the beloved Philip, simply smiled and chatted and then chatted and smiled. Did they think about nothing, Germaine asked himself a little angrily, these young men were now the future of the kingdom, had they no thought as to the wellbeing of their country? Thus observing his companions, Germaine had decided not to acquaint them of his opinions of the league nor of the attempt on his life and the connection of this event with his former friend and mentor, Gavron de Laude.

*   *   *

Germaine awoke instantly and stared ahead at the group of his companions who were gathered about the visitor. He knew instantly who the newcomer was; he could not mistake the colossal form which stood head and shoulders above everyone there, nor the huge head surmounted by the great conical helmet. It was Gavron de Laude come to visit him on his journey; it was Gavron de Laude and none other, and the question that arose in his mind was – how had Gavron traced him all the way to these remote woodlands. Germaine was surprised but not surprised – he knew that Gavron was capable of anything, and Gavron was the man who had sent assassins to kill him all that time ago in Valdelaine. He must now meet his would-be killer and pretend he suspected nothing. He leaped up and strode forward to meet Gavron with all the cordiality he could muster.

"My Lord!" said Germaine, as he approached the group. Gavron stopped what he was saying and looked towards Germaine with a great beaming smile.

"Ah! Germaine, my son!" boomed Gavron as they shook hands. "You look well, my son! Your time in captivity has done you no harm. Thank God you are free at last and back on your native soil. And among friends, my boy, among friends at last!"

"It is good to see you at last, my Lord!" Germaine lied, as Gavron was still shaking his hand and slapping his back.

"I thought I might never see you again, you look well, my Lord!"

"Forgive me for breaking in on your company," Gavron said looking about him. "But I had to come and see you for myself!"

At this the others moved away and allowed Germaine and Gavron to be alone.

"I knew you were back among us. And I could not wait; I had to see you for myself. It has been such a long time, my friend!"

"Thank you for such efforts on my behalf, Lord Gavron. It is a good feeling to be back among my friends.

"And you are among friends, my boy. And pray, what are your plans for now?"

"I make all speed, my Lord, to return to my father and spend some time in Anlac."

"I see. Good then, Germaine you go visit your father. But then, afterward hasten to me, my lad, in Bergmond; we have so much to talk about."

"Yes, my Lord," Germaine said with mock deference. He could feel the anger and loathing towards Gavron rise up within him. But he kept his true feelings at this moment buried deep under an outward show of acquiescence.

"We have indeed so much to talk about. And as soon as I have seen to things in Anlac, I will hasten to join you if you are in Bergmond or if you are with the army!"

Gavron was pleased, his cheeks and eyes bulged as he smiled down at Germaine.

"And Germaine!" Gavron said taking Germaine by the arm. "I have such plans, Germaine! Plans for you, plans for the war, plans for everything! Now that you are back among us, our fortunes will change for the better!"

You mean your fortunes, Gavron, and the power of the Raven League, Germaine thought within himself. The two men conversed for more than an hour. Under his most affable and charming exterior Germaine managed to quell the real emotions that raged inside him. Apart from his chagrin that Gavron should have found him, Germaine felt nothing but anger and hatred towards the man now before him. At times he simply wanted to run the giant through with his dagger, at times he wanted to challenge Gavron about the assassins he had sent to Valdelaine and then, to challenge Gavron to mortal combat here on the forest floor. Here, on the spot, and be done with it forever. But, all of that would have to wait for another day.

Gavron departed and Germaine saddled his own horse for the day's journey. He felt no stomach for a breakfast! As they were about to mount up Germaine called over to Philip.

"That was interesting!"

Philip was adjusting his reins and called back, "Why was it interesting?"

Germaine was now mounted.

"That Gavron came alone!" he said. Philip then mounted also.

"My Lord!" he said. "Gavron did not come alone! A small army awaits him two miles up the forest! Gavron is never alone!"

Germaine simply looked at his friend for an instant and then spurred on his horse. The early mist had cleared.

The rest of the journey homeward was uneventful, except for the strange little happening at the ford on the Plessey Stream.

It was a beautiful morning of strong sunlight. As he gazed downward from the hills to the ford, Germaine could not but be elated at the beauty and warmth that such a morning brings upon the heart. He sighed with gladness, nearly home and a good morning to be alive. Germaine turned his horse and one by one the little band of companions descended to the flat ground and the wide clearing before the stream.

It was then that they beheld a monk like figure stepping out of the water. On seeing them, the man raised his hand in warning, took a bell from the folds of his habit and cried out "Beware! Beware, my Lords! Lepers! Lepers!"

The company of riders stopped immediately. They could see to the far side of the Plessey a long line of wretched looking, ragged figures making their way down to the water and begin to wade across.

"God in Heaven!" gasped Edgar crossing himself. And then he added, "We can go around them through the trees downriver. The water is low." The others crossed themselves too, all young men who had experienced fierce battles, but, at even the distant sight they had, did not wish on themselves even a remote encounter with the wretches now emerging from the stream.

Germaine was about to turn his horse away but somehow caught Philip's eye; on his friend's face there was that strange expression, not smiling, not serious, but expectant.

"Come on!" shouted Romain back at them. "Move on!"

"You go ahead around the ford," Philip shouted back, but all the time, his countenance was fixed on Germaine. "Germaine and I will stay and watch!"

Again Germaine looked at Philip, his face aghast this time. He turned his mount to face away.

"My God! Philip, are you mad!" Germaine said sternly. "We cannot stay! You heard the monk! They're lepers!"

Philip continued just to stare motionlessly at his friend. Germaine, his mount now whirling about under him, searched Philip's face for explanation.

"So they are," Philip said. "They are lepers. That I can see. But we are men, Germaine, both you and I. And I say we stay, Germaine. And not alone that I say we meet them and give them food!"

When his horse steadied, Germaine simply sat, and the look of horror was still fixed on Philip who simply said nothing, but looked kindly at his dumbfounded friend. At length Philip just said "We stay" and with that he dismounted and tied up his horse at a tree.

The column of lepers had now crossed the stream and was now seated on a grassy bank in the warm sunshine. They were no more than fifty paces across the clearing from where Germaine was still looking aghast at Philip, who stood for a moment and then crossed over to where the sad wretches were huddled. Germaine dismounted slowly and stood by the sandy roadside; Philip was now greeting the friar and was handing over his satchel of bread, dried fruit and meat. Germaine shuddered as a tiny blade of fear cut coldly to his heart and the day seemed to lose its sunshine. Taking his satchel with him, he walked across the clearing keeping his eye on the monk, careful not to even glance at the grisly company seated on the ground. He handed his satchel to the holy man as Philip had done and turned to return to the safety of the far side of the clearing. But Philip, all in his armour and pale blue surcoat was down on one knee, talking to the lepers. "O Jesu!" was all Germaine could say, as he felt his heart and body revolt at the sight, and his heart beat strongly sending sweat and shivers all over his body. He gritted his teeth.

"And this is my friend, Lord Germaine," Philip was saying to an old withered lady, half of whose face was covered because half of that face was missing.

"Germaine, come and meet our friends whom God has touched!"

As he tried to move towards the lepers, Germaine felt his bones and body freeze like bars of iron, but his legs did shuffle him forward until he could only kneel on both knees a little further back from Philip and the danger. Swallowing hard, Germaine said, "I greet you, Mother."

He saw that Philip was now smiling at him, encouraging him gently.

"I greet you all, my brothers and sisters!"

There was a murmur from the throng before him, not a murmur of sadness nor of pain. It was a murmur of happy greeting. There was no sense of horror nor alarm, just a musical murmur of happy greeting.

"How are you, my friend," came another sweet murmur.

Germaine looked at the smiling young leper and stammered.

"I, I am well, my friends." Then he managed to say, "May God bless you all!" At this, another murmur of appreciation, of gladness even, and gratitude.

Germaine was feeling a little relaxed now and changed from kneeling to sitting. All this time, Philip had moved among the diseased people, with greetings and morsels of food, as if he was greeting old friends at a fair.

By now Germaine knew. He knew that he could look at them, and look at their eyes. He saw the marked faces, the half limbs, the fingerless hands, how death itself was making its slow progress here and there within their bodies. And still, they smiled and chatted, even asked Germaine if he were hungry. Blue, grey, green and brown were the colours of the eyes that looked out at him from the souls of these lost people who waited for death. 'Why not smile, why not joke, why not enjoy a conversation?' those eyes said, over and over again. 'It is good bread, my friend, and good meat too! And we're so glad to be here in the sunshine, with you! So glad, aren't we? So glad!' Philip finished and Germaine stood up and both knights then knelt again as the monk wished to pray a blessing over them. Then they were on their feet again saying goodbye, and the murmur followed them as they walked silently across the clearing to where their horses waited. The murmur of blessings from lepers.

Neither man spoke. Germaine hastily mounted and crossed the ford at a splashing canter, then urged his mount up the sloping path to gain the high ground west of the stream. Philip followed more slowly, and eventually stood his horse where the road topped the hill. He did not join Germaine.

Germaine gazed out at the country side below and wept, yes, wept for the first time in his adult life, a long silent weeping. "God!" was all he could say to himself in the emotion that burned inside him. After a long, long silence, Germaine called out to Philip who waited a distance away.

"Why did you do that!" he called. Philip's horse moved but there was no response from him. Only another long silence. Then, on the air came Philip's reply,

"Gavron made you a knight! But today, today mind, you are a man; more of a man than you have ever been before."

On the top of the crest, in the sunlight, the two knights simply sat silently on their mounts, sat and gazed on the land below.

At length, Germaine, shouted on the air,

"Damn you, Philip!"

"Oh! Yes?" came Philip's questioning reply.

"You look into men's hearts – as if you had the eyes of God!"

The sun went behind a little cloud and came out again, its rays beaming over the breezy countryside. Somewhere far below farm dogs were barking but up on the crest there was only the sunlight and the sound of the wind.

"I'll tell you something else!" Philip called steadying his horse. It was Germaine's turn to say,

"Oh! Yes?"

Silence again, Germaine's horse neighed loudly.

"You are in love with a girl!" came Philip's voice. A pause and then, "Ioni de Valdelaine!"

'Oh! God!' Germaine said within himself, dumbstruck. The horse beneath him shimmied, feeling the tension from the body above him.

When he did manage to speak Germaine shouted,

"Was it that obvious?"

"Not obvious at all!" came Philip's reply. "But, maybe, I do have the eyes of God!"

How long more they spent in silence neither could ever remember, but at length Germaine could hear the sound of plodding hooves as his friend moved away. For himself, Germaine was happy to stay a while more, just to breathe the air and be alone with his thoughts. But only a moment more; as it happened, he heard the hoof beats stop. Turning his head he could see Philip, quite a distance away on the road.

"And I know something else!" Philip roared back. God in Heaven! Germaine thought to himself; what is it now? He could see Philip, the horse beneath him swinging from side to side.

"You and I. We are going to fight –
We are going to fight –
The Raven League!"

Germaine's eyes tightened as he glared down the road; though, in the distance, he could not see the features of Philip's handsome face, the wide grin on that face was carried to him on the wind. For a moment Germaine stared after him, then his shoulders dropped with exasperated happiness. Philip knew; Philip knew everything. Germaine asked himself "Where? Oh where did I find this man – where on all this wide world?" No answer came, Philip had turned again towards home. And Germaine chuckled at first, then opened his jaws and his heart in laughter, loud and happy laughter. At length, when his mirth subsided he could only steer his horse silently and turn his face towards the mountains on the horizon, the mountains of Anlac, the mountains of home.

Chapter XIV: Rebellion

"Which of you is my son?" The old man's face did not move, but his eyes traversed the hall to examine the men who stood in the doorway with Germaine. Duke Anlac remained seated where he was by the fireplace. A cloak covered his nightshirt and a nightcap stood to one side on his head. Wispy white hair flowed down to his shoulders and his moustache and beard were discoloured by food and wine stains. The dogs at his feet stood up and growled, their movement scattering the food platters that had been left on the floor. As Germaine strode across the hall the old man did not move, but his eyes followed and watched with wonder. Son and father, neither man would have known the other. The old man stared at his son for a long time in the hushed silence.

"Alas! My son!" the old man coughed and spat towards the fire. "Alas you see what poor fortune has befallen us!" Germaine, still on one knee, was dumbfounded as the desolation of his home coming was sinking only gradually into his heart. "I can see that you are a strong young man. That is good. Your friends of the Raven League have been staying with us for some time now and have departed but two days ago. They neglected to tidy the place before they left." Germaine stood up and looked around to see that Philip and the others had departed and had left him in privacy with his father. Germaine spoke.

"My Lord, as truly as I am your son, I now have no friends among the league – but what has happened here? Where is everyone? Is there no one to look after you?"

The old man spat again, shrugged his shoulders and staring straight ahead, smiled bitterly.

"The place was garrisoned by the league after you were taken. They have taken away our servants and our furniture and helped themselves to all they could get. All of it, the work of that damned upstart knight, de Laude."

Germaine could only look down at the old man that was his father. Once again he was without speech, as the rage flared within him at the violation of his house.

"But how are you, father?" he blurted out finally. "What can be done for you?" The old eyes looked at him directly.

"I am fine," he said. "There is no need to fret for me. The peasants hide in the woods, they watch all the time. One of the women brings me food each day. I know it must be strange for you after all this time – to see me and to see this place as it is. But I am well and I forbid you concern yourself with me. Get some rest and refreshment for yourself and your friends. Tomorrow, yes, maybe tomorrow I will meet you again and we can talk. God knows there is plenty to talk about. Now, leave me and rest, you have had a long journey!"

Unwillingly and with his heart still in a rage, Germaine bowed to his father and withdrew, the dogs following him to the doorway. Outside he strode straight at the peasant man, throttled him and shouted "Is this all you could do for my father!" But Philip and Romain took hold of Germaine and drew him back from the helpless peasant. When they had calmed him they explained that his father would have no one in the house, or near him, save for the woman who brought his meal once in the day. His father had tried to pay them in silver for even this small service but they had refused any reward. The most the peasant folk could do was to keep watch on the place

and wait for times to change. Germaine placed his hands
to his face and then apologised profusely to the peasant
man. Philip and Romain led him away to one of the
chambers where he could be alone with his thoughts and
his rage. The others, Philip assured him, were already
gone into the woods to hunt for firewood and the evening's supper.

For Germaine and also for his companions the day
had indeed turned to disaster. The initial warmth he had
felt on first sighting the turrets of Anlac had turned to
dismay when they had found the village burnt and deserted. The main gates of the castle lay open, as did the
main door of the keep. When they had removed the
wooden beams that lay across the threshold, they had
found nothing but cattle sheltering in the hall on the
ground floor. The smell of filth was everywhere. Dust
abounded and the walls were devoid of tapestry or any
other ornament. A glance into one of the large chambers
revealed that the place was without furniture of any kind.
As they had mounted the first stairs a peasant man from
the village emerged on the landing and it was this man
who had escorted them to the landing outside the great
hall. He had knocked on the door and announced them to
the old man beside the fire.

When Germaine was summoned to his father's
presence, the next day, the old man was in a more con-
ciliatory mood. "Forgive me," he said, "for the poor welcome to your homecoming after all these years. I am, as
you see, too old and weary to manage things properly
here. But you must make yourself and your companions
as comfortable as possible here. Now listen to me – there
are important documents and things on the table there!"

Germaine moved towards the table and saw an assortment of documents and document satchels on the table. But then he turned towards his father once more.

"But, my Lord. What of you? What of your welfare here?"

The old man swallowed some wine, pursed his lips and spoke emphatically.

"Do not trouble yourself about me. I am as well as I can be with age and with the state of things about me! Go to the table and listen to what I say!" Germaine moved back once more to the table.

"The first things there – are the documents, letters from Campaldo, from Father Roland. Read them first and when you have, see that there are three books, also from Campaldo. In that satchel there you will find pages."

Germaine had already opened the satchel and took from it a thick wad of pages. They were all blank but he could see that they had been cut through in various parts of each page with little rectangular holes.

"They are templates," said his father. "You place them in order over the pages of the books. The holes will show you the secret words of whatever Father Roland wishes you to know. Leave them now. Finally those scrolls are the documents of your title to Anlac. I have sent copies to the king and the justice royal in Bergmond. However, so far I have received no letters of approval from that quarter. Methinks these rebellious leaguers may have a hand in the delay. You know your title is not safe till it is signed by the king, and the miscreants of the league have wormed their way to the king himself and to the courts of justice. Now take everything and take time to read through it all. Oh! Dear me, God but I am forgetful. The little book at the end of the table – that book you must leave till the last!"

"What is it, Father!" Germaine asked.

"The title of the book is 'The Lost Prince of Bergmond'. No matter the title you were never told of its contents – for your own safety, you understand. But now, that you are to be the future Duke of Anlac, well, you will need to know its contents yourself and then in time to come pass it on to your own son, whenever you have one."

Germaine was about to speak again but the old man raised his hand and said,

"No more for today, young man. Take yourself from here, as I am tired and would sleep. And read them well, my son!"

Germaine took the contents of the table, bowed and departed.

*   *   *

It was at this time too that the heart of Ioni de Valdelaine was lifted up higher than she could have ever hoped. One day a messenger arrived with a satchel of letters for Valdelaine and there, in the privacy of the room which had been her father's study, she sat down to open and read them. There was nothing new in this for Ioni, for as a matter of course, she had to read all correspondence and indeed write letters in return. Many were letters of petition for favours, many were records of taxation, some were advice on legal matters; there was one from her father requesting money and clothing, there was also one from Count Michael's official requesting requisitions for the army, cattle, horses and so on. Midway through her perusals she paused for a while to make mental notes of all she had read. She would have to send for Frère Benedict to help her to sort out so many diverse issues and to help her to pen all the replies. She sighed as she reached out across the table to pick up yet another sealed scroll; breaking the seal she unrolled the parchment and her eyes squinted as she began to read. Addressed to her as 'Lady Ioni' she began to read it and could make no sense of it though she had read several lines. And then her heart stopped and pounded and her hand began to shake. The letter was from Germaine. 'Oh God!' she thought, he found a way to write to her and get the letter through. She read on and on, she wept and wiped her tears, she laughed and leaped up and danced around the room for sheer joy. She held the beloved parchment to her breast, she kissed it and sat down to read it again and again. And she wept again, there in her very hand was part of him which had come back all this way to her. She placed the parchment on the table, knelt down and with her hands on the precious page she prayed. She prayed in thankfulness, she prayed for his safety and she wept again.

She arose, and with the letter clasped to her breast she stood by the window and her gaze brought her eyes to rest on the far off horizon to the west. He was there, he was alive, he was well and he remembered her. And he loved her.

Suffice it to say that it was the first of many letters between Ioni and Germaine. As it happened, Germaine had found a way to despatch letters to Count Michael's encampment where they were received by her own brother Jean who then sent them onward to Valdelaine. The details of these letters do not survive save for fragments which are today housed in the library of the university of Bergmond. At first glance, the texts on these fragments appear somewhat strange until the reader realises that they are poetic summaries or inserts. The texts make references which may have contained special meanings for the loving couple who penned them and a number of them can be reproduced here. One letter from Germaine to Ioni contains the following passage:

> *The thought of thee*
> *Is like a jewel*
> *Which I carry as I walk*
> *For now I walk through*
> *Strange landscapes and*
> *Strange new days*
> *And yet, because of you*
> *All things are familiar*
> *And all things are blessed!*

Upon examination, this fragment is certainly from one of the early letters from Germaine. A bemused Germaine has just returned to his homeland and yet feels he is walking through 'strange landscapes' in which his only familiar thought is Ioni herself. The 'strange new days' may refer to Germaine himself as he comes to grips with the dangerous political situation in Bergmond after his return from exile. These were dangerous times for him as we shall see, but his courage had not failed him.

Ioni seems to have taken up the practice of poetic inserts almost from her earliest letters, as this text shows:

> *The blessed messenger*
> *Was the angel*
> *Who brought such tidings*
> *That my heart shines*
> *I bless the messenger*
> *As I bless thee*

In another text Ioni dwells on the joy of the soul at finding the other person:

> *There was a soul*
> *That did not know herself*

Till she met thee
At last she found herself
Reflected in the other soul.
The world was wide and lorn
Till she found its heart in thee
The journey it was long
The road went here and there
From the warm womb of the mother
To the warm heart of the stranger.

Though not masterpieces of the poetic muse, these pieces seem to reflect the intensity and fascination that the lovers discovered in the beginning of their encounter and which had lost nothing in the time they were apart from each other. Some of Ioni's efforts are even somewhat amusing, especially as her first couple of lines are so nobly put together, but gradually she loses the measure and just lets her heart get the better of her poetry as the latter lines are just a tumbling outpouring of emotion:

Such sober days followed
In the wake of thy departure
Such sober days indeed
In the wake of winged times
We had in our togetherness
In the pain of losing thee
I loved loved loved
Till I thought I could love no more.
And in the morning I arose
And my heart loved even more.

The letters became even more frequent, lifting Ioni's heart and causing her such joy as she faithfully penned her reply and then happily awaited the next missive from Germaine. Those letters, Ioni buried away in the most secret place she could find, between the ceiling of her room and a supporting wooden beam right above her bed. At night before she slept she took them down and read and reread every one of them over and over again, extracting nourishment for the heart from every word and phrase. For her, this was her time for being with her beloved in heart and in spirit.

*   *   *

High in the tower of Anlac, Germaine sat in a room he had commandeered for his own use; it contained a writing table and some chairs; shelves had been installed to cope with the myriad of books and documents pertaining to Anlac and its estate; a fire had been kindled in the hearth as the early October evenings turned cool. By candlelight, he had perused the book sent to him by Father Roland from Campaldo. In spite of his haste to put his estates in order, this was the book which, for now, held most interest for him. With the help of the templates sent with the book, he had been able to decipher the names of almost a hundred men, from the most ordinary knights all the way up to the Duke of Anflair himself. These men were the 'sea of souls' mentioned by Father Roland when he had visited Germaine in Valdelaine, all that time ago. These were the men who had sworn their undying enmity towards the Raven League, and their desire to bring its power to an end, once and for all. As he gazed in the candlelight at the long list he had made, Germaine found that only a few had surprised him – they were the names of men he had previously deemed to be league supporters, and whose true loyalties he could never have guessed. In fact, here were one or two names in particular whom he could have sworn were ardent leaguers. First among these was that of Jan de Jubilad, a young knight and one of his own company of young bloods as they were called who had fought as a unit in the war. Germaine was doubly interested as neither he nor Jan had any liking for each other and had often quarrelled during their time at war. The other most interesting name was that of the gallant Stephen de Laude, the young nephew of the great Gavron himself, high master of the league, now striding the world of Bergmond itself as if he owned it. Strange, Germaine thought, even within great families, the league had caused its share of division. As he looked down the pages, Germaine was further impressed that Father Roland's list contained the names of men in high places, men appointed by the league but who secretly had no affection towards it. The name of the high provost of Bergmond, Laurence Greysteed, was there, as was also the name of the vice chancellor's secretary Eldwin Lande; both powerful men with access to the workings of power in the city of Bergmond itself. Brave men indeed for whom one wrong turn, one slip of the tongue would mean the horrors of a traitor's death. As he folded away the pages Germaine wondered 'Am I worthy of all these people. And how will they accept me, having been, until my capture, the foremost protégé of the league. Only time will tell – but if Father Roland has endorsed me, then their acceptance may come more easily'.

When he turned his attention to thoughts of writing to Ioni, he seemed to enter a different world, a world of energy and confidence that cheered his heart. Even the great distance that now lay between them did not diminish the joy he felt when he thought of her, and his letters of this time indicate only a radiating warmth and joy. Curiously, in all their time together Germaine had never acquainted his beloved with the troubles of his situation once he would return to his homeland. And even now he refrained from any mention of his true danger. She must have guessed, of course, from the attempt on his life, under her very eyes, all that time ago in Valdelaine. She must have guessed that all would not go smoothly in Bergmond for the future Duke of Anlac. For Germaine her guesses would be enough, and in his letters he would not risk increasing her anxieties for his welfare. "Are you well, my beloved Lord, are you safe?" were the questions she asked in every letter, and to each one he must reply that all was well. He had never confided to her that, beneath the conflict between Esmor and Bergmond there lay another conflict – Bergmond was now on the verge of civil war between those who wished for a good and decent life within the laws and traditions of the land, and those who by force and evil means sought to create a new society forever in thrall to the ordinances of the Raven League. In Bergmond, the politics of the previous decade had centred around the question of the royal succession. The grand masters of the league had long ago secretly decided that the next heir to the throne of Bergmond would come from the ranks of the youngbloods, the special force that the league had weaned and trained to knighthood, and from the best of which they would one day choose the future king. No matter that there were many others close to the royal lineage, who could validly bid for the throne, they would choose the successor to Leopold, they would choose the strongest and the one most loyal to the league. In fact Gavron de Laude was still hopeful that the name of his erstwhile protégé, Germaine, would be put forward. There was the issue, now growing more significant, given the king's decline in health, that Germaine had never taken the vows of the military order. Being the son of an Anlac this was understandable, but the boy might still be persuaded, so Gavron hoped. Far and away on the other side of the political unrest that troubled Bergmond were those people who felt strongly that some suitable prince from abroad should be invited to take the crown and re-store peace to the land. Approaches could be made to the royal houses of other lands. There was no shortage of princes in the Frankish royal household for example, nor indeed were the Rhinelands and Spain short of eager young princes. But the league had said no to all such suggestions; and mistrust, fear and anger seethed and boiled between the two parties. For years the abbot of Campaldo had worked in search of a compromise plan but to no avail. Campaldo argued that, following a great as-sembly of the nobles that a candidate might be found from among the nobles of Bergmond, but that he must not come from the ranks of the Raven League. Promptly, of course, the league had rejected this, adding that the monks of Campaldo should stick with their prayers and not inter-fere in civil politics. At any rate the day of reckoning with the league, for now Germaine was unsure as to how it would come. But Campaldo thundered on.

Germaine finished his letter to Ioni and fixed it with the wax seal. While he had been writing he had heard the sounds of hoof beats and voices in the courtyard far below. It would be Philip and the others returning home from a day's hunting. There was a tap at the door and Philip entered, his face smiling and red from the day's activities in the forest.

"How did you fare with the hunt?" Germaine asked as Philip threw himself in a chair opposite him.

"We fared well," Philip replied. "There will be meat and plenty of it for some time!"

Germaine reached forward across the table and picked out one of the letters he had been writing and handed it to Philip.

"Now, tell me what you think of this, my letter to Gavron." Philip perused its contents and as he did so his frown grew deeper with every line. It was a stormy, angry message of protest to Gavron, whom he blamed for the garrison of league troops who had been quartered on Anlac and which had so badly abused his father, his castle and estates. Philip paused for a while having read it, then placed it back on the table.

"Better not to send it," Philip said smiling.

"What!" roared Germaine, glaring furiously at his friend. "Not send it, not send it? What do you mean, Philip? I tell you I will have satisfaction from him for everything that has happened here!"

"Yes, of course," said Philip coolly. "But you still want to convince Gavron that you are his friend. And you – I mean we, need time to find our way – now is not the time to show your hand, Germaine. Now is not the time to antagonise him – let him still believe you are his, and his only!"

"And what do you suggest?" Germaine sighed holding up the page that would never be sent to Gavron.

"Let me draft the letter for you!"

"Very well, then, Philip," he said as he tossed a blank page across the table to Philip who promptly took the quill, drew the candle closer to him and began to write. After a moment Philip looked up at Germaine, tapped the quill on the side of his hand and smiled.

"We need to tickle the brain of the grand master. Build him up, show him that you are a right loyal son of the league!"

"Very well then, tickle the brain of the grand master, if you must!"

'Cherished and Glorious Baron Gavron, greetings…' began the letter and then it went on to say how happy Germaine was to be back in his homeland, how eager he was to meet the grand master again, and how he longed with impatience to take the field again in the defence of Bergmond. Towards the end of the missive Philip gently told Gavron of the sad news that had overtaken Anlac, how a band of renegade knights had taken advantage of the upheaval of wartime and had quartered themselves there until supplies ran out leaving the estate quite desolate. Philip then inserted his little masterstroke – begging the Baron to use his influence in restoring the estate by sending supplies and even money. The message concluded with the usual niceties and compliments. Indeed, as it turned out, it was as well that Philip had redrafted Germaine's original letter as, a month later, Gavron sent wagons of supplies and even better, he sent a courier with a goodly bag of silver and gold.

"I shall put you in charge as my secretary-in-chief," Germaine said to Philip when his letter had found its mark and Gavron had sent the gifts. Philip grinned.

"I have to make a statesman of you and I don't have much time to do it!"

They had been out in the forest together at a pond watering their horses, when the news of Gavron's gifts was brought to them by a page. They had smiled and laughed and Germaine said after a thoughtful pause,

"Philip, what better gift could God have given me!"

"Better than Gavron's gold? I know not, my Lord!"

Philip was splashing about in the pond scooping up water to wash his face and hair; he was still laughing at the fun of it all. Germaine mounted his charger.

"No," he said, also chuckling. "Not Gavron's gold!"

"What then, my Lord?"

But Germaine only gazed at him as he splashed about, hair and face all wet and smiles, and reached for his horse. Germaine wheeled his mount about and began the trot back to Anlac.

Oh yes, thought Germaine, it had seemed like a boyish prank, the letter to Gavron, it had truly felt like one at the time. But Philip had been right, an angry letter to the grand master would only have provoked mistrust. Germaine knew he needed Gavron's trust for just another little while.

Philip and the others remained on at Anlac and little by little as October passed the castle became once again a more comfortable place for everyone. In the village every effort was made to make the cottages habitable again, numbers of trees were felled and cut to make doors and roof beams. Germaine sent far and wide for thatchers to come immediately and restore the rooftops. Finding rushes for the work was not a problem as rushes were abundant by the streams and by the lakeshore. Each week Edgar and Romain would ride escort for wagons as they reached market towns and other parts of the estate. There they could buy what foodstuffs were required. The previous summer's crop destroyed, both the castle and the village folk were now reliant on these missions to keep starvation at bay. For the villagers, food could be prepared in large cauldrons and all could share a communal daily meal. The wagons brought bags of corn to be held as seed for planting when the spring would come. Invaluable were the flocks of geese, turkeys, ducks and chickens which were brought in from time to time – once eggs were laid, then each family could be sure of survival. Germaine's men also made long trips to buy cattle herds and teams of plough horses and slowly Anlac began to turn its back on its previous desolation and burgeon into life again.

Through all the work of restoration, Valdelaine never ceased to impinge itself on Germaine's memory. Hardly an hour in the day passed without some glimpse of the place itself and the characters who peopled it. In fact it now seemed like a dream or a long slow holiday of growing up, a time of living far from the urgencies of wartime and military life. So much insight had come to him in those years from individuals and from the homely complexity of the family life of that place. The quick humour and banter of Valdelaine and its people had placed his perspective on life into a new sphere which was a far cry from the strained ordinances of the Raven League, which had devoured the spirit of his childhood and youth. True, he had grown into the warrior he had always dreamt of being, but Valdelaine had taught him how the heart is warmed and healed and life is not lived in a constant state of winter. For long enough had he been the disciplined child of duty, and youthful war-pawn of the league, Valdelaine had come over his heart like a summer morning, fresh, warm and life-giving. It seemed comical to himself that those times, when all of those years lived amid the fanaticism of the masters, were not worth the sheer magic of Eleanor's laughter nor one of Ioni's smiles. He dearly wished that he was still a prisoner, for there never had been a prisoner more happy nor more free at heart. But now, by contrast, he must be free only to shoulder the many burdens of the estate into which he was born.

The great fief of Anlac was almost as large as a small country, ranging from the mountain country to the north, down to within fifty miles of the city of Bergmond.

At any given time the dukes could summon over three hundred knights to their blue and red standard and, over the centuries the knights of Anlac had taken ferocious pride in answering the call to arms. But this had all changed with the coming of the league and especially when the future heir, Germaine, was taken to be trained and educated by the league when the company of the Young Ravens, or youngbloods, had been formed. This was done to produce future leaders and strongmen who could take the ideals of the league on to the next generation. Stubbornly, however, the Anlac country had resisted the influence of the league, but as time went on its once proud knights were no longer sure as to their leadership. They were firmly opposed to the league but Germaine's departure at seven years had driven a wedge between them and their loyalty to the great house of Anlac. Those knights who were fighting in the present war did not do so under the banner of Anlac but at the behest of the league. The majority that had chosen not to enter the war and remain on their estates had, for the most part, not paid the four year's absence revenue owed to the great house in time of war. Thus the great house had fallen into a confused state of isolation, both actual and political. The old duke had been too old and feeble to force the revenues question, but now, it was no longer the duke who held the reins. Germaine intended to restore Anlac in every aspect of its former power.

*   *   *

Within a number of days after his first arrival home Germaine was visited in Anlac by four of his liege knights. Finding the place in such poor repair they were quite shocked and explained that of course they had been

aware of league knights at Anlac, that they had understood they were there at Germaine's own behest, and so
they never approached close enough to see the state of
things for themselves. Two of the four knights were
Germaine's closest neighbours, the other two were bound
to Anlac by ties of both blood and old friendship. The
elder of these was Godfrey Blackmane, a second cousin
of Germaine – a powerfully built man, his giant red face
and greying hair and beard, and his fiery eyes immediately set him forth as a natural leader.

Germaine welcomed them cordially though he was
all but stranger to them and they strangers to him; his
years with the league had seen to that. At his invitation,
they were happy to join him and Germaine introduced his
friends to them. Godfrey, seeing that the old duke was
not present, enquired after his health, Germaine assured
him that the duke seldom left his bed at this time but that
he was well and his spirits good. He went on to explain
the presence of the league knights at Anlac before his
homecoming.

"There is a veritable game of cat and mouse betwixt the grand master and me," Germaine said looking at
Godfrey with a twinkle in his eye. "He does me harm to
ensure my loyalty and in turn I pretend to be his loyal dis-
ciple!"

"You pretend," Godfrey said. "Am I to take it
then that you are not one of his minions?"

"You make take it as so. As to Gavron, I be no
more his friend. As for his league, I be none of their
company!"

Godfrey's eyes opened wide with surprise and
pleasure.

"You are no longer one of them."

"Exactly! I am nothing now, but the Duke of Anlac by proxy with my father who has given me permission to act as such."

Godfrey's great face melted into a smile and there were tears in his eyes as he looked about at the other Anlac men.

"My God!" he said. "That we should have lived to see this day, my Lord Germaine. And that Anlac may rule again like in the days of yore. Of course we are set firmly against the league and want nothing of their interference. And for the future, where will you stand, my Lord?"

Germaine leaned towards Godfrey and said smiling,

"So help me, before I finish, I intend to singe the grand master's beard, and burn his league!"

At this Godfrey's eyes opened wide as did his mouth in momentary surprise.

"Do you now, begod!" he roared, laughed, pounded the table with his huge fist.

"Well then, let me be the first to light the brand!"

Everybody laughed, and cheered, Godfrey got up and strode around to Germaine who rose up and the two men embraced.

"It's a long road has no turning, my friends. But now an Anlac, the Anlac, has come home to his birthright!"

"True, my friends, this is true," Germaine said. "But, by your leave, I must play cat and mouse a little longer! Lord Godfrey, and you my friends, I pray you return to me within a week and I shall have written messages to all the knights on our estates. I rely on you to deliver them. More than that I will send messengers to each corner of Bergmond wherever there is an Anlac knight, squire or page compelling each one to present himself here before yuletide or risk the forfeiture of his estate! More than that again, I shall also compel of each of you the revenue of not less than four years!"

"Spoken like an Anlac, my Lord," boomed Godfrey. "And by God you shall have it!"

Then Godfrey drew his sword, followed by the others and shouted "Anlac!" and the cry was echoed in loud voice by all present. Later in the courtyard, before his departure, Lord Godfrey confided in Germaine that the need was great to draw the entire duchy together again. Over the years the bonds of unity had been frayed with family feuds, boundary disputes and so on – nothing was needed more than a leader and a cause to unite Anlac into one again. And so Godfrey Blackmane departed with his friends with the promise to return within a week and deliver Germaine's summons to all the estates.

That was the very week when everything changed, not alone for Anlac, but for the whole of Bergmond. On a sunny October morning a solitary knight accompanied by a squire and page rode into Anlac courtyard. It was Germaine's adversary of his younger days, Jan de Jubilad. The two men met in the great hall and shook hands; before Germaine could say a word Jan spoke,

"I have come to offer you my services, my Lord, such as they are, if you will have me."

"You are welcome, Jan, and you will have all of my hospitality! I have need of men like you – for I presume you know where I stand."

"When you knew where we stood, we in turn knew where you stood – shall we say by means of the 'sea of souls' of Campaldo."

"I see," said Germaine.

"But I am also here on another errand, my Lord. That is to bear you bad news of a tragedy that has befallen our country. My Lord, Campaldo itself has been burned to the ground!"

There was stunned silence as the words sank in. Campaldo was gone, Campaldo of the Peace, Campaldo of the treaties, Campaldo that had looked down for centuries upon Esmor and Bergmond and which time and again had taken up the pieces shattered by war and forged them into peace once more. Finally, Germaine spoke,

"Not us surely? Not –"

"It was the league, my lord; though they deny it, no one believes them!"

"And the monks?"

"The abbot and seven of his brethren perished. The other monks escaped into the countryside."

"My God!" whispered Germaine, and then, remembering, said, "And Father Roland?"

"We do not know the names of the monks who perished. But Father Roland may be alive; if he is, then he is hiding among the peasantry! And to add to that, Count Michael is advancing on our forces to take the ruins of Campaldo for Esmor."

"Then I must write without delay – I have a friend on the Esmor side, he may track down Father Roland for us! It is a faint hope and a frail link, but it is all I can think of. And the country, Jan, what was the reaction, if there was one?"

"All of the east has come out against the league. There were riots in Augsad. Even league knights have been attacked – but the city of Bergmond is firmly in league hands. There is talk of a complete breach between the Duke of Anflair and Baron de Laude – angry messages have been exchanged."

"I see," said Germaine, thinking. "So the east and Augsad are up, Norland is already in arms, and soon Anlac will raise its standard – this gives us a more even hope of success.

"That's how it looks, my Lord. Bergmond, Jubilad and Pentevel and all the south is held by the league. As you say the east, Norland and Anlac will bind against it."

"Jan, I thank you for your pains in coming here. For now, this is your home and we are your family. As I said I have need of you, but first we will find you comfortable quarters."

And summoning a page, Germaine bade him find lodgings for Jan de Jubilad. Immediately Germaine began the letter to Jean de Valdelaine, informing him of the disaster at Campaldo and begging his assistance in finding Father Roland if indeed he was still alive.

*   *   *

Thunderous night, and lightning too, the great purplish flashes throwing their glow on the rain swept rocks of the Anflair Pass. Thunder in the sky rolling in the clouds above. Thunder on the ground as well, as the earth shook beneath the hooves of a hundred mounted steeds galloping through the pass, the sound of those clattering hooves reverberating against the high rocks in the narrow confines of Anflair. On and on, a hundred knights, all dark against the lightning flashes bounding onward amid the tempest. What awesome quest beckoned them through such wild country on such a night. Peasants in their hovels, waking and hearing the sounds crossed themselves with fear. None could have guessed the intent of such a wild quest that night would be Campaldo, the holy abbey of the high hills beyond the plain.

Word of the disaster reached Jean who was foraging near Vorlaine; it came via a messenger and the parchment was from Germaine written carefully in code. "The high place of holiness has fallen at the hands of evildoers," the message read. "All of the holy ones are killed or fled. You and I, though we stand on opposing sides of the ravine, are not of this evil. Beg you go to holy shrine and find the holy ones still alive. Your brother in arms on the other side." the message ended.

The destruction of the sacred Abbey of Campaldo sent waves of shock and revulsion through the two kingdoms. On hearing the news, the knights and men of Esmor had no doubts any more of the justice of their cause in this war. They were now fighting whatever evil it was that had violated the holy place which was sacred to the people of the two kingdoms. Indeed the shock was echoed far out beyond the frontiers to the wider world. Even the king of the Franks, the emperor, and Saxon English kings wrote to Bergmond in protest. The archbishop of Bergmond was emboldened to preach in protest at the murder of the abbot and some twenty of his monks and called on all men of good will to seek out the perpetrators and bring them to justice.

Gavron de Laude was furious. His secret orders to the knights involved were that only the abbot was to be killed. Gavron immediately had it put out that the massacre had been the work of unknown renegades who would be tracked down without mercy until they were all brought to justice. The imperative for Gavron to do this was quite pressing, not for any remorse nor moral outrage which an honourable man might possess. Gavron possessed none of these qualities. His reasons were political as the sense of revulsion at the crime was felt most among the Bergmondese themselves. Riots broke out in all the cities, in Bergmond, Pentevel, Augsad and Jubilad.

Hundreds of Bergmondese knights protested too. Only the knights of the league were silent at first, but then, hypocritically, joined the rest of the nation in its mourning. Many years later the knight Herold de Traloy, one of the men who had taken part in the destruction, outlined during his trial the facts of the case. Gavron had sent a hundred knights to Campaldo in a fit of rage to dispose of the abbot. But upon arrival the men had gone on a rampage of killing, looted the abbey and then burned it.

While Gavron now launched a campaign to distance himself and the league from any involvement with Campaldo, yet another disaster fell which was to have immense consequences for the war. John, Prince of Esmor, with his forces combined with the army of Count Michael led a major assault up the valleys to the east of Campaldo. The Duke of Anflair quickly sent troops to the scene under Baron Agron. The two forces met near a small town called Argenden, and Baron Agron's force was completely routed, Agron himself narrowly escaping capture by the prompt actions of some of his captains. After Argenden the Esmorin forces moved swiftly through the valleys until they took the vast country around the ruined abbey. Campaldo was now in Esmorin hands.

The Duke of Anflair, encamped near Augsad, summoned Gavron and showed him the contents of the letter from Prince John – both men were riled by the words "in the event that the king of Bergmond either cannot or will not protect the holy shrine of Campaldo, in the name of His Majesty of Esmor, I now take possession of the said place for my king and will protect it when the Bergmondese have failed to do so."

Anflair had his suspicions of Gavron as the real perpetrator, but of course could not prove it but made bold enough to say to Gavron,

"This was a bad mistake, my Lord – a bad mistake! You will see to it that our men – all our men, act properly and with proper authority at all times! It was always going to be difficult to win this war but this – this outrage has seriously hampered our chances! Campaldo was the kind of mistake that loses wars."

Gavron could only stare at the duke, his face bright red, as he tried to mumble something. The duke dismissed him and turned away.

*   *   *

It was again the turn of Sir Godfrey Blackmane and his companions – now there were eight knights in his company – to visit Anlac once more, where each in turn swore allegiance to Germaine and where they handed over the monies owing to the Anlac estate. Germaine had yet another task for them, for the letters of summons to all the Anlac knights had been prepared and each of Sir Godfrey's visiting knights received a satchel each containing summonses to all, region by region. On departure, Sir Godfrey questioned Germaine.

"What have you done to contact our knights at present with the army of the league?"

"They are ready, Sir Godfrey," answered Germaine. "But I have to select carefully the messengers who will scour the country in search of our men."

"I pray you, Germaine, leave that to me. I have many that I know who will be happy to do the searching and bring our lords and squires back to the banner of Anlac."

With that Germaine sent for the remaining batch of letters and had them placed in a leather satchel and handed over to Sir Godfrey.

"This coming yuletide will be the deadline," Germaine said. "Your men will need to make haste. God speed, Sir Godfrey!"

As he and Philip watched them go yet again, Germaine said,

"We will need to redouble our hunting sorties in the next few weeks, Philip!"

"You will have guests?"

"All of Anlac will be calling in the next two months!"

"Is it not time, then, to invite Sir Godfrey and other cousins and their families to come and stay here?"

"Yes, I had thought of that, but it slipped my mind! Till now we have been a house without women and children, but it is time to change all that!"

But it was not the Anlac knights who were first to arrive however, as that momentous autumn began to yield to winter. Seemingly, following the example of Jan de Jubilad, a number of squadrons of the young Ravens began to arrive at Germaine's doorstep to offer him their services, and they were warmly welcomed. At first Germaine was quite surprised that they should desert the league to fight with him, though as time moved on he could see plainly what had happened among them. There was not as much as a drop of friendship lost between them since the day they had lost him on the bloody slopes of Elvendene. The years of separation since then had the effect of augmenting rather than diminishing the esprit de corps which had imbued them all. Nothing had been lost, save their loyalty to Gavron and the league. Germaine was especially heartened by the warmth of the ones he had not known well, as much as by the warmth of those for whom he had little previous friendship. For all of them, their lives had been taken from them at a tender age to the service and ideals of the league. This school of hard knocks and discipline had taken their youth and early manhood. But the years of the war, with all its horrors and adventure, had shown them the possibility of another life beyond the strictures and ordinances of the league, sufficient to place the hard questions of life before their very hearts. When young men are thrown together in a dangerous bond, when they are proved together in hardship, there grows an unseen and oft unspoken bond between them that lasts forever and nothing can outforge it though a lifetime may pass. Hammered together in danger, conflict and even in mistakes and insight, a sacred brotherhood is fashioned. Anyone who might defy it will find it harder than steel. Unrelated even to personal traits, it is there simply because the next man was there also; he knows the harshnesses that were to be known and therefore he is blood of one's blood and nothing will be denied him.

*   *   *

Jean paused somewhere near the edge of the wood. The evening was still light and indeed the sun only beginning its setting in rays of red glory in the west. The sadness that had come upon his heart was momentarily lifted by the beauty of the time of day, the quietness and the cooling of the air. Then, somewhere, somewhere between the air and the cooler breezes he heard the words, "She is in the woods below. The woman is there, the woman is there." Where the words came from he knew not nor did he now care. He had witnessed this day more evil than he could know and yet, far off in his memory there was something familiar – as though he had known it all already, as though this awesome moment had been always there. But search though he might he could not fathom this déjà vu nor its source.

Shaking himself Jean took the horse's reins and walked the little brown pathway that led downwards and into the forest. How long he walked he did not know. Then suddenly in the light of a tiny clearing to his left he saw her seated on a great trunk of a fallen tree. She was looking at him, intent eyes stared out from under jet black hair, her dark skin old but still beautiful. She wore a great dark cloak which covered her form, and a hood which rested upon her head revealing just her face and some hair and always the long stare of the strangest set of eyes he had ever seen.

Jean's little trance was suddenly broken when two great wolfhounds bounded towards him snarling and showing their teeth. Jean's hand went instinctively for his sword but before he could draw it the woman gave a little shriek and both hounds stopped as suddenly as they had started, lowered their ears and tails and padded back to the woman seating themselves at her feet.

For Jean the whole scene was like something from a story of elfin beings and sprites. Tying his horse, he took the courage to leave the path and tread the undergrowth towards the woman. She did not move.

"God save you, Mother," Jean said on the evening air. "What do you abroad at such an hour?"

The woman's stare was still there, and something of a smile.

"God save you, young Lord," she spoke, a ringing musical sound on the air. "I am abroad this hour," she continued, "that I may meet someone."

"We are deep in the forest, it is almost night," Jean uttered. "There's no one to meet at this hour in this place."

Jean was now standing before her, she remained seated, a basket beside her and the two hounds resting at her feet. Smiling again she spoke again.

"I have met you."

"So you have, Mother," Jean went on, "but I'm hardly the one you were hoping to meet."

"Perhaps not," her eyes intent and smiling. "I was hoping to meet a young man called – Jean of Valdelaine."

Jean froze.

"And you are he," she said.

"Jesu mon garde!" breathed Jean stepping back and drawing his sword. She smiled again.

"You have nothing to fear, Jean," she said. "Replace your sword." Then she went on, "How can you be surprised to meet me – you knew I was already here."

Jean was aghast but replaced his sword.

"Mother!" he said, "I don't understand. Yes, something did tell me someone was here waiting for me in the woods. But I still do not understand. What are you, old woman? Are you a witch or sorcerer that can know such things?"

"Pray sit down awhile, young Valdelaine," she spoke. Jean complied and seated himself near her on the great tree trunk. Both knight and crone turned towards each other. She spoke again.

"Soon the night will be upon us," she said, "and the bat creatures will take to the air. And soon again the moon will rise to light the way for fox and badger in these woods. Soon also shall the two of us be gone our separate ways and neither sun nor moon shall find us here e'er again.

Jean was silent and then spoke.

"Pray tell me, Mother, what brought us here, for good or ill?"

"For good, Jean, for good only," she answered. "I am perhaps a witch or sorcerer as you call it. I serve only the old gods of this world, the gods who ruled the air, the woods, fields, mountains and streams. They were good gods in their way long before they were banished by your 'True God' as you call him."

Jean was enthralled and fearful.

"But how can I listen to you, Mother. I am a knight of the True God."

"Bear with me and listen, Jean de Valdelaine," she said, "for my gods have told me to meet you here and tell you things I know about you, in the past and in the future.

"What things, Mother," exclaimed Jean. "And how can you know such things."

"Who can tell the ways of God, or the ways of the gods?" she answered. "Who can say what spirits come to us in dreams? But this I tell you I have seen you in dreams. Once as a child, a child descending a stone stairway. A child descending to place himself between some demon, some unearthly entity, to place himself between danger and those he loved. Such love in a child is rare."

Jean was silent with sheer awe. Now he remembered that night long ago on the stairway at Valdelaine.

She smiled at him. "Now do you believe I speak the truth," she asked.

"I do, Mother," he gasped.

Then she rose for the first time and stepped towards him, she then knelt on the ground before him.

"I care nothing for myself, Jean," she said. "But pray listen to my words. Afterwards you may if you wish run your sword through me or let me go in peace. I have to tell you now that I know you may live a long and great life – but you will never be Lord of Valdelaine. I know also that the evil that visited you that night long ago in Valdelaine will be destroyed by you – my gods tell me that you must, from this night, fight the evil. Fight the evil, Jean. Fight the evil. That is all there is to be said."

They were both silent for a long time, the night had come; the bats were in the air. She spoke,

"Now, I am finished with you, Jean," she said. "If you are finished with me let us leave these woods together and part company below the abbey."

*   *   *

Once more, the following morning Jean took it on himself to wander about the ruined remains of the abbey. The roof timbers of the main church had fallen, tumbling downwards and crushing the many beautiful religious ornaments, the smell of charred timber was everywhere. While his companions took breakfast under the shelter of the almshouse, Jean meandered from place to place amid the ruins, vaguely trying to come to terms with the tragedy. This was Campaldo; known as a shrine of peace since before the time of Christ the Saviour, it had been famous far and wide for its healing springs of water. Kings and warriors alike had come to this place, great treaties had been signed here between kingdoms. In fact a treaty signed at Campaldo was said to be so binding that rulers would die rather than break it. This was Campaldo of God, Campaldo the Beloved, Campaldo of the Peace as it had been known down the ages. The sick, the maimed, the troubled in spirit had made their way here and all had been welcomed. And now it stood high on the hillside, a smoking ruin. Somewhere and in someone's agenda, the destruction of this holy place had been deemed to be a good thing. For Jean, the sense of shock which beset him when he first saw the outrage the evening before was now changing to feelings of grief and anger.

As he knelt in prayer before the shattered high altar, Jean noticed something that intrigued him. Clearly from the dust marks on the floor someone had come and had begun to move away the charred beams from around the altar. Already some soul had been here and had begun the work of clearance. He smiled grimly and thought of it as a labour of love but a task which would take many labours and many years to restore the holy place to its former beauty.

Only then did Jean recall the meeting the evening before with the witch of the forest and the strange and eerie way he had felt, called by an invisible voice down from the abbey and into the woods, there to find this strange creature. And he recalled her words,

"You will never be Lord of Valdelaine!"

And then later she had said,

"You must fight the evil, fight the evil."

Shuddering he crossed the courtyard and rejoined his companions by the almshouse.

"You will have to return to camp without me, I'm afraid," he told them. "I wish to stay here for some time longer."

"But why, my Lord, do you stay," one of them asked. "There is nothing you can do here!"

Jean raised his head and looked at them one by one.

"I believe not all the villagers were killed," he said. "Some must have escaped and are now hiding in the woodlands. Some of the monks may also be alive and in hiding hereabouts. I wish to find them."

"Then we will stay with you," said one of the men. "No one is safe alone, not even here!"

"Are you agreed to this?" Jean asked, and all of them nodded their heads.

"Then I will need to send one of you to Count Michael with word of our whereabouts," Jean said.

"I can do that for you, my Lord," said young Laurence, Jean's own squire.

"Thank you," Jean said to Laurence. "I will write to the count explaining our overstay here and even ask if he can spare some troops and workmen to come here. We need to make contact with the local people here, we need to find out if the abbot and other monks are alive. We need to begin to remove the debris inside the various buildings. We need to do many things!"

"Why is all this so important to you, my Lord?" asked Jovis. Jean placed his arm around Jovis' shoulder.

"Look at it, my friend!" said Jean. "This is Campaldo the Beloved, Campaldo of the Peace. The sooner the light of the faith beams in this place again the sooner people will hope for peace again. Word must go out to all – Campaldo the Beloved is not destroyed, its light shines again!"

Laurence was dispatched with the messages for Count Michael, and Jean and five of his men set to work on the abbey church while the remaining four set off to hunt in the woods and barter for bread in the outlying villages. By the first evening Jean and his men had cleared the church of debris, especially the timber which was used as their campfire. Masonry and broken stone and marble carvings were carefully stored in an outhouse. On their return the foragers brought food aplenty but no news of the people and monks of Campaldo. The villagers had been courteous but tight lipped, tense and cautious as if they trusted no one. Next day Jean and his team went through the abbey buildings and found that the fire had caused only light damage in many places but they still had hard work in removing all the damaged furnishings. At noon on the third day Jean was called from his labours to the front gate of the abbey where, there on the roadway below, stood a group of village men armed with pikes. One of these demanded to know who Jean and his men were and what they were doing in the monastery. Jean called down to the group huddled below and explained the original purpose of his visit to Campaldo and why he and his men had stayed on.

Unarmed and bareheaded Jean strode down the hill towards the group of villagers until he stood before them not ten paces away.

"Are you the people of Campaldo?" Jean queried.

"We are," replied one of them. "What is it to you?"

"I come in peace and goodwill," answered Jean. "I wish to know if any of the monks survived this outrage and if I may be put in contact with them."

Cautiously the village men backed away a few paces and huddled together with whispers.

"If the monks are alive," called one of the group, "how can we know they would be safe if you did find them?"

"I mean no harm," repeated Jean. "Take me with you, I will be unarmed, and let me find the ones who have survived. My men will remain here and will harm no one, I promise you."

The group huddled together and Jean retraced his steps to the gateway to meet his men and explain what he was about to do.

"Come with us then!" the call came up from the villagers. Jean strode down the hill to meet them and called back to Jovis,

"I may be some time. Go on with the work we started! And fetch me my cloak, my satchel and my horse."

Silently, Jean and the band of villagers strode down the roadway, through the village and up the hills on the far side. When the party finally reached the woods Jean was blindfolded and from there on had to be lead on by one of the village men. Another of them brought Jean's horse. An hour or more brought them to a small forest clearing where Jean's blindfold was removed. What he saw was like a village with makeshift dwellings, and men, women and children wandering about at their many tasks. Even the dogs came to bark at him and scrawny children came to squint up at him with curiosity. A tall burly elder approached and said,

"We are the people of Campaldo. What is it you want?"

Jean politely explained who he was and what he wished to know.

"Why should we trust you?" the burly man demanded.

"I have already trusted you," Jean replied. "My men are at the abbey. We are already clearing out the buildings there. We need what help we can get. And I repeat I wish to know if any of the monks are alive – the abbot for example, or Father Roland."

A look of surprise came over the faces of those around him.

"You are from far away and yet you know of Father Roland?" the burly man asked.

"Yes," said Jean. "He is known far and wide and has visited my house a number of times." A murmur went up from the villagers and then the burly man approached Jean.

"Stay with us then," he said, "and we will do whatever we can for you."

Then the man turned and strode away. He returned to Jean some time later and brought refreshments of food and mead for him. As he ate and drank, Jean assured the village elder that Campaldo was now under the protection of the king of Esmor, and that it was safe for the villagers to return and to begin rebuilding their lives there. The village man was pleased with this news, though he added no further comment except to say that he would accompany Jean to another village the following day where there was a possibility of finding Father Roland. Beyond that the man said nothing save to bid Jean a good night. Jean found himself at one end of the forest village bivouacked under a canvas shelter with some of the village men.

Early next day Jean was escorted by the village elder out of the camp and deeper into the forest. By midday they came to a clearing in the forest which eventually opened onto a wide area of tilled land and from which he could see a village in the distance. It was a prosperous place, by the look of it, and boasted a manor house and a little church.

On arrival at the manor house Jean and the company of Campaldo villagers were greeted by a number of people but most importantly they were welcomed by the manor lord himself. When greetings and explanations were over Jean was invited to dine with the lord and his lady. The lord, a big red-faced man with reddish hair, whiskers and beard had little to say and his plump lady wife merely smiled occasionally at Jean. It was understandable, Jean thought, the shrine of Campaldo had been sacked and burned. The shock of the outrage was only gradually sinking in with the local people and so they were not inclined to talk much, especially to a stranger. Towards the end of the meal a servant girl announced that Father Roland had arrived and wished to see the stranger. Jean rose from the table along with the lord and lady of the manor, the door was opened and a rather tall gentleman was ushered into the hall.

"May I present to you," the lord said, "Father Roland of Campaldo."

Jean reached out his hand and took the hand of the newcomer in his as he said,

"My name is Jean de Valdelaine. And as true as that is my name you are not Father Roland of Campaldo."

There was a moment when everyone there was taken aback, then the stranger smiled, and Jean, the lord and his lady laughed.

"You are right, my friend!" the stranger said to Jean, gently holding his arm. "But you understand, we are being very careful."

"Who are you, then?" Jean asked.

"I am a brother of the monastery," the man said. "My name is Brother James! I am sorry we played a trick on you, my Lord. But we are being very careful. Not to worry, soon you will have an opportunity to meet with Father Roland. First of all we have to find him ourselves, and then you will meet him!"

"Father Roland is alive then, I take it," Jean said. "I have with me some documents and other items that you can take to Father Roland as token of who I am. You can read them yourself." There were seated again at table and some wine was poured for Brother James.

"You can understand, my Lord," the brother said, sipping the wine. "We are all very terrified since this – this terrible thing has happened to our beloved abbey."

At this Jean reached into his satchel and handed some parchments across the table to Brother James, he then took the ring from his finger and passed that over as well.

"The documents and the ring carry the insignia of the House of Valdelaine," Jean said. "You may take them to Father Roland."

Just before noon, on the following day, Brother James brought Jean down from the manor to a roadway which ran between fields of golden corn. Brother James instructed Jean to wait by the roadside and that Father Roland would be with him presently. Then the brother said farewell to Jean and departed. Jean stood alone by the roadside and waited. All about him were the fields, and all he could see not far to the left was a team of peasants busy cutting and saving the corn. Perhaps half an hour had passed when he noticed one of the peasants stand up from his work, stretch his back and wipe the sweat from his brow. Then the peasant left the group and was now walking quickly towards where Jean was standing. When he was but a few yards away the peasant removed his cap and cowl revealing a fresh complexioned face, white hair, moustache and beard. Drawing closer to Jean he spoke,

"I am, Sir, Father Roland of Campaldo."

A rush of gladness ran though Jean's heart, at last he had found Father Roland, alive and well.

"Father, I am Jean de Valdelaine," he said smiling. As they shook hands the monk too was smiling.

"Yes, indeed Jean, I know you by your face, the family resemblance is striking! You have your mother's good looks, God rest her soul in peace."

Jean's eyebrows were raised.

"You knew her, Father!"

"Oh yes indeed, my son, a long long time ago!"

"Father, I have come to escort you back to Campaldo. It is safe to do so now, I have a troop of soldiers on guard there. Campaldo is in Esmorin territory now."

"Wonderful, my son, wonderful." Father raised his hand in a wave to his companions and they immediately left their work, striding across the field towards them.

"These are my brother monks, we have not been idle while we were hiding. We helped save the harvest for the good people of the manor.

And so without another word Jean, father and the group of monks started out on the journey back to Campaldo. It was the first step in the restoration of the monastery simply getting the monks to return.

As Jean and the little group of monks walked together, Father Roland chatted with him from time to time. But the monk's face was clouded with anxiety as though some dark secret clouded his mind. The pace of his walking seemed to indicate a great haste to return to Campaldo as though the monastery was still in great danger. Jean was lost, uncomprehending and, with every step, his sense of mystery grew deeper.

When they finally saw the monastery, the monks cheered with joy and began to break into song. But Father Roland's expression never changed. When they reached the monastery buildings the monks joyfully set to inspect every building, cleaning, tidying and making every effort to coax the place back to its normal self.

Father Roland did not join them, rather he took Jean by the arm and led him into the ruined church building.

"My dear Jean," he said anxiously, "I have sent for Peter the Blacksmith to join us. Just you, me and Peter. We have an urgent task to perform."

Jean was puzzled.

"What kind of task, Father?"

"Campaldo holds many secrets in trust for many many people of all ranks. When an abbot is elected, he, of course, knows its secrets. However within a year the abbot must entrust all this knowledge to another monk who is then entrusted with the care of such secrets. They are documents, legal, historical, sacred texts. They are objects which for one reason or another people entrust to us for safe keeping. These are regularly moved from one hiding place to another and only the one monk knows where exactly they are at any given time. I have been the monk of the secrets for many years. One of my secrets was placed in the abbey church. I need to see if it survived the burning."

At that moment they were joined by Peter the Blacksmith and then all three, Roland, Jean and Peter entered the abbey church together. Halfway down the nave Father Roland stopped and turned left. Reaching one of the stone pillars he began to measure a distance up the pillar from the ground using hand over hand to do so.

"This one, this one it is, Peter."

"Very well, Father," said the blacksmith moving forward with hammer and chisel. "Stand back please, my Lords, some stone chips may fly."

Father Roland and Jean stepped back as Peter began to chisel at the rendering between two stones of the pillar. One of the stones held a gargoyle which grinned hideously at them, while Peter hammered away at its edges until he had made it loose enough to be removed. Using his mighty hands he gripped the stone and began to slide it out of its place. When it was free of the pillar he lowered it gently to the ground. Father Roland rushed to the aperture and, raising his sleeve, he put his arm inside reaching into the pillar. He moved his arm this way and that until finally his hand found the object he was seeking. Deftly he coaxed the object upward and out of the hollow set in the pillar. What he extracted was like a roll of fabric. Frantically he placed the fabric on the floor, his hands twitching nervously as he opened the strings binding the roll. Finally he unrolled the cloth on the ground revealing sets of documents, parchments, pages of vellum. "Oh thank God!" he gasped as he saw that nothing had been destroyed.

"O, thank God," he said again as he rolled up the cloth again and held it to his bosom. He knelt there for some time slowly regaining his breath and his composure.

"Will I close the pillar now, Father," said Peter.

"Do that, my son, and may God bless you!"

Still clutching the bundle Father shuffled his way toward Jean. Father beamed a smile at the young man. "Thank God these are safe, Jean!" he said. "Now I wish you to accompany me to finding the new hiding place for these, it is in the crypt under the deepest cellars. May I prevail on you to find at least two torches, we will need them. There is no light down there!"

"Yes Father, of course. I'm glad you found what you wanted and in a sound condition!"

Father was now chuckling with joy, tears began to stream down his face.

"Thank you, my son. Ever since the night of the attack, every day and night I have worried and prayed for the safety of these precious things!"

An hour later, deep in the darkness of the crypt beneath the cellars Jean held the torches while Father replaced the slab of stone over the hole in which he had deposited his treasured documents. This was to be their resting place for the time being, at least. He stood up and brushed the dust of the crypt from his clothing. In the torch light he smiled at Jean. When the two men had climbed out of the crypt, then out of the cellars and into the refectory where they found some of the monks had happily prepared an evening meal, Jean whispered to Father Roland,

"These documents are infinitely precious to you, Father. If you will forgive me for asking but why could they be so important?"

Father turned to face Jean, placing the palms of his hands against Jean's upper arms.

"Why could they be important indeed, my dear Jean. All I can say to you now is that they will not see the light of day again until they are needed. Suffice it to say, dear boy, that they hold the future of Bergmond within their pages. When this time of war is over and when the league has been overthrown, only then will they see the light of day once more!"

Within a few days, all the monks came out of their hiding places among the peasantry and joined their comrades with great joy. The monastery life began straight away, work was restarted and the chanted hours of prayer rang out at intervals during the day and night. Jean had ordered timber to be brought in wagon loads and already workmen were busy building a temporary chapel for the monks. Jean's troops had worked with locals cleaning the debris from the church floor leaving the building clean and neat, though its roof was gone and the windows smashed by the heat of the fire.

After some days, Prince John arrived with a large retinue of knights, to the great joy of the monks. He wished to see for himself the damage caused, and immediately endowed the abbey with generous funds towards the reconstruction of the church. The prince charged Jean to remain at Campaldo for the time being.

"When I need you, I will send for you," the prince told Jean on his departure.

And so, Jean was to spend almost half a year in Campaldo living with the monks as they brought Campaldo back to life again. Meanwhile the army of Esmor was descending from the hills to rendezvous before the walls of the great city of Augsad.

Thus it transpired that, during his stay at Campaldo Jean found time and plenty to reflect on all that had happened. "You will never be master of Valdelaine," the witch had said. If this prophecy proved true, then the outcome of his life would prove so different from what he had mapped out for himself. The words of the witch could mean that he might be killed in battle and buried where he fell, far from home. They might also mean that, by some pernicious twist of fate he might betray his country and suffer the executioner's axe or the ignominy of banishment. For all his striving for goodness of life, he knew that evil was never far away, evil from without, evil from within. "You must fight the evil, Jean," the witch had said. Finally there was the possibility that, under some powerful illumination sometime in the future, he would step aside from his chosen course in life and thereby take up a new and unforeseen path which would be his destiny. As he sat and prayed amid the ruins of the abbey church, try as he might, he could not see what the future might hold for him. He was at peace however and resigned to waiting until all might be made clear to him.

*   *   *

Finally, as the weeks wore on, the Anlac knights arrived; singly, in small groups and in companies. Sir Godfrey, his wife and family and servants had taken up residence in Anlac which took the burden off Germaine's shoulders when it came to housing and entertaining the two hundred knights who came and went. There were joyous festivities and music in the great hall which well matched the delight of the Anlac knights in coming to know their future duke. The idea of a tilt against the league forces at some time in the near future was received well by eager swordsmen who longed to fight under the Anlac banner once more. But Germaine was careful to caution them from acting alone, the time to strike would come soon enough; he wanted them to await his call to arms until the right moment. Germaine knew that it would come soon, as he had in his possession a number of letters from Eldwin Lande, the vice chancellor's secretary in Bergmond. The first letter had warned Germaine that in the city itself the demand was growing that he should present himself to the king, the council and the ordinary citizens there. He was, after all, their long lost hero, and a hero's welcome he would certainly receive. The following two letters warned Germaine that the grand master Gavron was growing impatient with his long delay in Anlac. Finally a fourth letter warned Germaine that Gavron was about to take matters into his own hands, and send a force to Anlac to fetch Germaine thither. This was the moment he waited for, the moment known in history as the Rout of Pontefrane.

Of course these were the days of the aftermath of the destruction of the monastery at Campaldo and most of the league barons and army had repaired to the city of Bergmond and the surrounding country to brood over their blunder and sit out the crisis. From Gavron's point of view it was vital that Germaine should show his face in Bergmond, if not to rally the league cause, then to provide a welcome diversion for the capital city until the storm over Campaldo blew over. At that moment, Gavron did not know that Germaine had set himself on the course of rebellion, but Gavron, who trusted no one, preferred to have Germaine in Bergmond either way where he could keep an eye on him. And so Gavron busied himself preparing a small army to escort Germaine to the city.

Through the secret works of Eldwin Lande, Germaine was well advised beforehand, and in a declaration sent to all his knights he decreed that no league army, not even a foot soldier, was to be permitted set foot on Anlac soil. He continued to placate Gavron, of course, in letters claiming that affairs at Anlac were the source of his delay and asserting that as soon as his work in Anlac was completed, he would make all haste to join Gavron in Bergmond. Earlier he had sent secretly to the Countess of Norland assuring her that he would rise against the league soon and urging her to come into an alliance with him. He also assured her, if she did not know already that the dukes of Anflair and Augsad would eventually come out against the league.

From the moment the league force set out from Bergmond, Germaine had news of it. He decided to camp his force of two hundred near the village of Pontefrane. It was now early December, and in the company of Sir God-frey and a small troop of the young ravens, he waited on until the sound of drums heralded the league force as it marched through the village and crossed the bridge. There was a wide expanse of open ground north of the bridge, white with a light covering of frost and which was bounded by thick forest on both sides. The sound of the drums was louder now as the league column crossed the bridge and continued northward on the road where Germaine and his little party were waiting. Finally the column reached the spot where they encountered Germaine and friends.

The column halted as the commander Baron de Sever raised his hand. Germaine rode closer to encounter de Sever.

"Good morning, Baron," Germaine said affably. "What a splendid day for a bit of hunting. Have you and your men gone astray perhaps. I cannot think what business might take you this way.

"Good morning, Lord Germaine!" de Sever said scornfully and eyeing the small group of men in Germaine's entourage. "I bear orders, my Lord, to escort you to Bergmond."

"Whose orders are they, my Lord?"

De Sever sniffed contemptuously and answered,

"These are the orders of the grand master, Baron Gavron de Laude!"

"I see!" said Germaine. "As you must know, Baron, only the king can summons a duke – and you have no orders from that source!"

De Sever's face hardened.

"The league is fully within its rights to summon you and the king's summons is not necessary!"

Germaine looked at Sever in the eye,

"I answer to the king of Bergmond, God save his Grace, and to him only. So therefore I'm afraid, Baron, that your journey has been in vain. You may pause for refreshments in Pontefrane before you depart these regions. You are permitted in Anlac only by my permission!"

At this stage, de Sever's face was red with rage and he shouted,

"We in the league can move freely anywhere we wish!"

"But the law says you must receive permission to encroach upon my estate."

"Anlac!" said de Sever between gritted teeth. "What is the law – nothing. The league is the law, and I now order you to come immediately with us, and if you refuse then we can take you by force!"

While Germaine was replying "Then you must take me by force for I obey only the laws and statutes of the land and not the ordinances and evil practices of the league. Therefore you must leave now when you can!" Sir Godfrey had raised his hand in signal and a small army of Anlac knights emerged from the woods to the left and a similar army emerged from those to the right causing the league knights to turn outward in both directions, lances at the ready. One of the league knights went to raise a crossbow but he was killed outright by a bolt from Philip's crossbow.

"Stop, stop, you fools, hold your fire," de Sever bellowed at his men. "A fair fight, Anlac, let us withdraw a hundred yards or so and form battle line! The grand master shall hear of your treachery."

"If you wish, though I would prefer if you withdrew further and went back the way you came."

But de Sever dug in his spurs and galloped down past his column ordering them to face about, march a hundred paces and form the battle line. This delay gave time for Germaine and Sir Godfrey to don their armour which was hurriedly brought to them by the pages who had hidden in the cover of the trees. Germaine had been pressed by some not to enter the battle himself as he was wanted alive by the barons in Bergmond. But he had no intention of permitting his troops to enter their first encounter without himself at the very heart of those troops.

The winter sunlight shone across the wide fields north of Pontefrane bridge where the two battle lines were drawn up. The hour was almost noon and for some long moments an eerie hush descended on the scene and it seemed that even the birds in the trees had stopped their song. Finally Germaine looked to his left and to his right, raised himself from his saddle, lifted high the sword which glinted in the sun and roared the war cry "Anlac! Anlac!" His men took up the cry with a great roar and Germaine began the charge which swept across the field like a wave, the sound of hooves breaking the silence with its thunder and the first clash of arms rending the still air.

For sure, the league knights had the best of the early exchanges as six of Germaine's knights were killed instantly in the first shock. The long experience and sharpness of the league knights was driven into their every act and blow, and they quickly gained the upper hand as the Anlac men were unhorsed and scattered in large numbers. In fact the league line slowly began to move forward as the less experienced Anlac knights were pushed backward, slowly losing ground with each passing minute. But the sight of Germaine, sword raised high, screaming hacking and swirling in the midst of the fray was becoming sufficient to call his wavering knights to

heave at the enemy, and heave yet again. The young
Anlac knights lunged again and again, each time some of
them yielded up their lives in the maelstrom of blood
rather than allow the league one step further, their lack of
battle experience compensated by their ferocious willingness for the Anlac cause. Wounded men picked themselves up from the cold ground, took sword, axe, or even
a broken lance and then, in groups plunged themselves
headlong, once more into the fury. At last the league line
came to a blood drenching standstill as the fighting became even more murderous – the young Anlac men, no
longer quiet landsmen and farmers intent only on crops
and feudal dues, once blooded they were now frenzied
men of rage. On their own soil and in the sight of their
kinsmen they gave themselves up to vicious death rather
than retreat. In the thick of the fight Baron de Sever
paused, raised his visor and looked about; he was now
worried that his attack had ground to a halt and more than
surprised that his textbook tactics had failed against an
inferior but furious enemy. Every swing of sword, every
hack of battle axe had yielded gaps in their line, only to be
filled again by desperate charges of their horsed and unhorsed men heedless of their lives. Before de Sever could
think again, Germaine and his fanatics had broken the
league line and were cutting his force in two. He saw no
point in pursuing this useless slaughter, better he thought
it, to turn home for Bergmond and come back with a larger force and fetch the damned Germaine to Bergmond as
a prisoner. He signalled a retreat and his men began to
wheel about and canter back across the field towards the
bridge and the safety beyond. Like a great garment being
rent in two, the two forces disengaged all the way up the
line. For the moment the Anlac men could not pursue,
only catch their breath on the frosty air. Germaine found

Sir Godfrey, wounded but none the worse for wear. The men were falling to the ground from their wounds or to catch a breath – there were a large number dead, twenty knights for sure, and the field was scattered with wounded who needed tending, and Germaine saw his chance of pursuit was exhausted. The enemy were already in full flight towards the bridge.

We may wonder then, why this battle was called the 'Rout of Pontefrane' when indeed there was no rout and when the enemy withdrew in good order, leaving about a third of their number dead or wounded. But it was precisely at the bridge, the escape route of the de-feated leaguers that the second battle of Pontefrane, the rout, took place. It was not usual for common people to hang about when the locality was filled with armed knights, nor was it usual for them to assemble to observe battle save from a safe distance. But the common folk of Pontefrane and other villages had gathered to witness the hostilities and the bridge gave them a vantage point, high and overlooking the fields. But these folk had not come just to watch the proceedings, for they were armed with any kind of weapon they could find, pitchforks, scythe blades, sickles, clubs and sticks. They were villagers, peasants, woodsmen and blacksmiths and their blood was up. They knew the young Lord of Anlac had returned and by now they knew the men of the league meant him much harm. Thus when the retreating knights approached the bridge they found their way truly blocked by the motley army of common folk who closed ranks menacingly as they approached.

For a brief moment the knights had pause for thought, but then proceeded. Five of them abreast charged at the bridge only to be met by a stream of angry peasants who quickly surrounded them and eventually tore them from their horses and killed them in a hail of blows. Quickly the peasants ran back up the slope to the narrow safety of the bridge – a second troop of knights charged, their fate was much the same, once unhorsed some were trampled to death and others thrown over the parapet into the river. While yet another group of knights tried again to force the bridge and its mob, their companions, the remnants of the league army, seeing they were trapped decided to drive their horses into the waters of the river and thus cross over. A number of them succeeded and galloped away, but some hardy young men, sons of woodsmen began to run down the far side of the river bank and began to ply the crossing knights with arrows. If the water had been low the knights might have fared better, but it was winter time, and steering a large horse amid deep swirling water was not easy. Soon the arrows of the woodsmen began to find their mark; stung by these missiles horses panicked and threw their riders or simply swam for the safer shore. Even so, a few knights were making it across, singly or in twos at most, grateful to find firm ground and flee for their lives, leaving their companions to fend for themselves. Eventually some knights did cross in large groups and having gained the bank, turned right to assault the peasant archers who were causing them so much trouble. However the crowd on the bridge was very large and its rearguard had not yet had the chance to strike a blow, and seeing the archer boys in danger, they betook themselves down the riverbank in droves. There they set about the horsemen with such a fury that drove off their attackers who galloped away out of reach downriver, there they waited to see if the remainder of their force might cross as they had done.

It was too late however, as Germaine and his troops had taken up the pursuit and were already harrying the leaguers from their rear. Trapped by the river, the bridge and the village folk on one side they were now equally trapped by Germaine's arrivals. Straight away, and with little resistance, they fled for the river, splashing headlong into the waters. Seeing this Germaine sent a portion of his troops to cross the bridge to trap the retreating leaguers before they could reach the other side. As they emerged on the far bank, the leaguers now faced a squadron of Anlac knights and another bitter fight took place. A few leaguers managed to get away but not before Baron de Sever and many of his captains were killed. It was all over, and a great crowd of the common folk who had defended the bridge earlier came forward to greet and cheer Germaine. He rode among them acknowledging their cheers until he came to the bridge. There he dismounted, removed his helmet and vaulted up on top of the bridge parapet. There, surrounded from all sides by knights and the people he waited breathlessly until the cheering died down. Then from his high position on the bridge he spoke, his voice carrying over bridge, over river and over the fields.

"My friends, my dear friends and countrymen! Today by our deeds, we have sent word to all of Bergmond and beyond that we would fain be rid of the tyrants of the Raven League. We have much to do, but this day, and this place, Pontefrane, will be remembered as the first to strike at those nobles who have robbed our country and plunged it into a war, a useless war with Esmor. I thank you all, one and all for your brave actions here. We will carry the name of Pontefrane with us as we go, for soon we will march against them that hold our king hostage in Bergmond. Anlac has struck the first blow at the heart of the league and by God I swear I will not rest till Anlac strikes the last blow!"

He could speak no more for the crowd set up such waves of cheering that no one voice could be heard and he stood still before them, one hand on his hip, the other holding his sword aloft. The celebrations in and around Pontefrane began there and then and went far into the night. In thanks Germaine exempted the village from all tax for four years.

A full and merry yuletide was passed that year in Anlac, the first for many years; the sounds of laughter, merrymaking and music filled the halls, and Anlac became once more a place of joy. There was good news from other places also, the Countess of Norland, emboldened by the news of Pontefrane moved her household and her army as far south as she could dare. As well as this the Duke of Anflair had summoned a secret assembly of nobility to meet him in Anflair in the middle of January. Finally a letter had come from Ioni to say that all was well with her and with all her family, that her father had come home for a few weeks and that her brother Eris too had finally come home also to pass the yuletide at Valdelaine. Ioni's heart is happy, Germaine reflected, therefore my own heart is at ease, though ever and always longing to be with her again. There are few quiet moments in my life now, he thought, but in every one of them my heart goes to her. Ioni's letter had contained another happy piece of news. After Germaine's departure, Gilbert Belmont, younger brother of Leon had escorted the Valdelaine and Ronclava girls on their return journey, following their summer sojourn in Belmont. Young Gilbert and Cousin Fleur had formed a special attachment the outcome of which was that Gilbert had asked Uncle Robert's consent for him to marry Fleur. And Robert had granted it, the wedding date was set for sometime in the coming summer. So the dream that had so long featured her, Ioni, that of a marriage between the Valdelaines and the Belmonts, had come true, not for her, but for her cousin Fleur. From the letter Ioni was ecstatic for Fleur's good fortune.

And so, with the company of fifty of the Young Ravens, Germaine set forth from Anlac in the middle of January. The route taken, led them not south towards Bergmond, but at first eastward for three days and nights turning southward near the town of Adelburgh, thus hoping to avoid detection by the patrols of the league. Once the Anlac territory had been left behind, for added safety they travelled by night and rested in the woodlands by day. Germaine had left Sir Godfrey in charge at Anlac, and had left everything in a state of readiness for war. Fearing an invasion by league forces in reprisal for Pontefrane, Germaine insisted that every road, village, bridge and fortress be placed under complete alert, and patrolled at all times. When Sir Godfrey had quizzed him as to when to expect his return, Germaine hinted that he might be delayed at Anflair for some time, though for what exactly he could not say. He reminded Sir Godfrey that he was a relative newcomer to the anti-league cause and as such, might not figure greatly in the plans of the Duke of Anflair.

In the early hours of the winter morning Germaine and his escort arrived at Adelburgh but skirted it widely and turned southward. Some seven miles in that direction they came to Lorne Ridge which crosses the plain from east to west and which would deter the would-be traveller from advancing further, if it were not for the Giant's Gap, a great cleft which cut the ridge in two. Germaine and his riders dismounted to guide their mounts through the rocky floor which was covered in snow. Descending from the gap with the winter sunrise on their left, they made their way across the snow laden fields to the safety of the dense woodlands to their right. Once the woods were reached and the encampment set Germaine felt sure he had evaded any league forces that might be in the countryside they had passed. A good rest today and tonight and then they might proceed by daylight once more for the rest of the trek to Anflair. Their tracks across the snowy fields would have been easily detected and their point of entrance into the forest easily pinpointed except for the precaution they took by trailing beams of wood from the two last horses, thus covering the heavy tracks they had made. Besides this they did not make camp on entry to the woods, but continued to ride southward for two more hours on the sparse forest tracks before finally halting for the day. For any enemy searching, finding them would be difficult indeed. Deep in the wood four pavilions taken on the baggage wagons once erected provided some welcome comfort for the weary travellers.

*   *   *

Germaine was awake before noon and emerged from his pavilion shivering and eager to eat something by the fireside. Others too were stirring. But then Philip arrived on horseback returning from the edge of the forest where he had kept a silent watch on the Giant's Gap, two miles to the north; he had also watched for any activity on the Anflair road. The news he brought was bad, a number of league patrols had come down from the Gap, paused to search the snows for tracks, and then moved southward. For Germaine this meant his little company would be denied tonight's rest and would be obliged to sally forth from the woods before sunset and continue down the Anflair road through the night. He advised his young ravens of the change of plan and urged them to eat a hearty supper before their departure. He also warned them that there would be trouble up ahead.

That evening they travelled unimpeded for an hour until the sunset. The sky was clear and the red and golden afterglow was strong, and it was then that they spotted the enemy spread out in a long line, their dark forms silhouetted against the red glow on the horizon. So this was it, there was no turning back, and as they approached closer Germaine's men fanned out left and right. There was no hurry and there would be no charge from either side as the snow was too deep for the warhorses to move quickly. But as Germaine led his formation up the slope and closer to the foe, who were now but seventy yards away, he quickly noticed that the snow was much lighter on the high ground. Then the traditional stand, the drawing of the sword and holding it aloft. Then came the piercing cry "Anlac!" which rent the silence of the snowy air, followed by the roar of "Anlac" as Germaine and his ravens thundered at the league line.

In the waning twilight the charge and the sounds of clashing swords, lances and shields were sharp on the crisp air. Within moments, Germaine was whirling and weaving among the enemy, his sword crashing the life out of three enemy knights. Again his horse reared and already he was forcing a gap in their line to left and right. But not for long, strangely and suddenly his destrier was shot from under him with a crossbow bolt, and as he rolled away and stood up, sword in hand his attackers hesitated. The sight of Germaine, even on foot in mid-battle was enough to cause any would-be attacker to think again. In those moments he was brought a spare horse and lunged forward. But the league knights, amazingly, had begun to disengage and were soon galloping away west across the snowy field. Germaine followed them with his young bloods close behind. The deepening snow made it heavy going but Germaine caught up with some stragglers after half a mile. This last skirmish was fought in torchlight as darkness had fallen, and a further eight enemy knights fell before Germaine broke off the pursuit.

Even now, there was little time to lose and Germaine gave orders that thirty of his men should travel with the baggage wagons while he, Philip and the others would press on with all haste. The sooner they were truly clear of league territories, the better. But first he had to retrace his steps in the torchlight to find his fallen destrier and dismantle its harness, saddle and trappings. After a brief search over the snowy ground he found the unfortunate beast and, kneeling in the snow, began the work of unharnessing. To his left the company of knights had formed up with the baggage wagons. Half a mile ahead Philip waited impatiently with the forward detachment, the light of their torches piercing the night. As his bare hands fumbled amid the harness, Germaine froze. This was not the freezing of the effect of the cold – as his hands searched, it was his heart that froze such that it might as well have stopped beating there and then. Terror, anger and the frustration of sudden loss shocked and drained him. His fingers had found the leather strapping of his saddle bag – it was cut clean through and his satchel was nowhere to be found. In the half light of the torches, in the eerie cold of wind and snow he broke into a sweat, the sweat of terror.

Shaken to his inner core, he heaved the harness onto the wagon, gave some quick orders and mounted his fresh horse. As he galloped forward recklessly to join Philip up ahead his mind was in a whirl, though he struggled to steady it. The satchel had contained no more and no less than various letters and a book, some messages from the Duke of Anflair, all of the letters from Jean de Valdelaine – but worst of all, by far was his precious collection of the letters of Ioni de Valdelaine. Gone! Stolen, as if Ioni's precious heart had been murdered there and then. Oh yes, the league knights had fought a skirmish and retreated – but someone, somewhere had watched the entire affair, had ensured that Germaine's horse would fall and when the battle had moved on, had used the cloak of darkness to steal the satchel. It was grim, it was trickery and it was surely the work of Gavron de Laude! As he continued to gallop forward Germaine was beginning to sigh with relief – all the really dangerous letters had been destroyed; the correspondence of Eldwin Lande, of Countess Norland and of Father Roland, all of this, mercifully, had been destroyed. As he joined Philip at the head of the forward column his heart was easing a little, though his brain was whirling, searching his memory with a fire that was like a dragon's breath. He waved the column forward into the night, up ahead three outriders acted as snow guides, when they broke into a canter it meant the ground was good, when they slowed to a trot, the ground beneath was uncertain and so the main column followed suit and did likewise, on and on, through the surrounding darkness.

After midnight the moon rose and with its light they were able to move at a comfortable pace, able to see all the wide landscape bathed in the pale silvery glow. Germaine was glad he had left the larger squadron of his knights with the wagon for, in this light, they would be seen from miles away.

Germaine did not speak as he rode beside Philip, not a word had he uttered since the skirmish. His mind for the moment was preoccupied with his own thoughts which were giving him no rest. I have placed no one in danger after all, he reflected. All are safe, the companions of my recent intrigues, especially those like Eldwin Lande who lived within the walls of Bergmond and whose lives would be forfeit at the least error. No one is in danger, save myself, and I am not afraid for myself. But the letters of Ioni de Valdelaine are a different matter – belonging in a different sphere, they are a cause for which I would gladly charge the walls of Bergmond this very night, if I could. The theft of those letters is something else, a matter of one's heart and of the depths of one's private innermost soul. Gavron! You have undone me this night – you would have taken my life, and I am still calm, you would have stolen Anlac and all my birthright, and I am still well. But now, Gavron, you have truly overreached yourself and violated my heart and soul, and I am in a fury – a rage for which I would happily kill you, for which I will kill you. So help me God, it is my heart that has now marked you, Gavron – has marked you to fall. It is nothing that you did not know the contents of those letters, Gavron – for, no matter what their contents were those precious pages are now in evil hands, of this I can rely on you, Gavron. It is my heart that has marked you, Gavron – to fall, and it is my sword that will search for you until heart and sword are sated in your death! Onwards! In God's name, onwards to Anflair!

Chapter XV: Treason of Hearts

*W*ith the league forces in control of the city of Bergmond and the south, the rest of the country, especially the north and the east in open rebellion, Gavron was anxious to proceed with the trial of Germaine as quickly as possible. There were other considerations also, with the trial of so high a nobleman for treason, there was the hope that the city itself would come out even stronger than ever for the league, and its wealthy merchants to donate even more finance for the league's cause, beleaguered now by the northern and eastern rebellions. To this end Gavron found himself in the White Tower in late February ensconced in the chambers of the lord high justice of all Bergmond, Ugo de Chacanne.

"I wish you to have a care, a great care in this matter, my Lord Gavron," the high justice was saying, seated at his desk with Gavron seated opposite. "It is in your interests to be most careful in the matter of such a trial. It is a duke of the realm, a distant cousin of the king that you are seeking to try for treason! It is without precedence in the history of Bergmond. I can tell you also that the king is most insistent that the weight of evidence against Germaine should be compelling to warrant a trial in the first place."

Gavron shifted in his seat and lifted a satchel on to the table, from which he emptied a large number of documents.

"As you will see," said Gavron, "my scribes have been busy setting forth all the evidence of treachery in this case. Every detail, every point of law has been anticipated. Very many witnesses are prepared to testify against him. Not alone have we sufficient evidence of treason, but we have proof, amazing proof that he is plotting to take the throne for himself. Everything has been done!"

"It is most prudent of you, my Lord," replied Chacanne. "Should you need any more assistance in this matter perhaps I could recommend the city provost to review your case before commencement."

"Laurence Greysteed!" Gavron exclaimed. "I'm afraid he has left the city some time ago to see if some form of agreement can be brokered with the rebels. I seem to recall he went to Augsad to speak with the dukes of Anflair and Augsad. I hope he can knock some sense into them! Then we can all join together and drive the enemy back to Esmor." With these words Gavron took his leave.

Later, in another chamber of the White Tower Gavron met with his own chief officers, Barons Conrad, Agron and Niverd. Gavron acquainted them of his success in persuading the high justice of the merits of the case. He also reminded them of the great pains he was taking to ensure the proper procedures would be maintained at all times from beginning to end.

"You make it sound as though it is going to be a fair trial!" said Baron Conrad. Gavron turned to him, red faced, and rasped,

"Conrad, every procedure will be followed to the letter – to the letter mind, and beyond if that were possible. In this case, justice and fairness will have to be stretched to the limit. Remember, it is a duke of the realm we are trying, not some rapscallion little peasant! Everything must be done to order."

"So, it will be a fair trial," Conrad mused.

"Of course, as fair as ever there was!"

"Don't you think it's a little risky for us – a fair trial for him, I mean, supposing he is acquitted?"

Gavron rubbed his mighty palms together in glee.

"I have no doubt that the outcome will be the same, fair or no, condemnation for treason. But it is better for us to have him the subject of a seemingly fair trial, more convincing to the populace and the country at large!"

"So the fairness will be merely an illusion to persuade the masses?"

"Niverd!" said Gavron giving his companion a thump on the chest. "If we are ever to run this country again, if we are ever to see this crisis out, it is the illusions that will be our greatest ally! If we are ever to seize power, it is the illusion of the rightness of our cause – and the wrongness of others – that will be the key to ruling all Bergmond!"

*   *   *

After the miserable winter that had gone before, the city of Bergmond was in need of some festivity and diversion, and Gavron was adamant that the city should have its diversion in the form of the trial of Germaine. Early in the morning the citizens were treated to the spectacle of the great procession which left St. Mary's North Chapel, wended its way through many streets and finally reached its destination in the cathedral square. First came the royal heralds in their bright livery, sounding their trumpets with much gusto, then came the lords justices in splendid purple regalia, then came the mayor and aldermen of the city, followed by squadron upon squadron of mounted knights, all colours and banners fluttering in the light morning breeze. Last of all came a knight leading a fully caparisoned horse – but with no rider. This latter represented the absent Germaine. The procession came to a halt in the square; all stood facing the tholselhouse, which was to be the venue for the trial. On the steps of the latter building, a resumé of the charges was read out to the great crowd which had followed the procession and which now filled the square to overflowing, each one straining ears to catch the words of the announcing herald. Many eyes were on the executioner who stood on one side of the tholselhouse, his fearsome axe turned inward and away from the crowd. If a guilty verdict was reached at the end of the proceedings, then the axe man customarily held the blade in the direction of the condemned man as he was taken from the tholselhouse to the White Tower prison to await the date of his execution. As the trial was being held without a prisoner then the executioner would point his blade at a herald who would carry the con-demned man's coat of arms.

Only after the introductory proceedings were initi-ated in the main hall of the tholselhouse, the trial proper went ahead. Gavron and his fellow barons took it in turn to present the evidence against Germaine. The trial judges sat at a specially constructed dais at the end of the hall; down the sides ample seating was also provided for the dignitaries – clergy, and league barons who were in attendance. Absent, of course, was the defendant himself and with him, almost half the nobility of the country who had gone over to the rebellion against the league, and were far away in the regions surrounding Augsad. While his country sank deeper and deeper into division and crisis the king had grudgingly given permission for the trial to proceed – as far as the ageing monarch was concerned the last thing the country needed was a trial such as this. But

Gavron and his barons had been adamant, there would be a trial.

That the Anlac country had risen in rebellion and that the Countess of Norland had thrown in her lot with the rebels seemed to matter little. That the Duke of Anflair was frantically shoring up the defences of Augsad against the oncoming Count Michael and his Esmorin hordes, it seemed to matter naught. A good trial of a top ranking nobleman was what was most needed in this, the country's hour of peril. Give the people a trial, argued Gavron, and all would be well. Once Germaine was convicted of treason, the people and the cities would rally to the league's cause.

Perhaps, uppermost in the minds of Gavron and the barons was a memory, far off and yet vivid, of another great battle fought nearly thirty years before. Esmor had then, too, crossed the passes of the Ostmontane and descended on the city of Augsad. Then the city's defences were in good repair, but no one in Bergmond need have worried as the Esmorins had brought little in the way of siege material. The present king, then Prince Leopold, had arrived to save the city and faced the enemy before the walls of Augsad itself. He had personally led the great charge that broke the Esmorin line and put Bergmond's enemy to flight. Many of the people mentioned in this chronicle were there that day. On the Bergmond side, as well as Prince Leopold was Henry, twelfth Duke of Anflair and father of the present duke. Also present was the young Gavron de Laude. On the Esmor side were the very youthful Count Michael, and Henry and Robert de Valdelaine. With the passing of the years the memories of the Battle of Augsad were undimmed. Now, I'm upset I wasn't there myself!

The tapestry hanging still in Augsad Cathedral showed a depiction of the battle surmounted by the words: "Esmor mortuus est. Vivat Augsadia!" When the trial was finished and Germaine discredited, Gavron would turn his attention to Augsad and the rebels there.

The first issue to be heard by the court concerned what Gavron introduced as the massacre of Pontefrane. The document describing that event had been carefully compiled by Gavron's secretaries and in fact its contents bore only a slight resemblance to the facts. Along with this, Gavron produced knights and soldiers of the league who had survived that day. Their story was as follows. As the league column crossed the bridge at Pontefrane, their rearguard, waiting to cross were set upon by a great crowd of armed peasants who first encircled them and then began to close in on them. According to the accounts presented by Gavron, though the knights fought gallantly, killing at least a hundred peasants, they were finally overcome. The bloodthirsty countrymen then proceeded to block the bridge with wagons and carts cutting off any chance of retreat by the remnant league force, now on the far side of the river and coming under attack from Germaine. Finally when Lord de Sever called for the few to surrender, Germaine paid no heed and proceeded to massacre the league force. Who escaped did so by forcing their horses to swim the swollen river and flee to safety. Gavron's twisting of the truth of Pontefrane was reinforced time and again as successive knights and soldiers relayed the story to the shocked court assembly.

Three days later the court began hearing the second set of charges against Germaine and this was an interesting twist in the prosecution's case against him. Pontefrane, it seemed, was not the first instance of his treachery. Evidences were brought forward which purported to go back to the Battle of Elvendene three years before. According to Gavron's carefully selected witnesses, Germaine, in his charge against the Esmorin right, had contrived to have himself separated from the rest of his troops, that he might surrender himself to the Esmorin knights and go over to the Esmorin side. It was claimed that Germaine had lost faith in the campaign after its first year; it was also claimed that, contrary to the stories of the time, he was never a prisoner, but a most welcome and celebrated guest of the king of Esmor; his ransom had been a charade as he was, in reality, returning to Bergmond as a spy, with the intention of overturning the prevailing powers in Bergmond. And Pontefrane had been ample proof of his evil intentions.

A week later the court assembled to hear the reading of the letters of the mysterious creature Ioni de Valdelaine to her supposed lover.

"My Lords," Gavron spoke as he introduced the letters to the court. "On first hearing these documents read out, you will be forgiven for thinking them to be merely letters of some lovelorn female of Esmor. We intend to show your lordships, word by word and phrase for phrase, that these letters are a devious set of encryptions, codes for communications of a sinister nature between the accused and his Esmorin mentors. There is no love-sick maiden. I can tell you now that there is no such person as Ioni de Valdelaine. She does not exist, nor did she ever exist. As I will show you, these letters come from a source within the court of Esmor. Moreover, they will give clear evidence of a covert assurance that Esmor would support the traitor Anlac in any rebellious plans he might have against the crown of Bergmond. As if that were not enough, the letters go on to demonstrate the urgent desire of the king of Esmor, our enemy, ever more to encroach upon the territories rightly governed by his most noble majesty Leopold II, our beloved king. It will be shown that the traitor conspired with the Court of Esmor precisely to advance his own claims to power in this kingdom. My Lords, no words of mine can persuade you of the treachery of Anlac, but then no words of mine are necessary. When you have had ministered to you the burden and the meaning of these letters then you will know the truth of the charge of treason, for yourselves, beyond doubt, beyond all doubt."

Gavron was once more seated as the clerk began the reading out of Ioni's letters. The court listened intently as to the reading, and seeing in them what Gavron had told them they would see, they nodded their heads from time to time, hearing not the words of Ioni's heart, but only the gravity of the most heinous treachery. On completion Gavron proceeded in the course of the next number of days to have the letters read word by word, phrase by phrase, always pausing to impute to those same words a sinister meaning far from their original intention. The heartfelt words of love were torn to shreds steadily, and with great effect Gavron proceeded to misconstrue them time and again for his own purposes. This process was to take many days and was repeated in the examination of letter after letter, all the while the courtly audience more and more was becoming steeped in gullible belief. The heads nodded and whispers of confided concurrence followed every syllable, every line as Gavron's clever dissection proceeded.

If some uneducated child of ten had perchance gained entrance to the hall, that child would have heard those words and known them for what they were. As it was, no such child would gain entrance. But the learned lords and greybeards of this world did indeed hear those words and, with all their wealth of wisdom, could not see in them what they truly were.

*   *   *

Proceedings had gone very well so far for Gavron. Secretly he was intensely pleased, while overtly he maintained only an attitude of one who is seeking with all seriousness the justice of his cause. But he made an error, perhaps the greatest error of his life. His work in discrediting Germaine was succeeding within the great chamber of justice. Nevertheless he was eager, too eager perhaps, to ensure that Germaine was equally discredited in the eyes of the populace; this was a task he was at pains to accomplish during the trial.

"Hear ye!" called the town crier from the top of a wooden pedestal which had been erected in the middle of the great square of the city of Bergmond. "Hear ye! That this be the reading of the treasonous letters of the Kingdom of Esmor to the great traitor Germaine of Anlac. Hear ye!"

The midday sun shone on the faces of hundreds of ordinary folk who had been to market all morning. The stalls had been closed and shut up for the day and now all eyes were on the little man in official regalia as he unrolled the batch of letters. The crowd was noisy and in a merry mood ready for any diverting entertainment, and the little town crier had to strain his voice to a shout in order to be heard at all. A great jeer went up at the mention of the name of Germaine – once a hero in Bergmond, but now an enemy and traitor. Eventually the crowd became a little quieter with anticipation, but the first words "My beloved Germaine" were greeted with another jeer, ribald jokes and raucous laughter. The town crier proceeded, raising his voice as best he could but each and every phrase of the first letter was greeted with loud cat-calls and screams of derision. When the little man on the podium reached the end of Ioni's first letter, the crowds were as noisy as ever and full of merriment. And so it went on until somewhere between the fourth and fifth letter, the throng had grown quiet and the little man's voice carried strongly over the waves of up-lifted mesmerised faces, all now straining to hear Ioni's precious words. Word by word fell upon them, sweet and heart-felt, reaching long and sure into every mind and heart. All the jeering gone now, many smiled and nodded their heads; many simply placed a hand to chin, and pon-dered. By the last letter, a woman at the front of the crowd bowed her head into her hand and wept. There was a long silence as the crier began to roll up the batch of letters and an eerie quiet had settled across the square. Half in hope, half in mischief a man's voice came from the back echelons of the crowd.

"Read them again!" he called and there was a little murmur of approval. But the little crier continued rolling up the parchments, scornfully calling out to the heckler,

"Belay there, varlet. You have heard the words of treachery and let that be enough for you. Besides, be aware all of you, that I am paid but to read these letters just once and no more!"

From the midst of the throng a coin came spinning through the air landing on the timber of the podium at the little man's feet. As the crowd laughed the little man bent down and picked up the coin, bit it, and with good humour unrolled the parchments once more. Though the herald was small in stature his voice carried to the four corners of the cathedral square, and indeed the square was like a great vault filled with silence save for the one voice. It was not a sullen nor angry silence, rather it was the silence of an audience intent on every word spoken. The words, like drops of water from the purest crystal font, fell through the air upon parched and weary hearts, sinking down to the deep recesses, refreshing, warming, transforming darkness into wonder, warmth and joy. The people there stood intent, and captivated as though some immense drama was unfolding to their ears, sure that this was a moment in their lives which they would never forget and one which would never come again.

"My beloved Lord, I bid you pause a while and deign to listen to the outpourings of my own heart, for it is this heart of mine that is your truest household, for you live in this heart every moment of every day and you rule it by sun, moon and candlelight!

"You have no warmer hearth, no merrier fireside in all the world than in this heart of mine. It enfolds you, my beloved, it takes you within on the coldest winter night and gives you rest and comfort. Even now my heart flies to you that it may be entwined in yours. Yes! Again and again it flies to you across all the miles which do now separate us, across every field and forest and mountain of the fair land which first begot you. My Lord Germaine, they say that you are of Bergmond and this is true – then I too am of Bergmond, born again a second time in the light and glow of our love, and how I love that land, the fairest of all lands because it gave you birth – yes every stone and pebble, every river, plain and mountain – because of you they are all beloved to me. In you, Bergmond has stolen me away and I am happy, my own heart's love."

When the herald paused for breath a man in the crowd shouted,

"Them's fair pretty words, Master Herald, fair pretty words, by my soul!"

A great mumbling sound of approval went up from the bowels of the throng. The herald made a little bow and shouted "Shall I read on?"

In answer a thunderous shout went up from the assembly. More, they wanted to hear more!

And so it was, that day of spring sunshine pouring into the square that the innermost thoughts of the heart of Ioni de Valdelaine washed over the people like great waves of the sea.

"My beloved Lord, the day will come, indeed, it is not far off, when I must leave my father and his fair lands, in order that I may find you once more. Because my heart is yours, Germaine, I will leave this house, with my father's good will or no, and seek you, though it take forever and a day, find you that I may press you to my own heart. It is with pain and longing that I hope for that blessed day of days. When we two shall stand together side by side, inseparable, by light of sun or candle it matters not. My heart has decreed that this is what I must do – and I shall obey my heart and find you once more no matter what it costs, when wars are ceased and our fair lands are happy with peace once more..."

When the herald paused once more for breath, the sharp voice of a comely fishwife cut the air.

"In faith I ask, where's the treachery in these lovely words? For I see none! The fair lady loved her man Germaine – where be the treachery here?

There was a loud murmur of approval once again from the crowd.

"No treachery! No treachery here!" the cry went up from the audience repeated again and again for some minutes before the herald could begin reading again.

The climax of the readings came when the herald read a poem from Germaine to Ioni. Germaine had not yet had the opportunity of sending a poem to her and it would be quite some time before she would set eyes on the wondrous lines. Its lovely words were the last the great crowd had heard before a great cheer went up from every mouth. The original page is today presented like the poems in the university of the city, and is clearly in Germaine's own hand, though whether it is his own composition or merely lines written for him by some Anlac poet we will never know for sure.

May you be ever nature's child and sing
In union with your heart and with your star
'Tis well that you have loved the flowers of spring
For they have been a blessing as you are
And ever seeking love as love seeks you
And finds you at the turning of each way
Hoarding not the beauty nor the time
But spendthrift like the dawn of every day
Let light and heartsongs blend with all your years
And peace more deep than all the skies above
Fearing neither darkness nor the tears
For darkness came to us with only love
In you let seasons weave themselves anew
For life is for the gentle and the true

The little man read the letters five times that day by which time the legend of Germaine and Ioni was born. That night, when all the excitement had long died down, every scribe and scribbler in Bergmond worked until morning copying the precious words of Ioni. Far from discrediting them, the reading of the letters had made hero and heroine of the two lovers, and on the morning of the following day all the first copies had sold out to a public eager to retrace the magic of the previous day. Within a week the letters were on sale in pamphlet form and within a month it was possible to buy little leather bound booklets complete with one or two illustrations and bearing the title 'Treason of Hearts.' And as time went on the legend gained momentum; heroic stories, purely the invention of the writers were added with even prettier illustrations in colour.

The two lovers, of course, knew nothing of the events of that day in the great square of Bergmond. Germaine was far off in the passes of the Ostmontane, guiding the secret embassy of Count Anflair to the borders of Esmor. As for Ioni, she too was blissfully unaware of what was taking place in the great square. In that great moment, she was gazing from a high window in Valdelaine amused as she watched the antics of her milkmaid Maria feeding the hens, her sharp voice now scolding, now cajoling the greedy fowl. And Ioni was smiling at the homely little drama as Maria scattered the feed among the hens unaware that she was being watched from the window high above.

In the following days, when the legend was being born, that of Germaine and Ioni, within the great tholselhouse the trial was proceeding to its final stages and concerned itself with the most damning evidence of all against Germaine, namely, the Campaldo book of the legend of the Grotesque Prince. It was a legend that was well known for some generations now. Seventy years before, the then Queen of Bergmond, Isabel, gave birth to her firstborn son and to the horror of everyone present the little infant was hideously deformed. Half an hour later she was delivered of another male infant, this time the child was perfectly formed. The legend went on to say that a kindly knight living far away agreed to rear the deformed child as his own. The deformed prince, in spite of his hideous appearance grew strong and tall, even married and produced heirs of his own. The identity of the knight who had taken the child into his own family was never known, as he lived far off in some mountainous place. Somewhere far away then, lived his descendents who were actually of royal descent, princes of the royal line, oblivious of their heritage. Some forms of the legend held that the descendents of the Grotesque Prince could one day be found and would return to save Bergmond at a time of great crisis.

But the Campaldo version of the story was more precise and told a story that was even more amazing and, in fact, much closer to home. According to the Campaldo book, the Grotesque Prince was brought to the castle of Anlac itself where he was reared by the then duke as one of his own family. The book went on to tell how the identity of the Grotesque Prince was kept secret, and when he grew to be a man, albeit deformed but strong, he married one of the Anlac girls. A noble child was born, perfect in limb – this child grew up to become the Duke of Anlac as the old duke had produced no male heir. This duke was the grandfather of Germaine of Anlac.

The story of the Grotesque Prince was read out to the court and was received with stunned, shocked silence.

But Gavron was quick to awaken the hearers from their silence.

"This book," Gavron bellowed, "is merely another fairy story, a concoction, a collaboration between the monks of Campaldo and the house of Anlac. It was written to support the claims of the Anlac family, spurious though they are, to support, with a package of lies, their treacherous claims to the royal succession. It is a trick, my Lords! And doubly treasonous – beware the lies of Anlac, the ambition of Germaine of Anlac and the trickery of Anlac!

"Campaldo, my Lords, and Anlac are in treasonous conference to destroy the kingdom with their false claims. For where is the evidence for this piece of fantasy – I can tell you now, no such evidence exists – nor ever will! And therefore I urge you to condemn Germaine d'Anlac as a traitor, and I urge upon you for a sentence of death – a sentence of death! For you have no other choice, my Lords, you have no other choice!"

Gavron continued his summation and now proceeded to drive home his argument as follows,

"My good Lords, you have heard many things these past weeks that surprised you, shocked you to your deepest sense of outrage. What I say to you now, I must say even for my own conscience sake; many will know the story of it already. But few of you will know of the bitter anguish that has troubled my soul these past three years. It is an anguish that must be expressed within the proceedings of this court. It is an anguish that forces me to beg pardon of the almighty God in whom we all hope for salvation. Aye, and to beg pardon of his majesty the king, of you, the assembled court, of the lords and commons of Bergmond for what I have done to the Kingdom of Bergmond.

"This Germaine of Anlac was once the boy whom I took generously into my own home. As he progressed in wisdom and skill I loved him as my own son. I nurtured him, encouraged him, inspired him. In those far off happy days I watched over him as he grew from boy to man. With fatherly pride I saw him become what I thought was the greatest knight and the greatest hope of the realm. But alas for all of us, for the bitter truth is, that I nourished the viper that has grown to be the snake which has now come to turn on us and bite us. With a heavy heart, heavy for the grief it brings to our beloved Bergmond, I ask you for a verdict of guilty. You have no other choice, my Lords."

As it turned out, the verdict was that of guilty of treason and Germaine was sentenced to death. The following day notices were nailed up all over the city, messengers were sent to all those regions still in the control of the league. However the copies of Ioni's letter and Germaine's poem continued to be penned by the many late night scribes about the city – to be sold surreptitiously in the streets and markets of the city.

*   *   *

The king had been presented with the death warrant of Germaine and he signed it eventually with the greatest reluctance. Indeed, for the ailing monarch this was the second major blow within the space of eight months. The news of Campaldo the previous autumn had so shocked the monarch that he had never again risen from his sick bed. As if to compound his grief even more, Abbot Maelruan and the Irish monks of the Royal Monastery at La Fontaine had threatened to leave Bergmond forever, such was their sense of outrage in the wake of the

Campaldo incident. Mailruan's predecessors had come from Ireland a century before bringing with them learning, scholarship and religious reform; it was they who had set up the schools in the city from which sprung the now famous university.

In many letters the king made impassioned pleas to the monks not to abandon Bergmond at this time of crisis. Finally the king threatened to have himself taken from his sickbed, placed on a pallet on the ground before the gates of La Fontaine rather than part with the Irish monks. If then they still wished to leave, Maelruan and his brethren would have to step over the prostrate body of a king. Some of the monks were sons of Irish princes and this was something they could not bring themselves to do and thus were they prevailed upon to stay.

The Irish monks were under no illusions as to the dangers they might face by staying. As it was, the king's death seemed imminent – if his successor were to be of the league party then the days of La Fontaine might well be numbered anyway. It is to Maelruan's credit that he urged his monks to stay, as he knew only too well that a group of Irish monks would count for nothing in Gavron's pernicious scheme of things. As soon as the succession was decided in favour of a league candidate, then the best possible fate for the monks would be banishment, the worst would be martyrdom.

The crisis for Bergmond deepened, everywhere there was fear and gloom. Men's hearts and loyalties were tested to the limit. The enemy, under Count Michael was encircling the easternmost city of Augsad, the civil war between the league and other Bergmond lords was escalating. The state of Bergmond had never known such a knife edged crisis, what the future held in store was anybody's guess.

Late into the night, in the light of many candles Gavron sat back in his chair, taking time to ponder things. Late in December a group of high state and city officials had approached him looking for permission to travel to Augsad. Their object, so they told him, was to reach Augsad and endeavour to persuade the Duke of Anflair to reconsider his position of rebellion, and to make peace with the league, with a view to ousting the Esmorin forces near Augsad, once and for all. Gavron had given his permission and the mission departed, ostensibly, to persuade Anflair to come over to the league, but in reality every one of these officials were in the pay of the duke and, once they reached Augsad, they formed the secret embassy to Esmor. As we know, the embassy was well received and came back to Augsad with the good will and guarantees from the king of Esmor. By the time they returned to Bergmond they presented Gavron with letters from the Duke of Anflair, all at once refusing to join forces with the league but at the same time begging Gavron to make haste to Augsad and drive away the enemy.

All of that had been a week ago, and in his interviews with each member of the mission Gavron found the same message, come to Augsad and drive off the enemy. That done, the Duke of Anflair would negotiate peace terms with him to end any possibility of civil war and for the good of all Bergmond. All in order, thought Gavron but he was puzzled. What had taken them so long? They had departed in January and now it was mid April. That was a long time surely, he mused. Gavron was not a man to let things go – had something else happened to delay these officials in Augsad? The question grew larger in his mind. He reached out his hand over the table before him and found the page with the list of officials. He went through each name and rank, these were important men and he could not arrest them for further questioning without creating suspicions and provoking problems where there possibly were none. Then he turned his attention to the lesser of the officials, he might take one of them in for questioning regarding the long delay in Augsad. His eyes fell on the name of Eldwin Lande.

The following night Lande was arrested and secretly brought to Gavron for questioning. Eldwin Lande's answers were the same as before, but when asked about the reasons for the delay in returning he was somewhat vague, less precise. Something about the duke wanting to entertain the visitors, show them the preparations for the defence of the city and so on. Gavron listened carefully and then told Eldwin that he was free to go, but on reaching the gates of Bergmond castle, Eldwin was arrested once more and taken by carriage to the White Tower prison. From his cell Eldwin had no way of contacting his co-conspirators, no one knew of his arrest, not even his servants. Had Gavron arrested the others too? Did Gavron now know something about the secret embassy or was he still just curious about the delay in Augsad? Eldwin was now worried and a little frightened. Had someone betrayed the conspiracy?

On Gavron's instructions, Eldwin was questioned again the following day by the governor of the White Tower. He was then returned to his cell. Meantime his household began to make enquiries about his whereabouts. Gavron had a messenger sent to assure them that all was well, that Eldwin had come to him on important business and was at this moment engaged in special work for the state. Meantime the governor's report arrived and Gavron read it quickly – the governor had found all seemed well with his interrogation of Eldwin Lande. But, he added, there was something amiss, though he had no evidence from the interrogation, he was completely certain that something was not right and asked to detain the prisoner for further questioning. Gavron gave permission. If something was amiss with that damned mission, he was determined to find out what it was. And so he gave orders for Eldwin Lande to be questioned under torture.

The following morning Eldwin lay crumpled in his cell, his arms dislocated by stretching on the rack, the fingers of his left hand cut off and his toenails pulled out. In incredible agony and in terror of even more pain, he agreed to tell the governor everything in exchange for a quick death. By the time the governor's report reached Gavron, Eldwin was already dead, beheaded in his cell. Even Gavron could not believe what he was reading he was so surprised, appalled even by the daring of the men who had gone to Esmor to seek terms for Bergmond if Augsad fell. Gavron roared with rage and alternately laughed with delight as he paced the castle room that served as his office. "And the so called embassy was led by that little bastard, Germaine of Anlac," he roared. Then he stopped. He would have to act quickly. The other conspirators of the treacherous embassy would be placed under house arrest – for the moment, that was. He would visit terrible vengeance on them, all in good time.

It was time to act, he ordered the league army of the south to join forces with him at Pentevel. From there he would smash the enemy encamped before Augsad and send them running. He would then enter the city and arrest all the rebels starting with the Duke of Anflair and from him down. And Germaine, that bastard traitor, would be hunted down and hanged, disembowelled and quartered in Bergmond square. And Beatrice of Norland, the witch, would be taken alive at any cost, put in a sack and burned alive in Bergmond square.

"They must all go and now is the time to do it," he said to himself. "The king will die soon and all the apparent heirs to the throne will be dead too. And I alone will be king maker, the power behind the next throne. Aye! In time to come I will invade Esmor again and depose its king, and Esmor will be no more. Only Bergmond will survive into the coming ages. Of Esmor there will be nothing to tell!"

And Gavron did move his forces to Pentevel and within three days the army of the south joined him. His objective, Augsad. All that separated him from his objective was the hill country between Pentevel and Augsad. North of the hill country, the Countess of Norland was blocking his way. South of the hill country Count Michael was foraging and skirmishing. He would cross the hill country and, descending, would dislodge the Esmorin forces and take Augsad, leaving Count Michael and the Countess of Norland separated and outflanked.

Indeed during those last days of April and into the first days of May, Pentevel was a busy place, and noisy. However from the hills, Count Michael's spies could easily watch the build up of forces as the tents and pavilions and cavalry lines spread out for miles around Pentevel. As it happened Count Michael was not south of the hill country – he had a token force there, but he himself was in the hill country with his large force, watching and waiting. He had left a token force to besiege Augsad under Prince John's command, however the prince had not enough forces at his disposal to launch anything more than an occasional barrage of missiles from his catapults and mangonels to remind the Duke of Anflair that he, the prince, was still there.

Chapter XVI: Long Hills

"*A*re you sure of this, young man!" Count Michael bellowed. He was seated within his tent, his ruddy face, beard and shock of grey hair all lit up by large candles which had been placed on the trestle before him. His visitor, and the bearer of this latest news, was young Eris de Valdelaine, all hot, sweating and panting from his ride from Pentevel.

"As sure as we are both here this dark night, my Lord," gasped Eris, throwing his chain mail cowl back off his head.

"I had thought him far away to the North," prodded the count throwing back his seat and standing up to his full height, towering above young Valdelaine.

"Not more than four days past, my Lord," Eris was still gasping for air as he looked intently up into the face of his commander, "our spies in Pentevel assured us that Baron Gavron had entered the city and that his large force is now camped beyond the walls. Only yesterday I ventured as close as danger would allow. I have seen the encampment for myself!" There was a silence and the count sat down once more. Presently he spoke,

"I had hoped to trouble Pentevel," the count mused, "though we could not hope to take it with our small force." The count was mumbling but his eyes and face were those of a man with a thousand sudden thoughts. "And now, perhaps Pentevel, through Baron de Laude, means to trouble us!"

"Will there be anything else, my Lord," Eris asked.

"No, my young Lord," the count said kindly. "Go and take supper. But send me in my squires first!" Eris turned to go but the count said, "Meet me at first light. I will have work for you, now go!"

In the grey light of the following morning young Eris approached the count who was standing outside his tent with the other commanders. Count Michael's face was alive and smiling as he took Eris away from the group and placed his great arm around the young man's shoulders.

"No fighting for me, I take it, my Lord," murmured Eris, eyeing the count with a smile.

"My dear boy, if you do nothing else," the count's voice rumbled, "nothing else but find me Belmont, then you'll do a great day's fighting! Find me Belmont, young Eris, and bring him here. In God's name, find Belmont, though it cost you a thousand horses and a barrel of sweat! Now go!"

As with many a military encounter before and since, the Battle of Long Hills took the form of a great ambush rather than that of a pitched battle fought on open ground. Likewise, the conflict at the hills was not an action which was thought out in advance but was rather a result of good timing and quick thinking. Count Michael had camped part of his army among the wooded hills that lie between the cities of Augsad and Pentevel. With part of his force, the count had already placed Augsad under siege and, with the remainder he had hoped to bring pressure to bear on Pentevel also. He kept this second force well into the hills permitting only the occasional raid on league forces in the Pentevel countryside. A third force, much smaller than the first two and commanded by young Leon Belmont, was away on the plains to the North engaged in the usual foraging and providing a buffer of protection to the count's army in the hills.

The action of the battle was precipitated by the sudden appearance of Gavron de Laude at the head of a large force of leaguers. Before the early morning light, these had sallied forth from behind the safety of the stern walls of Pentevel and were making good progress along the Augsad road. From his encampment in the hills, a bare ten miles from Pentevel, Count Michael had awaited the arrival of Belmont's force, but waited in vain. With no sign of Belmont, the count quickly laid his plans; he had rightly guessed that once again he would have to make do with a smaller force on the day of battle. Anyone who was there that morning could afterwards remember the giant figure of the count, as he moved among his commanders and his men, shouting here, cajoling there and  laughing everywhere. This was the kind of moment he loved and it showed in the glint in his eye and in the smile on his lips.

De Laude and his force of leaguers had made good progress along the Augsad road and they had already reached the region where the road left the plain and was winding upwards among the lower wooded hills. Count Michael waited; he had deployed his force on open ground on both sides of the road, on a kind of plateau, at a distance of seven hundred yards from where the Augsad road finally crested the ascent known as Long Hill. Meanwhile Gavron's first detachments were now leaving the lower hills and were engaging with Long Hill, a straight stretch of sloping road about a mile long. The count and his men waited, gradually the drums of the leaguers grew louder, and soon the banners of their forward section could be seen fluttering in the morning light as they came into view cresting the top of Long Hill. Gavron of Laude was among the leaguers first on the scene and, on seeing the count's force straddling the road ahead of him, he deployed his knights for battle as best as the situation would allow and only just in time to meet the count's charge head on. The first clash of battle echoed loudly on the quiet morning air among the woods and hills. De Laude's force wavered and were almost sent reeling backwards, but fresh units of the league column had now crested the hill and were joining their forward comrades in the melee, thus stabilising Gavron's hold on the top of the hill. On the Esmorin side the count's charge was now firmly halted and the top of the hill became the scene of the bitterest fighting of the day. Time and again Count Michael pulled back his force, wheeled round and charged furiously at the league line which was forming and growing all the time as step by step new levies of leaguers were reaching the top of the hill and entering the heart of the fray. Even from the midst of battle Count Michael could see his danger as the league force grew stronger and began to mill around the open ground to trap him.

Halfway down the slope, in the shelter of the woods, Raxtene smiled and watched the great column of leaguers climbing Long Hill road to the pitched battle

now taking place on the plateau above. When Chief Raxtene stopped smiling and raised himself on his mountain
pony to look about at his troops scattered among the trees,
he lifted his sword and bellowed the ancient war cry of
the mountain people. Raxtene's men were now coming at
pace through the woods to the left of the road; these were
the doughty men of the mountains, long-spear men and
halberdiers to a man. Their ponies left behind in the forest, they were scarpering among the bracken and, with a
great roar, burst from the cover of the trees to attack the
league column as it struggled upwards. The league
knights in columns were no match for Raxtene's men and,
wheel and thrash as they might in the confines of the road,
they soon began to fall, horses and men, in the sudden on-
slaught of Raxtene's hordes. Soon the long pikes and
halberds of the mountain men had cut right across the
column and indeed had begun to cast the column backwards down the road. The leaguers then sent forward
some detachments of men-at-arms to deal with Raxtene
but they too were driven backwards down the hill. The
league army, much of which was still in column form
along Long Hill road was now cut in two, the force further down the road unable to join the force that was engaging Count Michael at the top. The lower section of the
column had come to a halt and all the time Raxtene was
pushing the unfortunate column further downwards and
away from the battle above.

All the accounts of the day gave credit to the bravery of the league knights. Some of the accounts, most no-
tably the poetic masterpiece The Song of Ernain, suggest
that the league knights did rally and did attempt an assault
up the hill; some even suggest that they succeeded in
breaking Raxtene's hold on the road midway down the
slope. This latter would have been nigh impossible given

the slope of the road which the knight's had to cope with, not to mention the piles of dead and wounded men and horses that littered the entire roadway. Some accounts suggest that groups of league knights left the roadway and entered the forest on both sides hoping to complete the ascent by means of woodland paths. Given the terrain in question and given the horrors that had already befallen the unhappy column, it would have been impossible to deploy large numbers of troops to maintain a serious assault on Raxtene, let alone to gain access to the top of the hill.

Up on the plateau the battle raged on. Count Michael had observed that the leaguers' members were no longer being augmented and he rightly guessed that Raxtene's men had done their work. On the other side of the conflict Gavron de Laude was moving steadily forward each time the count attacked and retreated, but he had no idea of the disaster that had befallen his troops on the slopes below. Count Michael had almost exhausted every trick he knew – the charges, the feigned charges, the feigned retreats. On two occasions he had summoned his meagre support of foot soldiers to hold the road against the league knights with pikes and spears. On one occasion he had even thrown baggage wagons and equipment across the road to hamper Gavron's progress. But still Gavron and the league knights came on slowly and ever so surely. As ever, Count Michael was the optimist, his voice now hoarse with the exhortations he gave his companions, but even the count had to have misgivings as he watched Gavron's men calmly remove the baggage wagons that cluttered the road, sufficient to allow Gavron's knights to file through and reform their line of battle. Count Michael grimly observed that his own line, throughout the day, had moved backwards almost half a mile across the plateau. What was it going to take, he wondered, to defeat this Gavron? But another disaster had hit the knights of the Raven League.

Shortly after Chief Raxtene's pike men had ambushed the league column, and further down almost at the bottom of Long Hill, Merdon's archers had made their appearance emerging from trees to the right of the road. Known as the 'Forletti del Infer' or the 'Elves of Hell,' from their green jackets and hoods, Merdon's men appeared calmly out of the woods, formed their companies and began to harass the tail of the column with showers of arrows. When the Raven League knights did recover from the shock of the arrows and attempted to charge at their attackers, Merdon's men simply lowered their long bows and disappeared into the trees. Within minutes the archers would emerge again from the protection of the trees at some new point and begin to ply the hapless knights with yet more showers of arrows. Gradually the Raven leaguers were forced to turn back down the road and on to the more open ground at the bottom of the hill. Even then, the Elves of Hell appeared once more and with shower after shower of arrows they succeeded in keeping the league rearguard at bay. Besides, the road above them was now choking with wounded troops escaping the fury of Raxtene's assault. The latter now felt sufficiently emboldened to move his troops against the confused remnants of the column below. Gradually knights, troops, horses, baggage carriages were spilling out on to the little plain at the bottom of the hill. Some units were turning to face the down-coming Raxtene but others were already making their way along the road to Pentevel glad to be out of reach of Merdon's arrows.

Raxtene's attack downhill was halted, not by the troops of the league, but by Raxtene's own pike men who, on discovering large supplies of food and wines on some of the abandoned baggage wagons, began to help themselves to a hearty meal while looting the same wagons for valuable weapons and spare armour. Lord Merdon, with his archers, could only look up the road aghast at the sight of Raxtene's warriors as they looted and sat on top of the wagons eating, drinking and singing mountain war songs. Merdon felt the urge to shower them with arrows, thought better of it and kept up the pressure on the retreating rearguard as it moved away towards Pentevel.

Through the morning Count Michael's knights had fought well but had taken a mauling at the hands of de Laude's men. Now the latter was preparing a final assault on the count's decimated force scattered over a wide space on either side of the road. Lances were raised, banners were raised and Gavron de Laude spun his charger round and round screaming at his knights to hasten the formation of his line. As Count Michael and his bloodied knights gasped for breath and prepared to counter Gavron's final charge, a fresh face young messenger rode up through the ranks from behind and handed the count a little parchment. The face of the count widened into a smile and then a hearty laugh as he held the parchment above his head and bellowed to his commanders,

"Belmont is here! Belmont is here!"

And the cry "Belmont is here!" was taken up and repeated all along the line with great roars and cheers. Gavron had already begun his charge, at first a walk, a trot and gallop, when Count Michael raised himself to his full height in his stirrups with sword held aloft and bellowed out his charge and his army trundled forward. The Raven Leaguers were now in full flight charging the count's line, but their cheers turned to shouts of dismay as Belmont's force descended upon them from behind a bluff of rock to the right. The three forces, Gavron's leaguers, Count Michael's and Belmont's fresh troops seemed to crash into each other at the same time.

When the attack is called and the charges begin to move forward the knights at the front take a line of sight toward the oncoming enemy. And still charging they pick, as it were, their opposite number and begin to aim the lance. Frequently however the knight has to change his target as the crush of other knights and their horses round, pushing the individual rider to left or right. So it happened with Jean de Valdelaine as down the entire charge he was pushed by his companions further and further to his right and straight towards the centre of the enemy line. Within fifty paces Jean's lance was now pointing at none other than Gavron de Laude. It was the lance of Jean de Valdelaine that crashed the chest armour, sending the man somersaulting backwards to be crushed to death beneath the hooves of the horses behind him.

All about, the melee had started; a melee of swords, maces, battle axes, all wielding instant death and showers of blood. The league knights were now retreating, many launching into new attacks to form a rearguard fight while the bulk of their troops could withdraw back across the plateau in the direction of Long Hill. But their retreat was stopped. At the top of the hill three squadrons, one of Raxtene's and two of Merdon's archers stood between the retreating leaguers and any hope of escape. Rather than risk death in an arrow shower from the Elves of Hell or having survived that, rather than meet death on the long pikes of Raxtene, the league knights called the surrender. And suddenly it was all over. The Battle of Long Hills was over.

In the hours that followed men and knights could only stare in disbelief across the plateau or down Long

Hill, numbed as they were by the shock of battle and equally stunned as, moment by moment, the sheer enormity of the victory achieved dawned and disappeared again. All the plateau, all down the road of Long Hill, and out on to the Pentevel road – all strewn with the bodies of dead and wounded. In places the bodies were piled high where the fighting had been thickest. On the Esmorin side, a hundred knights had died and a mere eighty men-at-arms in the entire battle. Of the eight thousand troops and knights that had left Pentevel at first light, only fifteen hundred knights survived and about eight hundred men-at-arms. In all, the conflict lasted but two hours and when men looked at the sun, after the final charge, they were surprised to find it was not yet midday. About three thousand five hundred knights of the Raven League had fallen.

In the late afternoon, when prisoners and wounded were taken care of and the grim work of burying the dead was begun, the most mysterious moment of all befell. Count Michael was called hurriedly from his tent and escorted on horseback down to the plateau to the spot where Gavron had fallen. Groups of guards stood by the spot in heated argument with groups of prisoners. The count dismounted and looked down at the remains of the fallen Gavron. One of the prisoners knelt down by the body, reached out his hand and lifted the visor of Gavron's helmet. But the face that rested in death beneath the visor was not the face of Gavron de Laude, it was the face of some other knight, fallen in battle in Gavron's place.

The news spread through the camp of the Esmorins, as did the mystery of Gavron's disappearance, and no one could solve it, from Count Michael and his commanders right down to the lowliest men-at-arms. It was not unknown in those days for kings, princes and even commanders to enter battle with other men dressed in their colours and coats of arms. But no one else had remembered any other knight in Gavron's striking black and white. It was almost sunset when the news reached Leon Belmont's encampment where his men were resting after the long morning dash to Long Hill. As he sipped some wine, one of Belmont's knights had a flash of memory. "Yes!" he said as he downed his goblet. Of course – the memory of it had been lost – in the final charge, but now he could see it clearly, and he rounded on his companions to tell them.

As they came out of the woods and began the descent to the final charge he did remember a detachment of knights on the league left who, on seeing the approach of Belmont, broke their line and wheeled about leaving the battlefield. That was all he could recall, but, as he spoke, his words jolted the memory of some of the others who recalled it also. Maybe as many as a hundred knights had turned and disappeared! Presumably Gavron among them.

Belmont's messengers, dispatched to Count Michael with the news, found him emerging from the tent of Jean de Valdelaine. Jean had been taken from the field by stretcher, his thigh reefed by a halberd in the fray. All the way to his tent Jean had been cheered and hailed as a hero. Count Michael heard the story of the leaguers who had deserted at the final charge. He put a guard on Jean's tent and went in to Jean to ply him with the strongest wine his aides could muster.

As Jean rested that night a memory gently floated into his mind; it was the memory of the witch at Campaldo and her words to him 'You must fight the evil, Jean, you must fight the evil.' That day at the climax of the battle, he, and no other, had been so placed in the exact location where he had killed the arch enemy. Was this it, he thought to himself, was this his fulfilment of the witch's command? He smiled to himself, not a gloating, triumphant smile, such was not his nature, but a wry questioning smile. Was this the fulfilment, or did the witch have some other destiny for him? Who could possibly know? And weary he slept.

Jean was finally told the truth some days later in the city of Pentevel, which had surrendered to the count's forces. As he nursed his leg by a warm fire in the hall of Pentevel Castle, he was approached by the count and some of his captains who gently broke to him the story of Gavron's escape. Any fear they might have had of disappointment for Jean was allayed as he simply looked into the distance and smiled a little. As they stood about him Jean only nodded and listened to them, his face was calm. More than anyone there could know, Jean knew that he had done everything a knight could possibly do to fight the good fight against the evil of Gavron de Laude. He had been robbed of his victory but now he knew in his heart that the real victory, and the real fight against evil, would be achieved in another way, another place. Not on the field of battle with its glories of this temporal world. My glory was not to be and this was as sure a sign for me, he thought, as any that might have come. Now, I know for sure what the witch in the woods of Campaldo meant. "Fight the evil, Jean!" she had said. He smiled broadly now as at last Jean finally knew the way he must go. Count Michael placed his great arm around Jean's shoulder and held him tight, relieved that Jean had taken the bitter news so well. How little Count Michael knew that day in Pentevel of what had finally sank into the core of the heart of Jean de Valdelaine.

A week later the Peace of Augsad was signed declaring an end to the war. Count Michael signed on behalf of the King of Esmor, the Duke of Anflair signed on behalf of the King of Bergmond. The treaty returned the cities of Pentevel and Augsad to Bergmond in exchange for the lands west of the Gavenne and for the territories up to and including Campaldo.

Chapter XVII: Our Souls to Shattered Things

*G*ermaine sat down with Philip on a bench outside a tavern on St. Stephen's Square in Augsad. The city was crowded and still in festive mood after the peace treaty. However, the question on everyone's mind was what had happened to Gavron, he had gone to ground and all attempts to find him had failed. As they drank their ale in the midday sunshine Germaine placed his hand on Philip's arm and leaned close to him.

"Philip," he said in a low voice. "I have asked you here because I have news of the gravest kind. Bad news, Philip, bad news. And another thing, I now know where Gavron is!"

Philip almost dropped his mug and stared at Germaine in utter surprise.

"Good God," he exclaimed. "Where is he and how do you know?"

"Gavron did not go westward as everyone thought. No, Philip – he went east into Esmor. And the awful thing is – he has taken Valdelaine! I received the message an hour ago. Here, read it for yourself."

Germaine passed the parchment scroll into Philip's hand.

'Anlac,' it said. 'I am at Valdelaine. I took it. Believe me, it was easy. They thought we were Esmorin troops returning from Long Hills. Anlac, I have your girl, Lady Valdelaine, and all her family. They are safe. The bargain is this – we trade. You want the girl, well you can have her. In return I want safe passage for me and my men out of Esmor. I want guarantee of safe conduct from here to the Rhineland. Get me this guarantee in writing from the Esmor crowd, signed by Count Michael, countersigned by the King of Esmor. In return you can have your girl, her family and Valdelaine fortress. Fail to get me this and your Lady Valdelaine dies with all her family. In that event, we'll hold Valdelaine for as long as we can and attempt escape when it suits us. Anlac, you traitor, if I ever come by the chance of killing you with my bare hands, I will do so. Gavron de Laude.'

Philip put down the parchment, his face for once was pale. "What do we do?"

"Now this minute find me Lord Verling. He is the only one to know what you have just read. As well as this, find me one hundred and fifty of our closest friends – find the youngbloods. Fully armed with every weapon we can find, horses, plenty horses – Philip, we are leaving for Valdelaine tonight. Tonight mind, Philip, not tomorrow, tonight! I'll do some searching myself. One hundred and fifty and leaving tonight. Now go and report back to me when you have found our men and all they need. God speed!"

Philip was gone and that night Germaine and his one hundred and fifty knights rode quietly out of Augsad, north eastward, Valdelaine their destination.

They made their way as fast as was possible, resting in secluded places by day and riding by night. It was vital that they avoided detection from any source. Germaine knew only too well that the Treaty of Augsad did not include intrusion into Esmor by troops from Bergmond. Therefore he left nothing to chance. Little by little he informed the others of their destination and their purpose. They were with him to a man – he was the hero they fought with and trusted. They did not halt their journey until they came to rest in a dense forest ten miles from Valdelaine. By this time Germaine had acquainted each and every man among them of their plan of battle.

*   *   *

A place of bright water, and quiet, where the river was wide and low, and the forest closed in on all sides. This was the ford where Germaine and his companions crossed over the Gavenne. Upon the great stretch of water, the reflected beauty of the place was disturbed only by the quiet splash of hooves and footsteps, all amid the warmth of the autumn afternoon. A mere seven miles downstream from Valdelaine, and neither an enemy sentry nor patrol to be seen; it proved an ideal crossing place. The men and horses, having gained the far bank, Germaine turned to his companions.

"We are sworn, then," he said grimly. "All here, we are sworn to secrecy now, and always?"

"We are sworn!" they mumbled in turn, glad to be back among the protective shadows of the trees. Germaine spoke again.

"I bear in mind that you are my closest friends. I bear in mind also, that you have come with me so far and, that truly this is my fight, and my fight only. If I win this then, I win everything that I love in this life. If I lose, I lose happily, knowing that I die in the attempt. But for you, dearest friends, for you this is none of your fight, and I am obliged to say to you that, if any man here will turn back and join the others – I hold it to be no fault. In truth,

I hold that man as dear and loved as the blood in my own veins."

Germaine looked around at their faces – Philip and Ernan, Leon and Jan and the others. It was Jan who spoke,

"In truth, Germaine!" he said quietly. "This is my fight, too, and I will have it no other way!"

"At any rate," Ernan grunted and cleared his throat. "I am afraid that if you go on alone, something bad might happen to you! Methinks these woods are full of naughty elves!"

There was a good laugh, and each man approached Germaine, and embraced him. As Philip approached, and opened his arms, he said quietly,

"We have watched over you for a long time now, it would be such a pity to leave the best part of it all to yourself alone!"

There was more laugher.

"Good then!" Germaine said. "We can rest here, and dine a little too! We can move up the riverside, and hour or so before darkness."

Philip looked about at his companions as food-stuffs and wine were removed from saddlebags for their repast. Philip smiled to himself. Not for the first time in their short lives had they followed Germaine into danger and uncertain outcome. Not for the first time had they attempted what seemed impossible. There were memories of the years of war that had been the lot of their youth. And the memories flooded back as they ate and drank; memories of Holgen fort, the Battles of the Lakes, Rocharden, Savron Field, the Race at Elvendene, the Retreat from Borderlands, and so many other adventures. Forlorn hopes were as nothing to these young men. By now, every man among them knew that if their chances of success were slim, then it was better to be with Germaine than to be without him. And there was heavy fighting to be done after dark, if Valdelaine was to be taken with a mere ten men.

"Remember, arms, not armour!" Germaine had shouted at them the previous night as they were making their preparations. "Weapons, weapons. Bows, cross-bows, axes, broadswords, anything that a hand can fight with!" And even now, as they relaxed in the shade of the trees, by the river, their bodies bristled with every kind of weapon strapped to their sides, backs, thighs and lower legs. Even as they finished their food and drink and stretched back to rest against the tree trunks, not one re-moved a single weapon. Some slept and some just dozed in the warm-cool quiet of the trees.

*   *   *

Germaine had chosen to divide his forces, but not equally however. Here at the ford he had taken with him a mere nine others. A small trusted band, who would traverse the woods on the northern bank of the river. The main body of Germaine's force, almost a hundred knights, had continued on the forest road south of the river. They were to move cautiously, but also they were to make their presence known to Gavron's scouts, who would assuredly alert the league garrison at Valdelaine. On reaching the river opposite Valdelaine, they were to emerge from the forest between the wooden bridge and the village, and there make a great show of strength. Just before nightfall, they were to turn about and return to the woods, ostensi-bly to make camp for the night. After all, Gavron and his men knew that a mere hundred knights would be incapa-ble of taking a fortress like Valdelaine. Gavron would readily conclude that this new enemy force were retreating to the forest, to await reinforcements.

As well as this, Germaine had yet another ruse to play for Gavron. For this attack, Germaine did not wear his own armour. Lord Verling, soon to approach Valdelaine on the south side of the river, was dressed in Germaine's full armour – colours, shield crest, plume banner and all. All of this would be clearly seen from the bridge, and from the ramparts, and Gavron would be sure of the false Germaine's whereabouts. But the real Germaine would actually be much closer, on the castle side of the Gavenne.

A little under two hours before sundown, Germaine and his band broke camp. Making their way among the trees, they were careful to keep the river in view. This would be their guide, which would lead them to the open fields which stretched before the great pile of the towering castle above. Jan and Philip acted as scouts, leaving their horses with two others. It was still daylight when they reached the first clearings, which opened onto the bawns as they sloped gently from the castle walls to the riverbank. Their horses had been left behind deep in the woods. From their vantage point beneath the trees, they were in time to witness the scene opposite the bridge at the south side of the river, facing Valdelaine. Young Lord Verling, sporting Germaine's arms and colours, was parading his men in full view of the fortress. He was careful not to approach too close to the bridge, which was protected by a goodly squadron of Gavron's knights. From beneath the trees, Germaine and his little band had a clear view to the castle walls and towers. All along the ramparts Gavron's troops stood in full armour. Just above the main gate, Gavron himself and his lieutenants stood intently watching the scene across the river. There, Verling was doing his utmost to impersonate Germaine, and repeat as best he could remember, Germaine's characteristic gestures. Back and forth in front of his men, Verling walked his horse. Then he dismounted, and stood for a time with hands on hips, surveying the bridge and the fortress. Then Verling took to walking up and down with arms folded upon his chest, stopping occasionally to study the enemy. Germaine was pleased – Verling was performing a perfect parody of himself, which would have been quite comical had the whole situation not been so deadly. Eventually, under a white banner, one of Verling's knights rode up to the bridge, and handed the captain a letter demanding the surrender of Valdelaine. The captain had the letter sent up to Gavron, the reply assured Verling's knight that any surrender was out of the question. Gavron sent down Baron Agron to the bridge, and Agron, in turn, bellowed out the refusal to surrender. A ripple of laughter went along the ramparts among Gavron's troops. Verling, with visor lowered over his eyes, trotted his horse forward towards the bridge and reined in a few yards away from the bridge. He roared out something to the effect that he was awaiting reinforcements, and would take Valdelaine, Gavron and all. There was more laughter from the bridge and the ramparts. Then Verling galloped back to his knights, who in turn wheeled about and trotted back along the forest road. They were followed, in their retreat, by roars and shouts of derision from the bridge and the walls of Valdelaine.

*   *   *

In the falling twilight, Germaine gazed long at the great pile of the castle. It all looked so familiar and beautiful to him while at the same time, in the afterglow of the evening, it was the strangest place on earth. On that other fateful evening so long ago, a winter evening of deep snow, he had first seen it when he had been brought here as a prisoner himself. He had looked upward at the rampart a moment, to catch his first glance of Ioni de Valdelaine. So much had happened in the time he had spent here; it had been a place blessed with great happiness, more than he had ever known. Above all, that time had been blessed, as the love between he and Ioni had taken root, grown and blossomed to an intensity he would never have foreseen. And now Ioni herself was up there, a prisoner somewhere in her own house, and was, above anything else in the world, well worth fighting for. All going well, he thought, take Valdelaine and rescue her by midnight, or die in the attempt. She is worth it, he thought, so worth it!

Of all the things that could have happened, in these turbulent times, this was surely the strangest of all. The bold Gavron, having survived the bloodshed and carnage at Long Hills, seemed to disappear from the face of the earth only to emerge finally here at Valdelaine, of all places. In a master stroke, he had taken the castle and its inhabitants. With the last of his godless followers he had defied one and all to come and take Valdelaine from him. Having lost all in the defeat of the league at Long Hills, he had taken Valdelaine as a final gamble. And he was now in a position of some strength. He had the Valdelaine family as hostages, and his trump card in any negotiations would be Ioni herself. Of course, the Castle de Valdelaine itself was another consideration. Even though the forces of the king and the forces of Count Michael were converging on the place, albeit slowly, it would take a long siege to take the place by force. Germaine had deliberately outridden all others, to be the first to challenge

Gavron's hold here. He knew only too well the temper and the evil of this Gavron de Laude. Even if Valdelaine was taken by force of siege, then the Valdelaine family would be murdered one by one, and then finally Ioni herself would die. In the event of the collapse of any possible negotiations for the Valdelaines' safety, then the king and Ioni's father would have to engage in a long and deadly siege. Germaine remembered from his time here that, in its long history, Valdelaine had never been taken by force. It may have been surrendered over the centuries but it had never been taken, not once. Perched as it was on the bluff of high rock, its walls brooded over the field that sloped to the river bank. From the bridge on the river, a great stone causeway with ramparts on either side led upward to the main gate. The castle was impregnable.

Finally, the now famous letters written between Germaine and Ioni had brought all of them together this night – Germaine and Ioni and the awful Gavron, who had found the secret letters. He had first used the letters in the trial of Germaine. When Long Hills was lost, he knew from the letters that Ioni's life would be worth the world itself to Germaine. He knew that Germaine would go to any lengths to rescue his lady. Gavron was no fool; in fact he was a genius, a genius of the evil kind. Germaine shuddered with disgust. Gavron was the one who had taught him everything he knew about warfare. Germaine, from his seventh year, had been Gavron's prize pupil. It was now time for pupil and master to meet.

The beautiful day had died with the sunset and as the afterglow deepened into darkness, a hush descended upon all things. The birds went silent. Through the forest and all across the wide countryside, the air had become still and hushed as though silenced by some invisible hand. As the darkness continued to fall, deep and sombre, all things it seemed, would obey the invisible hand, in timid and tenebral anticipation of the terrors of the night to come.

There was complete darkness, save for the sentries' torches on the bridge up ahead; Germaine and his nine trusted men made their way along the lower bank, with the higher bank sheltering them from any possible view from the fortress. Presently some fifty paces away, with the bridge now looming high, Germaine signalled to the others to crouch down low. He moved as though he was searching for something and, all at once, he stopped and sat down among the grasses and the reeds. The others came up level with him and sat around him. He could see their faces in the faint torchlight from the bridge. There was a pause.

"What to do now, Germaine?" whispered Philip. "It is not broad daylight, as it was the day we took Holgen fort."

Germaine smiled in the faint torchlight. He then spoke in whispers.

"Behind me, set into the riverbank here, is a large iron grate. It leads to a passageway underground, which goes across this field and up into the fort. Now, let us go!"

The iron grate was lifted and, one by one, they disappeared into the underground.

Twenty minutes later, Germaine and the others were inside Castle Valdelaine. In the darkness of the third stable, they listened intently to every sound. From somewhere away across the far side of the bailey came the sounds of men's voices in conversation. Gently, Germaine lifted the door latch and eased the door open. From behind the door, he could see a troop of Gavron's men seated around a fire some fifty paces away at the top end of the bawn. As he listened intently, it became clear to him that there were other troops down in the courtyard, by another fire. He pulled himself backwards into the stable and turned to the others.

"Two groups at fires – one up the bawn, another in the courtyard! Avoid them for as long as you can! Stay in the shadows! Whatever happens, cover Philip as he goes towards the main gate. Cover me, if possible, as I go towards the main door of the old tower. Take out the rampart sentries first!" Germaine whispered. "God speed you all!"

They were out of the stable, and into the cool night air. Hugging the dark walls of the stables, they moved silently away from the bailey and towards the courtyard. There, they could see a cluster of Gavron's guards, seated around a warm brazier. One last time, Germaine motioned to the others to watch the curtain wall for sentries on the parapets. Lightly, and on tiptoe, Germaine and the others tripped among the shadows until they found shelter by the wall of the old tower. From there, they could see that there was no way through to the tower door without arousing the interest of the troops at the courtyard and brazier. Jan and two of the others stepped calmly out of the shadows, while Germaine continued in the darkness towards the tower door. The guards at the brazier saw the three men coming towards them and gave them no heed, thinking they were some of their own troops. At the last moment, a mere five paces away, one of the guards at the brazier became suspicious, and stood up. He opened his mouth to cry 'Alarm' but, he was silenced by the blow of a crossbow bolt to his chest. The man fell backwards away from the brazier, and the others whipped round to see the three ghost-like figures stand before them. Some stood up, and others attempted to draw swords. All of them were taken down by a little shower of arrows that came from nowhere, out of the darkness. A sentry on the rampart above, leaned out over the parapet but he too was stopped, as a crossbow bolt thudded into his chest. His body went down on the rampart floor, crumpled in a heap. Philip and two of the others fled past the brazier, across the courtyard, and down to the main gate. Yet another guard peered over the parapet, and he too was taken with a cross bow bolt. The man fell forward over the parapet, sailing downward through the night air, hitting the ground with a crash. By now Ernan and Hilaire had sped up the rampart steps and, gaining the topmost, moved one left and one right along the rampart, sheltering by the turrets and then moving forward again. Disappearing round the rampart, they were to take the sentries there by surprise, one by one, and eliminate them. Meanwhile, Germaine had reached the main door of the old tower. Having overpowered the sentry there, he held the man in a vice-like grip, with a dagger to his neck. He banged on the door.

"Who goes there!" came a shout from inside.

"A visitor for Lord Gavron!" said the man help-lessly. The inside door bolts were loosened, and the door opened, revealing the face of the guard inside.

"Well then, who goes there –" was all the man could say, as a blow from Germaine's mailed fist knocked him senseless, and sent him reeling backwards. Germaine dashed into the interior of the castle.

Out in the courtyard, all was well; Jan posted two men to keep an eye on the troops out in the bailey, who were still seated about the fire, and were unaware of events in the courtyard and at the main gate. Philip and his companion were down there, busy with watching for sentries, and busy cranking the wheels that lifted the portcullis. Suddenly the door of an outhouse opened, and one of Gavron's knights emerged, a little drunk, and with a girl in his arm. When he saw the brazier, and the bodies lying around it, he also saw the crumpled body of the sentry who had fallen from the roof. He then looked straight ahead, in time to see Jan lunging at him.

"What the devil..." was all he had time to say, as Jan leaped at him, and ran a dagger through his paunch. The girl screamed.

A flame tipped arrow scythed its way in an arc, up over the wall, through the darkness, drowning itself with a hiss in the waters of the Gavenne. This was the signal for Germaine's knights who were waiting, in silence, on the far side of the river. Shadowy figures arose from the grass and sedge, and began to shower the sentries on the bridge with arrows and bolts. In the light of the bridge torches, they could be seen falling or cowering for shelter. Suddenly, from the woods came this nocturnal vision of about a hundred knights armed and mounted, thundering towards the bridge. The last of the sentries had barely enough time to brace themselves, or jump into the darkness of the waters below. Germaine's knights swept across the bridge, and began to mount the causeway that led to the main gate.

For a time, it had gone well with Philip and Arlen. The portcullis was finally up, but as they lifted the wooden beams that held the gates shut, they became aware of a group of three guards on the rampart above them who were trying to peer down into the darkness below. The attention of these guards was delayed momentarily by the emergence of the knight and his girl. As she screamed, they were hit man for man by bolts and arrows from Jan's men in the courtyard.

Up at the fireplace on the bawn the conversation stopped, as the scream was heard. There was a shrugging of shoulders, but two or three of the men took up lances, and came down the bailey to investigate. Jan motioned to his men to back down towards the main gate. As they did so they were seen by the men coming from the bailey, and a loud 'Halloo' was shouted. The game was up now for Jan's men; the surprise was over. All they could do now was to fight to keep the main gate open, and already Gavron's men were bearing down on them with lances and swords. Jan, Philip and the others, now in a line by the open gates, managed to take down the first onslaught of their attackers with what was left of their supply of arrows and bolts. However, the stables and outhouses began to empty themselves of Gavron's hitherto sleeping garrison. Now Jan, Philip and their companions were outnumbered three to one. "Broadswords!" shouted Jan, as another wave of troops launched upon them. Each man unslung his great broadsword, hitherto clasped to his back. "At them!" shouted Jan, and the eight men waded into the leaguers, their broadswords swinging and hacking and carving large gaps as the leaguers handswords were no match for the savage swinging of the murderous broadswords. Men shouted, men howled in pain, and men fell mortally wounded. For a brief moment, it looked as if Jan and the others might rout the superior league force, which began to withdraw back up from the gates. But in a moment, Gavron's men had changed tactics, and brought up lances and halberds to the front of their line, and with a great shout moved forward in a mass on Jan's men. Though they fought like men demented, their broadswords could only parry and hack at the deadly lances being thrust at them. The broadswords, light axes and daggers were thrown as the deadly lance thrusts pushed Jan,

Philip and the others back towards the great wooden
gates. Already, leaguers were in possession of the right
door pushing it outward to close it while the small band of
heroes stood, now with their backs to the left door, ready
to keep it open with their very lives. The leaguers now
lunged at them one last time. Jan and one of the others
went down instantly, mortally wounded. The others had
held their ground before the door. While their left hands
shot out to grab at the oncoming lance shafts, the right
hand was busily hacking at the attackers with the lighter
handswords. There were deft sidesteps when the league
men rammed their lances into the wood of the gate.
When Philip took a wound above his chest, and went
down, the fighting suddenly stopped. The leaguers had
turned in dismay for, coming at a gallop up the causeway
towards the open gate, were Germaine's one hundred
knights, thundering upwards out of the darkness, into
Valdelaine.

All around the courtyard, the stable yard and the
bailey, the slaughter began.

What followed was not a battle, nor even a melee.
It was a massacre, which started at the main gate, and
continued up into the courtyard, down into the stable
yards and up onto the bawn itself. The garrison, all on
foot, were no match for the mounted knights who pursued
them into every corner and against every buttress. And
for some time, the shouts and screams continued to echo
all about the place as, little by little, Gavron's outer garrison were cut to pieces. The nightmare scene was illumi-
nated only by the moving light of torches carried by some
of the knights.

Warfare by day is horrible, but the warfare of the
night seems even more awful. All of what had taken

place had happened in a brief space of time. In that time, Germaine, inside the old tower, was moving rapidly through the passageways that led to the rest of the fortress. He knew every inch of it by candlelight or in darkness. Every stone step, every archway, every alcove was etched into his memory as he sped along. Somewhere from outside came the sound of a girl's scream. Germaine sidestepped into the darkness by a buttress. Torchlight from around a corner up ahead cast shadows of an approaching guard. There Germaine waited and, as the guard passed, he pounced on him, crushed him against the passageway wall. The guard fell in a heap as Germaine pounded his head with a mailed fist.

While Germaine was dashing deeper into the castle, Alain, one of the two who had earlier climbed the ramparts, was now inside the main door of the old tower. But Alain stayed in the darkness near the door. A number of guards who approached were silently thudded to death by Alain's cross bows. Again he waited; he would have to do so until Germaine's knights were safely in the main doors. He busied himself pulling away the dead bodies of the guards, hiding them as best he could.

Meanwhile Germaine moved on more cautiously now, from dark shadow to dark shadow, like some nocturnal fiend. Again another guard emerged from a room and again Germaine pounced, leaving the hapless man dead. This time however, Germaine removed the man's conical helmet and lance and shield. From now on, if he was seen, he could pose as one of Gavron's sentries and pounce on his prey at the last minute. He was right; a glimpse round a corner showed him yet another guard standing by the door of the great hall. Nimble as a cat, he retraced his steps ten paces, and then with heavy steps and as much noise as he could muster, he turned the corner where he had seen the sentry at the great hall. As he did so, he whistled and called out,

"Hey, friend! Come out here and have a look at this!"

The sentry, thinking he was being called by one of his own, moved quickly and turned the corner. The man's eyes all but popped out as Germaine ran him through with his borrowed lance. Germaine caught the man before he fell, let him down slowly, and then pulled his remains into the cover of darkness. Now Germaine waited, and posed as a sentry himself. He knew he must wait here in the torchlight of the antechamber by the wooden door of the great hall. How the fight was faring with Philip, Jan and the others down in the courtyard and at the main gate, he could not know. So he waited there calmly leaning on his lance, his newly acquired helmet drawn down low over his mail mantle until it almost covered his brows. Beside him was the door to the great hall, and occasionally he could hear the sound of voices, men's voices, coming from within. Probably the second echelon of de Laude's knights finishing a meal, he thought. Gavron himself was probably not in there, he would have taken the upper hall as his feasting place, as well as his centre of command. Across the wide antechamber, the wide staircase led to the first floor and the upper hall.

Presently, Germaine tensed a little as he heard the sound of footsteps coming down the wide stairs. With an effort he calmly slouched over his lance, with as much nonchalance as he could muster. The personage who came down the stairs was Baron Richard, one of Gavron's most trusted henchmen. Germaine didn't even look at him, but saluted and shifted from one foot to the other. The baron just belched, grunted, and made towards the door of the hall. Then he stopped, and turned towards Germaine, who stood easy a few feet away.

"Hey! You fellow!" the baron belched again. "There are supposed to be two of you at this door. Where's your companion sentry?"

Germaine shuffled again from one foot to the other, cleared his throat and turned his face slightly towards the baron.

"Eh! He's gone to check with the guards at the main door, your Lordship!" Germaine growled in a deep voice, "Baron Gavron's orders, once every hour!" And he turned his face away.

The baron only grunted, and turned and opened the door. Germaine could hear much sound of conversation within. The baron passed into the hall and shut the door behind him with a crash. Germaine smiled; he would have loved nothing more than to have run Baron Richard through with his lance, leaving him pinned to the door. No, thought Germaine, I must bide my time.

He did not have long to wait. All of a sudden he could see through a slit window the flickering of torchlight along the outer wall. It could mean only one thing, Philip and Jan had kept the main gate, and already Lord Verling's knights were in the courtyard. Germaine turned and banged loudly on the door, with his fist, opened it, and yelled at the throng inside.

"Alarm! Alarm, my Lords. Attackers! Attackers at the main gate!"

There followed a moment's consternation among the league knights thronged at the tables. Every man dashed forward to grasp weapons and helmets; then the great hall seemed to disgorge itself of its contents as Gavron's knights poured out the doorway and wheeled round and down the passageway like a pack of hounds on the loose. Germaine, however, had not run ahead of them, like a good sentry might do. In the seconds allowed him, he had dashed across the antechamber and disappeared upwards, up the second flight of stairs which led to a broad landing and the entrance to the upper hall. The guards at that door challenged him but he only repeated the alarm. With the two guards, Germaine burst into the hall – there, at the far end sat Gavron and about ten or so of his chief commanders. The two sentries ran up the length of the hall to repeat the ill news that there was an attack in progress at the main gate. The giant Gavron pushed back his chair and stood up, his huge red face glowering in the candlelight.

"Well don't stand there like fools!" Gavron roared, his bellow echoing round the near empty hall.

"Go find out what is happening! Hugo, Conrad, get down there and find out what's afoot. Report back to me! I'll be down presently!"

The two sentries had already made their exit from the hall, and were clattering down the stairway. They were quickly followed by Baron Hugo and Baron Conrad. In all the haste, no one even noticed that the third sentry was not around anymore, forgotten in fact. But Germaine, like a phantom in the night, had disappeared once more into the darkness of Castle Valdelaine.

While all of this was happening, Alain had been keeping watch on the main doors of the old tower, ensuring no guards came to bolt it shut. All had gone well with him until the 'Halloo!' had been shouted by Gavron's men out on the bailey, and in the courtyard. Above him in the chambers of the old tower, the castle garrison was now being aroused, and men were beginning to exit those rooms to descend the spiral stairway which led to the main doors. He could no longer afford to tarry, as alone he could not take on the descending troops. So he found shelter in an empty chamber beyond the main doors. Meanwhile young Lord Verling and his knights had charged through the outer gates, and the carnage in the courtyard and bailey had begun. Verling himself, anxious to secure the main doors while they were still open, motioned to a troop of his knights to dismount and follow him. But he was too late; the castle garrison came down in great numbers, charging out the main doors, down the steps, and on to the terrace where Verling's troops had just reined in. Here in the torchlight, a terrific melee began. Time and time again Verling's men were driven back; but each time, reinforced by knights now regrouping from the massacre up the bailey, Verling was able to press the knights of Gavron back towards the main door. Here took place the bloodiest fighting of the night so far. The garrison men found themselves surrounded on three sides. And so began a murderous retreat to get inside the doors. Verling's men surged forward en masse to prevent the closure, and every sinew was strained on both the outer and inner sides of the doors. Several times they were heaved open, only to have them heaved shut again from inside. With one exhausting charge, Gavron's men inside heaved forward and shut the doors, and more than that, they barred and bolted them. This event gave both sides moments to draw breath.

But Verling did not rest. He ordered his knights to move back from the doorway, and to bring forward the baggage containing the lances and pikes. As each man sheathed his sword, and took lance or pike, Verling sent some men to search for a wooden beam or tree trunk, or both. He would have to batter the doors down.

Gavron de Laude paced up and down the wide landing outside the upper hall on the second floor. His commanders stood to one side, and kept silent. The cheeks of his face could not have glowed more red; the scowl he bore could not have been darker. Presently, a sentry came up from below stairs, and blurted breathlessly,

"My Lord, they have taken the main gate – the main gate, my Lord! They are running wild abroad the courtyard and the bailey!"

"Great Christ!" bellowed Gavron. "How could they have got in?"

"No one can say, my Lord!"

"How did they get in?" Gavron put the question again, this time to his commanders, who in turn looked at each other, and at him, and shrugged their shoulders. One spoke,

"All sentries were at their posts an hour ago. The gates were locked, the bridge secure!"

Gavron turned around to the baron who had just spoken.

"Well, our enemies were on the far side of the river and in the woods, there, at nightfall!" Gavron chewed on his words, and spat them out. "What happened then? Were they spirited across the river, over the bridge, and inside the rampart by some nightly fiend?"

His face glowing red and one eye now larger than the other, Gavron turned back to the sentry,

"Well, call the men in the old tower. Call them to arms!" he roared.

The sentry quickly turned, and disappeared down the steps of the stairway. Gavron looked about at the other barons with a glare.

"Fetch me my weapons and armour!" he bellowed. "It looks as though I'm going to have to go down there – and if I have to – if I have to kill that bastard Germaine, myself. I'll do it and then, then I'm going to find the other bastard that let Germaine in and I'll..."

Gavron did not finish the threat. From away and below came a sound like an explosion. Gavron's head swung around to the stairs. Yet another messenger, this time a youthful squire.

"My Lord!" he called, as he topped the stairs. "Take heed, my Lord! The main door has been breached! The enemy is in, my Lord!"

Gavron clasped his hands before his face, and his roar went almost to a scream.

"Great Christ! Where are the troops from the old tower!"

"It is they have been overcome at the door, my Lord!" shouted the squire. "The enemy is within, my Lord, and is already forcing the corridors below!"

And sure enough, the sounds began to float up from below, sounds of clashes of arms, the sounds of men fighting and dying. Gavron's armour and weapons had arrived and he was fitting them on with help from some of his officers. When he perched the great conical helmet on his huge head, Gavron looked at the others again. "Up to the next landing! Bring torches!" he growled. Then he and ten of his foremost henchmen mounted the stairs to the landing and antechamber on the third floor. It was darker and cooler up there, one torch had lit the area.

Meanwhile from far below, in the corridors and passageways of the ground floor, the horrific sounds of butchery carried right up the flights to where Gavron and his chiefs waited. These passageways afforded no room for sword play; no, it was lances, pikes and the ugly heads of halberds that were the weapons of the slaughter. In relays of three or four abreast, Lord Verling's men charged forward in the torchlight, finding their targets and running Gavron's troops through with their deadly arms. A deadly pause, while men stopped for breath, or screamed in the pangs of death, and then with a shout, another relay lunged forward and the slaughter was repeated. Foot by foot, step by step, Gavron's troops were forced backwards until they were forced to retreat up the stairs, or into the great hall.

Yet another messenger, breathless from climbing, found Gavron on the landing on the third floor.

"My Lord!" he cried. "They are forcing the stairs below! Take care my Lord. The landing below is full with our men!"

Gavron beckoned to four of his stalwarts. "You four! Go down and steady the men with the bedlam down there!"

The four drew their swords; their weapons and armour clanked, as they disappeared down the spiral. Baron Agron turned to Gavron.

"Now what?" he growled.

"Now this!" de Laude glared at him. "Now we play our trump card, we bring down the lady of the castle! Go up to the chamber and bring me down Ioni de Valdelaine!"

Baron Agron drew his sword; he ascended the upper stairs as fast as his legs could carry both his paunch and his armour. From the opposite side of the landing, in twos, Gavron's men were appearing from below.

"My Lord, Germaine has forced the stairs, and is now forcing the landing below us!"

"Great Christ!" Gavron bellowed again. "Tell the men below – tell them we are bringing down a hostage to

Germaine – we are bringing down the Valdelaine girl! Tell them, tell them!"

Gavron paced up and down once more. Even his own men, having retreated up the staircase were standing all to one side of the landing; the sounds of slaughter continued to rise from the landing below.

"God's blood!" roared Gavron. "What the hell is keeping Agron, and the girl up there?" And he barged over to the foot of the stairs above. The silence from above was eerie, but presently Gavron could detect the sound of footsteps coming from the darkness above. Gavron smiled an evil smile.

"Now we have them!" he chuckled. "Now, we'll show Germaine and his cohorts that we have his lady hostage!"

The footsteps from above became louder, and also the sound of someone being forced downward. Then a pause; and then and unearthly sound as, tumbling and clanking and crashing, the dead body of Baron Agron came careering round the last of the spiral, and slumped to a halt at Gavron's feet. Gavron jumped high and backward, blood squirting from both sides of the dead man's neck. Gavron and the others backed away from the nightmare apparition. Gavron stared in horror and turned visibly pale. Slowly, the whites of his eyes grew large, as his gaze went upwards toward the ceiling and, all over his face, came the question 'What is up there?' He was expecting Agron with the girl. What he got was Agron – dead. What the hell is up – there?

"What is up there?" Gavron breathed. "Great Christ! The place is cursed tonight! If Germaine is below – then what is up there?"

Gavron's commanders looked at each other; slowly drawing their swords, the four of them stepped

lightly to the foot of the dark staircase from which Baron
Agron's body had come. They began to climb, with all
the care and stealth they could manage. When they did
attain the antechamber above, all they found was the dead
remains of the sentry who had guarded Ioni's door. The
keys to that door were gone! Then they divided their
numbers, two of them descending again to report to Gavron; the other two ran from one door to another, finding
all were locked. They pounded on each door, and their
pounding was met only with silence. They looked at each
other in disbelief and shrugged. Who could know
whether the girl was in her own room, or in one of the
others, or had she been simply spirited away like a phan-
tasma in the night? What kind of witchcraft was it that
now seemed to threaten Gavron's scheme to escape, with
Ioni as a hostage? One of the two descended.

Gavron cursed and breathed fury, as he heard the
news. Below him, the din of the battle on the staircase
was becoming more intense. Verling's men were taking
desperate runs up the staircase, thrusting their lances in
the narrow confines of the stairs. Occasional crossbow
bolts were finding their targets, and men fell and slithered
down the bloody steps. Some bolts simply ricocheted
against the circular stone wall, almost doing as much
damage. Such flickering torchlight as could be afforded,
gave barely enough of the fickle light needed to fight an
enemy. From below, there would be a lull in the noise,
for a moment; and then one or two of Verling's knights
would give charge up the steps, the poor light glinting on
their spearheads. Those above would hack at the surging
lances with swords and axes. Men would fall, and their
bodies were kicked downwards or hastily pulled upwards.
Another pause, another shout, and another heaving charge

upwards, contesting every bloodied step; and so the carnage went on.

At length, during one of the deadly pauses below, Gavron, torch in hand, appeared atop the steps and bellowed down.

"Parley! Parley! I say." He repeated the bellow again. "Parley! Parley! What say you below?" Below Verling's knights looked at each other, and nodded.

"Very well, Gavron!" one of them shouted. "Parley it is! Our weapons are down! What do you want?"

"Look, down there, you know I have the girl, the Lady Valdelaine!"

"How do we know you have her, Gavron? Show her to us, let us hear her voice!"

"Put down your weapons," Gavron replied. "You come up to us, and see for yourself!"

There was some manly laughter from below.

"Gavron!" came a voice. "You bring down the Lady Valdelaine to us! Our weapons are down!"

There was a pause.

"Very well then!" Gavron shouted. "I go to fetch her from her chamber. Make no move and keep your weapons down. Remember, one stroke, one shot and the Lady dies! Wait! Wait! Until I fetch her myself, and then I'll bring her down – but don't forget – my life and her life!"

Gavron turned, barging his way through his own men. He reached into the pouch that hung at his belt for his own key to Ioni's chamber. He whipped a torch from the hand of one of his men and began to mount the steps to the floor above. What the devil is happening, he thought. I'm outnumbered, cornered, and now I have to find the Valdelaine girl as well. He called upward to his knight above, but got no reply. As he gained the topmost steps, the antechamber came into his view. He beheld, there on the floor, not alone the body of his sentry, but also the body of his knight. He blew the air from his lungs hard with exasperation, the sweat was beaded on his face. On the landing below was the last remnant of his followers, all the rest of Valdelaine was taken in Germaine's nocturnal onslaught. And the girl, Ioni, his only hope of getting out alive, was in one of these rooms, but in which one?

He stood in the archway at the top of the staircase. He placed the torch in a holder on the wall; the key to Ioni's room was tossing up and down in the palm of his hand. Ten paces away, and straight in front of him, was Ioni's room. Slowly, slowly the door of that very room seemed to move a little, and then it creaked and whinged, and fell finally open, revealing in the candlelight from within, the figure of Ioni de Valdelaine herself! Gavron's jaw could drop no more; his head was pounding, and his sight and hearing were becoming blurred and bleary. Maybe the horrors of the night, maybe the strong wine he had with supper. Whatever, she stood there, just inside the room, like an apparition, dressed in her veil and long blue gown. Her right hand held a sword.

"Great Christ in Heaven!" Gavron gasped. "How did you... how?"

Ioni's voice, came from within the room and then seemed to come in eerie waves along the stone walls, as if from another world.

"You have come for me, Lord Gavron!" Ioni paused and took a deep breath. Her voice carried again, as she brushed her hair back from her brow, and with her right hand, raised the sword.

"Then I am here, my Lord! For you, there are two choices in this! You may choose to take one more step and your life is over!" Ioni breathed again, her head quivering a little at every sentence. "There is another choice, my Lord. You may leave my house forever, and live to face trial for your crimes!" Her voice seemed to linger elfin-like along the walls. Or so it seemed to Gavron – he was seeing her and hearing her, but the sight and sound were more like a dream than real, a strange eerie dream in the quiet, darker upper reaches of the tower where the two now faced each other.

There was a long pause, as Gavron's brain tried to make an iota of sense of what was happening. Then, slowly, great God, so slowly, his right hand was now drawing the glinting blade of his sword out of its scabbard. He looked about to the left, and to the right, and gradually the look of horror that had been on his face simply mutated, and finally came to settle in an evil smile.

Eyes large, and fixed on Ioni, he took a full step forward towards her. Nothing. The evil grin dripping from his lips widened, as though he had surprised himself! Then his foot shuffled along the stone flags, followed in turn by yet another step. Another pause and his eyes went sideways and up, as if he was expecting trouble from some quarter. Pleased, he began to step towards Ioni again, sword in hand. A door creaked behind him and the sound stopped him in his tracks. Still facing her, his eyes first went sideways, and then the huge neck allowed his head to turn around. It was Germaine, standing in the archway behind him; he wore no helmet, no armour, and seemed completely unarmed.

"Ha?" came the gasp from Gavron's throat, as his lips curled downward. Somewhere behind that awesome face, Gavron's brain struggled, in vain, to make some sense of what was happening. Somewhere else in that brain, his plans for his next move were already trickling.

The girl before me, and him behind me. She has a sword, and he is unarmed. But beware, take the girl first, and, who knows what Anlac's little bastard has in store? No. Take Anlac! And then, take the girl anyway! Gavron chuckled, shook his head, and with sword in both hands, now turned his colossal form to face Germaine.

"Anlac's little bastard!" Gavron chuckled and bellowed with laughter. In a lightning flash his scowl came back, and he lunged forward at Germaine, with arms aloft, sword held high. Germaine bent low, one leg forward and bent; then with all the force of his body, thrust his shoulder into the middle of the oncoming giant. Germaine then lifted, and the giant went high and over him, vaulting through the air, and crashing down into the stairway behind. In the force of the movement, Gavron tumbled onward, downward, crashing and thudding, and every crash and thud sending Germaine's poniard deeper and deeper up under his ribs, to his heart.

Two floors below on the first landing outside the upper hall, Verling's men waited patiently in answer to Gavron's call for parley. The sooner Ioni could be brought down alive, the sooner they could negotiate with the baron for her release. On the next landing, the remnant of Gavron's league troops were thronged, almost to stifling. The nearest of them to the stairwell above drew back in horror, as the body of their commander slithered down the last few steps, and then lay still, mouth agape, and dead eyes staring wide. Some gasped, but none moved, as the sound of footsteps came faintly at first, from above. Every eye was fixed on the stairway, its stone walls showing the flickering light of a torch. In the silence, the faint swish of the lady's dress was audible, and then, there before them, sword in hand, stood Ioni de

Valdelaine. Their surprise plunged to numbness, as the form of Germaine appeared behind her.

"Most of you know me," said Germaine. "My name is Germaine of Anlac. Put down your arms!"

At this, there was a long silence which was eventually broken by the sound of a sword clattering to the floor. Then another, and another, and finally, with a great crashing sound, every weapon there fell to the ground. There was a parting of the crowd as Ioni, followed by Germaine, walked through the middle of the throng to the downward staircase opposite.

From below, the knights of Verling's force were becoming impatient. What was keeping Gavron, they wondered?

"Above there!" Lord Verling shouted. "What keeps Lord Gavron and where is the Lady Valdelaine?"

The voice above them came down deep and sure.

"Gavron de Laude is dead! This is Germaine, you know my voice. I come down now to present to you the Lady Valdelaine!"

The sound of slippered footsteps and the swish of a lady's dress material – first they saw the slippers, then the lower folds of the dress, and finally the full form and face of Ioni de Valdelaine. Close behind her came Germaine himself, all blue eyes and smile. The men could not restrain themselves as they raised a loud and long cheer. This, in turn, was echoed by other cheers from all quarters of the castle. When there was silence again Ioni spoke, her head quivering in emphasis.

"I thank you. I thank you, my Lords, for your brave and noble service to me and to my house!" was all she could say.

At this, there was a clanking of armour as every man there knelt before her.

An hour later, the family of Valdelaine was re-united once more in the upper hall. Raymond and Robert, Ioni's uncles, had been discovered in the dungeons and released. The brave and doughty Raymond was still quite stunned by the ordeal, and looked a good deal worse for wear. Poor Uncle Robert, almost comically, seemed more calm than Raymond, and was no more confused in him-self than was normal for him. The women of the family had spent the captivity in the upper chambers of the old tower, and had been fortunate to be among the first to be rescued on that awesome night. Now reunited together, they were all embraced by Ioni. There were long and grateful embraces; there were tears, many tears. Even Aunt Blanche wept now, though in the days and nights of the captivity she had never flinched. Eleanor, Clara and Fleur spent long moments in Ioni's embrace. Anna was still asleep in the arms of one of the maids. A number of his fellow knights sat away by the fire with Germaine. Out of respect for the family they spoke little but were happy to slake their thirst with wine and mead.

Soon, all the family were seated at table and par-took in a light supper. Blanche and Eleanor sat on either side of Lord Raymond, comforting him, while further down the table, Fleur sat with her father Robert, holding his hand and talking soothingly to him. Fleur also cradled the sleeping eight year old Anna against her breast. As for Ioni and Clara, they could neither sit nor eat, and were more than content to act as maids, attending to the needs of all those at the table, and those across the hall seated by the fire.

Anna awoke from her sleep and lifted her head from her sister's breast; she blinked, yawned, and rubbed her sleepy eyes. Fleur beamed a reassuring smile into the child's eyes. Anna looked about the table, and looked at everyone there, rubbing her eyes again.

"Look Fleur, we are all here together again!" Anna mumbled, and looked away a little before saying, "Where are the bad men?"

"Hush Anna!" Fleur smiled again. "All the bad men have gone, and will trouble us no more. We are safe again!"

Anna looked at everyone, pleased and happy. Feeling sleepy, she began to nuzzle back again to Fleur's breast, and to much loved sleep. But for a fleeting moment, her gaze crossed the hall to the great fireplace and the strangers who sat there. She took a sharp intake of breath, and turned her head as though to say something urgently to her sister, and then suddenly changed her mind.

"Ioni!" Anna called out. "Where is Ioni?"

"Hush Anna!" Fleur whispered at her. "Cousin Ioni is busy, she's looking after all of us tonight!" But Anna continued to call out "Ioni! Cousin Ioni!"

Further down the table, Ioni put down some meat platters she was serving, turned, and strode up to Anna, wiping her hands in her apron. She knelt down before the child, who was still seated on Fleur's lap.

"What is it, Cousin Anna?" Ioni smiled. "What ails you, my love?"

Anna drew breath and leaned out towards Ioni to whisper in her ear.

"Ioni, is this a dream? Are we all in a dream or something?"

Ioni chuckled, a little puzzled at her cousin's question.

"What speak you, my child? We are certainly not in a dream. This is all real; we are all here together again!" Ioni reached out to hug the child.

"But Ioni!" Anna said, holding back the embrace. "This must be a dream, Ioni, for I can see Germaine! Germaine, Ioni! Over there by the fire. Is it a dream?"

Ioni's eyes went wide, and her mouth dropped as, embracing Anna, memories of another time came flooding back to her. Oh God, the child remembered Germaine, of course she did; had they not spoken of him together in the long days after he had gone. Of course, of course!

"It is no dream, Anna," Ioni murmured. "It is Germaine!"

Ioni embraced her cousin once more, then arose and strode out of the hall, for a moment, to calm herself, and wipe the tears from her eyes.

All through the night the work went on – the work of removing the dead for burial, the work of tending to the wounded, and the work of washing down the blood that was spilt on walls, floors and steps. Servants and villagers toiled through the hours, cleaning and spreading fresh straw and rushes everywhere the slaughter had raged. Germaine's knights refused any special hospitality from the family and simply slept on floors and benches, in nooks and crannies everywhere. Lord Verling alone refused to rest and spent those hours supervising the work. Only when everyone else had gone to rest, an hour before dawn, did he find himself a cloak and, wrapped in it, buried himself in some out of the way corner to sleep, after all was done. Philip, weakened from his wound, had been taken to the chapel room on the ground floor of the old tower, a makeshift bed had been set up for him and he was placed in it and made comfortable. Ioni knew Philip from Germaine's stories of him and knowing there would be no sleep for her that night took it in turns with Eleanor to watch over him while he slept, or rather while he drifted in and out of consciousness. Eleanor had refused to retire also, as well as tending Philip she was solicitous for Ioni's welfare. Her cousin, she knew well, was not squeamish, but the horrors of the previous hours might take sudden hold on Ioni, as realisation dawned on her of the full impact of what had happened, possibly leading her into shock and collapse. Eleanor kept her cousin busy with whispered chatter and distracting tasks, all the time helping Ioni's mind remain in focus. Frequently Eleanor would tell her to look in on Germaine and stay with him for a while, his sleeping presence before the fire would fortify her heart.

Ioni sat on a little stool gazing down into that long lost face; at one stage Germaine cried out in his sleep and she spoke soothingly to him until he slept calmly again. For a long time she gazed down at him from where she sat repeating over and over in whispers "I love you, Germaine." The noise and the hubbub had finally given way and silence prevailed all through the castle. Her own eyes now began to close. She awoke with a start, and shivered. I must have nodded off, she thought, and noticed it was now first light. I must go down to Eleanor and check on Philip. She rose, wrapping her cloak about her in the morning chill, sauntered out onto the passageway, pausing at a window to see the day dawn. Soon the sun was up, radiant and lovely. Presently she heard the swishing sound of skirts and the patter of slippered feet approaching up the stairs. That would be Eleanor coming from the chapel room to fetch her down to help with Philip. She turned and saw Eleanor's form in the archway.

"How is he?" Ioni whispered the question. Eleanor said nothing in reply but stepped over to her and took her in her arms.

"What is it?" Ioni whispered.

"He is gone, Ioni. He died but a moment ago!"

A weariness came over Ioni, and Eleanor took her back into her embrace again.

"I am truly sorry!" Eleanor whispered as Ioni shook with tears. Presently she lifted her head, wiping her tears with her kerchief.

"What will I tell him, Eleanor?"

Still holding her, Eleanor said, "Let Germaine sleep, there is nothing he can do for Philip. He is gone, Ioni, he is gone! When he awakes I will tell him and take him to the chapel room. Meanwhile you go and rest."

"I cannot rest," Ioni said. "Please permit me to stay with you till Germaine wakes. This will go hard with him, I know."

Eleanor responded, "Give me some moments to call the maids and help prepare his body for burial. Better still, come with me and we shall return to Germaine as soon as possible." Wearily Ioni followed her cousin, hand in hand.

Soon the house was stirring again, the maids were up and, in the kitchen Margreth was preparing a breakfast. Germaine awoke and, with his other knights, partook of some breakfast, after which Ioni and Eleanor beckoned to him and together broke the news of Philip's death. The two cousins escorted him to the chapel room, there he sat by the bedside gazing long into the peaceful face of his beloved friend. He reached out his hands and placed them around the cold hands of his dead companion and bent his head low on Philip's breast. Having passed an hour there he emerged from the chapel room where Ioni and Eleanor were waiting for him. They had been joined by Alain, who the previous night had sheltered in that same room until Lord Verling had forced the main door of the castle. The two girls embraced Germaine who then asked Alain to report to him within the hour and account to him for all who had survived. Sixteen in all had died that night, including Philip; Jan de Jubilad and another sixteen had been wounded and were being nursed. The sixty eight youngbloods who had survived the fighting were still asleep or having breakfast in the great hall. Lord Verling was alive but wrapped in sleep in the corner.

Gradually the family began to make their appearance – Lord Raymond, Aunt Blanche, Clara and Anna, all coming to terms with what had happened, each in their own way. Germaine begged leave of Ioni to walk in the fields, alone, but not before Anna had come running along the passageway and had heartily jumped up into his arms. Despite the protestations of Ioni, Germaine took Anna by the hand and together the three of them walked the morning fields. It was Germaine's way of coping with the shattering events of the night. Anna could still chatter away with him, beguiling his mind with her amusing ways.

Chapter XVIII: The Dawn of Wonders

*I*n the week or so that followed, Valdelaine returned to something of its previous normality.
Germaine, Ioni and all of the family gradually settled
back into the rhythms of everyday life. Needless to say,
the two lovers were allowed plenty of time together, now
that the story of their secret love affair was public knowledge. People rejoiced and were happy for them. Anna
took on the role of chaperone. This she enjoyed thoroughly, ever careful to keep herself at a discreet distance
from them either within the castle confines or when they
strolled together by the river or in the woods. What a
change it was from the old days when they simply had to
conceal their affection and when they simply had to run
the gauntlet of being discovered – if that had happened,
the consequences would have been difficult to say the
least. Now their hearts felt the relief of being together all
the time, without disapproval from any quarter. At last
Ioni's father, Lord Henry, arrived, much to Ioni's delight.
She lost no time and broached the story of her love for
Germaine to her father. Lord Henry was at once fascinated and pleased for them, to Ioni's great joy. She in
turn brought Germaine to meet her father who willingly
gave his consent for them to marry, though he did say he
needed time to arrange a suitable dowry now that she was
to marry a duke and have the title Duchess d'Anlac. But
Germaine quickly waived the dowry insisting that Valdelaine had already done so much for him and had given
him so much. But Lord Henry insisted on giving something to his daughter, she would have all the beautiful
gowns and jewellery that could be mustered and all the
money that could be collected at short notice.

They were married, Ioni and Germaine, in the church of St. Catherine's Abbey. The throng included the Valdelaine family and sixty five of Germaine's knights. Eleanor, Clara and Anna were bridesmaids, and Fleur was maid of honour, resplendent in gowns of purple and gold. Ioni of course wore white, the beautiful white gown trimmed with black and gold material at the neck, cuffs, with a girdle of the same material – it was of course the wedding dress of her mother Marie de Valdelaine. Frère Benedict read the nuptial mass and performed the ceremony – he seemed more happy than ever in his life, ecstatic that his beloved mistress had found happiness at last. While it was her father who gave her away, it was Lord Verling who stood witness for Germaine. The ring was the ring of Anlac which he had given her years before as a token of trust between them. She had returned it to him the day he left Valdelaine, the day she feared she might never see him again. Not nervous in the least but glowing with happiness she ascended the altar as Lady Valdelaine and came down those same altar steps as Duchess Ioni d'Anlac. When the Mass ended, happiness carried the congregation flowing out to the lawns of the abbey where the wedding banquet had been prepared. Toward the end of the meal when all the speeches of congratulations and thanks had been made, Germaine took Ioni in his strong arms and lifted her high in the air; she clung to him for dear life, laughing all the time. A great throaty cheer went up from his knights and everyone laughed heartily, none more so than Aunt Blanche.

At three o'clock the cavalcade began to move off with Germaine and Ioni at the head, on horseback, retracing their journey back to Castle Valdelaine. At their approach they were greeted by the common folk from all the manors and villages of the estate. On reaching the inside of the castle everyone broke away, the ladies to rest, the men to huddle together, chatting and drinking ale which flowed in abundance until the night's festivities commenced. There was music, dancing, mummers, dancers and acrobats for entertainment.

As the festivity proceeded there were a number of gifts and surprises for the wedding couple. Lord Verling presented them with leather bound copies of the augmented 'Treasons of the Heart', the book containing the letters of Ioni and Germaine and the imagined story of their love. Surprised and amused, the happy couple began to peruse parts of the little tomes, for both of them had been until now oblivious of its existence, and they were surprised to hear it was now avidly read and popular in the two kingdoms and beyond.

There was another surprise, more exalted in nature than the romantic 'Treasons of the Heart'. Lord Henry had left the great hall momentarily and returned in the company of a messenger from the king himself. This dignitary stood before Germaine and, bowing, presented him with a wooden box with beautiful carvings and brass ornamentation. On opening the box Germaine found it contained a large gold medal suspended from a chain of gold. Dumbfounded Germaine took out the medal and chain only to find a parchment with the king's seal upon it. Breaking the seal he began to read its contents. The king of Esmor had conferred upon him the Chivalrous Order of St. Michael – the highest honour that Esmor could confer. The king's messenger then read out the citation, his voice loud, now that the merriment had hushed. The messenger recounted Germaine's many deeds of valour and chivalry; he was now a knight of Esmor, with the freedom of Esmor. At the end of the citation Germaine was given a quill and signed two copies of the declaration, one for

himself and one for the king. He sat back in his chair as
the music and cheering began, speechless and full of puzzlement and wonder, for never before had a knight of
Bergmond been bestowed with such an honour. Ioni
leaned over to him and gently took his hand in hers and
Germaine placed his arms around her. Someone placed
the chain around Germaine's shoulder and the bright gold
medal hung at his breast.

There was yet another great surprise that night,
this time it was for the lady Clara, now seventeen and tall
and beautiful – a surprise of a personal nature for Clara,
and indirectly for Ioni. Earlier that day, while the wedding proceeded at St. Catherine's, a knight in resplendent
armour, accompanied by a retinue of squires and servants
and followed by three wagons of war booty, rode into
Valdelaine. To the consternation and then joy of those
present who received him, it turned out he was Claude de
Chalons. He was the man whom Ioni had banished to the
wars after his brief dalliance with the then very young
Clara. Against the odds, he had ridden away in disgrace
from Valdelaine to the wars, banished by Ioni and grieved
for by lovelorn Clara. He had fought at Augsad and Long
Hills and had survived. He had won many honours and
was now a wealthy man. At a signal from Lord Henry the
revelling stopped again, Claude appeared in the doorway,
strode up the hall and bowed to Lord Henry and the other
family members. Clara had failed to recognise him as he
stood in full armour before them. "Remove your helmet,
Sir," Lord Henry called out to him. His hands went to the
helmet and lifted it; he shook his head as he lowered the
helmet to his side. Clara jumped up and screamed for joy,
left her place at the high table and ran to him, screaming,
laughing, crying and threw herself into his arms. Then
she freed herself and shouted, "This is the man I love!

Everybody please listen. This is the man I thought had died in the wars. And now here he is. Everyone please be happy for me!" There was loud applause and long echoing to the roof of the hall and happy laughter too at the exuberance of Clara's outburst of love. But Ioni, still in Germaine's arms, could only think of the day she had broken Clara's heart by sending Claude away. Little did she realise that sad day that she had unwittingly saved his life. She had saved his life after all, for if he had stayed in Valdelaine he would have been slain in cold blood, as were all the other household knights when they had finally surrendered to Gavron and his butchering barons. Now, after all was said and done, she had saved him, for himself and for Clara. She might have cried with joy, but she did not, safe and happy as she was in the arms of her husband.

*   *   *

The journey itself was taken in leisurely fashion, for now at last Germaine and Ioni felt no need for haste. Man and wife they rode at the head of the cavalcade of thirty knights and four wagons which, as well as carrying provisions, pavilions and tents, also conveyed Ioni's maids and the Lady Anna. Down the forest road they went, that magical forest which Ioni had known since childhood and was now passing her by, its memories descending upon her like the red and golden leaves that trailed down from high above and were strewn before her at every step. All sorrows, all the heartaches of the parting from home and loved ones, all were instantly assuaged by the presence and energy of the man beside her. That presence enfolded her heart with a glow of happiness that was boundless.

When, after some hours, they emerged from the woods into the bright green country south of the river, the outriders galloped ahead and found the ford and crossed to the northern banks of the river, leaving the Gavenne to flow westward for some miles and then turn majestically in its long journey southward through the Golden Plain of Esmor. Their destination being westward, they parted company with the great river for the last time and set camp for the first night of their journey. On the morrow they entered the notorious Fens of Aren and spent the day keeping to the firm ground between the maze of little lakes and ponds. By evening they had cleared the fens, unmolested. With solid ground beneath them again, they made good headway. Already they had begun the long slow ascent towards the high Borderlands country. And they set camp again.

The nights were spent under tent cover between them and the stars above. These were nights that Ioni's heart would treasure forever as she lay there in the arms of Germaine, at one and the same time in the wilds of the world of the night, and also happy, comforted and content in the arms of her husband. Often in the night she heard the howl of wolves coming from distant woods but she smiled and snuggle ever closer against him, the heat of his body and the fur coverings lulling her into happy sleep.

Beyond lay the pleasant country. Three days they spent crossing the high Borderlands country, dotted here and there with little villages, before catching sight of the first of the king's border fortresses, namely Fontrue. However they had little time to enjoy the view as the wind began to rise sharply and storm clouds quickly filled the sky. They arrived at Fontrue beneath darkened skies booming with thunder and letting loose lightning bolts from all sides.

As they dismounted inside the fort, Ioni's rain washed face, lit by the glow of many torches, turned to Germaine with a smile and a little laugh. "So far, so good, my love!" she shouted above the din of the storm. Minutes later, standing before a great fire in the hall they laughed again, thankful to be in from the cold and rain.

They were greeted by the commander of Fontrue, Sir Charles de Fayenne, and his wife Lady Lucy who escorted them to the dining hall. There was good food to warm them – venison and pheasant with plums and apples followed by goat's cheese and oatbread. The wine and ales were plentiful too, and the guests were soon happy and full of good cheer, oblivious to the storm raging outside. Ioni retired early with Anna and her maids. Germaine sat by the fireside chatting with Sir Charles and Lady Lucy, who was saying "Isn't life peculiar, my Lord Germaine. You departed from us those years ago – a prisoner in disgrace, an outcast. And now here you are once more – the hero of two kingdoms! What a happy outcome after all..."

"Similar thoughts flashed through my mind, Lady Lucy, as we approached the fortress. As you said 'Isn't life peculiar after all!'"

Soon after Lady Lucy made her excuses and retired for the night. The men stayed on by the fire, chatting and drinking until they began to grow heavy with sleepiness and the embers began to fade.

Suddenly their languor was shattered by a loud banging on the hall doors, and in from the thunderous night of storm came six knights who tramped down the hall and stood ominously before them. By now Germaine was on his feet facing them. One of them spoke, "My Lord Anlac, forgive our intrusion, we bear you messages from the Royal Council and from the Duke of Anflair!"

With that one of them opened a pannier satchel and took out two sealed scrolls.

"Do you men know what these messages are about?"

"No, my Lord, our duty was only that we find you and convey them to you!"

One of Germaine's knights brought a brass candle holder with three candles, while Germaine proceeded to open the parchment scrolls and read them. Sure enough one was from the Royal Council and the second was from Henry, Duke of Anflair. Both letters however contained precisely the same message.

As soon as he set foot on Bergmondese soil Germaine was ordered to desist from further progress on his intended journey, whether to Anlac or to the city of Bergmond. As soon as he set foot on Bergmondese soil he was to turn immediately southward and proceed to the city of Augsad and to remain there at the council's pleasure. On reading the letters a second time, Germaine sighed deeply and scratched his head in puzzlement. What was the meaning of this, he asked himself. No reason was given for this change of plan, none whatever.

Then he showed the letters to his own knights to see if they could make any sense of them. All were puzzled, surprised, annoyed. The people of his own Anlac were expecting him, the city of Bergmond too, and its people. As well as this, his place at this time was with the ruling Royal Council. So why delay him in Augsad? Nobody knew.

Then true to form, Germaine shrugged, smiled, and bade his companions a good night. In a few moments he was with Ioni beneath the fur covers of their bed. In the golden glowing warmth of her body, under the comforting cover of the fur, they each held each other. Gently slipping down the dreamy drowsy slopes of slumber, they felt safe and happy, lulled from outside by sounds of the dark howling storm. It was still raging and gusting in the turrets and towers; in the battlements around and beyond them the storm faded from their consciousness as they fell into the comforting arms of sleep. In the course of the following day the storm slowly blew itself out. Germaine and Ioni had been invited to stay and rest for a few days. Germaine therefore decided to withdraw from others simply to ponder on the possible reasons for the sudden change to their plans. Was there something sinister behind this extraordinary command? Why was he to be detained at Augsad? Had Anflair and the council decided to ignore the compelling evidence of his own claims to the throne and opt for someone else instead? Henry, Duke of Anflair perhaps? Henry was a worthy and noble man, and experienced courtier, diplomat and soldier. He had excellent personal qualities and was extremely popular among the nobility and people alike. But then and therefore it was unthinkable that, untrue to his own character he would play turncoat and bid for the kingship, ignoring the better claim of Germaine. Of course there was another consideration – had the Royal Council and other factions among the nobles actually banded themselves behind Anflair, and persuaded him, against his own conscience, to accept the crown, pledging him their support and loyalty? It was not unheard of in history in situations like this, that the true heir would be excluded by a faction supporting their own candidate. In such a case the true heir was forced into exile at best, at worst he was imprisoned, tried on trumped up charges, found guilty and sent to a traitor's death.

If all his surmisings proved true, then Germaine was in a dangerous position. Anlac and others would rally round him and civil war would ensue. The last thing Bergmond needed was a civil war now, when war with Esmor had just been concluded, and when the Raven League had just been destroyed. And so, bothered as he was by all these surmisings Germaine kept them to himself – neither had he burdened Ioni with the strange news that had come the previous night. He would be obliged to tell her though once they had cleared the Borderlands, for then they would be turning south on the long road to Augsad. But how to tell her was the problem – it would have to be done tactfully and without burdening her with the worst of his forebodings. Perhaps he would be presented with a fortuitous opportunity to tell her – if so, let it be soon!

*   *   *

In the morning Germaine invited Ioni to come riding with him, but as they journeyed onward more than she expected, she turned in the saddle to ask him where they were going, should they not be getting back to Fontrue? Germaine only smiled and said,

"I wish to show you a special place, Ioni, special to you and to me!"

Presently they came to a stream which flowed south through cultivated fields, and there in the distance stood a village with a little church spire.

"Is this the special place, Germaine?"

"Yes, Ioni. This is it. But I will explain gradually to you why it is special. Ioni, the village yonder is Elvendene."

For a moment the name meant nothing to her but then it burst upon her. Elvendene, yes, the scene of the great battle three years past.

"Elvendene!" she said. "The scene of the great battle!"

"Exactly, my love. The very place."

They rode onward and she followed him up the slopes west of the stream. He circled the horse round and round and called to her.

"We were here, Ioni, on top of this slope. We descended to the stream and charged across. Your countrymen were on top of that rise on the far side."

With that, they trotted down, crossed the stream and began to mount the other slope rising from the flat ground either side of the Elven. Every now and then Germaine turned, eyed the little spire of the village, seemingly taking his bearings from it.

"Somewhere around here, we met the Esmorin line and there was some sharp fighting. Look, Ioni, we were driven back down about there! We then made another attack – I was so far in front, I became separated from my men. Now let me see!" he said trotting over and back across the crest of the rise. "It might have been here, Ioni – it might have been here that I was knocked from my horse. My men were unable to reach me, so thick was the fray. Imagine, Ioni, somewhere here I fell."

Then he paused and looked at her as though he had rediscovered a buried treasure.

"Somewhere here I fell – and that, Ioni, was the end of my old life and it was the beginning of the new life, the new life that was to bring me to you. Had I not fallen here – I would never have met you. Imagine!" He had now dismounted and she was gazing down at him, her face lit with joy.

"And I would never have known you, my beloved Lord!"

He stepped forward and took her hand and kissed it.

"Thank heaven I was taken here, and so brought to you!" She was still smiling, "Indeed, Germaine, it is a special place, thank Heaven for it!"

Some days later, when they had reached Borderlands castle, and were happily settled in there, Ioni broached the subject with Germaine of his recent silence.

"Something has troubled you since Fontrue, my Lord, and you have given yourself over to silence. May I know the source of your silence, my lord? I am your wife now and if your mind is burdened – let me hear of it, that I may heal it!"

Germaine looked at her, took a breath and sighed. He smiled at her.

"I received some weighty news that I must now unburden into your heart, my love."

She reached up and kissed him, held his hand and sat him down. He told her everything that had happened at Fontrue. He told her of his ponderings on it. Finally when he was done, he looked at her, but she was smiling at him.

She smiled happily. "If I loved you as a defeated prisoner then I can love you always, whatever befall us."

He smiled. "I had expected the Duke of Anflair's claim to be better than mine, others too. I never thought of it, it never bothered me... but now, now there may be a very different destiny for us, different from anything I might have dreamed. After we find out in Augsad – you could be 'Queen of Bergmond' – or you could still be plain old 'Duchess of Anlac'. What do you think?"

"Whatever the titles, they do not bother me – whatever robes we wear they don't matter, as long as we are man and woman to each other in truth and love."

Germaine was holding her close in his arms.

"This revelation has come upon us of a sudden. I'm not sure this is what I ever wanted. In fact I'm quite sure I don't want to be king – no, Ioni, what we have together is the most splendid thing of all and I could care for no more than what I have with you."

She lifted her head from his chest and looked up at him and said,

"We have already come a long journey together – the journey to Augsad and what it may hold – is nothing compared to the journey we have already made unto each other and unto this day. Let us go to Augsad and see what happens then!"

They departed Borderlands and little by little descended from the high moors and crags of the Border country. Once they were sure they had crossed the frontier country and were safely into Bergmond country they turned southward on the long journey to Augsad.

"My first time out of my own country. My first time in Bergmond," Ioni mused. Germaine was reading her thoughts.

"I bid you welcome, my beloved Ioni, to my native land. But be not dismayed for you are a duchess of this realm and as such you will not be a stranger – for as you know our legend has gone before us into the hearts of the people here!"

"At long last, I am happy to be here, Germaine, happy to be in Bergmond. All of Esmor, all left behind as though it never existed. I am content, I am content!"

Though they had set camp early that evening, everyone sat about the campfires eating drinking and conversing until the sun went down. In the twilight the ladies retired, and the men too began to get up and stretch their arms and legs and think of their night's sleep. Suddenly, without warning, from the west came the thundery sound of hoof beats, all ears strained, and every sword was drawn. As the sound grew closer the outline of a large troop of horsemen could be seen cresting a nearby hill, with no loss of pace they thundered downward toward the little encampment. Germaine, standing out at the forefront was about to cry "Alarm!" when a great shout went up from the oncoming troops. To everyone's relief they could now hear more distinctly the familiar cry "Anlac! Anlac!"

"Put down your swords," Germaine shouted, and before he could say more he heard the great booming voice he recognised. It was that of his own cousin Godfrey Blackmane. The troop now slowed to a trot and as they then came at a walk Germaine could now see in the light of the fires, the very face of Blackmane. As they dismounted he began to recognise all of them – they were the men of Anlac. Sir Godfrey plodded forward, took Germaine's hands in his and gave him a great bear hug of an embrace.

"Welcome, Sir Godfrey!" Germaine gasped.

"By God, Sir, it is good to see your Grace alive, and well!" Turning to his own men he said, "Gentlemen, let me present our duke. Ah yes indeed, this is the pale wan youth who a year ago, in my very presence, swore he would singe Baron Gavron's beard! And from what I hear, not alone did he singe his beard but he cooked his goose as well!"

There was laughter and good cheer as each one of Blackmane's men came forward to greet Germaine.

"Aren't you a bit out of your territory, Sir Godfrey?" Germaine said laughing. "A bit far from our Anlac. May I ask as to what brings you to this neck of woods, so far from home?"

"Enough of that for now, my Lord. We would eat and drink for we've ridden hard from Bergmond city!"

And so the campfires were stoked up again and piled with logs and the hungry travellers were devouring every scrap of food brought to them. Soon after Ioni appeared outside their pavilion, just to see what all the commotion was. On seeing her, Germaine waved to her to join the company.

"Sir Godfrey, gentlemen, may I present to you – my wife of late, the Lady Ioni de Valdelaine – now the Duchess of Anlac!"

And hungry though they were, to a man they stood up, came forward and knelt before her. In the firelight she looked beautiful, the blue dress, trimmed with mauve and gold, the jewelled headband, glistening and glowing, and of course the beautiful face gleaming in the light.

"I greet you all, gentlemen, and I am honoured by your presence here. I thank you for the pains you have taken to be with us!"

Sir Godfrey boomed on the night air, "All the pains were well worth while, dear lady, especially now that we have had a look at you!"

There was laughter and cheers as the men rose from their knees.

"By the good God, Sir," Sir Godfrey said to Germaine, with a twinkle in his eye. "She's a ravishing beauty! If I may be so bold, Ma'am, it is no wonder he fought like a tiger for you!"

Sometime later Sir Godfrey and Germaine sat together in conference in a pavilion which had been made available for them. It was Sir Godfrey who spoke and Germaine listened, silently taking in every word.

"By God, Sir, the city of Bergmond has been buzzing with excitement these past four weeks – rumours and counter rumours about who the next king will be. The Council of State and the Lords Justices have been busy examining each and every claim. Henry Duke of Anflair is close to the blood line, so too the Duke of Augsad. However, your claim has been presented in your absence by Father Roland – er, Abbot Roland of Campaldo. He sought me out in Bergmond and I accompanied him as he presented your claim to the throne. Over the span of a week he presented the most extraordinary set of documents pertaining to the Anlac claim, your claim, my Lord."

Sir Godfrey paused a moment, helped himself to some more wine and then continued speaking low in the candle light which illumined his great face.

"My Lord, you will of course recall the legend of the Grotesque Prince of a hundred years ago. By the blood of Christ, my Lord, I have to tell you now that it is no legend! With my own eyes I saw the documents, the letters of the then king and queen, complete with their signatures and royal seals – to your great great grandfather requesting him to take the deformed child into his family and rear him as one of his own. I also saw the documents of your ancestors accepting the little prince, again all complete with signatures and dates and the Anlac seal. By God, Sir, it was the most extraordinary thing I did ever see. Then there were documents from a later date committing all these letters to the care of the monks of Campaldo, to be held in secret and in perpetuity and only to be revealed in future ages if the royal line were ever to be threatened with extinction. The last documents confirmed you, my noble Lord, as the direct descendent of this lost prince. It would seem that the blood now coursing through your noble veins – is the very blood of the royal line. My Lord, the prince was your grandfather. In spite of his deformities he grew strong and well and eventually married your grandmother, Duchess Elizabeth of Anlac!"

Germaine sat pondering for a long time, the only sound the night breeze outside the pavilion. At length all he could say was, "My God!" and then he asked, "Was there any final decision on the matter?"

"No, my Lord. When we left Bergmond to find you, no decision had been reached!"

"You know my return to Anlac was diverted to Augsad. I'm on my way there now. Do you have any knowledge of why I must go there and wait the Council's pleasure?"

"Alas no, my Lord, but if you will permit, we will accompany you there for your own safety, if your safety is in danger at all."

"Of course, Sir Godfrey, you are my right hand. We can speak more in the morning, my Lord. I must bid you good night!"

"Good night, my Lord." Sir Godfrey turned round, "Germaine, your claim is the strongest, and you and I and all Anlac may have to fight for it. And by God, Sir, we will fight for it to the last man alive!"

When they set out on their journey the following morning, Blackmane confided to Germaine that, in the early hours before dawn, he had despatched two of his fastest horsemen. Their mission, he told Germaine, was to ride ahead as fast as they could, and on reaching Augsad, they were to find out what this mysterious detour was all about. If they were to discover that Germaine was in any danger they were to ride back with all haste to warn Germaine and himself, thus giving them the chance to turn away from Augsad altogether. They would then turn northwest for Anlac, they would be safest there. It was a good plan, Germaine thought, and so, for the moment they continued their leisurely progress to Augsad.

Onward, southward day by day, with the peaks of the Ostmontane visible on their left, they finally reached the great rolling open countryside north of Augsad. They halted in the midmorning sunlight some seven miles north of the city. Still they were unable to see the towers and spires of the city because of the gently undulating terrain before them. The morning was sunny and warm, soundless and calm, as they dismounted to refresh themselves and take in the scenes about them.

Germaine and Ioni stood together apart from the others. The previous day, when Sir Godfrey's messengers had not returned to them with news from the city, Germaine had sent on word to the city authorities that contrary to the orders given him by the council, he would not enter Augsad without guarantees of safe conduct. Therefore he would wait where he stood and proceed no further. He did not have long to wait, however, as presently two riders crested the slope before them and then galloped downwards to greet them. When the riders reined in before them, they dismounted, stepped forward, and smiling, they bowed deeply. Blackmane and the other knights had now gathered in a crowd about Germaine and Ioni, eager and curious at the presence of the two strangers, one of whom now spoke.

"My Lord Germaine, My Lady, gentlemen, I am sent from Augsad to beg you wait a little here where you all stand. I bid you all welcome and will not tread upon your patience much longer – for, my Lords, my Lady, not far behind me, Augsad approaches!"

Scarcely had these words time to sink in when Germaine, Ioni and the rest of their escort became conscious of a strange sound coming from beyond the long rise before them. The road swept away from them and up the slope between the stubble fields to where the sound was coming from. A strange low, indistinct rambling sound, growing slowly clearer in the silence of the morning. Suddenly a number of riders topped the slope, they were then joined by others, and others again, and yet more again, their numbers swelled to a mighty host of people topping the entire crest for hundreds of yards either side of the road. As one, they went silent for a time until they were joined by what appeared like an army now visible where the road crested the hill. Then, as before the great rumble of voices resumed as the throng began descending the slope. Banners and flags waved above them and drums beat loudly as the slope brought them closer. Finally they reached the level ground four hundred yards from where Germaine and his party stood. Ioni's mind was now racing, what could all of this mean, she asked. Blackmane, too, stood dumbfounded by the sight of the oncoming mass and glancing upwards still more crowds and banners were appearing over the hill top. The entire populace of Augsad seemed to be coming over the rise. But Germaine's eyes were like steel as he focused on what had looked like the 'army' in the crowd's centre on the road, slowly becoming more defined as they approached ever closer.

Then, Germaine quickly reached to Ioni taking her hand in his and then placing his arms around her.

"My love," he said earnestly in her ear, "Ioni, look at the centre, at the road, can you see it. Can you make out the figures at the front, the bishops, the archbishops?"

Ioni shuddered and nodded. Germaine spoke again. "Now, in front of the archbishops, make out the figures of two pages, acolytes – and between them they are carrying a box, a purple coloured casket, a casket Ioni, can you see it?"

"Yes, my love, I see it!"

"Anflair is there, by God they are all there! Augsad, the Royal Council – great God, Ioni! Do you understand what this means?"

Ioni nestled closer to Germaine and looked up at him, "Yes, My Lord, I think I do!"

At three hundred yards, the great concourse halted, while a brace of trumpets were brought up front and their sound rent the morning air.

Germaine closed his arm about Ioni's shoulder and said,

"My beloved Ioni, there is still a few moments left before they reach us. In those moments we can still mount up, turn and gallop away, never to come back. We can find a quiet valley somewhere in the world where you and I can be together for the rest of our lives – but we must do it now. If not, well then you know what future lies before us. Do you understand me, my love?"

Ioni took a deep breath and said,

"I – shall we say, understand you, my Lord!"

At the third blast of the trumpets the massed crowd began to move again, clanging, jingling, the drumming now thunderous, the cheering now louder, the sound of the footsteps of thousands raising the dust high in the air, and all drawing ever closer, ever closer, with every beat of the heart.

Chapter XIX: Remembrance

*A*h dear, I can only picture it in my mind – that autumn morning north of Augsad nigh on fifty years ago. I was not there myself, I was elsewhere as I shall reveal eventually. Therefore I rely on the memories of others who were there and who were close enough to see what happened and hear what words were spoken. And the years have passed and the night grows late as I bring my poor chronicle to its end. Be assured, though, that it is the true chronicle.

The great throng had now drawn up to where Germaine and Ioni stood. Silence. The acolytes stepped up, bowed and placed the casket before them on the ground, opening it as the archbishop of Augsad approached. He bent down and held a crown aloft, its gold and jewels gleaming in the midmorning sun. His voice came loudly over the hushed air.

"Germaine, Hugo d'Anlac, accepte tu la couronne du Bermonne?"

Silence, and then the voice of Germaine.

"J'accept."

Then turning to Ioni the archbishop held aloft the other crown.

"Ioni, Leonine de Valdelaine, d'Anlac – accepte tu la couronne du Bermonne?"

"J'accept."

With that the entire assembly let up a thunderous cheer that went on and on for some time. When silence was restored the throng knelt there in the fields in obeisance to their new king and queen.

The archbishop said,

"You both shall be crowned in the cathedral of Bergmond within a fortnight from now. You are first to come to Augsad, then in slow stages by way of Pentevel and Jubilad in triumphant procession to the city of Bergmond. And now pray kneel as I give you my blessing."

Together they knelt.

"Benedicat vos omnipotens Deus – Pater, Filius et Spiritus Sanctus. Amen."

"Amen!" echoed the crowd.

Over the next two weeks they proceeded to Bergmond, escorted by crowds everywhere they went, who threw basketfuls of flowers before them as they moved ever closer to their destiny. By all appearances the coronation was both a solemn and joyous occasion, and the city was in a state of festivity for more than a week. Of course most of the attention was on Ioni, people intently curious to catch a glimpse of the lady of the legend – until now only a character in the book 'Treasons of the Heart' but now real there before them in flesh and blood. Everyone said she was even more beautiful than the book described. She waved to everyone, stopped to talk to many, she laughed a lot and smiled even more and thus endeared herself to her subjects in Bergmond. Though far from Valdelaine now, she was still the same Ioni – gentle, calm and smiling. Germaine, who accompanied Ioni everywhere she went, was no less honoured by the people – he was now hailed as the Warrior King, the hero of the long war with Esmor, and the hero of the rebellion against the league. The holy monastery of Campaldo had long kept his lineage a secret, but now it was no longer a secret and his lineage and right to the throne proved beyond all doubt.

*   *   *

Ah! Me! As I said the hour grows late as I, Jean de Valdelaine, struggle to finish this humble chronicle. Here in the new monastery church of Campaldo, I write these last pages of the story. The readers will be curious to know what became of the other characters of these extraordinary times.

Let me begin with my beloved father, Lord Henry de Valdelaine – he lived for another thirty years, in which time he completed a beautiful church in the village of Valdelaine in thanksgiving for the safe rescue of his daughter. He did something else he had been promising to do for years – he began the construction of a stone bridge across the Gavenne at Valdelaine. He is buried with his wife Marie in the abbey church of St. Catherine.

Of course when I became a monk, I forfeited any claim to Valdelaine. Eris therefore became lord. He returned many times to Norland and won the hand of the eldest daughter of the great countess. She still lives and Norland is at peace. Eris Lord Valdelaine has four children, three girls and one boy, all grown up now and married, all of them.

The young Anna served as lady in waiting to Queen Ioni for the rest of her life. Despite the offer of many suitors Anna never married and still lives in the royal palace.

Anna's sister Fleur, as you know, married one of the Belmont boys and had five children.

Here I must bring tribute to Fleur and Anna for providing me with the details of their young lives at Valdelaine. Most valuable to my research was the long correspondence with the Lady Eleanor de Ronclava, who lives. Eleanor married the second son of Count Michael,

Jean Louis. They have children and grandchildren, too numerous to mention!

Here I must give a brief account of my life – after the battle of Long Hills, I knew that I must enter the monastic life at Campaldo. My friend, Abbot Roland governed the monastery. I recall the first seven years there as the happiest of my life – given over to prayer, penance and meditation, which brought with it a joy and peace in my soul that I had never hitherto known.

After that, I was sent to study theology and philosophy at the University of Bergmond. I had a good teacher in Maelruan – the son of a prince in his own homeland, he was a prince among teachers, and I learned well.

By the time I returned from Bergmond I was teaching the young monks all I had learned in Bergmond. Soon after I was 'promoted' to Abbot Roland's second in command, with the title of prior. After the abbot's death I was elected abbot twice. However I left a great amount of administration to my prior as I became more and more involved with the building of the new abbey church. In those years I spent most of my time among the masons, carpenters, wood and stone carvers, always enjoying their company. Then I was merely the abbot, but they were the masters of their crafts and I loved to see the skill and mastery they brought to their work. The abbey did not want for funds for the work, for my sister, the queen, always made sure we were able to pay our way until it was finally completed. After my final term as abbot I devoted myself to writing – I wrote a treatise on church building and renovation and when this was completed, I began the chronicle of our youthful years and the extraordinary times that were thrust upon us. Here in the abbey we were visited many times by the king and queen. In their marriage they were blessed with four children, Marie and Leonine the princesses, Henry and Hugo the princes.

Even as I pen these last lines, Germaine and Ioni are with me, not just in spirit but in fact. From where I sit, here in the abbey church, I see in the candlelight where they are buried beneath the high altar. The inscription on their tombstones reads:

Hic jacet Ugo Christienus, Rex Bermonensis.
Hic jacet Leonina, Regina Bermonensis.

The rest, translated, reads:
"Here together do we lie,
And await another Kingdom."

22321852R00355

Printed in Great Britain
by Amazon